The Boy Who Lost His Name

Ethan Locke

ELocke

26·1·18

What's in a name, anyway? Is it just a label that someone else – probably your parents – landed you with? Or is it central to who you are?

How important is your name to you?

And what would happen if it was taken away from you? Would you still be you?

Dedicated to my wife, Rachel, without whose support (and child-minding) this book would not have been possible.

Chapter 1
Be careful what you wish for

You've always felt funny about mirrors. Sylvia Plath said that they were silver and exact – but they're not, of course. They are a new dimension; they warp and bend reality into shifting translucent ribbons. People see what they want to see – not reality at all. Or sometimes they see something that they really don't want to see: something that looks back out at them and raises hair on the back of their neck.

Let's face it, there's nothing truthful or honest about mirrors. They lie and cheat and deceive; what you see inside of them isn't the world as we know it, Jim, it is something... Else.

So look again.

Look hard this time.

Watch as your world and all of your pathetic self-delusions and blind beliefs swim around with something... something in your peripheral vision. Something that you know is there but you really, really don't want to see it.

Look now.

See your face?

I am I am I am.

Here here here.

You are not you after all.

No.

I am you. And you never really existed. Gone now, winked out like the multi-coloured sheen on the side of a soap bubble.

I am you. Your life is mine now. Sorry about that.

If it makes you feel any better then you can reassure yourself that your loved ones will never notice that you're gone; there'll be no tears or grieving. In fact, some of them might prefer the new you.

Only that probably doesn't make you feel better at all, does it?

The boy gazed into the mirror. It was a grimy thing, grafted onto a cheap bathroom cabinet, its edges chipped and flecked with blemishes.

Still, despite its shabbiness, the boy continued to stare, as though looking for the answer to some great mystery at the heart of creation.

Dark eyes stare back, levelly: big eyes where the depth of brown is almost black. What big eyes he has; what deep pools. But they give nothing away. The boy wears his face like a mask; poker-player; inscrutable always.

His pale face is framed by unruly dark hair; it is overdue a trim – and, let's face it, a wash. His nose is slender; his mouth thin-lipped and pressed firmly shut as though trying to hold something in. A dark smudge of fuzz has sprouted between his mouth and his nose, marking the journey into adolescence. The boy runs a finger over it experimentally before sighing. There was only room for one man in this house.

Downstairs the shouting was just beginning: Carl was angry about... something: the state of the house; his dinner; his beer not being placed for long enough in the fridge... Pick one and insert a tick. His voice was rapidly gaining volume; it didn't take much to ramp him up. Soon he was screaming fit to burst and then there was a loud thump – an impact. A chair being thrown into the wall? The coffee table booted over? His mother? Possibly, for now he could hear her voice, normally low and placating, beginning to keen, like a weeping widow. Only she wasn't. A widow, that is. Unfortunately.

A small crease appeared on the boy's forehead, fracturing his habitual mask. His head cocked sideways and for a moment his eyes seemed to swell and burn with intensity.

"I wish Carl would die and leave us alone," he announced.

His voice at least was perfectly calm, as though he was reciting his times tables. Then he sighed again at the futility of it all. His stepfather was six foot two and in in rude health. He wasn't going anywhere. The boy turned abruptly away and headed back to the sanctuary of his small bedroom. There was no way he was going down there to get caught in one of Carl's rages. That would be stupid. She had married him and brought him into the house: she could live with the consequences.

So the boy left the tacky, cheap mirror, in a spirit of resignation. But had he not been distracted, he might have noticed something: a fractional drag between his movement and that of his reflection. For mirrors, as you may know, are queer things. There are those who tell you that they are merely treated glass

5

– but this is not the whole truth. Mirrors, you see, are portals; things move across them like creatures in a pond; creatures for whom a mirror is not a means of self-regard but instead a window. Had he but known it, something was looking back at the boy from behind his own image; something had noticed him and for reasons of its own was interested in what it saw. And heard. Oh yes, the boy's words had been heard and somewhere deep in the heart of that mirror a cold intelligence was drawing its own conclusions – making its own calculations.

Be careful what you wish for, boy, for there is always a price to be paid.

As luck would have it, Carl's rage ended abruptly with his exiting the house. The boy knew this from the crash of the front door as he stormed off into the night. If he followed the usual routine, he would head for the nearest bar where he would drink far more than was healthy. This was well and good in that it provided a temporary reprieve, but it would probably lead to further problems when he returned home, tanked with lager and angry with the world.

The boy took the opportunity to forage in the kitchen for food: eat quickly, while there was time and opportunity. He loaded a plate with toast, slathered with butter, and a chocolate bar found at the back of the cupboard. He could hear his mother's low weeping in the next room, but shut it out. As he turned to go, she appeared in the doorway, grimacing slightly and holding her side. He didn't look at her, but at the space slightly to her left.

"Oh, you're hungry. Would you like me to fix you some sandwiches?"

The boy shook his head.

There was a pause. The boy stood calmly with his plate; his mother groped for normality, for something to say to this stranger in front of her.

"Have you got any homework for school?" she ventured, slightly awkwardly as though she was addressing a matter of extreme delicacy.

"No. Finished it all at lunchtime in the library."

The lie came easily, as they always did: no hesitation; entirely plausible.

"Oh. Well, as long as you're sorted. I know you like to get it done out of the way."

"Yes." he agreed. "Well, I'm just off to eat this, then there's a book my English teacher told me to read."

"Oh. Alright then, love."

And that was it: he darted past the woman in the doorway, with his head down, moving swiftly back up the stairs. In the safety of his room, he devoured his food, before thumbing through a graphic novel he had borrowed from the school library. Not with a ticket, mark you. The librarian was an old lady who had neatly categorized him as a quiet, bookish boy: polite but liking his own space. There were much bigger fish than he trying to drop large stones in the placid mill pond of her domain. She hardly noticed him most lunchtimes – especially if it was raining and hence rammed to the rafters. Which made it easier to borrow things that he liked the look of: books, magazines, a nice new pen...

The boy stretched out and yawned, resting a hand on his flat stomach. Soon, he was asleep, dreaming of garish cartoon villains, of beautiful women, of screaming and shouting...

Ah.

Perhaps not.

The screaming and shouting was much closer to home after all. It appeared that Carl had returned from the boozer and his mood had not sweetened. Quite the contrary.

A tirade of slurred abuse preceded his unsteady ascent of the stairs. Then a stumble and crash brought him in a heap through the boy's door and onto the floor. There were a few moments where the man and the boy regarded each other with some surprise. Carl never bothered to come in here: his pathetic stepson was beneath his notice. The big man's mean little eyes struggled to focus as he took in his surroundings. So focused was he on reaching the top of the stairs and his wretched wife, that he seemed surprised to find himself here at all; he was like a man who had opened his front door only to discover a tropical rain forest had sprouted in his hallway.

"Wha..? Where?" He grunted in momentary surprise..

Of course, the boy had applied himself with great diligence to avoiding Carl's notice. He wanted to be invisible to him and was extremely put out to have him here as an unexpected guest, crawling on the carpet.

Alas, there was no accounting for bad luck and reflexes dulled by alcohol.

And that was it: the penny dropped: Carl's eyes went *ka-ching* as he realised where he was and who was staring at him from the top of his bed. He also noticed the general chaos of the room itself: books, comics, papers all strewn around the floor; several plates containing food remnants in various stages of decay. He was not impressed, it seemed, and his nostrils began to flair ominously. For all his faults, Carl had a passion for cleanliness.

"You..."

Words failed him; instead, Carl gestured wildly at the room, his sweeping arm like that of a Roman Emperor sending men to their doom.

"Look at this filth," he cried, his voice unaccountably and, God-forbid, rather amusingly high-pitched, like an angry Duchess. Too late the boy realised that he was smirking. Instantly he doused the expression from his face. But the damage was done.

"You think this is *funny*?" howled Carl, his voice cracking up a full octave. "I'll show you *funny,* I'll wipe the smile of your face you little..."

And with that, Carl surged to his feet, a great slab of irate muscle, quivering with rage, and stinking of booze. This was most unfortunate! All of the boy's careful planning had been designed to negate the possibility of him falling victim to Carl's violent wrath. Hadn't he spent the last year avoiding him at all costs?

The boy's eyes darted around frantically for a means of escape, but there was little room for manoeuvre in his small refuge – even for one with his speedy reactions. He was caught, like a rat in trap. Carl's belt jangled noisily as he removed it, before gripping it with a particularly grim smile. The conquering hero.

"Let's see if you're laughing after this," he said, nodding wisely, as if marking a moment of personal perspicacity; taking a step forward he filled the doorway and blocked his stepson's escape route entirely.

The boy's muscles tensed to leap, to twist him out of the way, like a cat; they each stared at the other, trying to anticipate which way to move when the appearance of another figure in the doorway added a wholly unexpected dimension.

"Put that down, you drunken oaf. You'll probably end up wrapping it around your fat neck. Get out of there before you embarrass yourself. Have you any idea how pathetic you are, trying to beat up a little kid?"

The boy's eyebrows shot up, his usual composure deserting him again. His mother was standing in the doorway, hands on hips and a cold sneer of contempt on her face. Now there really was going to be trouble. What on earth was she thinking? He had never heard her so much as hint that Carl might be wrong about something – not that it did her any good if he felt like knocking someone around.

Speechless once more, Carl pounded one meaty palm against the side of his forehead, shaking his head in complete disbelief. His eyes goggled at the gratuitous insults piled upon his worthy head. Such injustice! Such disrespect!

"Are you *mad*?" he squawked, gesturing wildly at her.

The boy's eyes shot over to his mother; he couldn't muster much attachment to her, but even so, this could end up with her being hospitalised. She didn't seem to care. She just stood there, all sassy, wearing jeans and a top that he couldn't remember seeing her in before. And then the strangest thing: she *winked* at him. She winked... like... like there was some hilarious shared joke between them. It wasn't even a *don't worry, this is all going to be OK* wink. It was a full on, cheeky *can you believe this guy?* wink. Carl saw it too, and was not impressed. With a strangled cry, he surged out of the bedroom, belt falling to the ground, arms outstretched, hands reaching to crush, to gouge, to punish.

Somehow the door snicked shut as he exited. The boy sat there, eyes like saucers, the hairs on his neck standing up. Just beyond his door, he could hear harsh, bestial panting and snarling, the sound of flesh against flesh. He waited for his mother's screams to begin, but there was nothing. Instead, there was a sudden roar, which transformed quickly into a blood-curdling scream.

Crash, crash, crash...

The sound of a heavy body falling down, down the stairs; the sudden slam as it hit the bottom, accompanied by the sound of splintering wood.

The boy remained where he was, rooted to his bed for long minutes. Finally, he roused himself, and, opening the door with infinite care, he stepped out onto the landing. It was empty, but there, at the bottom of the stairs lay Carl. His upper body was jammed through the splintered stair rails at an interesting angle. One appeared to be sticking up and out through his chest, and a bloom of blood was spreading around its point of exit. Carl's head was twisted at a crazy angle; his eyes were covered with the film of death; the florid colour which blotched his face was already leeching away.

The boy stared in frank amazement.

To his right another door opened, and his mother emerged, shaking like a terrified animal in a pink towelling dressing gown.

"What… what happened?" she husked, her breath coming in great sobbing gulps.

She edged closer, and wept openly when she saw him.

"I'm sorry," she gasped, "I could hear him shouting at you, but I put the pillow over my head. I wanted to come out to help you, but I was too frightened. Can you forgive me?"

She seized the boy in a desperate embrace which he did not reciprocate, but he tolerated it nonetheless. His gaze shifted from the corpse to his shaking mother.

"But, you did come out. You were out on the landing. You told him to stop."

His words emerged haltingly, as though he tasted each one for effect.

"Didn't you?"

Unable to vocalise a response, she simply shook her head, which was now buried in his shoulder.

"I should have. Oh God, I should have. What happened? Did you fight at the top of the stairs?" She pulled herself back to cup his face in her hands, large brown eyes searching his, desperately. "We can sort this out... we just have to tell the police what happened... that it was self-defence..."

The boy regarded his mother very carefully indeed. *She's telling the truth,* he thought. Which meant that either something very strange was happening, or that he was losing his grip on reality.

His face closed shut. Snick.

"No," he finally replied, calmly. "He said he was going to teach you a lesson and ran out of my room. He must've tripped down the stairs. He was pretty well oiled."

Mother and son stared at each other for some moments, each trying to weigh the other, trying to judge the credibility of the other's words.

"He fell without any help from me," asserted the boy, for once entirely confident in his truthfulness. He thought about starting to tremble, to cry. Wasn't that what he should be doing? It might also convince his wild-eyed mother that he didn't happily, joyfully, push his stepfather down the stairs to his doom. He thought about it, but rejected the idea almost immediately. It would be so out of character as to make her more, not less suspicious; and, in all honesty, he could simply not be bothered to expend such effort for Carl. Instead, he regarded his mother without flinching.

"I wasn't there when he fell. But I'm not sorry. I'm glad that he's dead."

And suddenly, without any warning, he really was trembling, and his eyes scorched with burning tears.

No! he yelled inwardly, fighting desperately to regain control.

His mother's eyes softened and she seized him in a savage embrace, her own body wracked with sobs.

"My poor baby, my poor baby boy..." she crooned into the top of his head.

"No!"

He broke free, flailing wildly, taking great gulps of air as though returning from a deep and perilous dive. He stepped backwards into his room, roughly wiping his eyes on the back of his hand. He felt his face resolve itself into its usual bland configuration before turning his dark gaze on the woman, still sniffing and reaching for him.

"Call the emergency services. We can't just leave him there. It'll look suspicious if we wait too long."

She sighed, and wrapped her arms around herself in lieu of any other willing recipient.

"I know," she said, in a small, defeated voice. "I'll go and call them now."

He nodded at nothing in particular, eyes drawn once more to the fallen titan below. His mother already forgotten, he took a couple of tentative steps downwards. Then the tiny furrow appeared again on his brow. *I wish Carl would die...* And now, rather obligingly, he had. He glanced over his shoulder; he could hear his mother's voice, low and husky, coming from her bedroom.

Out of sight (surely?) the boy lowered his defences. A bright, savage grin appeared on his face, changing it utterly. Eyes glittering, he moved swiftly down the stairs. Carl's face had taken on a grey waxy sheen; blood crusted around his mouth and chin, as though he had vomited it up. The boy's foot itched to kick his foe, to stamp on his prostrate form. He restrained himself, though – such marks would be swiftly noticed by any pathologist worth their salt and could raise entirely avoidable questions.

Be invisible. Don't draw their attention.

Instead, he leaned over Carl's cadaver and whispered in his ear: "Thanks. For dying, that is. That was really decent of you. I won't miss you, obviously; in fact I hope you're being tormented in some netherworld, with a pitchfork up your arse. So long and good riddance."

Perhaps he had hoped there would be some trembling sliver of life left in the man, some remnant to register his words and to be hurt by them. There wasn't of course – though he did feel all the better for having said what he said – what he had always dreamt of saying but couldn't for want of a fat lip or a black eye.

He was back at the top of the stairs when the woman, his mother, reappeared, her dressing gown tightly tied; her face drawn with tiredness and worry.

"They're sending some people: police and ambulance," she informed him.

"Good," he acknowledged, with a curt inclination of his head. And they both stood there in silence until the sirens could be heard on their final approach.

"I'll let them in," volunteered the boy, sliding shamelessly down the bannister before leaping off the now warped rail like a gymnast. To his stepfather he gave nary a glance, but stood there in the hallway, watching with interest as the blue lights gyrated through the frosted glass of the front door, bathing him with their cool, dancing love. He smiled at that and closed his eyes briefly, savouring the moment. Freedom. No more Carl. No more Carl... ever! Then the sirens stopped and there was a knocking at the door. The boy recast his face, making his eyes go big like a character from a manga comic. He wasn't big for his age and could probably pass for twelve instead of his actual thirteen. He sidled gravely to the door, pained sorrow splashed garishly across his features.

"Hello. Yes officer, there's been a terrible accident. It's my dad..." Pause for shuddering breath, as though battling down the grief; rub at the eyes roughly...

The boy thought briefly of Mrs Maher, his drama teacher at school. She was a big, horsey woman with short coarse black hair who insisted on walking around the 'studio' barefoot. She was rumoured to be a lesbian. The boy didn't know – or care – about that; she was OK, for a teacher: not a sadist and no written work. She used to shake her big lumpy head and bulge out her eyes at him during role plays, declaring, "always the quiet ones..." It was a bit awkward, to be honest. He'd let himself get carried away, pretending to be someone else. He was bloody good, of course – pretty much the only subject where that was the case – but it didn't do to draw too much attention to oneself... He used to hold himself back after these initial raptures and she soon lost interest. Well, God knows old Maher would be lobbing bouquets at him had she been there to witness his sensitive portrayal of a grieving son. Not too over-the-top, mark you – that would be, well, crass, and not as convincing. He even allowed a female officer to put her arm around him and give him a long hug. And he did not like to be touched, this boy, to be the subject of intimate physical contact. It made him feel trapped – in fact, quite nauseated, if it persisted for more than a few seconds. But on this occasion, he took it, and even played along, sniffling a bit on her shoulder. He didn't want to seem cold, after all: that might make them question what their eyes and hearts were already explaining away as a tragic accident; another casualty of alcohol abuse. They wanted to believe this, not just to reduce their paperwork, but because they found themselves looking at a scrap of a kid and his distressed mother, weeping over the body of their fallen patriarch. What pathos therein! How truly pathetic in every sense of the word. Why is it people in positions of authority are so terribly affronted by the appearance of strength in others? The boy wondered if they even realised how much they liked to be the ones in control, bustling about, giving their orders, issuing pronouncements on what had clearly happened. These two clearly wouldn't have the will or the water to try anything funny; have you seen the size of the guy?

But the thing was, they were right – on that bit, at least. It would never have occurred to the boy to shove Carl down the stair, thus ending his brutal dominion. Even his dark imagination had its limits. So what had happened? The police said it was a freak accident, but the boy was inwardly sceptical. He remembered his mother, winking at him as she taunted Carl. *She would never have done that!* And yet... there she was. His troubled gaze drifted over to her, sat rumpled in her dressing gown like a big, bedraggled flamingo, snivelling into a cup of tea which she periodically slurped at. *Would she? Could she..?*

No. He remembered her face a she came out onto the landing. Either she was a better actor than he was (doubtful) or his mind had started to project visions to confuse his senses. Perhaps she had had some sort of episode which she then edited out of her memory. He had read an interesting article on psychotic behaviour once at Grandmother's house. *Hmmm…* No. Definitely not. He had never seen anything like that in all the years he had known her. He doubted she would ever be that interesting.

So…?

Something cold ran down the back of his neck, like the gentle caress of fingernails.

I wish Carl would die…

Ridiculous, thought the boy. Pure coincidence. Then he wondered if *he* had had a psychotic episode: had he done something without realising? And that was even scarier, like imagining someone else inside your head, pulling all of the levers while you were stupefied and out of it; a kind of grotesque *brainjacking*.

He stood up sharply, the blanket falling off him to the floor.

"You know what, I think I will have that cup of tea with lots of sugar in it. Yes. Please." His words were coming out too quickly, and he began to shake for real, again, like he had upstairs. Luckily, this brought out the maternal instinct in the policewoman, who gently sat him back down, and explained that he was in shock.

Oh! Thought the boy, *maybe I am!*

He sat still and troubled, sipping at the hot, sweet beverage duly brought to him, and resolving not to think any more about... stuff that couldn't be explained. Maybe he had simply dreamt it. Yes...that would be it. Nodding to himself, the boy decided to take any awkward, unpleasant ideas, lock them in a box and bury that same box deep within a subconscious level of concrete.

Ah! That's better. He smiled and enjoyed the tea which was, he had to admit, a bloody good brew.

Chapter 2
A Wish Has Been Made:
The Price Must Be Paid.

Ah! The sweet rapture of a wish fulfilled... The line had been cast, gossamer light, threaded with starlight and the promise of a Carl-shaped hole in his life. How eagerly he reached for the bait: just the right sort of gentle twitching and he was there, making rash wishes. Silly boy! Don't you know that making wishes puts you in my power? You should have thought of that before you sailed across my silvery depths. But you're a canny one – that's what I noticed about you straight away. Not a foolish bait fish; you have potential. Your body is dark to me and beautiful; your mind is black oil on glass. You have such wile, my pretty, slippery little fish.

Enjoy your triumph. Soon I shall begin to reel you in. Gently, o so gently at first, you won't even realise. Only when the net rushes towards you – and by then it will be too late, boy of mine...

It took some time before everyone had gone. A forensic team appeared and had taken numerous photos of the scene, along with samples, swabs and prints. At least, that's what the boy assumed they were doing. The truth was, he wasn't particularly interested. Kids at school ran wild over crime shows and how they were going to study forensics at college; the boy thought it sounded terrible: really, really tedious. All of that measuring –

and the miniscule care needed to spot a speck of dust in just the wrong place. He'd rather watch grass grow.

Work was not something he was looking forward to at any rate – at least, not the type where you had to expend quantifiable effort in order to get paid. Really? One of the few things he appreciated about school was that there was little in the way of discernible consequences if one chose to do as little as possible.

That being said, school was still something that had to be endured: lesson after lesson with some greying teacher trying to pour their potted wisdom into your head. It was like Hamlet, where the guy had died after his evil brother poured poison in his ear. Only instead of toxins, he was dying of boredom; school was a vast, beige sheet of mediocrity – with the occasional pinprick of interest. Like fratricidal Danish brothers. That at least had elicited a response when his English teacher had meandered off on one of his many tangents. As for things like maths, or physics – well, they were irredeemably awful. Sitting there, awash with disconnected formulae, the boy had found himself pondering stories of animals which chewed off their own leg in order to escape from a trap. Then there were the people: the loud-mouthed braggarts; screeching girls, plastered in foundation; squinty eyed little nerds, surveying them all with contempt. How he loathed them. In fact, school's only good point, over the last year, was that it had offered a refuge from Carl, who spent almost as much time avoiding work as the boy himself.

Well, now that he was off the scene, perhaps the boy would re-evaluate that particular equation: the maths department would be proud of him. He smiled and stretched out in bed. It must have been 4.00 am when the law left, taking Carl with them, zipped up in a big black bag. He had felt a weight lifting from him, as a doe-eyed policeman had gravely told them, "We're taking Carl out of the house, now. There are procedures to be followed. Once you've spoken to an undertaker and the autopsy has been carried out, then you'll be able to see him again."

Yeah, right, like the boy was going to want that. They could just sling that black bag over the bridge and into the river for all he cared.

The boy's smile broadened as he imagined Carl floating like a particularly large turd inexorably towards the estuary and the sea.

Ha ha ha!

Ha ha ha!

The boy jerked awake with a start. For a moment he thought he heard a second voice laughing just slightly after him, as though delayed by a fraction of the second. It was quite disconcerting. His heart pounded for a few moments – he wasn't sure why. It was as though, on some primal level, he sensed that something was *wrong.*

The room was softly lit by the lamp in the corner. He was covered by his own duvet, now. His mother was sitting nearby, sipping a coffee and watching some late-night talk show. She smiled reassuringly at him over her mug.

"You OK love? Having a bad dream?"

The boy rubbed at his eyes before muttering that he was fine.

"It's OK," she continued. "It's been an unusual day. No surprise if you're feeling traumatised."

There was something in her intonation which caught at him. It was a little too cool; too matter-of-fact.

"Er... Yeah. Well, I think I'd better go to bed now – get some proper sleep."

"Righty oh!" she chirruped. "Careful you don't slip on the stairs!"

And with that, she actually snorted with laughter into her coffee.

The boy gaped for a moment, and she winked conspiratorially at him – just like she had before, when... And then it happened: the penny dropped. He felt like someone had just tipped a bucket of iced water all down him, head to toe. He gulped, his Adam's apple bobbing.

"What's up?" she drawled, "somebody died?"

More laughter, this time wild and raucous and not like his mother at all.

Not like his mother.

Because... this wasn't her, was it?

The boy grasped weakly at the back of the sofa.

"Who are you?" he managed to enquire, in a very small voice.

"Me? Why, I'm your own sweet Mammy, aren't I?" she fired back with a wicked grin. "What's the matter? Cat got your tongue?"

She looked straight at him then, a mixture of contempt and pity swirling across her face.

"You're not my mother."

It came out baldy, not an accusation, but a simple statement of fact. She wasn't; he felt it, without any hint of doubt, in his bones.

She regarded him still, coolly, appraising; her eyes seemed to take on a savage brightness, luminescing as he watched.

"No. Of course not."

And now, although it still looked like her, the voice was altogether different: a cold, high falsetto that sent a further dose of ice through his veins.

He darted for the door, filled with a desperate urge to flee. God knows he was fast, but she was there in the doorway before he could take a second step.

"But… How did you…"

"Oh, now wouldn't you like to know! Actually, you probably wouldn't. The process is long and more than usually painfully unpleasant. Poor lovely. You're going on a journey. It's what they call a steep learning curve. I don't know whether you'll survive to come out at the other end of it, but things are going to change around here. They'll change forever. Soon, you'll know the truth."

Her eyes were glittering gold now, but the pupils were vertical slashes, like a cat; like a predator. He went to take an involuntary step backwards, but her hand shot out, grabbing him by the throat in a grip like iron.

"Don't make me angry!" she whispered, leaning closer to his face. "When I lose my temper, I like to throw things around, like dollies down the stairs."

Her eyes gleamed; her head cocked quirkily from side to side as she spoke and he felt himself being lifted of his feet, legs dangling, kicking in the air; the hand like marble on his throat, cutting off his air, starving him of oxygen, choking the life out of him...

Then, somehow, he screamed, his voice raw and full of terror. He screamed so loud, he woke himself up. He was lying there on the sofa, under the blanket that the policewoman had given him.

The door flew open, his mother appearing wild-eyed and white-faced.

"Sweet Jesus! What is it? What happened?"

She rushed to his side, causing him to shriek again, this time like a girl discovering a large and hairy arachnid on her pillow. He found himself involuntarily scrabbling backwards to get away from her, almost falling over the back of the sofa. She froze, shocked and conflicted, and shoved her fist into her mouth. Tears welled in her eyes at this apparent rejection – at his revulsion.

"What did I ever do to you to make you despise me so?" she murmured softly, almost to herself, before half-turning away.

His breathing slowed and he regained control. He felt gingerly at his throat for bruises, but found none.

"No," he said, awkwardly, "it's not... It was just a nightmare, OK. It's not you..."

He frowned at the carpet near her right foot.

"Oh. Alright."

He sensed the hurt in her voice. She wanted to believe him, but, on a deeper level remained unconvinced.

"Well, shall I make you some nice warm milk?"

He accepted it, just because. He even let her hold his hand and then put him to bed like he was a little kid again. This was his mother, after all. The guilt he felt, on some level, for the fact he didn't really love her, certainly didn't respect her, made him do these things without pushing her away from him.

He was so tired. He had to sleep.

To sleep.

Perchance to dream.

That's when he began to realise just how much trouble he was in...

The boy twitched and tossed; his brow continually furrowed, and he muttered thickly into his pillow.

Carl regarded him placidly. He was wearing his mother's pink dressing gown, and was sipping genteelly at a cup of tea.

"You know," he suddenly declared brightly, "there's something special about you. That's why you've been noticed. I'm not sure what it is, but She wants you."

He smiled sweetly, taking another careful sip of tea.

"Who wants me?" demanded the boy.

He was wearing grey shorts and a matching blazer with red bits around the edge of the lapels. It seemed perfectly normal to him, as he gazed across at Carl in the large wood-panelled room. His stepfather crossed his legs, but remained straight-backed on the ornate, bird-patterned couch. He reached out carefully, dropping another five sugar cubes into his tea.

"Who's who, dear boy?" he replied, with a puzzled expression.

"It's no good asking him," called a dry voice. The boy looked across the room to see Mr Hayes, his sometime maths teacher, dancing elegantly with his Grandmother. Mr Hayes was wearing a dinner suit, beautifully pressed. He retained his familiar circular grey fringe, though, and his face had the same chalky pallor that it exhibited in the classroom. When he spoke, tiny strands of saliva stretched at the corners of his mouth.

"He's just a pretty face," continued Mr Hayes, remorselessly.

The boy turned back and was unsurprised to find that Carl was applying lipstick. He smiled coquettishly at him, before pressing his lips onto a tissue to remove any excess colour.

"Don't be foolish!" spat his Grandmother, as she whirled past him. She was clad in some kind of grey dress, which seemed to float around her. At her breast sat a gleaming emerald brooch in the shape of an eye.

"This gown is made from cobwebs and moonbeams!" she informed him, crisply. "I made it myself for a few copper pieces and a small blood sacrifice. I'd like to see that shiftless mother of yours come up with something half as grand!"

"I'm lost," said the boy, sadly.

"I know," replied his Grandmother, turning her head mid-waltz, to eye him disapprovingly. "You should be more careful. Now you have left the path. Beware of the beasts that lurk in shadow."

"How do I get home?" he asked, plaintively.

Grandmother stopped dancing all at once. She stepped smartly away from Mr Hayes, who immediately froze, before bending at the waist like a broken automaton.

"Life consists of many journeys," she told him. "You will sometimes find yourself on strange new roads. You have taken an unexpected detour and now your road leads you somewhere else."

"But to where, Granny?"

Grandmother's face soured at that. She clicked her tongue.

"I am Grandmother, with a capital G," she reminded him. "And now your road is leading you on to a new existence. Don't worry; you won't be lost for long. A guide is coming. And then you'll find your way to Her."

"Her again!" said the boy, crossly. "Who is She? How will I get there?"

Grandmother turned to the far wall of the room, which was adorned with an enormous gilt-framed mirror. It must have been thirty feet by ten.

"They're coming for you. You must be a brave boy, now."

The boy stared, entranced. As he did, the mirror seemed to bend and distort, like one of those fairground mirrors. There was a sound, like many people who had held their breath exhaling at once. The mirror no longer reflected the ballroom, but looked out into a tangle of verdant vegetation, studded with exotic pink blossoms. Steam began to roil out into the room and he heard a woman's voice lifted high in song – a beautiful, terrible song, in a language at once alien yet speaking of power – the power to strip him down to his raw component parts and remake him from scratch.

His Grandmother swayed like a sunflower, her eyes closed in apparent ecstasy.

"She is coming," she intoned. "She is coming!"

Her eyes shot open: they were luminous gold and slashed with a vertical line of black. Somewhere just beyond his sight came a laugh like the peeling of bells. It rippled through him, lifting him from the ground; he felt like he was about to pop, like a bubble, spraying its flimsy essence around the room.

That's when the buzzing started, insistent, dragging him back, eyes sticky with tiredness and stale tears, to his bedroom and smells of sweat and old food.

He stared for a few moments.

"Where am I now?" he said, to no one in particular. "Am I here?"

He was, of course. Here, that is. He heard his mother slowly descending the stairs, to answer the door. The sound of hushed voices, punctuated by his mother's occasional, quavering utterances. He supposed it was all Carl-related. Shaking his head, he massaged his temples. These dreams, they were probably some form of stress. What he needed was a distraction; some r and r. His eyes drifted over to his gaming console. He had had to be careful with that when Carl was around: once he hadn't heard him come back in, immersed as he was in a near future post-apocalyptic killing field, and Carl had screamed about the noise of gunfire, along with promises to hurl his console out of the window. A promise which was entirely credible, the boy knew. Now, he could indulge to his heart's content – and he did. The game's storyline was vaguely satisfying, but what really drew him in was the fact that he was so bloody good. His reflexes were almost unnaturally fast: few of his cyber-foes ever managed to get the drop on him before they had been shot/stabbed or occasionally garrotted. Variety is the spice of life, after all.

The boy's perceptions shifted back into the zone. He was pleased to find that he was better than ever, reacting just that split second before the competition. The hours blurred by before hunger finally made him stop for a break. He ventured downstairs, half-surprised to find that evening had leaked into the house. His mother had resumed her vigil over the television, which, let's be honest, offered her more warmth than her son. He paused, nostrils twitching, mildly caught out to find her smoking. This had not occurred for a long time. He considered pointing this out to her, but decided against: it could start a conversation of more than usual tediousness, and in all honesty, he didn't really care whether she smoked or not.

"Never trust a person without an obvious vice," his Grandmother would pronounce from time to time, when sharing one of her iron-clad aphorisms.

This time, his mother did not attempt to make eye contact.

"I left you some dinner in the oven. I did call up to you, but I don't think you heard. I couldn't face going up the stairs."

He turned silently away to inspect whatever votive offerings she had left for him.

"Oh," she continued, "I called your school to say that you wouldn't be in for at least a week. Under the circumstances. I said you were too upset."

She coughed at the end of this communication, a strange noise somewhere between a laugh and a sob. The boy turned his great dark eyes on her. In the shadow of the unlit kitchen doorway, they were starless voids, sucking in and swallowing any hint of light. Whatever thoughts were flitting around beyond them were drowned entirely in their depths.

"Thanks," he said, flatly, before inspecting the oven. A shop bought lasagne reposed therein, waxy and rather sad now in its cooled form, molten cheese set like old lava. He turned the oven back on and waited for it to return to life. His stomach growled as the smell of food began to circulate the kitchen. The boy's mind did indeed flicker, thoughts flying around in cascade of cerebral energy. He found himself contemplating the faded flowers on the kitchen wallpaper; his finger absently traced the petals. He imagined them trembling beneath his touch; the smell of thick perfume cleaving to his nostrils.

The kitchen wall seemed to indent, just for a moment, like a particularly convincing piece of stage backdrop in a film or a play, but then it was back, solid brick, as it should be.

The boy snatched his hand back. Then the anger kicked in; he cursed his own stupidity, his tiredness. Maybe he really was upset on some level? Maybe this was some sort of delayed shock? Either way, he was determined to restore control. He would not be subject to the whim of misfiring neurons or the swirling depths of his subconscious. No. He would sort himself out. Pronto.

The lasagne barely touched the sides as he consumed it.

Rest. He needed to rest.

And hopefully no more weird dreams.

He wiped his plate down under the tap and left it to dry in the rack. His dark brow knitted now with preoccupation, he barely managed a grunt in his mother's general direction as he went back up the stairs. He went directly to the bathroom, where he relieved his bladder before cleaning his teeth. He stared at his reflection in the shabby old cabinet mirror. The whites of his eyes were a little bloodshot and he was more than usually pale. But no strange blots or stigmata had broken out on his forehead. He looked a bit rough, that was all.

And it was while he was busily convincing himself of this that he found the hairs rising on his arms. He suddenly felt, with absolute certainty, that he was being watched; that he was not alone… Clutching his toothbrush like a stiletto, he spun around, full circle, in the tiny bathroom. No one. Of course there wasn't: you couldn't swing a cat in here, let alone hide some sinister intruder waiting to sneak out, spy or surprise him from behind. He let out a small, nervous laugh before returning to his night-time ablutions. What a fool he was! Too much nervous energy built up. Perhaps an eight hour online killing spree wasn't the best psychotherapy after all. He grinned ruefully at his reflection, which grinned dutifully back at him. Then came the feeling, again, a chill conviction that he was being watched. But… by whom? There was nowhere to hide; this had been established already. How could anyone be watching him? He frowned at his reflection… or at least, he thought he did… only he couldn't have done, because there was his reflection still grinning, rather wickedly back at him. The boy dropped his toothbrush and stared wide-eyed into the mirror; the face there seemed to be doing as it was told now, and gazed back out in vision of neurotic anxiety. That was good, wasn't it? That was what happened when you looked in the mirror. Only then the image gazing back out at him went and spoilt it all by winking at him. Lightning quick, but the boy was almost sure it had happened. And he didn't have any nervous tics that he knew about.

"Holy Jesus!"

He stumbled back wildly, actually falling into the bath. He lay there for a couple of minutes, his chest heaving at the utter *aberrance* of what he had just seen.

That wasn't him. In the mirror.

"There's something in the mirror," the boy murmured to himself, as though trying the concept out for size.

Carefully, he extricated himself from his prone position in the tub. He edged away towards the door, assiduously avoiding the bathroom cabinet. His mind kept telling him that the whole notion was impossible; it was trying to rationalise it away: that's what minds do and it's a much underrated function in the world at large. However, this time, the boy didn't believe it himself. That was NOT his reflection.

It was something else, and it was looking out at him.

The boy shuddered. He felt like an insect, secured to a board by a long and vicious pin. Twist as he might, there was surely no escape. Was there?

Still shaking, the boy climbed into bed, having checked underneath it first.

He really was in a bad way, for he found himself rummaging in the drawer of his bedside table for the little blue box his Grandmother had given him a couple of years ago. In it was a silver crucifix on a chain. The boy carefully secured this around his neck. He had never been one for religion, believing too much in human evil and the need for self-reliance. But tonight he was a humble supplicant, drifting into a fitful sleep whilst clutching the cross of the Saviour.

Back in the bathroom, the cabinet mirror gleamed dully in the orange lamplight emanating from the street below. Whether there was still a face gazing out, grinning, winking or otherwise, we shall never know, for there was no one in the room to see it.

Chapter3
Laid to Rest

Of course, there are many types of death. And how the mortals obsess over them! They fail to appreciate that 'death,' as they call it, is not some simple cessation of existence: it is a change of state. One form is left behind, like a sloughed skin, and the essence is remoulded into something new.

Death is not THE END.

It is not permanent.

Those sneering philosophers who would have you believe so are blinded by their own myopic hubris.

You're not so easily off the hook. Some of you will wish you were. But alas, death is a dream; a fantasy. The margins between it and life are barely discernible; it is so easy to lose oneself.

So easy...

Are you so sure of your existence right now? How certain are you of your reality? What if you were to wake up and find yourself somewhere altogether darker..?

● ●

The days passed by far less pleasantly than the boy had hoped. He had looked forward to a week of wanton self-indulgence at the end of which was the rather tiresome chore of having to attend the funeral of someone whose death he actively welcomed.

What he got was a week with a sharp edge.

The boy had slept, after a fashion, following his unexpected encounter with the mirror. He had awoken feeling less than fully rested, however, and with a sense of deep unease. Still, in the drear light of a March morning, his fears and near hysteria from the night before did seem a little ridiculous. Obviously reflections can't operate independently: mirrors are just glass objects which reflect back whatever passes in front of them.

Aren't they?

See, the mind, as mentioned earlier, is a wonderful and resilient machine. It slowly but surely transposed a web of disbelieving rationality over his nocturnal escapades, which helped to draw their sting.

That being said, he left the bathroom cabinet open when cleaning his teeth from then on – and he also retained possession of his Grandmother's holy chain, despite scoffing at the very idea of such superstitious nonsense. He would wear it as a kind of accessory, that's all – he liked the cool gleam of the cross and the chain around his pallid throat. If it offered any deeper, psycho-spiritual comfort, then he was keeping that to himself.

Needless to say, his mother's half-hearted invitation to visit his erstwhile stepfather at the chapel of rest was declined, to neither person's surprise. He supposed she had to ask him, even though they both knew the idea was practically laughable. He had to wonder if she had any internal doubts herself: had any of her initial love survived the brutal reality of marriage? Was there some glimmer of affection for the man who had terrorised her? Or did she simply undertake her pilgrimage out of a sense of duty or social expectation?

Such folly. He would have none of it. He had to go to the funeral, though – there was just no way round it. He felt the unshakeable weight of expectation bearing down on him and despite his best efforts to slip out from under its crushing mass, it had him pinned.

Thus it was that, after a week of restless lurkage in the house, and a rigid quota of cyber- slaughter on the grounds of his mental health, the boy found it was the night before Carl's final big outing. His mother had dutifully informed him of the arrangements: a simple secular service at the crematorium followed by a wake for friends and family at Carl's favourite pub. A funeral was one thing, but the wake sounded like an ordeal too far: several hours of hanging out with Carl's dodgy mates and his mother's sister's awful family – dull, sneering wretches the lot of them! He didn't care how much expectation rested on him, he'd vault over the coffin to escape that if need be. It must have shown on his face, somehow, despite his best efforts not to react. Well, almost best efforts: he had calculated that if he was too deadpan his mother might choose to overlook what she knew damned well were his true feelings under the guise of ignorance. Therefore, he injected just a dash of revulsion into his expression on hearing of the plans. His mother sighed deeply, and looked just a little more crushed than usual before making him an alternative offer: it appeared that Grandmother had also found the prospect of a wake at The Crown an insalubrious one and had duly excused herself. If he wished, he could spend the afternoon with her instead. It would do him good, his mother intoned, with just the flicker of a smile, to spend an afternoon with the old lady. She was always asking after him and complaining of how infrequently he visited, so this was their chance to have some bonding time.

The boy allowed his mother her small grain of victory: God knew she'd had few enough of them in life. He knew perfectly well that she expected this to be an uncomfortable few hours for both him and his Grandmother. His father's mother would transfix him with her cold judgemental gaze and he would take perverse enjoyment in disappointing her expectations whilst returning her lack of emotional warmth with interest.

Still, needs must, so the arrangements were put in place.

And so it was that, as life began to blossom all around, they marked the end of his stepfather. Carl's big day was blessed by watery spring sunshine. The boy played the part of the loving and supportive son and accompanied his mother in the hearse. As the vehicle sedately negotiated the curves through the Garden of Rest to the doors of the crematorium, the boy found his attention focused on a bed of crocuses, purple and gold, craning up towards the distant sun. He wondered vaguely if Carl had left any money behind, but doubted it very much. A cool breeze ruffled the dainty flowers, but they sprang up again. Amazing really, to think how his meat-headed stepfather had been felled, just like that, at the height of his silver-back dominance – in his own domestic arrangements, at any rate. And yet he and his mother, each fragile in their own way, had weathered the storm and lived on to fight another day.

The boy closed his eyes and smiled, letting the sun caress his face with its benign rays. It was only his mother's strained cough next to him that reminded him that this was a funeral and that he wasn't supposed to be feeling happy and relaxed. Appearances, again.

Assuming an all too believably doleful expression, the boy squinted up through his dark fringe as various people began to appear. The undertaker informed them that all was in place and everyone was waiting within. They were the last to arrive, as was the tradition.

Sighing, the boy allowed his mother to link arms with him.

This was going to be bloody awful.

And just then, scowling over the undertaker's inky shoulder, he saw something completely unexpected. A boy, perhaps a year or so older then him, perched on a stone monument. The sun glinted from loose curls like spun gold. But this was no cherub. This gilded phantom was looking straight at him with a grin of more than usual wickedness. As he watched, the interloper produced a cigarette from what had been apparently empty fingers and flicked it into his mouth. Then, with an amiable nod in the boy's direction, he struck a match on an angel's arse and lit it. The whole thing must have taken about five seconds. The boy didn't know whether to feel shocked or amused; when he felt a reciprocal grin spread wolfishly across his face, he realised that he had, on some level, made up his mind. This disrespectful cad had pricked his interest. Unusually, the boy had seen another human being and actually felt inclined to initiate further communication. This was quite something: the boy found very few people to be of interest – and even fewer to be likeable. But he sensed in this character a kindred spirit – another spiritual nihilist who had only contempt for the rules laid down by society.

39

However, this was an inopportune time to be making introductions. Another cough – this time from the undertaker - recalled him to the present. Reassuming a dour cast, the boy followed his mother's lead and the two of them entered the building, preceded by the broad-shouldered mortician.

The boy adopted the same blank disinterest that got him through his more tedious lessons at school. A couple of people spoke about what a good bloke Carl had been – a fantastic mate, apparently – and some woman he'd never seen waffled on about favourite memories. No one had asked him about his memories of Carl – though apparently they had been a loving father and son. Which to choose? The time he passed out on the lounge floor and wet himself? Or perhaps the touching moment where he had punched his mother in the stomach so hard she had thrown up. The truth, of course, was that his favourite memory of Carl was finding him staked at the bottom of the stairs. Now that was something worth enshrining; perhaps he could write a poem about it and stick it up in their garden of remembrance.

And then, finally, it drew to a close. To the sound of some horrendous rock track – one of Carl's favourite songs, it transpired – the coffin moved serenely off through some mauve curtains and on to oblivion. The boy watched its progress and found that it reminded him of being in the supermarket and watching the items moving down the conveyer belt ready to be scanned.

Beep!

Goodbye Carl.

Beep!

And on to the next one.

At the end of the service, his mother went off to receive the condolences of those who had gathered for the occasion. Grandmother, positioned on the same bench as them, as she was 'family,' grimly offered her support. The boy expected she would be as much comfort as an iron bar – but then again, even that would be better than nothing at all, which is what his mother would get from him.

"You may wait for me outside, if you wish," Grandmother decreed, sweeping him with her bleak grey eyes as if expecting nothing less.

So he did. He turned and walked out, indifferent to the wounded, mute pleas of his mother for a bit of human solidarity at this miserable time. He shut that right out. Nor did he spare a glance for his scrawny, whey-faced aunt, mouth puckered into a rictus of disapproval. He caught a glimpse of Graham, one of his cousins, a bit older than him, directing an unpleasant leer at him through blubber-lips, but he didn't care about that, either... They could all go to hell. He slipped on, past large beer-bellied men, slowly moving out into the aisle, and hard-faced women wearing too much makeup.

Out. Out into the sunshine. He had never been an outdoorsy sort of person, preferring the dank solitude of his bedroom, but on this occasion, it felt just right. The sky was a clear duck egg blue; the breeze was fresh and pure. And now he was free. In an uncharacteristic moment of expressiveness, the boy closed his eyes, twirled around gracefully and emitted a laugh of pure delight.

Somewhere nearby, a pair of hands clapped.

Immediately his eyes flared open and he assumed his customary slouch, face shutting like a door. There, leaning against the wall, and chewing gum ostentatiously, was the youth he'd spied earlier. The boy appraised him, coolly, not giving anything away. He was wearing skinny jeans, a T-shirt with some sort of weird abstract pattern in red and a faded denim jacket. A pair of hip trainers adorned his feet; they were black and red. One foot was placed casually behind him as he leaned against the brickwork. His hair was fairly long: almost shoulder length, and wavy in texture. The sun illuminated various shades of gold. But it was his face that really stood out. Whereas the boy was singularly unremarkable and faded into the background without a second glance, this character was striking. His face was mobile, with full, smiling lips and white, even teeth; his eyes were glittering green with flecks of gold. He looked, thought the boy, like a young movie star.

"So-o-o…" drawled the princely figure before him. "I thought people were supposed to be sad in this place. You are at a funeral, right?"

He flashed a smile that was like the sun emerging from behind a cloud.

The boy shrugged.

"Yeah, it's my stepdad's. He died last week. Fell down the stairs and skewered himself on a broken rail."

He didn't know why he felt the sudden urge to reveal all of these details, but it felt… liberating.

"Wow!" said the youth, his eyes round wells of emerald as his fine eyebrows disappeared under his fringe. "Call me perceptive, but I sense you didn't get on so well with your stepdaddy?"

The boy barked out a laugh entirely devoid, this time, of humour.

"No. I didn't. I hated him, actually – he was a complete dick."

There: he had said it, and it felt good. The two of them stood for a few moments, grinning at each other. Then the stranger broke the spell by moving towards him. He extended a hand: an oddly formal gesture, and for a moment, the boy blinked at it, stupidly.

"I'm Evan. Evan Greenway." he announced, in a grave voice. "Always nice to run into good company at a place of death."

The boy smiled shyly, rather taken aback. He couldn't remember anyone ever saying that he was good company, let alone someone who radiated an edgy kind of cool from every pore. He took Evan's hand and shook it, returning his introduction.

"Where you from, Evan?" he enquired, conscious that he'd never seen him at his local school. "Maybe we could…"

It was at this point that the boy became aware of voices: people spilling out from the building just behind them both. There were rough voices kept unnaturally low and the occasional nervous squawk of laughter. Someone nearby lit a cigarette, the acrid smell wafting around him.

"Looks like the party's breaking up," observed Evan, wryly.

The boy's heart gave a tight little squeeze. He thought… he thought he might have made… a *friend.*

He's going to go, now. He's going to go and I'll never see him again. The thought reverberated around his head with fatalistic certainty. *Stupid! People like me don't have friends like that anyway – the guy's just bored and looking for kicks.*

Remember: the mind is very good at protecting its owner. The boy was so self-reliant and contemptuous of those around him; he was happiest in his own company. Wasn't he? He didn't need anyone else – or any friends who couldn't be relied upon. Did he? And just for a moment, the established self-conviction slipped, revealing a desperate chasm of pure loneliness and misery.

Well, no point in getting maudlin. It was just some kid he'd bumped into in a graveyard – or whatever these places were called. Easy come, easy go…

Out of the corner of his eye, he saw his Aunt staring accusingly at him. Podgy Graham took a couple of steps towards him and then hesitated, as though suddenly nervous of intruding.

"Well, I'd hate to keep you from your family – difficult times and all that. See you around, twinkle toes."

And with that, he gave the boy's dark hair a quick scuff: not hard, or mean, just a playful, affectionate gesture. At least, that's how he chose to interpret it.

Without a second glance, Evan turned on his heels and walked off, golden head high, laughing to himself about some private observation. The boy noticed how people looked as he went past, and some of the men actually moved out of his way before they realised what was happening.

The boy sighed as he felt his cousin's shadow loom over him. Graham was fifteen and six feet tall. He liked to play the hard man around smaller, younger kids – like the boy, here – but was known as being all mouth and no trousers where those of a similar age and size were concerned.

A doughy hand fell on the boy's shoulder and pulled him round.

"Some use you are!" Graham seemed happy to share his thoughts at this point. "There's your mum, bawling her eyes out, and where are you? Scuttling out here chatting up some trash from the estate. You're a disgrace!"

He followed this observation with a prod from a meaty white finger.

A flame lit inside the boy. Of course, by any objective standard, Graham had a point. He was a bad son; he had abandoned his mother to shake all of those hands alone. And he really didn't care – he didn't care whether she was upset or not. She was just there, a featureless fixture in his life; a person for whom he felt neither love nor dislike. Fair cop, really. But how dare he describe Evan as trash? From the estate? What the hell did he know? The boy was incensed at the sheer, obvious injustice. He was worth ten – no, twenty, Grahams. He shone with some sort of light – some sort of energy. Then he bit back his sharp reply; he damped down the anger, resisting the urge to seize Graham's finger and snap it like a twig. If he was capable of such a feat, that is: the boy would be the first to admit that he was no strongman. He was fast enough to grab the finger, but imagine the embarrassment of standing there, huffing and puffing, trying to break the bloody thing to no avail while everyone looked on and Graham's broad face broke into a smug beam of amusement. Then there was the additional irony, not lost on the boy, that this complete stranger with whom he had conversed for about two minutes, had evoked a stronger emotional response than his own mother.

The boy let Graham stare at him and prod him again. He gazed slightly to the left of him, blandly observing the gravel path.

"I felt too upset," he lied, throwing in a good sniff for added effect. He shook slightly, like a frightened dog, and brushed at his eyes. Graham vocalised his disgust through some sort of noise in the back of his throat, rather than verbally. It evinced his contempt for his worm of a cousin. But it had the desired effect, drawing the self-righteous anger from his frame, and causing him to step back as though afraid such worthlessness might be contagious.

His retreat was hastened further, back to his vinegar-faced mother and sister, by the arrival at the boy's side of Grandmother.

Grandmother had a way of sliding suddenly into view without any warning. This had frequently resulted in irksome embarrassment and awkwardness, but on this rare occasion, he was pleased to see her.

The old lady stood ramrod straight. Her steely hair gleamed under a dark net, arranged into some complex kind of bun. Her taut figure was clad in a smart black two-piece suit, and a black velvet choker adorned her throat, decorated with a silver edged silken flower at the centre of which was a gleaming pearl. It made him think of the eyes of dead fish, for some reason. She must have been well into her seventies, but her face was largely smooth and unwrinkled, like some Nordic priestess whose complexion had resolved itself into a condition like fine leather over the years. Her eyebrows were still dark and beneath them, a pair of grey eyes, the colour of northern seas in winter. They were utterly without feeling or warmth and had an unpleasant knack of weighing you up in the manner of a pitiless slave trader, interested only in the worth of an investment. These same eyes now surveyed Graham. She gave nothing away; didn't say a word, but the three of them knew that she had weighed him up aright. Graham retreated just slightly too quickly to be dignified, reminding the boy of a nervous hippopotamus making a break for the safety of the water without wishing to seem like he was doing so.

Grandmother watched him go.

"Fool."

The word issued forth quietly, but with complete contempt.

"Me or him?" enquired the boy, innocently.

Grandmother turned her bleak eyes on him.

"Ever the wit," she observed, with no hint of finding him funny. "On this occasion, him. Though you are equally deserving of the title. Always ready with a quick word or two; never ready when it counts." She tilted her chin even higher to look down on him. "But then, you are my fool, not theirs. That lot can keep their airs and graces for people who can't see through them. Now enough of this idle chatter: I left a joint of beef in the oven. Come."

And he did, as they both knew he would, wondering how anyone could be as unpleasant and unlovable as his Grandmother. He almost admired her for it on some level. It must take years to hone one's persona to such a sharpness that it slices through all emotional self-defences and leaves the recipient feeling hollow inside. Maybe one day he could achieve this glorious state of being himself.

Chapter 4
Grandmother's Cottage

Follow the breadcrumbs, my dark heart. They are golden and delicious. They would have to be to catch one as wily as yourself. But then, everyone has a weak spot somewhere, don't they? One simply has to keep testing the defences, ever so gently, until one finds a bit of give.

I have found the chink in your armour, sweetling.

The path has been reset.

The trap is baited.

Soon, you'll be just where I want you...

The boy sat glumly in a high-backed armchair: it was richly upholstered in red damask and was crowned with an elaborate lace antimacassar. Heavy red drapes hung at the window, along with net curtains, helping to enhance the sense of gloom which pervaded the house. This was the parlour. It was tastefully decorated with dark wooded furniture and designer wallpaper with some sort of floral design. Poppies and wild flowers – that kind of thing. He was noticing the wallpaper, and the various landscape paintings in gilt-edged frames because there really was nothing else to look at. On the sideboard, next to a tray bearing a cut glass decanter and some posh-looking wine glasses was an imposing radio, housed in a dark walnut casing. Grandmother did not have a television set (as she called them). She did not have a television on principle: apparently they rotted the brain. She would occasionally listen to music but her preferred mode of recreation (again, her words) was reading. As in newspapers – or *books*. Yes. Books. Big papery things in covers. Not even with comic strips in them.

From the kitchen, he could hear various culinary sounds: the clanking of pans; the clatter of cutlery. His stomach let out an appreciative growl as the aroma of roast beef circulated around the house. Whilst she had many shortcomings as a Grandmother, he had to admit the old warhorse could cook. It was only rarely that he actually got what could be called a 'proper' dinner, and most of those were due to her. She took a pride in it. Big slabs of meat; roasties; a range of veg cooked just right and oodles of rich brown gravy. Much better, they both agreed, than anything his mother could knock together in the kitchen.

A few more minutes passed before she called his name: it was time to take his station in the dining room. He walked on through and deposited himself in a carved wooden chair at a table dressed in snowy white linen. The shape of the chair made it almost impossible to have anything but a rigid posture, but he contorted himself into a slouch, despite the additional discomfort, on principle. He had his reputation to live down to, after all.

Grandmother sat opposite him; a slight flaring of the nostrils and an extra tight compression of the lips told him that she knew exactly what he was up to, and that he had hit his mark. They stared at each other across the table and their steaming plates like a pair of warring generals, each trying to outmanoeuvre the other.

"I don't suppose," began the old lady, initiating the first skirmish, "that you're terribly upset about your stepfather's death."

The matter-of-fact way in which she said it might have been shocking in any other context.

The boy waited until he was chewing a large and succulent piece of beef before responding, as he knew she hated him speaking with his mouth full.

"No. I'm not. Good riddance to bad rubbish – isn't that what you say about people like him?"

A slight nod acknowledged his tactical move: using her own words against her. Smart. Her mouth quirked slightly.

"Quite so. I never knew what your mother saw in that uncouth layabout. Still, she always did have terrible taste in men."

Ah. A slight on his mother and, by implication, his actual father. She was trying to unbalance him – to press his buttons and see how he reacted.

"Yes: he was a complete tosser." He paused to check that his vulgar expression had hit home. Judging by her pained expression, it had. "But you're right about her. She does have bad taste. Still, she chose to marry him – on her head be it. You know, I suppose, that he used to knock her all around the house?"

Grandmother's visage was grim.

"Not for certain, but I had my suspicions. I take it you didn't feel the need to intervene?"

The boy guffawed at this.

"Me? Intervene? How, exactly? I suppose I could have leapt in front of her to take the worst of it. But why should I? People make choices and they live with the outcome, good or bad."

"How callous you have become," observed Grandmother, with what just might have been a hint of approval. "You're right, I fear, true heroes are rare in the world at large. Better someone else suffers rather than you, yes? It's a craven attitude, but one likely to result in your survival."

Pause. Sweet smile.

"Which would, of course, be a good thing, wouldn't it, my dear?"

He mustered his own most sour face in response to this stiletto through the ribs. He had often considered his relationship with Grandmother to be an odd one – aberrant, even. Weren't Grandmothers supposed to be sweet and nurturing? His was cold and hard, and he strongly suspected that she hated him for some reason. Still, it kept him sharp. Messed up though it was, this was probably his most open relationship. Perhaps they were kindred spirits on some level. He didn't think that he was a terribly nice person either, if he was honest. But it was nice to be able to look the enemy in the eye; to circle each other, looking for an opening. There was an honesty in their mutual antipathy which was lacking in any other area of his life.

He offered her a nasty smirk.

"I'm glad you think so, Granny. And yes, I agree. People who sacrifice themselves for others are really dumb. What's the point? Gratitude won't bring you back, will it?"

He paused then and shot her a defiant glare.

"I'm going to survive it all. I've been dodging other people's crap all my life and I've become pretty good at it. The next time she brings some stupid oaf home to be my stepdad, I'll follow my real dad's lead and check out of the hotel."

"Hmph!" His adversary remained unmoved by this speech and he sensed that he had lowered his guard, revealing a little too much of his actual feelings. "All very worthy I'm sure. And yes, I daresay you would slither off into the shadows, just like him: as soon as life became difficult he vanished, leaving it for others to deal with the mess he left behind."

The boy contemplated her, curiously.

"It's funny," he mused. You don't love him – or even like him, do you?" He gestured to a faded black and white photo on the dresser. It contained the image of a young baby: big dark eyes; moist lower lip. It googled uncomprehendingly at the camera. Its face was framed with dark hair. "That's the only photo I've ever seen of my dad. So."

Time for the gloves to come off now. Since they were being so brutally honest with each other, there were questions that had always drifted around in his mind, but he had feared to ask them: maybe now was the time for a bit of honesty after all.

"So. What did he do to you? My father? What did he do to make you hate him so much? Why aren't there other photos of him around the house? First day at school picture? Eighteenth birthday. Where are they? Is that why you hate me, too? I don't care, of course, but out of curiosity, is it? Because of something he did?"

"Aah!" Grandmother fixed him with a stare so intense it made him shiver slightly. A chilly bleakness crept over her taut face, as though it was suddenly freezing before his eyes. Her eyes glimmered like dying stars and without warning, he felt a crack in the stiff lacquer that she presented to all of the world. For a moment he thought of the ornate cases into which the Egyptians had placed their mummies. He wasn't sure he wanted to see what was actually inside. "We're going there, at last, are we? I wondered when we would make this little journey. It was only a matter of time, I suppose. Some things can't be kept secret however hard one tries." Her voice assumed a haunted resonance, echoing, or so it seemed, from the past – from somewhere – or *somewhen* – else.

"My father!" The boy rapped the handle of his knife on the table, hard. He was close to getting an answer for once, and didn't want this moment to slip away. "What did he do? Why can't you stand your own son?"

The room went eerily calm as his Grandmother surveyed him, her face still frozen, immobile. Finally, something shifted within her – like a gear suddenly snapping into place. She leaned forward, eyes drilling holes in him.

"That, my dear is simple." She paused to skewer a potato with unnecessary brutality. "You see, he wasn't my son at all."

Chapter 5
The Truth Will Out

Ah! The truth! Such importance you mortals place upon this notion. Of course, I feel bound to point out that the entire concept is wholly subjective and prone to revision. Who really knows the truth? The truth is there is no truth. And sometimes, when it seems that there might be, you hope with all your pitiful being that it's not true at all – please let this be a lie, a hoax, a hallucination. It is really rather amusing how you idealise the truth as some precious moral certainty. My oh my: if you knew what was really going on out there you'd never sleep again!

Please don't come to me, whining about the truth, until you're big enough to cope with it.

Well, of all the things she might have said, he hadn't anticipated that one. The boy found he was staring at his Grandmother with his mouth hanging open like an old trapdoor. For her part, the old girl continued to eat a roast potato with a faint smile, as though she had just passed some pleasantry about the weather.

"I don't understand," said the boy. "If my father isn't your son, where on earth did I come from? Did you adopt, of or something?"

"Oh no," she replied, equably, "nothing like that. I never wanted that – it had to be my flesh and blood, you see. I would never have knowingly cared for someone else's child."

Then, sadness suddenly floated across her steely old brow, making her look uncharacteristically human.

"I so desperately wanted a child. A child to show how much I loved my Harold, God rest his soul. We tried for years and then, just when I was on the verge of giving up, it happened: I fell pregnant. I loved every moment: the cramps, the morning sickness, the bloating. I had life in me and I loved that baby, oh, God, how I loved him. When he was born, he was just perfect. We called him Paul and we loved him with all of our hearts. I can still see his smiling little face; I can still smell his hair. And the love that glowed in his eyes when he looked into mine; that precious, precious memory."

The narrative paused as Grandmother seemed to disappear, her eyes somewhere else. A reverie fell upon the room.

The boy twitched, nervously. Never had he seen such raw emotion from his Grandmother. It was… discomfiting. He waited, and when there was no cessation in the lull, he coughed, gently, and spoke, in a very quiet voice.

"Yes, Paul. But that was my dad. Paul. Your son. And you loved him then. So – what happened?"

The old woman's gaze slowly returned to him and then her face seemed to drop, as though someone had cut the ties that kept it tight and close fitting.

"They took him," she intoned, in a voice so low he had to strain to catch it.

The boy felt unaccountable prickles on his skin.

He wasn't sure he wanted to know the truth after all. This was taking him in an entirely unexpected direction.

He swallowed, before forcing himself to enquire: "Who? Who took him?"

Her stare didn't waver.

"The Others. The Others took him. I don't know who they are or why, but they took my beautiful boy and they left me something else in his place."

"What do you mean?" The boy's voice squeaked involuntarily. This was too much – too weird. It was creeping him out. It seemed he didn't want the answers after all. But he had to ask, all the same – something drove him on to ask those awful bloody questions. He couldn't stop himself.

Grandmother's expression began to tighten. The clockwork was beginning to whirr back into life, as though a mysterious hand had wound it up. Her eyes shifted from empty pools of grief and longing to something more... speculative. She now gave him a measuring look, before shrugging.

"I've gone this far, you might as well know the rest, I suppose, much joy it may bring you."

That's when he realised how angry she was: angry with her child's supposed abductors; far more angry with him for tearing her open and forcing her to show her hidden wounds and vulnerabilities. She knew damned well he didn't want to hear any more, she could see it in his anxious, pasty white face, but she went on anyway, grinding him under the weight of her terrible Truth.

"We made a little playroom for Paul. I would lock him in for his safety when I needed to do chores around the house. He loved it. There were lots of toys and musical instruments for him to play with. It was bright and the wallpaper was decorated with choo choo trains. The toy box was like a pirate's treasure chest and there was a sweet old dressing table that one of my friends had given to us. It was painted blue and Harold stencilled the drawers with pictures of little red soldiers.

One Saturday, we had arranged for some of Harold's work friends to come over for dinner, so I was busy in the kitchen. I wanted to put on a show for them you see; Harold was due a promotion at the time. I was preparing vegetables at the sink, when I heard a sudden bump and a cry – no, a scream – from the playroom. I rushed upstairs as fast as I could, fumbling at the lock. It was so quiet. I was calling all the time, calling to my little baby, telling him that Mummy was coming. I flung the door open and…" Here she had to stop for breath, for despite her self-control, she had felt herself swept along by the tide of these past events.

"And?" whispered the boy, all eyes.

"And there was the baby, just sitting there, looking at me quite calmly." She paused, anticipating his next question. She raised her hand to silence him, before, leaning over the table once more and hissing with sudden fury, "but it wasn't Paul. I don't know what it was, but that was not my baby. A mother cannot be deceived so easily. That… creature just sat, looking at me. Watching, watching, always watching."

She paused again, before giving a smile completely lacking in warmth. "Harold had to cancel his dinner party. Men are so simple. He looked at that baby and saw his own son. They are clever, you see, in their facsimiles, for it was physically identical. But I knew, oh I knew. Harold convinced himself that I had had some sort of breakdown. He made me go to see doctors; I had to endure various treatments, suffer life through a veil of tranquillisers so that I no longer knew where I was. Perhaps that even helped to numb the pain, I don't know. After a while, I gave myself a shake. I couldn't really blame Harold or the others for thinking me mad: my story was, after all, preposterous. I would think me mad, too. So, I took a deep breath and got on with it. I raised that baby, fed it, clothed it, put it to bed. But I never accepted it, not in my heart, for it wasn't mine."

The boy thought deeply. He actually felt a twinge of something which might be compassion. He looked at her again, with the small crease back on his brow.

"Have you ever thought that they might be right?" he asked, tentatively. "What if... what if you really were ill? What if the baby really was yours?"

Grandmother pressed her lips into a hard line before cracking them open to reply.

"It wasn't mine. I looked into its eyes and saw nothing – none of the love, none of the wicked humour that my Paul had. He wouldn't play with the toys that Paul had loved: his drum went unbeaten; his little teddy bear was left to gather dust on the floor beneath the cot. And he smelt wrong. That thing was NOT my child."

Her tone left little room for debate, but still he persisted. This was not necessarily to bring comfort to Grandma, but to himself, for the alternative was to accept what she was saying – and he really didn't want to do that.

"But, listen, you said yourself, he was in a locked room. It was still locked when you got up there. How could anyone have got in to take him?"

She looked at him for a moment, like a benign teacher might regard a well-meaning pupil who has just proffered a statement of unbelievable stupidity. Then, she started to laugh, little gasps at first, rising to a howling crescendo as her shoulders shook with fierce energy. Tears appeared on her cheeks as the fit took her. After a few minutes, her laughter faded and she took deep, gulping breaths to steady herself. The boy was rooted in position, more petrified by this display of wild matriarchal mirth than if she had suddenly screamed abuse at him.

"Oh, my poor boy," she sighed. "So very naïve. There are more things in heaven and earth, as they say."

"What?" snapped the boy, prickled now by her patronising tone. "You're talking about ghosts now? Because only ghosts could float through a locked door – and even then, they wouldn't be able to float your baby back out through solid wood!"

"They didn't use that door, silly," she replied, indulgently.

"But… what then… Oh! You mean the window?"

"On no, that was locked too: we were worried that Paul might manage to climb up and fall out."

"Then… What? What door?" demanded the boy, losing patience. Maybe, beneath the surface, Grandmother was actually cracked. Maybe she was ragingly insane. Maybe? He wasn't sure if this brought him comfort or not.

She gave him another cool look, appraising, testing.

"They took him through the mirror," she informed him, matter-of-factly.

The boy felt the blood physically drain out of his face as though someone had pulled a plug on him. He let his knife fall from now nerveless fingers. He fought the sense of blind terror that was beginning to rise up inside him.

"But... that's impossible... isn't it?" His voice quavered and he found his eyes filling with tears. It couldn't be true; it... just... couldn't.

"It is true."

Grandmother leant across towards him, earnestly taking his unresisting hands into hers.

"That afternoon, when I ran upstairs into the sun-dappled playroom, I saw him, you see." She looked to check that he was following her. "Paul, I mean. Just for a second, I saw his face in the mirror over the pretty blue dressing table. His little hands were pressed against the glass; his face was red and he was screaming in sheer terror. But I couldn't hear anything. Mirrors are sound-proofed, it would seem. And then he was gone. Something snatched him away from me. That's how Harold found me, howling, breaking my nails clawing against the surface of the mirror." She paused sadly. "Poor man; no wonder he thought me mad."

Sighing wearily, she released his hands, and dabbed the fast-flowing tears from his cheeks with a napkin.

"So you see, that boy I raised was never mine; he was not my son at all – just a replacement for the real child that I loved and they stole. Like a doll, I suppose."

The boy shook for some moments, dimly aware of the snot running down his upper lip, and he wept. He wept, because he was thinking of the bathroom mirror, and Carl dying and all of that, not because he felt sorry for Grandmother. He knew, on some fundamental level, that it was all true – and that, more meaningfully for him, there really had been something in the mirror that night, looking out at him. He caught his breath, trying to calm himself, and he suddenly noticed something.

"There are no mirrors in your house." He spoke, haltingly, because he was distressed, but he stared wildly around the dining room, trying to ascertain the truth of his observation.

"No." confirmed Grandmother, as she began to mechanically clear the table.

The boy turned sharply to look at her again, as if with new eyes, another thought bubbling unwanted into his head.

"But... if that baby wasn't your son. Then... then I'm not your grandson, am I?"

The old lady smiled at him. Putting down the plates for a moment, she leaned across to ruffle his hair.

"No." she said. "You're not."

Chapter 6
Seven Years' Bad Luck

The thing about doors is that they are everywhere. Think of this world as a vast colander: blocking a hole or two here and there really won't make a great deal of difference. Planes of existence are permeable, you see. It may be theoretically possible to seal one off, but this has never happened to my considerable knowledge.

There are doors everywhere; some you know about and some you don't.

You can't shut out a rising tide by locking a door: it will seep in anyway.

That's what we do. We seep through. Nothing much you can do about it.

And soon I will transform from the abstract to something rather more concrete.

Watch your back, my darling. One day we shall have our formal introduction.

When the boy got home later that evening, he waited until his mother went to bed, sad-faced and yet somehow not entirely convincing as the grief-stricken widow. The wake, it seemed, had been a cathartic experience for her and if she had had a few drinks to help her along, then that helped to induce a state of particularly heavy sleep. He stood poised on the landing now, listening to her rhythmic breathing and occasional snores. Satisfied, he moved into the bathroom, where he produced a screwdriver. Working steadily, he removed the cabinet doors and took them out into the garage, where he draped them in a cloth and smashed each mirror with a hammer. The shards were neatly cleared away via a dustpan and brush and deposited in the bin.

There had once been a mirror in the lounge, but as luck would have it, Carl had broken it in a drunken rage by hurling a beer glass into the wall. He couldn't remember why, but he wasn't complaining.

A couple of mirrors still existed in his mother's bedroom, but he never went in there, so figured they weren't too dangerous to him. Besides, it would be tricky enough explaining the bathroom cabinet away, let alone those in her room.

Instead, he retired for the night, feeling slightly foolish for believing his crazy Grandmother but also secure in the knowledge that he had taken the actions required. He had blocked the portal. He was safe.

A shaft of moonlight broke across the bed and traced its finger across the boy's forehead. The curtains shifted uneasily, as if teased by a breeze: except the windows were shut. A frown slowly forming on his brow, the boy's eyes cracked open.

His face felt warm – in fact, so did his body. He became aware of wisps of steam floating into the air above him. Then his other senses kicked in: there were cheeps, squawks and whirs; the air was moist and a rich perfume hung upon it – a thick, voluptuous scent that somehow made him think of decay. Turning his head, he saw the base of an enormous tree trunk to his left, festooned with purple vines as thick as his arm.

To his right he heard a hiss and cricked his neck around to see a wide black feline face curling its lips at him. Golden eyes glowed in its face and dagger-like fangs dripped saliva onto the forest litter. The boy stared with some surprise. The creature bore some resemblance to a black panther, except that it was significantly bigger and had six legs instead of four. Just behind this formidable predator, stood a slender feminine form. She was wearing clothes which fitted very closely and which seemed oddly organic in their appearance. Her hair was red as autumn leaves and the sides of her face were decorated by swirling black tattoos or war paint which faded out into faint speckles at the temple. In the midst of these fantastical designs a pair of green eyes glittered, surely too big and too green to be human. The tip of a pink tongue was nestled in the corner of thick, mobile, crimson lips as though to denote a certain puzzlement. She cocked her head to one side and then moved forward in quick, lithe steps. That was when he noticed that the staff she carried actually had a very sharp end and was in fact a spear. A spear which seemed intimately linked to the supple musculature of her arm.

"Hello?" he ventured, feeling rather awkward.

By way of an answer, she took a sinuous step towards him, her eyes fixed upon him and bright with savage curiosity.

"What are you?" she murmured in a silky voice.

The boy had an unpleasant inkling that she didn't give a damn what his answer was, but was simply trying to distract him while she positioned herself for a strike. His own eyes narrowed and his muscles tensed. His instincts were right. With a blur of movement, the spear was suddenly launched towards him. Fast himself, the boy sprang aside, before rolling smoothly into a crouching position.

The huntress grinned, revealing twin rows of pointed teeth.

"Clever boy," she whispered, teasingly. "You're a fast one; smart, too. Why don't you run, now? Maybe you can escape me."

Not waiting to be asked again, the boy surged up with surprising vitality and flung himself through the undergrowth. Big wet leaves slapped at him as he charged onwards, head down, weaving to avoid obstacles. His breath came in great gulps. He had no idea he could run this fast!

Somewhere behind him he heard a wild bubble of laughter, followed by an ululating war cry. Luckily, this soon seemed to fall away as he swept through the verdant foliage, a dark blur against the green. He ran and ran, exhilarated by the chase. His muscles seemed to burn with raw power; it was wonderful; it was truly liberating. Eventually, he came to a stop in a clearing; he breathed slow and deep, maintaining control, and taking stock of his surroundings. Gnarled, mangrove-like trees stood sentinel around the clearing's edge. To his left a clear pool was fed by a spring. It burbled happily, festooned around its edges by small blue flowers. Loping over, he bent to take a drink. And that was when the spear took him. Passing through his right shoulder, it threw him to the floor in a glorious blossoming of agony. Across the clearing, a red-haired apparition strode confidently towards him, a gleaming, curved knife in her hand. He tried to rise, but the pain was too great.

"Quiet now," she husked, gently, and actually stroked his trembling face, "you gave a good chase, and I'll speed you on your way." The knife glittered, like a cold slash in the weft of reality.

"But you are prey, boy. Remember that. The hunter will always come for the prey."

The knife moved again, swiftly, against his pulsing throat now, cold; so cold. She leaned in and whispered into his ear.

"No matter how many mirrors you smash..."

There was a burning slice and then the images around him began to fade.

He woke screaming.

Just a nightmare.

Just a nightmare.

Nothing to worry about.

The boy was sweating profusely.

He quickly turned on the light and gradually calmed his breathing.

Going out onto the landing, he could still hear his mother snoring. Funny. He almost wanted her to emerge now and to offer him some maternal comfort.

He went to the bathroom, and, staring at the now blind cabinet, splashed water over his face before drinking great gulps from the tap.

It would all be alright in the morning.

Except that it wasn't. In fact, it got off to a terrible start when his mother flipped out about the bathroom cabinet and it went downhill from there.

The trouble followed him to school in maths. Maths. Ugh! The bane of his existence!

First, Mr Hayes remembered that he had yet to hand in his homework – in fact, any of his homework. Now normally, a well-placed distraction worked wonders. The boy was fairly confident that Mr Hayes was of that school of teachers who believed if pupils didn't want to do their homework, then that was up to them. They were wasting their own potential, not his – in fact, they were saving him work: hurrah! Less marking! But not this time. Mr Hayes' watery blue eyes gazed wistfully at him, as if coming to a belated and tragic realisation. It just wouldn't do, apparently. Worse, he actually asked him to remain behind after class to discuss the matter. The boy closed his eyes and breathed deeply. He wasn't one to be precious, but having to spend any more time than was absolutely necessary in this soulless classroom, with its faded displays of geometric shapes and dreary equations, probably dating back to 1983, was almost more than he could bear.

In the event, Mr Hayes commiserated with him on the death of his father. His chalky face took on a mournful visage, like a professional undertaker. But then he moved closer, closer than the boy liked, and he leaned towards him to stare into his face.

The boy fought to remain still; his flesh tingled with the desire to at least back-up, if not run straight out of the door. Stale old breath roiled over him, with a grave-like stink. He was forced to make eye contact – lord how he hated doing that – and then he actually reached out to clumsily pat his shoulder. The boy flinched at this, and shook slightly, like a young gazelle straining to leap into the bush. It probably didn't help his cause which, Mr Hayes assured him, was quite hopeless. The sticky strands of saliva at the corners of his mouth stretched impressively as he relayed his determination to winkle work out of the remiss student in front of him – it was the least he could do, to make sure that he honoured his father's memory. The boy was fairly sure that Carl would not have spent long hours lying awake at night contemplating his stepson's progress in mathematics, but it didn't seem politic to point this out.

Instead, he was forced to nod, seriously, and to give an equally earnest assurance that he would turn over a new leaf: his work would be completed on time, or he would spend his lunchtime in the maths department until it was. Great.

Heavy of heart, the boy trudged down the now silent corridor. Sounds of feral joy echoed faintly from the playground as lunchtime loosened the chains of academe. The boy glided past the external doors and moved, like a grieving spectre, into the sanctuary of the library. There, he actually produced his maths book and for the first time that year attempted the homework. It was not the epiphany Mr Hayes might have hoped for. Numbers and figures swam confusingly across the page, defying him to understand them. After ten brain-aching minutes of scratching vainly at the page, he hit upon a better idea: there, secreted in a far corner was Novak, another of life's social misfits. However, whilst the boy actively elected to give homo sapiens a wide berth not everyone shared his sociopathic desires. Novak – and he wasn't sure whether this was his first, second or indeed, real, name - wore a perpetually sad expression as one who longed for a kind word – or any other kind of social interaction. Of course, that wasn't likely around here. Novak was clever: really, insanely clever, and he was treated with universal disdain as a result. It didn't help that he was nervous and had a tic; nor did he have a clue about his personal appearance. The boy had heard that his parents were immigrants; this came with its own nasty little subtext, of course. The other kids laughed at the cheap tackiness of his attire, not to mention his school bag. Had the boy ever attended a PE lesson (he hadn't) then he would have seen an additional forum for Novak's ritual humiliation.

However bad things are, there's always someone worse off than you, right?

The boy grabbed his stuff and moved over to the corner.

"Mind if I sit here?" he heard himself ask and almost chuckled at the unbelievability of it all.

Novak, who had been engrossed in a really boring-looking book, looked up, blinking in apparent confusion. He stared at the boy and then around the immediate vicinity, as if to check that he was actually being spoken to. His left eye spasmed a couple of times.

The boy forced his lips into something approximating a smile and sat himself down, positioning his rumpled maths book strategically. He wondered aloud how to tackle the mystical equations inflicted upon him by Mr Hayes.

Novak might have had the social awareness of a wombat, but even he picked up on the hint. In no time, he was chattering away about algebraic formulae; the freak actually seemed to be enjoying himself. The boy had enough self-discipline not to seize Novak by the neck and shake him about. Instead, he made his eyes very big and round, and wondered, in a tone of innocent hope, whether Novak might be able to show him how it was all done...

And then it was all over. The awful maths was complete: thanks Novak! The boy made sure to be pleasant to him: after all, he might need his assistance again at some point in the future, especially if Mr Hayes decided to prolong his crusade to save his mathematical soul. For now, though, he was free, and, having hovered with Novak for the minimum possible time after he had served his purpose, the boy slipped away to prowl the book stacks for some interesting graphic novels. He smiled to himself. Crisis over. For a while, he had worried that his usual strategies might be failing him. But now things were back under control; there was no need to worry after all. Which was true – for a couple of days. The maths work was handed in to an approving Mr Hayes, who promptly seemed to lose interest in capitalising on this tactical success. The boy went back to his usual position of near invisibility at the back of the room. At home, his mother had recovered from the shocking fate of the bathroom cabinet, too. In an inspired moment, he had tearfully explained to her that he hated himself and that he couldn't stand the way he looked. In a moment of self-loathing, he had removed the mirrors. Rubbish, of course – handily picked up from a TV feature on teenage self-image by a well-meaning breakfast show. But it was enough: she bought it, and even promised not to replace the cabinet for a while at least.

Yeah. He was smooth. He had to admit it. It took an early bird to catch him out. Someone very fast and sharp. Not some musty maths teacher, or his pitifully gullible mother. No one was going to get the drop on him again, after all of the crap he'd been through lately. They'd have to be a ninja...

A six foot, two hundred pound ninja.

Called Ricky Fosseway.

Ah.

Ricky liked to think of himself as the toughest kid in the year. He was certainly tall and thickset – but this was more fat than muscle. He had a particular fondness for pasties and crisps, both of which he was to be seen feasting upon on most break times. This did his complexion few favours, for his face was ravaged with large, angry spots, rising like mottes from his pale, greasy skin. Ricky had equally greasy hair, somewhere between dark blond and light brown, and his eyes maintained a perpetual and suspicious squint. You noticed the meanness in them rather than the colour, which was fairly indeterminate. Ricky's academic career had much in common with the boy's – he had an aversion to work which was quite impressive. His tactics were rather less subtle, however, for he preferred Neanderthal belligerence rather than avoiding too much attention; power over finesse. And, if success is to be measured by results, then he was indeed successful: pretty much all of his teachers had written him off as an odious slug who was not worth their trouble. He would get his just dessert come the exams – and then in life at large.

Ricky's third predilection, in addition to processed carbs and work avoidance, was the infliction of suffering. Every now and then, he would pick a target – a bit like employee of the month, except that this was an honour you really didn't want. Poor old Novak had enjoyed much close attention from his burly schoolmate, who showed a genuine interest in human psychology belying hidden depths of emotional intelligence. Indeed, it was hapless Novak who served as a conduit on this occasion.

The boy had decided to keep channels open with Novak, just in case he had use for him in the future. Unfortunately, Novak responded to this by thinking that he had acquired a friend. This was most... vexatious. He kept coming to talk to him, first in the library and then in class. The boy was adept at keeping these encounters brief, but it was a different story when Novak actually decided to sit with him in English. (One advantage of maths was that, due to Novak's brilliance, they were in different classes. A curse upon the English Department, with its well-meaning policy of mixed ability...)

The boy blanched, even paler than his usual wan tones, and gave a great inward groan. People were turning around and looking, before sniggering and making comments. They were all noticing him. Novak was oblivious and was holding forth, at some volume, about mathematical equations – perhaps he would like to work on them with him again at some time? This was getting worse. To the left someone openly guffawed. The boy massaged the bridge of his nose and closed his eyes, wishing that Novak would shut up and go away. When he opened them, he was disturbed to make eye contact with Ricky Fosseway, who was staring at him like a scientist might regard a new lab rat. Something in his eyes moved and flickered, and the corners of his mouth quirked slightly. There was no hint of friendliness in it, though, that smile, and the boy's heart sank a bit further. He anticipated what would happen next, so at the end of the lesson he killed a bit of time by asking the teacher for some advice on story writing. Miss Harris was a pretty, young teacher, full of hope for her young charges, and, after getting over her initial surprise, chatted away to him with as much enthusiasm as Novak, who was, infuriatingly, waiting for him at the door. When he could delay no longer, he headed for the corridor. Maybe, just maybe, he had read the signals wrong; maybe Ricky wouldn't be...

Oh.

Of course.

He had waited a little way down from the room, to ambush him at the corner. Yes. An ambush predator – that was a good way of classifying him. A deceptively gentle hand rose lazily to the boy's chest to arrest his progress. Novak, still chattering at the boy's back like a parakeet, emitted a startled squawk and scuttled past, clutching at his bag protectively.

Thanks for the back-up, Novak. Not that the boy had ever lifted a finger to defend him – better someone else suffered the attention of the class sadist than him – but even so!

"So..."

Ricky's plump lips broke into an unpleasant smile. The boy stared somewhere over his left shoulder and waited for the inevitable witticism

"It looks like Novak's found some love, at last. How long have you two been an item?"

Fosseway's dim-witted sidekicks chuckled at this hilarious pronouncement. Hurr hurr…

"He just sat with me today. I don't even like him." replied the boy in a flat, bored voice. Which was true, as it happens.

"Not what it sounds like to me. Sounds like you been meetin' up, whisperin' sweet nothin's about maths shit."

The smile became a grin.

"Ahh. Pretty cute, really, eh lads?"

Hurr hurr.

Ricky's large paw moved to cup the boy's chin. He casually pinched his lips, before patting his cheek gently. Then he leaned forward, right in the boy's face; his warm, pasty-breath washed across his face. To his credit, the boy remained perfectly still; he hid his revulsion completely, even when Fosseways lips brushed his ear as he whispered "I'll be watching you…"

Then it was finished. Fosseway and his goons strolled off like nothing had happened. Only it wasn't really over at all. The boy knew how this worked. Fosseway liked to tenderise his victims. Having marked him out as the current target, he would let him stew for a while before striking again, just when his nerves had started to relax and he was wondering if it was a one-off.

It wouldn't be a one-off. It never was. Like Billy Bones, he had been given the Black Spot, and all that lay before him was to be Ricky Fosseway's plaything, like a big, fat, mean old cat with a mouse.

The boy sighed and sloped off. He ignored Novak, who was hovering at the bottom of the stairs, and was now clamouring about Ricky – what had he said and done? Was he OK.

"No," said the boy, fixing him with a cool stare. "It's not OK. I'm not OK. Just leave me alone and never, ever, sit next to me again."

He was dimly aware of Novak's face, collapsing like papier-mâché left out in the rain. But he didn't really care about the feelings of others anyway, and certainly not Novak, who had gifted him the tender mercies of Ricky Fosseway.

The boy headed for the library and Novak, thankfully, did not attempt to follow him.

Chapter 7
A Friend in Need

Poor lamb! Did the nasty bully hurt you? Yes?

An interesting specimen, that one. He understands that cruelty is an art form. He studies his prey and anticipates its next move and where he is likely to find it hiding. All qualities which I can admire. Still, the fact remains that he is an oaf. There are times when a crude tool can be of use, but all in all, I prefer to operate with some subtlety. My prey – my chosen ones – they walk smiling into the web, embracing the trap as though a joyful opportunity. They don't suspect the truth until it's too late. And by then, they're caught.

But don't worry, little one. I have great plans for you – and I don't like others making free with my vassals. Treat this as a test of your abilities; evolution, after all, is meant to make a species stronger in the face of adversity, is it not? Hone your reflexes, child; polish your deceptions that they might gleam darkly in the light.

Soon, now; very soon.

It went on, pretty much as he had expected. The boy was very good at staying low; he was a master of avoidance. But this added level of challenge seemed to whet Fosseway's appetite still further. He would be walking to class, purposefully late so as to avoid his tormentor, and there he was, released to go to the toilet. Nothing said, no acknowledgement – until the slap to the face, just as they passed each other by.

The boy maintained a steady pace, neither speeding up nor slowing down. The truth was, he could have easily avoided that slap – but he figured that would just annoy Ricky, and would probably lead to greater pain in the long run. So he took it; he took it and said nothing.

Sometimes days would pass without incident; then Ricky would be there, at the end of lunch, and he would be pressed up against the wall by the throat, while Ricky smiled his smile and breathed in his face, and told him how much he enjoyed their little conversations. His two cronies would nod and chuckle in the background, like approving grandparents. Then, with a parting punch to the stomach, he would be left to go his own way.

The ambush points varied in time and place. Sometimes there would be an encounter as he walked to school; at other times it would be in the toilets at break; once or twice, it would happen in a lesson, whilst the teacher was distracted or had left the room to get some exercise books. It was impossible to get used to, and that was the point. Ricky had found a new type of victim: one who was silent and refused to react. He had made it his mission to get that reaction – to break the boy until he wept and was begging for mercy. His long experience told him this would be a tough nut to crack, but he was happy to raise his game and meet an added level of challenge. The teachers should be proud of his personal ambition!

For his part, the boy did what he could to minimise the damage. He was sure that he managed to avoid as many encounters as those which were inflicted upon him. And he began to hate

Ricky Fosseway, more even that he had hated Carl. For Carl was just a drunken lout who liked to lash out, just to remind everyone that he was the master of the house. He didn't have Ricky's grasp of strategy or sense of purpose and application. No. Ricky moved with conscious malice and delighted in every successful strike against him. The boy knew what he was after, but couldn't give it to him – he wouldn't expose his inner core to such a pig.

He even thought of finding himself a mirror and making another wish – but so far, he had resisted it. The truth was, though, that he couldn't take much more of this. That's when he decided to cut school out altogether. After all, he had never enjoyed going there at the best of times – and now, it was unbearable.

He set out from home as usual, in his uniform, but instead of heading towards his seat of learning, he would head into the city park, where he would find a quiet spot to while away the day. It was early summer, and the weather was nice, so it wasn't too much of a chore. He missed his school lunch, of course, but had had enough forethought to bring some peanut butter sandwiches with him. He found a sheltered spot, hidden from prying eyes by some bushes, and lay there, drowsing in the sunshine and doodling in his books. In his heart, he knew this couldn't continue indefinitely, but he didn't care. This was now, and it was delightful to enjoy a bit of peace and sanctuary.

Two days were whiled away in this fashion. On the third, though, his fortunes shifted. As he ambled home, at roughly the right time, so that his mother would remain blissfully ignorant, he wondered when he would have to face the music. His school were fairly slack at making contact when someone was absent- usually they only did so after three or four continuous days.

Might they have phoned his mum today? Would she be waiting for him, with a look of angry disappointment on her face? This was not something that he particularly relished, but it suddenly became an inviting prospect instead of what lay ahead – for there, enjoying the sun at the park gates, like a wily old crocodile, stood Ricky with his entourage. The boy involuntarily slowed. Was there to be no escape, then? It was as though Ricky had some sort of sixth sense; perhaps he could scent his prey like a hunting hound, enabling him to run his quarry to ground.

He gave the boy a cheery wave, before walking to meet him like an old friend.

"Fancy seeing you here!" Ricky joshed, when they closed to a few feet of each other. "I've been missing you around school – our little chats. Looks like you been trying to avoid me!"

The words were spoken lightly, but there was a nasty glint in his eyes.

"I just fancied a…" the boy began to answer, before being cut off by a swift knee to his groin. Coloured motes swam in front of his eyes as the pain washed through him; gasping, he doubled up, clutching at his injured person. He thought there was a high chance he might actually vomit over Ricky's scuffed old shoes.

Then he was up again. Really up: Ricky had wrapped both hands around his throat and had lifted him casually into the air, like a rat to be shaken around. His grip tightened, just a little, and the boy coughed and choked, his eyes watering profusely as the pain of his injury combined with the sensation of choking.

He was dimly aware of an accompanying *hurr hurr*.

Ricky's full attention was on him. He pulled his face real close, and hissed between his yellow teeth.

"You think you can hide from me in the park all day? Well you can't. You're mine, now, and there's nowhere you can go. Not in this world, anyway. So you think on that, you little turd, and be very careful what you do tomorrow. I expect to be entertained. You're going to entertain me tomorrow, aren't you, turd?"

His voice was low; his eyes gleamed with feral joy; his lips almost grazed against the boy's when he spoke, adding a whole new dimension to his intense discomfort.

Fosseway smiled: the cat that had got the canary. He was immovable; he would never stop. The boy's life was doomed to perpetual suffering. He felt a hollow despair descend as he was forced to face this undeniable, bleak truth.

Just then, from another plane of existence, came a light, melodious voice.

"Why don't you just put him down, now? I'm sure that little guy just isn't worth all of this trouble."

The boy blinked stupidly.

Ricky's eyes flashed and he snarled, savagely. The boy was dropped, cast to one side like so much trash.

He shook his head, and looked over to the source of the voice.

Standing just behind them both with perfect poise, was Evan Greenway. The sun caused his hair to radiate a corona of light; his eyes glowed the colour of new-grown grass. He nodded amiably at the pair of them, and smiled a dazzling smile. All seemed well with the world and the boy felt his despair lift like an early morning mist.

Even Ricky seemed momentarily spellbound. He stared at this apparition, uncomprehendingly, his jaw gaping slightly, pike-like. For a second or two, it almost looked as though he might acquiesce to this request, made with such good humour. But the moment was fleeting.

"Who the..." he began to growl, threateningly, and then his jaw snapped shut into a square of twitching muscles. The boy saw that his pupils had somehow hardened into nasty black dots, like a variant of a sniper's target system. He felt the first stirrings of concern. He really hoped that Evan knew what he was doing. It would be awful if Ricky beat him to a gruesome pulp.

"Hi, I'm Evan," said Evan, grinning a little wider, and, with no apparent sense of peril, offering his hand for Ricky to shake.

Ricky gawped down at the proffered limb as though Evan had waved a jewelled sceptre at him. His jaw continued to work; teeth ground ominously.

"You're dead, you ponse!" spat Ricky in reply. And then, without bothering to generate his customary hints of doubt or fear, he swung a large meaty fist.

One moment Evan was there, looking as though his flawless face was about to be beaten all out of shape, and the next he had moved just fractionally to the right. Ricky's momentum carried him forward, and there was a sudden blur of movement followed by a dull crunching sound.

The boy took a few seconds to register what had happened.

Ricky's nose was now flat against his cheek; it looked as though someone had hit it with a frying pan. Blood ran like a tap down his face, dripping onto the floor.

Hurrr... The sound of his fan club petered out abruptly into shocked silence.

"You... You broke my dose!" howled Ricky, shrieking a little more when he reached to touch the damaged protrusion. "Gahh!" And with that war cry, he lumbered forward, arms flailing wildly.

Evan casually blocked one of these whirling fleshy appendages, before landing a single, savage strike to Ricky's kidneys. He hit the floor, mewling like a frightened kitten, doubled up in agony.

Evan's smile never faltered, as he knelt next to the fallen ogre on the ground.

"Now you listen to me," he continued, pleasantly, "you fat sack of lard."

With that, he nonchalantly reached down to seize Ricky's crotch in a vice-like grasp. He gave a sharp experimental twist, which evinced a primal cry of pain.

The boy glanced around, worried that Ricky's mates might try something while Evan was distracted, but they both stood there transfixed, the colour and cockiness gone out of their face. They looked petrified. The whole thing had taken less than thirty seconds.

He looked back at the floor to see that Evan was whispering something into Ricky's ear. Ricky's lumpish face was pink from pain and exertion, but whatever Evan said caused it to drain to a chalky white colour –and, for the first time, he saw the glint in his eyes change into something resembling genuine terror.

Then Evan withdrew. He smiled and winked at the boy, before rising in one fluid motion. Stretching like a cat in the sun, he beckoned.

"Come on then: what're you lying around for while I do all the work? Let's go get ourselves a drink. My treat – you look like you could use one! I might even stretch to some chocolate cake."

He reached down and hauled the boy up. They left the park through the gates, and the boy noticed with some pleasure that Ricky's mates leapt out of the way like startled wallabies. In his small world, Ricky Fosseway had encountered another, even more dangerous, beast than himself. Nature was cruel but hey, it's a Darwinist world.

And so it was that a dark chapter in the boy's life came to an unforeseen close and he found himself sitting at an outside table at Josie's Café. His pain and humiliation were washed away in the late afternoon sun's golden balm, which drizzled over the two laughing, animated youths. The boy slurped happily at a large strawberry milkshake, before taking a bite out of a decadent slice of rocky road. Now this was the life! Opposite him, Evan reclined lazily in a wicker chair. He grinned at the boy before gnashing his teeth and pulling a cross-eyed face. The boy giggled, strangely, giddily, light-hearted. The waitress, whom he vaguely recognised as having left school the previous summer, came to check, for a third time that all was well with their order. Josie's was fairly busy, basking in the warmth of the day; the boy rolled his eyes at Evan who assured the girl that they were fine.

"Must be after a tip," he drawled after she had been called over to another table.

"She's after something, alright," piped the boy, suddenly bold in his humour, which rippled around him in waves, like heat rising from the road on a hot day.

What on earth was happening to him? Maybe this was another form of delayed shock?

Evan wrinkled his nose in protest at this familiarity, and pouted indignantly.

"You, sir, are a cynic," he intoned. "I'm sure that our waitress is just unusually conscientious."

"Uhuh. That's why she split a pot of milk over that fat guy cos she was gawping at you."

Evan sighed, exaggeratedly, before flicking a strand of dark gold hair from his face. "I'll admit that my good looks and animal magnetism sometimes cause people to lose focus. What can I say? We all have our crosses to bear. I can't help being gorgeous."

At this, he pulled a rueful face, eliciting more peals of laughter, perhaps just slightly too loud, from the boy.

"Yeah, right," he snorted, "we all have our delusions!" And then he thought he might have gone too far, and quickly bent to slurp more milkshake, hoping to hide the flush that shot across his cheeks behind a curtain of black hair.

Evan gave a low, bass chuckle, almost reminiscent of a purring cat. "Somebody's getting a bit big for his boots," he asserted coolly. "After my daring rescue today, you could at least show some worshipful gratitude!"

The boy, couldn't help it: he looked up and was instantly locked into place by a pair of too-green eyes. They seemed almost to glow in the light and somehow reminded him of something – but he couldn't quite think what. For an odd moment, he felt like an insect, caught in a green-gold resin, slowly enveloped in warm sweetness before it realised the terrible danger it was in. Then Evan stuck out his tongue and the moment was broken.

"What was that, anyway?" demanded the boy, swiftly changing the topic. "Are you a boxer or something? I've never seen anyone move that fast in a fight. Not Ricky, anyway – he's usually juggling a pasty and a cream cake in between clobbering some poor sap over the head."

"I can handle myself," replied Evan, so coolly and matter-of-factly that it was a simple statement of fact rather than arrogance.

When the boy raised his eyebrows and continued to stare at him, he elaborated somewhat further. "Look, when I was younger, I used to go to a gym for some boxing. This guy I knew thought it'd be good for me. I was a bit wild then, see. He thought it'd help me channel my energy and aggression. And then I got talked into learning a few kung fu moves by someone from the gym. It was pretty cool. I won a couple of junior competitions. But I don't go there much anymore. Too many irons in the fire."

"Wow!" said the boy, "you're like some sort of karate kid!" He grinned, Cheshire cat style over his almost empty glass.

"Actually, kung fu isn't the same as karate," replied Evan, rather earnestly. He opened his mouth as if to begin a lecture before seeing that the boy's lip was wobbling with barely repressed mirth.

The boy bowed gravely to Evan. "Thank you, Mr Miyagi. Please do explain. Ah!"

"Arse!" grumped Evan, scowling, but his eyes were twinkling and, in the face of the boy dissolving once more into giggles, he had little option but to grin in shared humour.

How nice it was, thought the boy to no one in particular, to laugh – to actually feel a connection with another person. To have something that could be described as a social experience. The realisation of the void inside him, suddenly, disorientatingly exposed by half an hour of friendly company, was like someone shining a torch into an unseen chasm into which he could have fallen at any time. It made his head spin with vertigo. His smile almost faltered.

Evan quirked one eyebrow. "What's up with you? You look like you got a toothache."

Don't mess this up, thought the boy to himself, desperately. *Please don't mess this up!* He got a hold of himself and forced a smile, "Nothing!" he said, "I guess I still feel a bit shaky."

He almost believed himself – but he wasn't sure whether Evan did. He just cocked his head to one side and smiled in that infuriatingly knowing way that the boy had come to notice about him.

"If you say so," he agreed, equably. "I guess you did take a knee to the balls. Bound to leave you feeling a bit off-colour." He volleyed a jaunty smile at him in such a way that even that painful memory was cause for a laugh.

With that, Evan slurped the remainder of his milkshake and looked at his watch. "Listen numb-nuts, I got to go now. Gotta sort something out." He glanced up and could hardly have missed the stricken look that flashed across the boy's face before he swiftly crushed it. "Don't worry, dork – I got your back. You don't need to worry about school any more. That guy won't go near you again."

"How can you say that?" the boy blurted, not meaning to challenge him rather than to state what he saw as a fact. Then the gloom settled heavily on him once more. "He's going to be mad about today – really mad. And you're not around in my school. I'd say I'm toast."

"Oh ye of little faith! I told you – I've got this covered. He'll leave you alone. You've nothing to worry about."

The boy half-shrugged. He wanted to believe, he really did. Evan seemed so certain. But he knew human nature. Ricky had been humiliated in front of his victim and he would have to pay a steep price for that. Then Evan got up to go. He found himself sagging over the table, almost as though he had been kneed in the groin all over again. That was the trouble with fun and friendship when you didn't normally have either: when they're taken away it leaves you feeling completely empty – like a balloon with all the air let out.

Evan paused dramatically. "Wow! Look at that face! Did someone die in your dessert? Has a meteor hit your house? Is it broccoli soup for dinner tonight? Lighten up a little! It'll be fine, right?"

"Yeah. Course," replied the boy, unable to disagree with him.

"There you go. And do you know what?"

"What?"

"You'll be able to tell me all about it tomorrow. See you here at half four?"

The boy rose from the ashes of despair and his pale face shone with delight. He revived like a newly watered flower.

"Really?"

"Really, really," grinned Evan.

The boy knew he was breaking all of his own rules about getting close to people (they always let you down; always hurt you) but he just couldn't help himself. He was almost pathetically happy.

"OK," he confirmed, trying not to answer too quickly or to allow his voice to shoot up in pitch.

"Sorted then," replied Evan, grinning wickedly. "Got yourself a date."

"Get lost, fool!" the boy half-yelled, whilst giggling perhaps a little bit awkwardly.

"Here: in case you need to ring me to console you in your darkest hours."

And with that, Evan was gone, moving swiftly down the pavement, amongst the evening crowds, like a bright leaf caught in a stream.

The boy looked down, blinking to see a coaster, bent in half and inscribed with a number. A mobile phone number. He had no idea when Evan had written it down – he certainly hadn't noticed him – but he wasn't complaining. He clutched at that coaster like it was a fifty pound note, and, draining the last of his milkshake, he moved off. For once, he felt like he could face pretty much anything. He let the softening sun wash over him and he smiled.

Chapter 8
Good Times

I am told that there is a certain type of shellfish in possession of formidable defences: its shell is heavily armoured and notoriously difficult to open. It dwells in frigid northern climes and has evolved in response to ice and hardship. Apparently, soaking it in warm water will cause it to open, just a tiny crack – and then, one can slide a knife into this teensy opening before prising the whole thing apart.

Sometimes, when a creature has been toughened beyond caring by a life of wretched misery, a touch of joy can be a dangerous thing.

Just imagine that, now. I'm sure you take my meaning.

And now we come to summer: the season that gets all the glory, with its sleepy, heady days and bright blue skies. The flowers bloom amidst the narcotic hum of insects and everyone basks in the sun's golden rays.

I'm afraid I don't care very much for the sun. No. I really don't. I prefer the dark, damp recesses of the world where I can move at my own pace and the cold keeps me sharp.

But then, everything has to conform to a certain cycle; there are rules. And I can tolerate the thought of summer, if I must, for it is necessary to ripen the wheat.

Shine, hated sun, and do your work.

Soon, it will be time for the harvest.

Do you know what? He was right. Whatever Evan had said to Ricky Fosseway – or indeed done to him – he never laid another finger on him. In fact, he actually seemed to avoid eye contact; it was now Ricky who scurried off at the end of class, as though anxious to escape trouble. Only at one point was there any cause for alarm: the next day at school after Ricky had been felled, one of his scabrous hangers-on had squared up to the boy in the corridor. He had poked him in the chest before beginning to tell him how dead he was, in a reedy, nasal voice. What happened next left both of them equally surprised: Ricky appeared around the corner; his gimlet eyes swiftly appraised the situation and his face suddenly composed itself into a mask of horror. Charging headlong down the corridor, he laid his huge hands upon his unfortunate minion before bodily tossing him aside. There was general confusion at this, which rapidly deepened. Sweating now, and panting somewhat, Ricky loomed over his now cowering lieutenant and snarled, in a quivering voice. "Never, ever, touch him. Is that understood?" He turned to survey his other boot-lickers. "Understood?"

There was a general chorus of assent, reinforced by much nodding of heads.

The boy could hardly believe it; neither could the other kids in the vicinity. From that day on, all sorts of rumours began to spread and the boy occasionally found other kids staring at him with nonplussed curiosity. What had he done to Ricky Fosseway? The rumour was that he had some tough friends: someone had battered Ricky and put the fear of God into him. Who would've thought it? Still waters ran deep, they said...

The boy didn't give it undue thought: all he knew was that his life was suddenly much brighter. He was being left alone to mind his own affairs – and now he had a friend to confide in – a cool, funny friend at that. As school came finally to a close, he made his way to Josie's Café. It took all of his willpower not to run there. As he approached, he became aware of a certain trepidation. The previous night, he had sent just one brief text to Evan before going to bed: *Thanks again for helping me out. See you tomoz.* Such caution in his dealings with others was ingrained into the boy. You can't trust people, no matter how nice or friendly they seem. At least you know where you stand with those who are openly foul to you; the dangerous ones hide their intentions with fake smiles, biding their time before they stick the knife in.

Anyone would think that the boy didn't like people! He was, of course, a prime example of misanthropy. But there was no denying that Evan had come riding to the rescue – that had to earn him some credit. And he was fun to be around: and that, the boy was surprised to find, earnt him even more. So, when he strolled casually into the café and found no sign of Evan, he played it cool. He got himself a shake and sat outside. He smiled to himself, a rather twisted smile. It was stupid to trust anyone – remember that? Stupid. Evan Greenway was just too good to be true – a passing mote of sunlight flashing across the dreary plane of his existence. What would someone like him see in a boring, awkward nerd anyway?

Pulling out his art book, he began to draw: strange apparitions appeared on the page – huge vines with vibrant fleshy flowers. In their shadows, strange creatures – or beings – lurked, merging with the gloom around them.

The boy liked drawing: it was therapeutic. This, however, had an edge to it, like drawing out a particularly deep splinter. He knew that these images were emerging from his dreams – or even, if he wanted to be melodramatic, from his subconscious, and he wasn't sure how that made him feel. He watched as fragments of dreamspace slowly took shape on his pad. It was as though he was drawing one world through into another through the medium of his drawing. His eyes narrowed with concentration and the pencil moved faster, slowly fleshing out a savage feminine face, staring right out of the page, as if challenging him not to believe in her.

He paused to consider his creation. It certainly had an energy to it, as his art teacher would have said. Not that she would have liked it – she was obsessed with drawing pictures of flowers and fruit. Yes: fruit. Why the hell would anyone want to draw an apple, over and over again? To be fair, this did have flowers in it – but they certainly didn't look like Mrs McConnell's carnations. The boy allowed himself a brief – and rare – smile of satisfaction. It was good – really good – and he knew it.

"Wow! Looks like we've got a Picasso in the house!" There was a silvery laugh and suddenly Evan's hand was resting lightly on his shoulder. He bent lower to have a closer look. He smelt of mint and fresh-cut grass. The boy frowned. He was normally very observant: how had Evan managed to sneak up on him like this? He must have been really focussed on his drawing.

"Yeah. You're in the presence of real talent here, karate kid." The boy kept his eyes on his paper and his voice was remarkably even and non-committal. Anyone watching would have perceived a supreme level of apathy. But inside, the boy's heart gave a joyful leap. His rescuer had turned up, just like he said he would.

Evan sauntered into the café to get himself a drink – and a particularly large slice of chocolate cake, thanks, he asserted, to the charm exerted over the lady behind the counter. He draped himself carelessly over a chair and directed an amiably rueful smile at the boy.

"Sorry I'm late. Kinda got caught up with some stuff. You know what it's like."

"It's fine," the boy assured him. "I like my own space – helps me to think."

"Ah! But what thoughts are running around behind those big black eyes of yours?" enquired Evan, grinning. "All sorts of weird shizzle, by the looks of it. What is she, anyway? Some sort of alien?" He nodded at the sharp lines of the huntress' face.

The boy tapped his pencil against his lip and frowned.

"It's a working theory," he mused, tentatively. "Maybe you're right?"

He looked up, smiling softly.

"Yeah. I usually am. Got an eye for detail, see." There was a brief pause, punctuated by Evan slurping his drink, before he suddenly exclaimed, "well, come on then. What're you waiting for?"

The boy's face clouded with puzzlement; he looked quizzically at Evan only to find himself being assailed by a toothy grin.

"Eh?"

"Come on – let's see how good you are – draw me!"

The boy lapsed into a smile and he found himself shaking his head.

"I don't normally do portraits – not of real people, I mean. But I'll give it a go, if you like."

"I do like. And if I actually approve of the end result, I might even allow you to hang out with me again. Or," he quickly added, as the boy raised his eyebrow with mock incredulity, "I might let you share this unreasonably large wedge of chocolatey cake."

"Fine," the boy laughed. "I'll see if I can manage to fit your fat head onto the page."

Evan chortled merrily at this, but positioned himself even more artfully in his chair. He placed his chin between his thumb and forefinger to make him look more thoughtful.

The boy rolled his eyes and began to sketch. He didn't know what was with him today. Mrs McConnell used to warble on about 'muses' in her art lessons, but that was a load of rubbish. Wasn't it? The pencil flew rapidly across the page, lightly sketching out the outline of Evan's face before it began to add details. Slowly, his nose took shape, then his eyes. The boy was particularly pleased with these, as he had managed to catch a sense of the roguery that lurked within them. Soon his was adding in the smiling mouth and a mop of tousled hair. When he was finally satisfied, he put his pencil down and looked up, pleased with his effort. The café was half-empty now and the sun had shifted somewhat across the sky.

Evan perused his artistry with exaggerated attention, sticking out his bottom lip and wrinkling his nose. "Yeah," he said at last, "I spose that's pretty good."

"Arse," replied the boy. "It's bloody fantastic. Now where's my cake?"

"Ah! The artistic temperament! Here, here! Please don't start throwing your pencils around!"

The boy happily consumed the remainder of Evan's cake, as the café tables were cleared around them.

Evan gazed up at the shifting sun as its rays turned to slow-pouring treacle. "OK Dali, I need to make tracks," he declared, springing out of his seat.

"K," acknowledged the boy, coolly. "See you around."

"Yeah, you will, probably. Listen, I'm busy the next couple of days – but what're you doing on Saturday? Fancy hanging out again?"

"Sure."

"Cool. I'll be in touch. In a bit, dog shit."

And with that, he was gone.

The boy stretched and put his things back into his bag. He paused briefly to look at his portrait of Evan, before smiling and closing his eyes as he yawned. This guy just wasn't for real; he thought he was something, alright. That he would just drop everything to fit in at his convenience. But he knew that he was right: he'd meet up with him on Saturday, wherever he chose. After all, this was the only friend he had.

High, white, fluffy clouds drifted lazily across a china-blue sky. The boy lay back with his hands cupped beneath his head. He watched contentedly as a wreath of smoke curled and writhed upwards, slowly expanding and losing its cohesion as it dispersed into the air. Distant sounds of play permeated the heavy air of the park.

"That was a good one!" drawled Evan.

There was a faint, hot sound as he drew on a cigarette; the tip glowed fiercely, and then Evan's mouth formed an elaborate O as he blew forth another smoke ring.

The boy chuckled. "Nice one, fish-face."

Evan pulled his lips into a sour expression and shot him a look of disdain. "You have no appreciation of skill," he declared. "This has taken me many hours of dedicated practice."

The boy closed his eyes and let a smile spill across his face. "I've always deplored idleness," he said, deploying one of Grandmother's phrases in a prim tone. "Why don't you do something useful with your life instead of lying around inhaling toxins?"

Evan propped himself up on an elbow, a look of shock on his face. "I hope you aren't suggesting that I should be *working*?" he spluttered.

"Huh! I doubt your body could stand the shock!" The boy's eyes were still closed, but his smile broadened. "But perhaps you could find a good book to broaden your mind."

"You know what? Maybe I should've helped that meat-faced bruiser paste you around the park. How about that for a work-out?"

The boy opened one eye.

"Ah! But then you would never have known the joys of my company. Also, Ricky Fosseway lacks my artistic skills – he wouldn't have been able to please your vanity like I have."

Evan nodded in agreement before grinding out his cigarette and flipping the butt into some bushes. "You have a point, my padawan – that must be why I put up with your constant stream of unsolicited criticism."

The boy giggled and attempted to kick him – but of course Evan easily avoided the blow, before contorting himself round to get him into a headlock, which was rapidly followed by a fierce rub on the scalp with his knuckles. The boy protested volubly, yet couldn't help but laugh in between his yelps of discomfort. Without warning, Evan released his head, and spun round, pinning the boy to the ground like a wrestler. He grabbed his arm and bent it back.

"Submit, weakling!" he growled in an approximation of an angry voice.

The boy squawked, but looking up, he could see the mischief glittering in his friend's green eyes. Suddenly, he relaxed, and smiling, said "OK, OK! I submit. If it makes you feel better." And then, without really thinking about it or understanding why, "it's not like you'd really hurt me, anyway."

"Are you sure about that?" replied Evan in a low voice, but he let him go all the same.

"Yes," he said, "I am." And he was, too. "You're my friend. You're… you're a good guy."

The boy was surprised to find the words escaping his lips with such abandon. Normally, he liked to self-edit before speaking. For some reason his voice became husky when he said it; he didn't really understand why.

Evan stared down at him, looking into his eyes, and his face took on a troubled caste; the flashing eyes darkened to a dark sea-green. They were frozen into position for a few seconds and the boy felt suddenly tense; nervous. Then Evan broke his laser-like gaze, got up and moved a couple of paces away.

"No, I'm not. I'm not very good at all, to be honest." He looked back around, frowning slightly, but thoughtful rather than angry. "You should be careful of me, you know. I'm nothing but trouble."

The boy shrugged, shaking out his aching arm. "Probably," he answered. "But do you know what? I don't think I care. For once, I'm having fun. My weird dreams have almost gone; I'm… happy. So – if you are trouble, I guess I'll just have to be fast on my feet to avoid it when it comes."

Evan stared at him again, strangely expressionless. Then his lips parted into a bright white smile. "You fool!" he whispered. "You don't know what you're letting yourself in for. Don't say I didn't warn you."

Leaning down, he gave the boy a light punch on the arm, before yanking him up to his feet.

"What now?" asked the boy.

Evan gave a grin of pure wickedness; putting an arm around his neck, he marched him along.

"Now, my friend, we are going to have some serious fun!" Spinning him round, Evan's eyes crackled again with currents of wild energy. "You had better buckle up, my good sir – because this is going to be one wild ride!"

Chapter 9
A Change of Heart

Of all the things in this creation, change is, ironically, the one constant. Everything changes; nothing can remain eternally in stasis. Time effects its own changes of course, like a river eating away at a rocky bed. But that's not all: people can be changed by their environment too – by the company they keep.

Just look at him now, my introspective little misanthrope. How he loathed humanity and tried to have as little to do with it as possible. No more! Even his mother has noticed a difference in him: a brightening – an increase in confidence – and, dare we say it, sociability.

Very good. Because, if someone has been through significant change once already in the near past, then they're more likely to survive the changes which find them when they least expect them. Think of it as preparing a piece of meat. A crude analogy, granted, but one which seems apt, here.

Let's soften you up, sweetheart.

You have many changes ahead of you, and only the most adaptable of subjects actually survive.

Bubbles tickled the boy's nose. It wrinkled and his mouth puckered into a grimace.

"This stuff costs how much a bottle?"

"About thirty five quid, I think."

He pulled the bottle away from his lips and swilled liquid around in his mouth for a few seconds before swallowing. He promptly hiccupped and his eyes watered.

"I'm not sure I like it, Evan."

"That's because you're an ill-educated heathen," replied the older boy, snatching the bottle from him and taking a hearty slug of its contents. "This stuff is what they crack open at posh weddings to toast the bride and groom, I'll have you know. I consider it part of my mission to educate you in the finer parts of life."

"Gee thanks," replied the boy, feeling slightly warm inside and a touch giddy. He took another slurp and grinned. "It kind of gets better the more you drink. Like pretzels."

"You drink pretzels?" enquired Evan, with a look of astonishment.

"No, fool, I mean – it's moreish..."

"Yeah, I guess. Now let's break into some of that chocolate."

It was high summer. The boy had broken up for the long school holidays the week before. He had been hanging out with Evan for over two months now and it had undoubtedly changed him. His mother had taken some time to get used to the idea of her son having a friend and actually going out instead of festering quietly in his bedroom. She had even asked if he would like to bring his new friend over for tea – and when he refused, she began to worry that he had fallen in with bad company. He assured her this was not the case – but maybe she wasn't so far from the mark. After all, Evan Greenway turned out to be quite the accomplished thief.

His secret was to act like he owned the outlet in question. He would brazenly waltz out with stolen items in stolen bags, and would often chat with a member of staff – and a couple of times even store security - as he did so. The boy would watch from a distance while these encounters were underway, and would see a familiar, slightly star-struck expression come over their faces. Only the most hard-bitten actually asked to see any receipts, and they barely looked when Evan dug out an old one to wave under their noses.

It was incredible, really, the boy had to admit – though he wouldn't dream of saying so to his friend, who was quite full enough of himself as it was, thank you very much.

"How do you do it?" he had once asked as they devoured some luxury sandwiches from a high-end supermarket. "I mean, aren't you nervous? That one of these days someone might actually check your receipt and realise that you're a shyster?"

Evan almost choked on a piece of hand-carved salt-beef. "A *what?* You unappreciative wiener!" he spluttered. "I, sir, am a bloody artist, not some shyster. I play people, for your information, like a bloody maestro. And the best part is, they don't even know they're being played. THAT is how good I am!"

The boy had feigned amazed bedazzlement and begged forgiveness on bended knee.

"Pardon me, o gracious one," he had intoned, solemnly.

"Yes," sniffed Evan. "That's more like it. You know what? You may kiss my ring."

They had both chortled at this low joke and the matter was dropped. But there was... *something* about Evan. When he talked to people, they were happy – really happy, some of them. And when he moved away, their faces took on a strangely wistful look, mingled with a sense of confusion, as though they were recovering from particularly severe jet-lag.

It wasn't long before Evan had dared him to partake in some larcenous behaviour. Of course, what worked for Evan would not work for him. Whilst golden-balls radiated charm from every pore, the boy remained a dreary teenager; he was gauche and came across as either awkward, boring, or a winning combination of the two. Still, he had been set a challenge, and he wasn't about to let Evan think that he didn't have the guts to rise to it. Instead, the boy perfected his own technique. Whereas Evan relied on being noticed and assaulted people with excess charisma, he took refuge in his very dullness. People didn't give him a second glance: he was just some pale, miserable-looking kid with black hair hanging limply over his face. He did his best to live down to their expectations, but you could bet that, after he had passed through the checkout with a couple of cheap items, he would have concealed several others about his person; it seemed that wearing baggy clothes conferred additional benefits on top of their obvious comfort. Sleight of hand, Evan called it, and almost complimented the boy on the speed and subtlety with which he could decant small objects into his pocket.

Now here they were on a late July afternoon. They had got the bus out of town, loaded with goodies. Evan, it appeared, lived in one of the outlying villages, and knew a great spot for a picnic.

The boy was intrigued: Evan was always tight-lipped about his home-life; he didn't know why, but suspected that there were problems at the root of it. Either, way, the boy was oddly bashful about quizzing him: if he wanted to keep his secrets, then so be it.

The truth was, the boy would never risk genuinely offending or upsetting his friend – he would never do anything to hurt him and simply wouldn't countenance the terrible possibility that Evan might, in his own mercurial way, bin him off. He wasn't stupid. Evan could make a new friend any time he wanted. The only mystery at hand was why he seemed to enjoy hanging around with a nonentity. Because that's what he was. He didn't think it was pity – Evan wasn't the sort. Maybe he was wittier than he gave himself credit for: Evan certainly seemed to laugh at his constant banter, and he was fairly sure, if he didn't like someone, you wouldn't see him for dust.

So, now that enigma was conveniently parked to one side, and certainly not fully addressed, the boy found himself being led away from a bus stop on a winding rural road and down through a hedge into some fields. Giggling, they had run through a field of cows, whooping loudly as they did so, and howling with laughter as the large herbivores scattered mooing before them. Then it was their turn to run from an angry farmer who had appeared around a hedgerow, waving his fist and shouting things that sounded suspiciously rude – although it was hard to make them out over such a long distance.

"Come on! Flee!" yelled Evan, barely containing his mirth, and yanking him over a stile.

Together, they had run through two fields of lush, waving wheat, green heads fully formed and heavy with seed. They soon left the farmer behind, overweight and middle-aged as he was, and slowed to catch their breath. The boy bent over, resting his hands on his thighs, and panting deeply. He was annoyed to find that Evan was merely stretching and looked as though he had barely broken a sweat.

"How can you be so fit? You disgust me!" the boy wheezed, slowly straightening up. "Do you think we lost him?" He peered back towards the top of the field, shielding his eyes from the sun with his hand.

"Probably," asserted Evan, looking around to gauge their position. "But let's make sure: we should lie low. I'm hungry and I need a drink; this looks like a nice spot for a picnic."

The boy looked at him in some confusion.

"What? Here? But what if that guy…"

Laughing, Evan took his hand, "Shush!" he grinned, "you're like an old woman. Just do what I do!"

And with that, he leapt over the nearest rows of wheat, and proceeded to jump on, like a demented, spring-loaded jack-in-the-box. The boy, still having his hand clasped tightly in Evan's, had little choice but to emulate him. After about two hundred metres, Evan suddenly hit the deck, pulling the boy down with him. They lay there, trying to stifle their laughter and gazing up at a hot blue sky. After a few seconds, the boy realised that Evan was still holding his hand. His laughter petered out, and he felt himself suddenly flushing. His heart did not seem to be slowing down all that much, despite having had a couple of minutes' rest to get his breath back. He looked away, and then shyly back at Evan, whom he found to be looking straight at him with a wicked grin on his face. Winking, he gave the boy a squeeze, before slowly releasing his hand. He seemed to take just slightly too long to do it, his fingers briefly trailing over the boy's as he pulled his hand away. The boy shivered in spite of the heat and felt his chest tighten as he struggled to maintain an even rate of breathing. Just to his right, he heard Evan's low throaty chuckle, as though amused at some sort of private joke, which jarred on the boy with surprising and grating resonance. He was being played with – deliberately made to feel… odd… and uncomfortable. Sometimes, he just wished that Evan did not regard the whole world and everything in it as a source of humour. Now he was just trying to make him feel awkward and embarrassed so that he could wind him up at some later point.

"Get off!" snapped the boy, pulling away from Evan with some spirit. He didn't enjoy the feeling that he was the butt of some private joke. He half sat up amidst the green wheat and got down to the business of unpacking his rucksack. He needed something practical to do, to focus on.

"Alright, alright," said Evan, in a low, purring voice that was full of knowing amusement. "No need to get uppity." He gave the boy a dig with his toe. "Get the booze out – we'll start with that."

The boy turned sharply to look at him, suddenly spiky in his uneasy feelings and the sense that he was being mocked – or worse, toyed with, like a wounded mouse.

"Sometimes, you can be a real dick!" he snapped, before stopping up short, surprised at himself. They looked at each other, the boy, biting his lip, suddenly worried that he had gone too far, that Evan would simply get up and leave him to find his own sorry way back home. He gazed anxiously, trying to read how Evan had reacted, but those impossibly green eyes returned his gaze, framed by slightly raised eyebrows and still dancing with whimsical humour.

"I'm sorry," muttered the boy, suddenly feeling hot and embarrassed again. "I... don't know why I said that..." His eyes suddenly smarted and he had a horrible feeling that he might weep. He looked away again, quickly.

"Hey," replied Evan, quietly. "It's OK. Don't be mad or peed off – you're right. I can be. It's just my nature, you know."

And with that, he actually took the boy's hand in his again, and held it gently for a few seconds.

"Come on: don't be mad. Let's just enjoy ourselves and make the most of the summer. These summer afternoons... we'll never get them back, you know."

The boy looked around again and they smiled at each other. "Fool!" he said, but was grinning now, as he aimed a light punch at Evan's arm. Evan took it and nodded to the rucksack.

"Come on already. That stuff's going to be evaporated away if we wait much longer." The boy rolled his eyes, but bent to the task of removing the cork from the champagne. It went off like a gunshot, making him jump, and splashing foam over his crotch.

They both giggled at this. "There are so many things that I could say at this point," began Evan, but was silenced by a dangerous look from the boy.

"Yeah. But you're not going to. Especially not about popping corks. Now let's see what this stuff tastes like."

With that, the boy lifted the bottle to his lips and took a deep swig. And yes, he discovered that the bubbles tickled his nose – but we've already established that, haven't we? What's really significant here isn't the champagne at all – although it could be argued that it was a factor. What was really significant was the complex processes of emotional alchemy which had been set off in the boy and which were now being fused in the crucible of his heart.

The sun drifted slowly across the sky. Under its fiery gaze a decadent rite of indulgence was being practised. An eclectic selection of nuts, crisps, a pasta salad and half a dozen chocolate bars were alternately washed down by a couple of bottles of champagne – one of which turned out to be pink, of all things! Evan had finished off with a cigarette – one thing that the boy wasn't about to emulate, having tried one and almost vomiting.

A big, silly smile was splattered across the boy's face as he lay there, his head resting on Evan's chest, slowly rising and falling in time with his breathing. He opened his mouth to emit a loud, bubble-fuelled belch, and snorted with hilarity.

"Classy!" commented Evan, amiably. Annoyingly, he seemed to be only slightly affected by the bubbly. When asked why, he pointed out that *one* his companion had quaffed most of the booze and *two* he had acquired resistance through a young life of sinful excess. The boy had protested but had soon become confused about what he was protesting about, so contented himself with lying back and using Evan's chest as a pillow.

The boy felt warm and rather giddy – but in a good way. He suspected that the bubbles were now dancing around inside him. Perhaps it was this which caused him to forget his earlier caution and, as the air moved sleepily around them, he crossed his own line.

"Evan, why don't you talk much about your family – and where you're from? Is everything OK? I mean, are you OK?"

There was a long pause. He knew that he shouldn't have stuck his nose in, but alcohol was sending blissed out swirls of hedonism to permeate his brain and dull his normal self-control.

"It's complicated," Evan suddenly replied, in a short voice.

The boy rolled around so that he was lying sideways and looking up at Evan's face. It looked troubled. His delicate brows were sketched into a frown of concentration.

"Do you want me to shut up?" the boy asked. "I mean, I know it's none of my business, but I always think you might be in trouble and..." Here he stopped abruptly, knowing through his slightly foggy state of awareness that he was revealing too much.

"And?" Evan glanced over at him, lips curving into a slight smile.

"And... I wouldn't want that. You, in trouble, I mean. I... I hope you're not..."

He trailed off, lamely. Evan ran his forefinger across the boy's forehead, moving his fringe away from his eyes.

"My family are… unusual." He glanced away, casually, but he was clearly thinking about how he was going to proceed. The boy looked on, all eyes.

"They don't always fit in: socially, I mean. In fact, they're pretty weird and not especially nice. If I'm being honest! I don't especially like them myself."

He looked back at the boy and grinned, but unusually, it didn't reach his eyes.

The boy mused on this, surprised to find that it was something he could identify with quite easily – at least in terms of lacking affection for his family.

"Well they can't be that weird and anti-social: they produced you, after all!"

"Yeah. But I'm the golden sheep of the family… Must've got all of the good genes. That's why everyone loves me – like bees round a honey pot." Here, he stuck out his tongue, mischievously.

"You are one of the most big-headed, cocksure, annoying people that I've ever met," laughed the boy.

He sat up, slightly woozily, and shook his head. He felt really funny; what was that phrase of his mother's? Tipsy? He laughed to no one in particular. Then he looked down. Evan lay sprawled on a bed of squashed wheat, one arm bent back under his head and the other resting on his stomach. His shirt had ridden up, exposing several inches of toned, golden skin. His loose waves of hair shone, burnished by the sun and he toyed with a blade of grass in his mouth, manipulating it with his expressive lips.

The boy felt blood rushing to his head: an intense blast of emotion swept through him, almost unmanning him. He was just about back on an even keel when Evan went and looked directly up at him. Those eyes – those terrible eyes. They seemed to glow they were so bright sometimes. And that was now. The boy tried to look away, but he couldn't. Evan's gaze locked with his, fierce and reckless, and, horrified on some subconscious level, the boy found that he was beginning to bend low, arcing downwards as though caught in a twin pair of emerald tractor beams. There was nothing he could do. His heart leapt and sang; it pounded wildly in his chest – so much so that he was surprised it didn't provoke comment. And then, awash with sunshine, champagne and desperate affection, he was kissing Evan on the lips. He tasted of cigarettes and chocolate and salty sweat.

This was terrible. Wasn't it? Or was it possibly the most wonderful moment of his grey, crappy life? He didn't know what to think, so he closed his eyes and made everything even more awful by whispering "I think I might love you, Evan Greenway."

Then, the moment passed. Time, which had slowed to a crawl, as if to take in this exchange, resumed its normal speed. At the same instant, the boy sobered almost instantaneously, aghast at what he'd done.

Eyes flaring open, he pulled sharply back and sat up like a startled hare.

"Oh! God! I'm... I'm so..." he began to stammer, and the terrible heat of utterly crushing embarrassment rolled over him like a wave.

He had one true friendship – one great friend – and now he had ruined it all in a moment of madness. He didn't know why he'd done it. He didn't even feel like that about Evan – did he?

Amidst this torrent of conflicting emotions came an unlooked-for sound. Evan stretched out on the ground, like a cat, and emitted a long, bubbling laugh. He jumped up, eyes showing no hint of anger or disgust, just merriment.

"You broke my grass!" he complained, discarding the mangled stem to the ground. Then, looking at the sky, he cried "come on, it's nearly time for the last bus back to town. We need to move."

With that he ushered the boy into flinging their things into the rucksack and hurried him back through the fields. He let it happen: the frantic activity prevented him thinking about *that*. It certainly appeared that Evan wasn't thinking about it – he was just carrying on as if nothing had happened. Well, he supposed that was better than the alternative: anger, disgust, hatred. He had seen what Evan had done to Ricky Fosseway: he didn't want to be a target of his anger, that was for sure. If he wanted to play it cool, that was fine – in fact, the boy swiftly acknowledged, it was probably for the best. He had to be practical about these things.

So it was that, a short time later, the two of them were standing at the bus stop, the boy once more panting for breath.

"Do we have to run everywhere?" he moaned.

"Good for your fitness," retorted Evan. "And besides, the bus to take you home will be here in a couple of minutes.

The boy shielded his eyes and peered into the distance. While he was doing so, he muttered, awkwardly, "Listen, Evan. I'm… I'm really sorry about… you know. I… I don't know what came over me. Please don't hate me."

It was pathetic, really; he knew it even as he spoke feeling like he had died a little inside.

In the distance, the bus could be seen, trundling through the summer haze.

Evan laughed lightly next to him. "Don't be stupid – I don't hate you!" And then he reached out and gave his hand a squeeze. They stood there for a few moments.

"Listen," said Evan, "do you really want to know more about me? And my family?"

The boy looked around, surprised.

"Well, yes."

"OK then. I'll let you into my secret, weird, life. But be warned: once you know, that's it: you can't ever unknow a secret." He paused, and looked at the boy with uncharacteristic earnestness. "You might not like me after that. You know, sometimes ignorance really is bliss."

The boy gazed back, spellbound. Was this really happening? Evan was letting him in – him! Boring, nerdy, perpetual victim – and he was going to trust him with his secrets. He was going to lower his defences and let him in.

He tried to modulate his voice as he answered: "OK. Yeah, that's OK. And you don't need to worry about me – I'm sure it's not that bad. I'm very difficult to shock, you know!"

His composure faltered somewhat in the glare of the grin which Evan lavished upon him, and he felt his treacherous heart tremble once more.

"You're alright, black-eyed boy!"

Then they looked down. The bus was almost upon them. The boy was surprised again to find that they were still holding hands.

"See you tomorrow, loser," rasped Evan in a strangely low voice. And then he followed this up with a rough hug.

The boy dimly remembered buying a bus ticket – and indeed, had vague recollections of the journey home.

His heart was aflame inside him; it was bursting out of him, and forcing his mouth into a broad, face-aching smile. Unbeknownst to him, other passengers smiled indulgently back at him. That kind of joy is infectious, you see.

He was very, very happy.

Chapter 10
Bait

You know what they say about curiosity, don't you? Well, it's not entirely right: I don't want to see this little pussy cat die. Not after all of the investment I've put into him. Still, once I have him in my possession, I will have to do some digging – quite possibly literal digging. In his flesh. If he is strong, he will survive; if not, well, he wouldn't have served my purposes anyway.

If he lives, one of the first lessons he must learn is the fallibility of human emotions. Whilst they fascinate me, I can't say that I yearn for some of my own. The truth is that love – and hate, for that matter – are far more dangerous than the fleeting influence of alcohol. They dull the senses, blinding the subject to approaching danger or opportunity.

The only use for emotions is as a tool to be employed against a potential target – something that can weaken them or tip them into some reckless course of action. Thus disabled, the most deadly of marks becomes vulnerable.

The moral? Use emotions as and when you can; cultivate them, like a delicate flower. But never indulge in your own neurotic narcotic: the raw stimulation it produces is illusory; it will soon pass, leaving you weaker than before – assuming you're still alive when you emerge from the other side.

We need a cool head in our line of work.

There is no room for emotion or spontaneity: only good planning.

Existence is a chess board, you see: one wrong move and the game is over.

I do not intend to lose this game. I play to win. And I have my eye on a new piece to aid in this endeavour. If he survives, that is. If he survives… no mere pawn, this one… something… higher.

You're so close now.

The line has been baited and you've taken your first big bite.

Now to pull you into the net.

Come along, my sweetling; come to Mama.

In the midst of his joy, the boy didn't feel that anything could touch him. Perhaps that was why he was so surprised by the dream – an uncomfortable reminder of darker times. Having closed his eyes with but one face dancing in and out of focus, and a feeling of warm contentment, the boy once more found himself picking his way through an exotic alien jungle.

She was waiting for him, as he knew she would be, perched this time on a rock smeared with some sort of purple lichen. Her six legged companion was absent now, but she looked no less dangerous. Her crimson hair was restrained by a sort of elaborate alloy circlet which framed her brow. It had a liquid gleam to it, like mercury, but was sketched out with shimmering whorls and symbols.

The huntress drew a long, thin-bladed black knife. It did not reflect the light. She held it parallel to her eyes and regarded him coolly over the top of the blade, her wild green eyes devoid of any hint of compassion – but unsettlingly intelligent.

"You have come again to be hunted," she observed, with no emotional inflection in her rich voice, which dripped like poisoned honey from a deep red mouth

"I'm not afraid of you. This is just a dream. You can't hurt me."

"Is it?" she countered. "Can't I? Are you so sure, boy?"

"I can outrun you. I'm faster than you."

"Spoken like prey."

Fierce defiance rose up in the boy's breast.

"Not for you. You be careful: I have a friend. He's strong – stronger than you."

Unsettlingly, she grinned at this, showing her pointed teeth.

"Fool. There is only predator and prey. There is more than one hunter – more than one way to stalk and bring down prey. Especially when it is quick and watchful."

With that, she jumped lightly down from the rock. It must have been ten feet high, but she landed with gymnastic poise. There was not a hint of fat or softness to be seen; she was all lean, hard muscle. She moved towards him slowly, curving off slightly to his right. Like a skittish deer, he backed away, skipping slightly backwards.

"I track my quarry and run it down. But you have been marked out by another hunter: one which uses bait. She will not come to you; no; you will go to her."

"This is just a dream," insisted the boy, wondering why the words rang so hollow even as they left his mouth.

"No. It's not. You're not here physically yet, but soon you will be. For now, it is just your mind and your spirit which are being drawn here, for their essence is part of this place."

The boy closed his eyes. He thought of Evan's grin; of his rough hug. It gave him strength; it made him feel brave. He opened his eyes and she was there, right in front of him: close enough to kiss. He hadn't heard her move. Her inky blade pricked the base of his throat.

The boy locked eyes with her. He made no effort to run or pull away.

"You don't scare me anymore. You're not real. This is a dream: you can't kill me, not really."

There was a hiss of breath; was it irritation or laughter? It was hard to tell.

Her eyes gleamed, the slanted pupils expanded slightly as though sucking in the light. Her breath played gently over his face: it smelt of flowers, thick, opulent flowers. And death.

Her lips grazed his cheek.

"Little lamb, little lamb. Will the lion lay with thee?"

The boy shivered.

"Poor little lamb. There are worse things than death, you know. Soon, you'll be wishing that I was the one hunting you; you will wish for a clean death – clean and quick."

Her voice was low and sensual; words vibrating, bubbling from her throat, oddly reminiscent of a purring cat.

"Wait!" he cried. "Who – who is hunting me if not you?"

"You'll know soon enough. A nasty, milky spider, hovering in the darkness, weaving, weaving her webs to catch the unwary. She will suck you dry. But now I am become like one of those dwellers in the darkness, talking to my prey. Quiet now. Be at peace."

And with that, she rammed the knife up through his throat, right to the hilt.

The boy woke with a gurgling cry. He instinctively reached for his throat: the flesh was smooth and uninjured.

Just a dream he thought to himself. *Like I said.* He clutched his silver crucifix nonetheless but it wasn't Jesus he thought of as he went back to sleep.

The boy was jolted awake by the chimes of his phone. He cracked open one eye and reached for it. It was 9.43. There were only two people who ever texted him, one being his mother to let him know if she had to work an unexpected shift, or asking what he wanted for dinner. The other was nothing but trouble. The message was, as he knew it would be, from the latter.

Hey! Meet me by the chippie at 11.

The boy smiled happily as he rolled out of bed. He flung himself through the shower to wake up properly and munched his way through a bowl of cereal. He had planned to leave it for twenty minutes or so before replying, but had only waited five: what, after all, if Evan took his delay as meaning he wouldn't be there and changed his mind? Still, he didn't break his neck to get there and arrived 'fashionably late,' as Grandmother would have said.

Evan was perched on a low brick wall, working his way through a bag of vinegary chips. The morning was fairly overcast and he was wearing some sort of retro sports jacket over his customary T-shirt and fitted jeans. He nodded amiably as the boy slouched towards him.

"Morning smiler!"

The boy pulled his most hangdog expression and grunted.

"You'd be miserable too if you had to face a morning with the guy I'm meeting up with," he proclaimed in a mournful voice.

A chip bounced off his forehead.

"Huh! You should be grateful that I lower myself to bring a little joy to your lowly existence!" His voice rang with indignation but he was grinning, which made the boy grin back like an idiot, even though his words were rather too close to the bone.

There's many a true word spoken in jest!

Grandmother, again, thanks oh Queen of Cliché...

The boy sat himself next to Evan on the wall, close, but not actually touching him. He availed himself of Evan's chips and they exchanged insults until they were gone. Then they ambled around for a while, spending time and money at the arcade, before swinging by a couple of shops, where they managed to pilfer a comic book and some chocolate. They ended up in the park, picking through their loot.

"You should do something like that," observed Evan, nodding at the artwork of the comic. He flicked a cigarette into his mouth, winked, and lit it, shielding the flame of his match with a practised hand.

"Yeah, maybe." The boy looked at him, admiringly. "You are just too cool," he observed, before cursing his loose lips. "But maybe you shouldn't smoke, you know? It's like, really bad for you..." He trailed off as Evan shot him a dark look.

"Thanks for the life advice kid, but I know what I'm doing and I don't need any lectures right now, OK?"

The boy glanced away. Why had he said that? It was the sort of thing his drippy mother might have come out with.

Because he was trying to cover something else, obviously...

"Yeah. Course. Sorry."

He shivered as a cool breeze cut across him: spoilt by days of summer sunshine he had left the house in just a shirt and jeans. He wrapped his arms around his knees and stared at the flowers being ruffled by the weather.

Behind him, Evan clicked his tongue in apparent annoyance.

"Come here fool! Why didn't you wear a hoodie or something? Didn't you look out of the window?"

"No. I just ran out the door without thinking."

He blushed slightly as he realised that this was exactly what he'd done. He hoped Evan wasn't too good at reading between the lines.

"Hm. Well, you can share my jacket for a bit if you like. As long as you don't whine about my ciggy smoke."

"OK. Deal." The boy gave a quick, anxious smile, but shuffled up to Evan, who shrugged one arm out of his jacket and wrapped the material around him. The boy closed his eyes, enjoying the moment of close contact, but not wanting to show it."

"You could catch your death!" cried Evan, shrilly, as he encircled him with his left arm.

"OK Mum, thanks for the lecture," said the boy, smiling softly and hearing a reciprocal chuckle from his friend. "But I know what I'm doing, ta. No need for life advice." He tilted his head back, looking upside down at Evan, who leaned down towards him before stopping himself.

"I'm not sure that's true," he asserted, with a wry tone. "Be careful what you wish for..."

Something stirred uneasily in the recesses of the boy's mind, but he pushed it back.

"Right. But sometimes, you just got to take a risk, don't you?"

Evan's arm squeezed him and they both laughed.

"You're getting very bold in your old age. OK then, how about you put your money where your mouth is?"

The boy looked up again, quickly, wondering what he meant, but he saw a wicked look on Evan's face, the sort of look that presaged a dare of some description – most probably involving some level of risk and illegality.

"What did you have in mind?" asked the boy, raising one eyebrow.

Evan never broke eye contact.

"There's a place near my granny's house. She reckons there's some stuff in it – like old coins, silver and stuff – it got left there a long time ago – like by some tribal chieftain or something... She says it's cursed – there's bad spirits and it's dangerous. But I think she's just trying to put me off having a look down there. I want to check it out, but I need another pair of hands in case anything gets too hairy."

The boy returned his stare.

This was a test, wasn't it?

"OK," he agreed, casually. "Where is it? I'm ready when you are."

"Well, that's the thing. It's underground – quite deep down. How are you with enclosed spaces?"

"OK normally – but if I'm stuck in one with you, I'm not so sure."

Evan stuck out his tongue.

"Yeah," he said, drily, "I can see that you like your own space."

The boy giggled a bit, burrowing even closer into Evan's flank. "Except when it's cold, of course," he replied, giving a look at contrived innocence.

"Fool!" said Evan, but his voice was surprisingly gentle and beneath the jacket he gave the boy's hand a squeeze.

They lay there for a while in companionable silence. The boy was just about to ask some more about the mysterious treasure site – like where it was – when he felt it. There was a strange vibration in the air: it made his ears want to pop and sent tingles through his skin. Confused, he looked up at the sky, but it remained unchanged; two small children ran past shrieking with laughter, apparently unaware of any strangeness. Puzzled, the boy looked up at Evan, only to find his face a tight mask of anger – possibly more than anger. His green eyes blazed with barely restrained emotion and his mouth was set into an uncharacteristic straight line. His head swivelled to and fro and the boy thought for a moment that he was actually sniffing the air. Suddenly his eyes locked on to some large shrubs about fifty metres away. As the boy watched, someone stepped out from behind them. For some reason, he felt a surge of uneasiness, as though somewhere in his reptile brain an alert was sounding – that primal, hard-wired instinct which recognises a threat.

"What is it?" he asked Evan, annoyed to find that his voice had come out in a higher pitch than usual.

Evan abruptly pushed him to one side, positioning himself between the boy and the nearby figure.

"Stay here!" he commanded, in a tone that brooked no questions or complaint. The boy felt his heart rate increase, pounding in his flesh like a startled animal. He nodded

126

acquiescence. Shivering and now not only with the cold, he stared mutely at his friend, but Evan was rising, his attention focused entirely on the person who waited now, just in front of the bushes, some forty meters away. The only comfort he could draw was that Evan, although his face bore the marks of intense concentration and anger, showed no fear.

The boy redirected his attention to the mysterious figure. It looked like a young woman in her late teens, possibly early twenties. She was strangely dressed in what looked to be a deep blue hooded cloak. Long strands of very dark hair could be seen framing her face, which was dark and of a Mediterranean appearance. Her eyes were partly in shadow, but they seemed to reflect the light so that they almost glowed inside the hood like a cat. She stood there calmly, arms hanging limply by her side.

There was something wrong with her. The boy knew it to be a fundamental truth. She was a jarring affront to the laws of his universe.

Gulping back saliva, he looked back at Evan. He was also standing in a loose posture, with his arms to one side, but his fists, unlike hers, were tightly clenched. Occasionally he shook slightly, as though maintaining a strenuous gymnastic position.

He had absolutely no clue what was going on, but he sensed some sort of tension or energy shimmering in the air between them.

Suddenly it was all over. The tension just disappeared. Evan unclenched his fists and the young woman's cupid's bow mouth turned into a knowing smile.

Evan turned to look at him, before calling to him.

"Go home. Go now. I'll text you later, OK? Don't worry, everything's fine. I just have a few things to sort out."

The boy stumbled shakily to his feet. "OK. If you say so."

"I do," said Evan firmly. "Oh – and don't answer the door unless I'm ringing you from the front step to say it's me."

"But..." the boy was inexplicably afraid now. "But I'll be able to see it's you from the window before I open it."

"Not unless I actually ring you," said Evan, sharply now. "This is important or I wouldn't have said it." He turned his searing gaze on him. "Promise me!" Then, a little more softly, having seen the boy's face, "Please?"

The boy nodded, dumbly. Licking his lips, he finally coughed out, "Yes. Alright. I promise."

Evan smiled wistfully at him. He looked tired, like he hadn't looked when they'd run through the fields the other day.

"Good man. Now scoot. Go on. I'll be fine. It's just some... family business I need to take care of."

The boy's eyes flared in surprise and he stared again at the woman who simply watched them both with an enigmatic smile. Then he turned and began to walk quickly. Truth be told, he had to fight down a sudden urge to run. Looking back, he saw that Evan and the stranger had walked towards each other. They seemed to be in an animated conversation, with Evan's body language showing anger whilst hers was casually mocking.

What the hell am I getting mixed up in here? The boy suddenly remembered Evan's warning about his weird family. Maybe he should have left well alone. But then he thought of those wicked eyes and the strong arm of Evan Greenway, and he knew that he was well and truly caught.

Chapter 11
In For A Penny, In For A Pound.

How very tiresome! I was not expecting that another interested party would try to get their hooks into the boy! It seems that I underestimated their intelligence and indeed their willingness to take to the field. I must presume that they too have some sense of his potential. Still, no need to do anything rash; my plans have been set – with great attention to detail, I might add – and are running to schedule. If I can throw them off the scent for just a short while it will suffice.

I must move in quickly now. They do not yet realise his true significance or they would have sent someone with greater power to monitor him.

I am calm. All will be well.

What is that human rhyme? The one about a spider and a fly? I cannot quite remember except that there is a sense of inevitability that the fly must succumb eventually to the spider's cunning.

Step into my parlour, pretty little fly.

Let me hold you in my loving embrace.

Let me remake you in my own image.

The boy had brooded on the events of the day to the point of neurosis. Who was the mystery woman? Why had she made him feel so strange? Was she dangerous? Would Evan be alright?

Of course, once he was back home, he began to realise that he may have over-egged the pudding. The feeling that had seemed so strong at the time – the feeling of wrongness – was probably just a reaction to the suddenness and strangeness of her appearance. The way she had just stood there, watching and not moving or speaking. Yeah, she had upset his nerves for sure – but, odd though she was, she hadn't actually done anything scary, so he needed to calm down and put it all in perspective.

Still, after an hour or two had passed, and he had chewed his finger nails into rags, he had sent a text, just to check how Evan was. Eleven slow minutes crept by, leaving him with his heart increasingly in his mouth, before a brief reply had appeared: *Yeh. All sorted. Don't sweat it Dali. See you tomorrow.*

He knew that was as good as it was going to get, and it certainly did reassure him – at least Evan was OK. He still felt stressed, though, and he wasn't entirely sure why. Something had knocked him off-balance, and it wasn't a feeling he enjoyed. Even his mother sensed there was something wrong, despite his best efforts to hide it and began to ask him annoying questions. Complaining of a headache, he excused himself and went up to bed for an early night.

Had he slept, this would have probably done him good. Unfortunately, his sleep was plagued with uneasy dreams: half-images and distant voices drifted in and out of focus. After a period of disorientation, the mists seemed to clear all of a sudden and everything came into sharp focus; he found himself in a quaint little parlour, perched on an ancient-looking red velvet sofa. There was an old-fashioned coal fireplace, and a mantelpiece decorated with ceramic animals – rabbits, cats, dogs and some fairies sitting on large toadstools. An older lady, probably in her late sixties appeared with a tray containing two glasses of lemonade and a plate of creamy scones. She was a little overweight and her fading red hair was tied loosely back, but was difficult to restrain. Her eyes were very blue and surrounded by laughter lines. She looked friendly and pleased to see him – like a Grandmother was supposed to look.

Placing the tray on a scuffed side table, she stood, passing him a glass of lemonade.

"Here you go, my lovely, it's home-made this! Just what you need on a hot summer's day."

She beamed at him and picked up the second glass for herself. "Help yourself to scones: I made them for you, too, specially."

With that, she sat in a creaking brown leather armchair, facing him.

He swigged the lemonade: it did taste good! Reclining on the clapped-out but ridiculously comfortable sofa, he eyed the scones hungrily. This all seemed so real, so natural, that for a moment he almost forgot he was dreaming. A latticed window, framed by flowery curtains, presented him with a view of blue sky and a pretty garden, studded with lupins, delphiniums and snapdragons.

They chatted comfortably for a few minutes as he tucked into a creamy scone. She told him not to worry about the crumbs he dropped – the cat would hoover them up when she came back in. They laughed about how annoying his mother was and when she asked him about Evan, it seemed like the most natural thing in the world for him to tell her all about him – how cool he was, and funny – and how he had saved him from the school bully, like a knight in shining armour. Her blue, blue eyes twinkled with merriment as he described Ricky Fosseway being flattened.

"He sounds like a real charmer, this Evan boy," she chuckled and then gave him a knowing look. "You love him, I suppose?"

He stopped, mid-chew, to stare at her, surprised by the directness of the question. But then he warmed to the topic – it was nice, after all, to be able to be open and honest about his feelings.

"He's the only thing that's good in my life," he confessed, simply, "it's like someone came into a miserable old house and turned on the lights and the heating. He makes me feel happy like I've got something to look forward to when I get up in the morning."

The old lady, smiled and nodded, but she looked rather sad – and a bit worried, too. Leaning forward, she gently took his right hand in hers.

"Don't put all of your eggs in one basket, sweetheart. People like this Evan are like comets streaking across the sky – so brilliant, so beautiful. But they're fleeting – and they can cause such terrible destruction. Don't give him your heart without any reserve, or it'll get broken for sure."

The boy almost choked at this: he did: he felt a great lump work its way up into his chest, where he thought he might have a heart attack, the pain was so intense. Tears sprang to his eyes.

"Don't say that!" he cried, but in a tone of desperation rather than anger. "I couldn't bear it."

"Ahh," she said, and squeezed his hand comfortingly. "Then I see that I'm too late. Poor boy. He's got his hooks into you, good and proper." Then she nodded, appreciatively. "That was clever of her."

With that, she rose from her chair and kissed him, gently, on the head. She carried with her the smell of baking and of wild flowers. He didn't doubt but that she had good intentions. Resuming her seat, she looked seriously at him.

"Now, then, tell me about your family. I want to know all about them. Shrugging, he complied. After all, they meant nothing to him – not like Evan, on whom he'd already spilled the beans with alacrity. So, he told her all about his mother – that didn't take long. Carl took even less time. Then she asked about his father, and he had to tell her how he had run out on them when he was just a baby. He didn't enjoy telling people that – it made him feel ashamed; rejected.

"Just upped and went, did he? Poor child!" But her blue eyes seemed to suddenly sharpen, despite the exclamations of sympathy. "And your father: did he have any family of his own? They say that such behaviour is often linked to a child's upbringing."

He laughed at this. "Well, I'd be tempted to run away if Grandmother was bringing me up. But she's not like you think: everything's above board and ultra-respectable where she's concerned. Except that..." And he thought back to their last conversation, and the information she had revealed. At the time, he had believed her right enough – hence the bathroom mirrors – but now, he wasn't so sure. Maybe she was just delusional and he, at a vulnerable moment, had been taken in by it all.

Shrugging, he decided to recount the strange tale anyway.

The old lady listened to this attentively. "Shocking!" she murmured, when he got to the bit about the baby trapped in the mirror. "Well I never! How terrible! Your poor Grandmother!"

It was his turn to stop to reassure her now.

"Oh don't worry too much – I'm pretty sure she was delusional. Grandad thought it was some sort of post-natal thing and he was probably right."

"Wouldn't it be lovely if that was true!" exclaimed the old lady, leaning back in her chair and smiling sadly at him. "But I'm afraid it's not true – the delusional hypothesis, that is. Everything your Grandmother told was quite correct. Her son was taken from her and another baby substituted in his place. Which could explain a few things, by the way..." At this, she tapped a finger on her lips and appeared to be deep in thought.

The boy goggled at her in surprise, still not convinced.

"Hmm. Well, let's see if we can't get to the bottom of this. Young Evan: has he told you anything about where he's from? Or his family?"

"Well, no except that they're weird, apparently. I think I saw one of them yesterday. Some woman in a cloak."

"Oh?" She said, her ears pricking up at this. "And has he asked you to do anything out of the ordinary at all – or tried to take you to an unusual place?"

The boy looked at her in surprise. What was it he'd been saying about confined underground spaces? That was a coincidence! He frowned and thought how he should begin to answer this, when she suddenly grunted and looked towards the window.

"Ah! It seems that our nice little chat is going to be cut short! And it was so lovely talking to you!"

He followed her gaze. Outside, the summer sky had darkened, but not as it might with the onset of a storm – it had gone black in a matter of seconds. There was a deep rending sound and the house shuddered.

The old lady seized his hand, and stared into his eyes. "Remember! Remember to be careful. Beauty is not the same as goodness – you can't trust him!"

She was having to shout by the end of the sentence as the windows suddenly imploded; huge, black tree roots coiled into the breaches like they were alive. One snaked towards the old woman, but with a wink of her blue eye, she was gone and the armchair was smashed to pieces.

"What..?" began the boy, stunned by the suddenness of the attack. But then a root grabbed him: it coiled around him with astonishing speed, rising over his body until it had covered his mouth and eyes.

Breathe... can't breathe...

And then he woke up, choking and gasping for breath, finding that he had somehow wrapped his duvet tightly around him. As usual, he was unscathed – physically, at least.

The first glimmers of light were eking away at the curtains. Falling back onto his pillow, he dozed fitfully, never quite wanting to fully surrender to sleep, until he got a text at six in the morning which woke him up entirely.

Can't sleep. You awake?

I am now!

Then his phone actually rang. Blearily, the boy answered it

"Are you trying to kill me?"

"Rise and shine! It's gonna be a wonderful morning!"

"Huh! So you've not been locked in a box by your relatives, then?"

"They tried," replied Evan gravely, "but they were unable to contain me!"

The boy giggled, croakily.

"I bet they couldn't! Listen, I'm just glad you're OK"

"Hey, stop that, brown-eyes, you're making me tear up!"

"You're such an idiot!" complained the boy, but he lay there with a ridiculous grin on his face all the same.

"Yeah, yeah! Stop whingeing and listen up. You doing anything today?"

"Other than visiting my therapist and sketching a portrait of the Queen? Nah! Should be able to fit you in sometime this evening."

This provoked a throaty chuckle.

"Wow! You're on fire today! I thought I'd ring early on the off-chance that your normal acid responses might be dulled by fatigue, but no such luck."

"Nope. Somehow you can irritate me at any time of the day or night."

"Now there's a thought," chortled Evan, causing the boy to flush with embarrassment. "Anyway, enough of the banter. I ended up crashing with a cousin in your neck of the woods last night. I'll call for you around half seven and treat you to breakfast. Whaddya say to that?"

The boy pretended to hum and haw for a few seconds before agreeing with an over-the-top display of reluctance.

"OK then – but does this mean I get the afternoon off? There's only so much of you that I can cope with in a day."

"Funny guy! Keep on churning out the jokes – I'll be along in a Kevlar vest before you know it."

And then he was gone.

The boy sat for a moment like a startled rabbit. Evan was coming *here.* He felt unaccountably nervous and self-conscious and had to sternly remind himself that he had never been invited to Evan's place, so he had no cause to feel awkward. Even so, he rushed into the shower and from there to the kitchen to clear the dishes from the previous night. His mother almost died of shock when she appeared in her pink dressing gown in the doorway.

"What's going on?" she squawked, her eyes out on stalks. "You're WASHING UP!"

"There's no need to raise your voice," he huffed, testily, "I just thought I'd try to help out."

"Oh." She said, and had to sit down. "Well while you're in such a helpful mood, you can make me a strong coffee. I think I might be in shock."

"I'm surrounded by comedians today!" scowled the boy, making her a drink anyway. "If you must know, Evan's calling round for me. We're going to go for breakfast together." He was annoyed to find that his ears had gone red, in spite of his attempts at nonchalance. A smile kindled into life on her tired, careworn face.

"Ah! That's nice. So I'm finally going to meet the mysterious Evan." There was a hint of mischief in her eyes.

"I suppose you'll have to," he muttered with ill grace, "unless you want to sit upstairs till we've gone?"

"Oh no, boy of mine, I wouldn't miss this for anything. I'm staying right here." And with that, she positioned herself at the kitchen table in the manner of a woman who would NOT be moved.

Assuming the resigned air of a prisoner with no hope of release, the boy joined her at the table with a coffee of his own. He didn't want to be falling asleep over breakfast! And when there was a smart rap at the door, both mother and son made a run for it, with mother barging him aside in a very undignified manner.

"Oh hello!" she crooned, "You must be Evan. We were just having a coffee – why don't you join us before you whisk him away? One for the road?"

If he was surprised, embarrassed or impatient to get going, Evan Greenway didn't show it. He was wearing a faded denim jacket and a weird white t-shirt with a giant tongue on it. A pair of expensive sun glasses shielded his eyes from the bright morning and he stood there on the boy's doorstep with a sense of practised ease, like he called round at the same time every morning.

"Thanks! That'd be great," he agreed, affably, pushing his glasses up into his tousled golden hair and sauntering through to the kitchen. There he was engaged in a determined conversation by the boy's mother, who had her own concerns that he might be involved in drugs or petty crime. The boy cringed each time his mother said something ridiculous or embarrassing, which was pretty much every time she opened her mouth. Evan didn't seem to mind, though, and after ten minutes or so, mother was chuckling raucously at his jokes and had begun to assume the slightly dazzled expression that the boy had seen in others on so many occasions.

Eventually, Evan excused himself to use the toilet before they headed off, and the boy found his mother beaming at him in an uncomfortably conspiratorial manner.

"He's bloody gorgeous!" she hissed, giggling, as she leaned over the table to share her thoughts in a very loud stage whisper.

"Mother!" reprimanded the boy, primly.

"I can see why you like him," she continued, her voice lowering slightly and taking on a shy edge.

The boy looked sharply at her. "He's a good friend, that's all," he snapped.

"Oh come on, love," she said, smiling at him now, "this is the twenty first century. I suspected from the way you talk about him and try so hard to make it sound like he's a pain, when all the time I've never seen you so happy. But having seen you – you can't take your eyes off him, sweetheart! You were staring at him like a moonstruck cow!" She couldn't stop herself from giving a peal of brassy laughter at this.

The boy, flustered, stammered, trying to string a suitable sentence together, but failed.

Then, even worse, she took his hand and squeezed it. "I just want you to be happy. It doesn't matter to me whether it's with a girl or a boy. Don't worry, you can count on your old mum. In fact, I positively approve. If I was twenty years younger, I wouldn't mind a bit of him myself!"

"MOTHER!" shrieked the boy in a scandalised voice. He didn't know what he took the most exception to out of all of the preceding comments, but his outrage simply seemed to make his mother chuckle all the more boldly.

He was prevented from saying anything else by Evan's return.

"Hey! Who's been making funnies in my absence?" he enquired innocently, whilst shooting a wink at the boy, just to add to his increasing sense of mortification.

"No one!" he cried in a strangled voice. "Come on – let's be making tracks – I'm starving."

With that, he grabbed Evan by the arm and practically frogmarched him to the door. Mother followed them, smiling broadly.

"Have fun boys! And Evan?"

"Yes?"

"Look after my little lad, won't you?"

Evan sketched a bow.

"I'll bring him back to you unscathed and content."

"Oh, I don't think he'd mind a bit of scathing, would you love? Just be gentle with him!"

Her rowdy laughter followed them down the street. The boy thought he might actually die from embarrassment. Evan's expression was partly hidden by his sunglasses, but he was grinning and laughing softly to himself.

"God! I am so sorry – she's a nightmare!"

He blustered away as they walked, but Evan simply laughed out loud.

"Oh hush up about it! She just has a sense of humour. You need to relax, you sour old puritan!"

And with that he put an arm around the boy's shoulder and hugged him close as they walked. On some level, the boy felt nervous about what his neighbours might assume – but on most levels, his worries and outrage were simply subsumed into a golden mist of delight, like hot iron suddenly plunged into a quench bath.

A short time later, they had ensconced themselves in a hip coffee bar, where Evan ordered them each a portion of French toast – something which the boy had never had before and which amazed him with its decadent glory – and hot, fresh coffee, which tasted nothing like the own-brand instant stuff he drank at home. They chatted and laughed for an hour or so and Evan shared a few stories about his loonier relatives – notably a female cousin who wore an entirely unsuitable level of clothing to the scandal of her neighbourhood and his grandad who kept a number of stills in his cellar for the purpose of brewing excessively strong alcohol.

He had a way of telling funny stories that reduced the boy – who was not known for his ribald sense of humour – to tears. His timing was spot on – as were his facial expressions and gestures. The boy was subject to the full power of his charm and attention and he basked in them like a flower in the sun.

As they finished the last of their coffee, Evan leaned back on his chair and composed his face into a mask of insincere innocence.

"Well, I guess that's it, then. I should probably head off to the frenzied clutches of my insane family and leave you to it. I seem to recall you saying you couldn't cope with me for more than a morning."

The boy smiled shyly at him, and lowered his head so that he was peering up at him through his fringe.

"Oh, it's OK. I haven't gotten completely sick of you yet."

"Is that right?" chirped Evan, with exaggerated delight, before grinning at him. "OK. How'd you fancy another trip out into the countryside? The sun is shining, and I know a really cool place for lazy summer days. You up for it?"

The truth was that the boy would have followed him on a jaunt to the local abattoir, but he made a show of sucking his teeth and deliberating until Evan kicked him and threatened to leave right there and then.

"Seldom have my generous social offers been so underappreciated!" he declared – but by then, they were already on their way to the bus stop.

It was shaping up to be a hot day and the bus was humid and sweaty, but half an hour later, they were free of its confines and walking through the centre of an outlying village. Evan called into the local post office, which also doubled as the village shop, and bought them some sandwiches, pop and crisps.

"Wow!" said the boy as they emerged back into the glorious sunshine. "You actually paid. With money and everything!"

"Oho! Yes, thank you Dr Watson, I did. This is the place where my Granny comes to do her shopping – you might call it my local. I like to do my bit for village commerce," he replied, with a wide smile. "Now come on – we've got something of a hike coming up, so we'd best get moving."

"Whoa! A major hike? How come this was left out of the proposal until I was stuck out here in the middle of nowhere? I'll tell you now, if you think I'm running all over the place again in heat like this, you can do one!"

"Oh, my little urban mouse," sang Evan, grabbing him and spinning him around, to the surprise and alarm of a passing pensioner, where's your spirit of adventure?" Then, leaning closer, he whispered "we both know that you wouldn't be anywhere else right now, but right here, with me."

"You," pointed out the boy, "are an arsehole."

But he knew he was right all the same.

Chapter 12
Falling

On the cusp of something new, are we? Feeling like your world is suddenly full of hope? How fragile are the dreams of mortals – these... humans. So easily warped and manipulated. I have to say that I was surprised by the subtlety of my enemy – it's not like her to be so devious! To enter his very dreams for the purpose of interrogation... Such audacity! I am almost impressed. Still, she hasn't learned anything of immediate import – and she's still too far behind to catch me up now. For when it comes to subtlety, I invest many years in the slow weaving and interweaving of my webs. This particular subject has been almost thirty human years in the making. I don't think I'll be thwarted now, at the eleventh hour, however clever and fast-thinking her operative is in his world.

This one is mine, my dear: he has been nurtured and monitored until his time has come.

Try if you like, but you'll not be able to save him now.

I have staked my claim – keep your meddlesome minions out of my way or they will share his fate - or worse.

It was quite a hike for a town boy who thought walking for twenty minutes to reach the cinema was approaching marathon standards, but he liked the company and the sun was beaming down, so he restricted himself to occasional cries of 'are we nearly there yet?' not least for the comically irritating effect they had on Evan, who scowled and grimaced at him with increasing ferocity.

The village was soon left behind, and the boy found himself being dragged through a patchwork of fields before arriving at the edge of some woodland. The trees were big and widely spaced, so that great profusions of wild flowers were able to grow, brought to life by the dappled sunlight. Evan started to tell him what different plants were called, until he saw the ironic curve of the boy's mouth.

"OK laughing boy, what's tickling you now?"

The boy's eyes shone with impudent mirth.

"Well," he replied, "I'm trying to adjust my perceptions..."

Evan stopped and turned to glare at him.

"Here we go!" he grumbled, "I'm sensing a moment of intense wit wafting over in my direction..."

"No! It's just that... well, back home, you're like this uber cool rebel without a cause, with your smoking and your fight moves. And suddenly, out here, you've morphed into David Attenborough."

"I," said Evan, with frigid dignity, "am merely trying to share some of my natural lore with you. I should have known," he continued, testily in the face of the boy dissolving into open laughter, "that I was casting pearls before swine!"

"Yeah, OK gramps, you keep it coming! You should have warned me to bring a note book or something. What's next, you going to start on the mating habits of the lesser spotted flying squirrel?"

"There is no such creature, as I'm sure you know," said Evan, coolly, before leaping to grab his tormentor in a headlock and knuckle his scalp, eliciting alternate yelps of pain and laughter. "Have you anything else you'd like to say to me now?"

"Yes," said the boy, squinting up at him, "are we nearly there? I'm knackered!"

"Huh! Yes, weakling, it's about ten minutes away now. I think I preferred you when you were sullen and wouldn't speak to anyone for fear of being caught in a conversation. You've become irritatingly keen to share your thoughts and what passes for humour."

"That's your fault!" crowed the boy, gleefully, to which Evan had no answer, and was obliged to release him without further scuffing.

"I've created a monster!" he cried, dramatically, but he looked rather pleased about it all the same. "Come on, then, whingebag – stop dragging your heels!"

With that, he stuck out his tongue and set off at a jog, forcing the protesting boy to keep up with him. As before, he noticed that Evan was infuriatingly fit, and showed no obvious sign of being out of breath, whereas he was huffing and puffing like an old steam engine. Together, they flew, whooping and (in his case) panting through the thick banks of flowers; everything was so alive – there was so much growth and energy here; the very air was filled with the scent of flowers, ferns and wild garlic. There was almost too much of it, the boy thought, his senses almost overpowered by the rank fecundity of nature. Then suddenly, the trees gave out to a softly yielding grassy bank, studded with yellow and white flowers, and leading down to a slow-moving river.

Grinning with delight, he crashed down next to Evan on the turf, still panting for breath and wiping sweat from his brow, but the length of the journey now forgotten.

"Wow! I gotta hand it to you – this is a pretty sweet spot!" he exclaimed, turning his open, smiling face towards Evan, who was already smiling back at him.

"Yep! Didn't I tell you it was a nice place for a lazy afternoon? And what's more, I've raised your fitness level to get here: everyone's a winner."

The boy shot him a look and wrinkled his nose. He thought about drawing attention to Evan's smugness, but, mellowing now he had arrived and could laze around all afternoon, he decided to leave it.

In the meantime, Evan busied himself setting out the goodies he'd bought from the village shop. The boy was thirsty after the long walk in the sun, and was glad of a drink. Soon they got to talking and exchanging stories about school and family. Evan had, as he'd begun to open up about himself, recently revealed that he was home-schooled, something which the boy thought sounded fantastic. He was supposedly a year ahead of him in his studies, though he showed little interest in academic matters.

"How come you're home-schooled, anyway?" the boy enquired.

Evan had made a pillow of his denim jacket and had his eyes half-closed. He looked very relaxed, the sun streaking splashes of light over his face as the tree branches above moved slightly in the soft breeze. All around them, birdsong rose and fell in vibrant bubbles of sound and the river gently lapped at its earthen banks.

"Hmm, that's... complicated," said Evan, in a drowsy voice.

"Does that mean you're not going to tell me about it?" asked the boy, after waiting a few seconds, with what could only be described as a satirical edge to his voice.

Evan cracked one eye open and pulled a face.

"Did you take a high-powered annoyance tablet when you got up this morning?"

"Yeah. Right after some wise guy woke me up at the crack of dawn cos he couldn't sleep."

Evan smiled at this and closed his eye again.

"So, it's partly a family thing: the council would class us as Travellers, see."

"Oh!" said the boy. Maybe that explained why Evan seemed to have such a free rein, although if he was honest, he didn't really know what Travellers were meant to be. "And what's the other part?"

"The other part, Mr Persistent, is me. You may not have noticed this, but I don't take well to following orders. Or rules. It became very clear, very quickly, that I was ill-suited to the demands of a formal education. So I stopped going and got my ma to sort all the paperwork stuff out with the council. She's good at that – like you wouldn't believe with rules and regs and official bureaucracy. And now," he continued, turning his head towards the boy and opening both eyes, "unless there are any more questions for the prosecution, I'd really quite like a bit of a kip."

The boy laughed quietly at this and flopped back down. The idea of a nap was pretty appealing to him, too, given the night he had had previously. He decided that if he ever actually met Evan's mum, he would do some research on how one opted out of school for 'home education.' As far as he could tell, this simply meant that Evan spent his days doing whatever took his fancy — whether that was feuding with his extended family, shoplifting or giving bullies a damned good thrashing.

"I wish I could do that!" sighed the boy, softly, but Evan was already asleep, his chest rising and falling in a regular pattern, his face a mask of tranquillity. The boy glanced over, somewhat enviously. *I wish I could doze off as easily as...*

When he woke up, the sun had moved across the sky: he must have been out for at least an hour if not two. It was just as well they'd had an early start. His friend was sitting up and smoking a cigarette. He nodded companionably to him when he yawned and raised himself to his elbows.

"Feeling better?" he asked, casually flicking away some ash.

"Well, no, since you ask!" replied the boy. "I feel half-asleep still, and I'm starving hungry!"

Evan grinned and tossed his cigarette butt into the river with practised nonchalance.

"Well, let's get to eating then. See, I was a gentleman and waited for you to wake up. I could've just sneaked off with all the grub and left you here to starve. Some skinny dippers would've been shocked to find your tragic skeleton."

"You should get a medal for gallantry," observed the boy, drily, as they both fell upon the food.

Food always tastes good when you're hungry, and this was no exception. Soon, they were lying down again, rubbing their bellies contentedly. The boy couldn't help but notice that this time Evan was a little closer to him. Obviously a coincidence; or maybe he was imagining it.

As they lay there, the boy turned things over in his mind.

"Evan," he ventured, hesitantly.

Something in his voice must have registered, as Evan turned towards him and offered what was almost a look of concern.

"Mmm?"

"Do you ever have really weird dreams?"

Evan chortled at this. "Heh! If I told you what sort of things appear in my dreams, you'd be leaping in the river! I might even be arrested."

The boy sighed and shook his head.

"Listen, jackass. I'm trying to confide in you here – can you manage a bit of deep and serious for a minute or two?"

"Ah. Apologies, then. Go for it."

Evan raised himself up on his elbow to look down on him, with a suitably grave face.

The boy stuck out his tongue in response, but went on to tell him about his dreams: the huntress, the jungle, the kindly old woman with her scones.

"It's just that it seems so real – and it's recurring. I feel like it's an actual place – that some of these people are real." He paused to stare at Evan, who was frowning at him. "Do you think I'm weird?" asked the boy, in a small voice.

"Well, obviously!" replied Evan, nodding seriously, and easily avoiding the kick that was aimed at him. "Look, everyone has intense dreams from time to time – and they can seem real. That's dreams for you. When I was a little kid, I used to dream about a tall thin man in a black top hat. He used to follow me everywhere and I knew he was out to get me. I used to wake up screaming. But it passed, eventually. It was just a dream, that's all."

"I do wake up screaming, sometimes," confessed the boy, in a low voice. "Maybe I should see a doctor. I mean, I'm fourteen now, not four."

There was a little pause again, and he was surprised out of his introspection by his hand being gently held. Evan traced his finger lightly over his palm.

"Hey. You're not weird. Don't sweat it. So what if you don't go along with all of the sheep out there? And so what if you have crazy dreams? It just means you're different from the crowd – and you've got an imagination – and a sense of self that most people can't possibly get. You're alright."

153

The boy looked up into a smiling pair of green eyes, which definitely seemed to be closer to him than they were a few seconds ago. He gulped, and moved slightly away, sitting up as he did so. The look of genuine tenderness and even, possibly, *affection* on Evan's face made him feel nervous – he didn't want to do anything stupid again, so discretion was the better part of valour and all that.

Evan released him and rummaged around in his jacket before producing, like a conjurer, a large metal object, like a flattened bottle.

"I think you, my friend, might be in need of some medication – and I have just the stuff here!"

"What is that?"

"It's a hipflask."

"Yes, I know that, I mean what's in it?"

"Aha! A fiery elixir, guaranteed to wash away all unpleasant feelings of bad dreams! Have a swig – Dr Greenway's orders!"

The boy took the flask and opened it, before having a sniff. The contents were unmistakably sweet but the fumes also made his eyes water.

"So-o, just so that I know you're not giving me battery acid, can you please confirm what I'm about to be swigging?"

Evan grinned.

"Sure: it's my Granda's homemade mead."

"Mead?" asked the boy, "what the hell is that? Isn't that what the Vikings used to drink?"

"Meh!" shrugged Evan, "I've got the looks and the charm but not much history. All I know is that it's made from fermented honey."

"Oh, OK," said the boy. God knows he had a sweet tooth and was quite partial to honey. He lifted the flask and took a deep gulp. The sensation was like burning petrol, albeit with a sweet flavour, and he almost choked and dropped the flask, had not Evan's reflexes saved the grass from being napalmed. He coughed and spluttered for a few seconds, before catching his breath and wiping tears from his eyes.

"Jesus, Evan!" he croaked, "you could've warned me!"

Evan reclined next to him and chortled in a most unsympathetic manner.

"Yeah," he agreed, cheerfully, "I should probably have told you to take small sips till you get used to it. It must be getting on for forty per cent proof!"

The boy shook his head, which already felt like it had been wrapped in a couple of inches of cotton wool. Grandpa Greenway's mead sure did have a kick, and his stomach now had a warm glow. He imagined the mead sitting there like some sort of radioactive material from a comic book. Mind you, it did have a nice after-taste: rich and sweet, like a high summer afternoon.

Evan had a couple of swigs himself, and a relaxed expression slowly spread across his face.

"Ahh! That stuff hits the spot!" he declared to no one in particular. "You want some more?"

The boy surprised himself by taking the flask back. This time, he took a very small sip. In such a limited amount, he could appreciate the fiery liquid without his head being blown off. He swilled it round, much to Evan's amusement, like some sort of posh wine critic, before swallowing it.

"Yes!" he enunciated, in an unconvincing upper class accent, "this has a splendid aroma and bisquet!"

"You mean bouquet, philistine," laughed Evan, as he relieved him once more of the drink to partake himself.

In the space of ten minutes, he was wrapped in a warm fuzzy glow. He wasn't sure that he'd be able to walk a tightrope, but Evan was right about it taking away his darker feelings. Now he felt happy.

The sun glinted off the bottom of the flask as Evan lifted it to his curving lips once more. The boy watched the Adam's apple move in his golden throat as he drank, before quickly turning away.

No. Don't be stupid. I'm not making an idiot of myself again. I was lucky he let me off the last time.

"What's up with you?" came his voice, husky with mead. "You look like you've just eaten something nasty."

The boy laughed, not entirely convincingly, and declined Evan's offer of another drink.

"Good stuff this! It'll put hairs on your chest!"

"I'm not sure I want hairs on my chest," said the boy, but he found he was gazing back up at him and smiling again.

"Yeah, me neither. I'm too fair for a hairy chest anyway I reckon."

The boy flushed and screwed up his eyes to find himself suddenly thinking about Evan's chest.

Oh my God! What's wrong with me?

He hissed, sharply exhaling and trying to control his imagination. He dug his fingernails into the back of his hand.

"Hey! Are you OK?" Evan's hand suddenly appeared on his forehead, stroking back his fringe and feeling as if for his temperature. "You look like you're gonna vom!"

The boy cracked a fairly broken-looking smile. "Yeah! It's... it's the closeness of your ugly mug! It's turning my stomach!" he groaned, before emphasizing the fact by clutching at his abdomen in mock pain.

"Huh!" responded Evan, before shooting him a sly look. "That's not what you said the other day!" But he withdrew his hand and fell back on his elbows, looking down at the boy where he lay.

Inside, the boy was mortified. This was the first time Evan had actually alluded to what had happened – he couldn't even say between them, as it was all him. Poor Evan had just been lying there minding his own business, after all.

"Oh God!" said the boy, with some feeling, "why do people drink? Alcohol just leads to one big mess after another! I swear I'm going to stop now before I even get started."

Evan grinned. "You need to chill out, mate! A bit of booze is OK – it just loosens things up a bit, that's all – makes you more relaxed... and honest."

The boy shot a frightened look up at him. What was he getting at? Was he making fun of him? He wasn't sure whether that would actually be worse than his being angry and disgusted with him. Those green eyes met his gaze and twinkled.

"What?"

"What what?" countered Evan.

"You're thinking something!" accused the boy.

"Maybe I am..." said Evan, leaning back on his elbow and leaning a little closer towards him.

"Well... stop it, OK! You're making me nervous."

"So-o-o?"

"What!"

"Did you mean what you said the other day? Or was it champagne-induced hysteria?"

"I... I'm not sure what I think... I mean feel..." said the boy in a quavering voice, turning his face away to hide his confusion.

"You seemed to know back in that field," continued Evan, implacably.

"I'm sorry..."

"I didn't say I was complaining."

Startled, the boy turned back to find Evan's face very close indeed now. His eyes glittered and his mouth had quirked into a suggestive half-smile.

"Oh."

"It was just a bit of a surprise. I've never been kissed by another boy before."

"I've never been kissed by anyone!" returned the boy in a squeaky voice. He lay there frozen, like a butterfly pinned to a board by two green pins. He could neither move nor relax. The air around him seems to resonate, as though something momentous was about to happen.

"We can do something about that," murmured Evan, in a tone like thick-curling smoke. His eyes were verdant orbs of fire, and he bent just a little lower, so that the boy could feel his breath on his cheek. "If you'd like?"

The boy considered the possibility that the mead might have damaged his brain – or that he might be dreaming again. It was so very difficult to tell what was real and what wasn't. He was simultaneously terrified and euphoric.

"OK," wobbled out of his mouth, "if you're sure you don't mind."

He winced inwardly: anyone would've thought Evan had just offered to help him with the washing up.

The face above moved lower, his mouth curving slightly wider in a wicked smile and then it was happening: he was being kissed. Not just a peck on the lips, but a slow, deep kiss which quite sucked all of the oxygen out of him and left him resembling a freeze-dried cadaver afterwards.

Evan raised his head and his face shifted into a lopsided grin. "So; how was that?" he enquired.

"It was OK," burbled the boy.

"OK?" replied Evan, quirking one eyebrow.

"Yes – uh... very nice."

Evan's quiet laughter was like a silver bell ringing; he looked younger, more innocent, with his beautiful face hovering just a very few centimetres above.

"You're not doing wonders for my self-esteem," he confided, his grin spreading out all the way across his face. "Maybe I need to work on my technique?"

"Oh. No. It was fine. Don't worry. Very... uh... good," came another gibbering response.

"Oh shut up," he laughed, and bent down to kiss him again.

The boy felt his whole body shake: it was like all of his Christmases had come at once. He revelled in the second kiss, allowing himself to think that this might really be real. When Evan finally broke off, the boy found he was gasping for breath like a drowning fish on the riverbank. He wheezed, and clutched at his chest.

Evan's brows knitted together in an expression of surprised concern.

"Are you asthmatic? Do you have an inhaler or something?" he enquired.

The boy giggled and cried a bit at the same time.

"No! I'm just… really, really happy. I never dreamt that something like this could happen to me."

Evan rolled his eyes. "Why not, you dork?"

"Well… I mean – look at me and look at you! You look like one of those guys they have in American teen movies – only better! And… you're really cool – I don't mean hip cool, although you're that too, I mean cool cool – like – really funny and nice to be with…" The boy stopped to catch his breath again. "Oh God! Now I have verbal diarrhoea!"

Evan giggled. "It's all those years where you moped around scowling at anyone who tried to talk to you – you have a backlog of words to get out. And anyway," he continued, in a softer voice, "don't put yourself down. You're cool too: you do your own thing and won't compromise to fit in. That takes courage. I could almost admire you for it," he whispered, with a wink. "And do you know what else?"

"What?" said the boy, in a high, desperate voice, hanging on every word.

"You're not so bad-looking yourself once you get past all the hair." So saying, he ruffled his hair, whilst pinning the boy's shoulders down with his arms.

"Thanks," said the boy. Never had his eyes shone like this – with such unadulterated joy. He tried to rein in his smile, but couldn't, so instead, he just lay there gazing into his lover's eyes, whilst linking his hands around the back of his neck as those glorious lips drifted down once more.

And so the summer afternoon passed by like a slow dream: the liquid notes of the birds, the drowsy humming of bees. The boy's fingers wound golden curls around themselves as he lay there drinking in slow kisses, rich and heady like summer wine.

Chapter 13
Crossing the threshold

And so the pieces move across the board. This one is almost in the bag: but will he be worth all the trouble? Will he turn out to be a knight, a bishop or a rook? There is, of course, only room for one Queen around here, that goes without saying.

Once again it comes down to the nature of the operatives on the ground: extensions of my will and indeed my adversaries. I gather Lady Thyme has dispatched one of her best under orders to keep the boy from me. She will soon learn that her efforts are futile – and, if all goes to plan, possibly fatal. I do hope so: little pleases me like the annihilation of an old enemy – it's just so invigorating.

Tick tock clock.

Time is on my side and brings me my dark heart's desire.

He must have dozed off again at some point during the afternoon, for when he opened his eyes, he found that he was lying on Evan's lap and gazing up at him, whilst the older boy stroked his hair back and smiled down at him.

"Welcome back, sleeping beauty!" A wild grin lit his face and he hauled the boy to his feet and spun him round a couple of times, causing him to yelp in alarm.

"Look!" continued Evan, pointing vaguely at the sky. "It's nearly tea-time." Then, pausing, he let go of the boy's hands and said "you know, my grandparents' place is near here. I don't suppose…" He paused again and looked surprised at his sudden stalling. "Whoa! What's this? Why do I have butterflies all of a sudden? This must be your fault!"

The boy beamed back, delightedly.

"Maybe you've fallen under my dark power?" he suggested to Evan.

"Nah! Probably the booze," he countered, cackling like a pirate when the boy leapt at him, only to be caught and spun around in the air, shrieking with abandon.

"Anyway," resumed Evan, casually, as he dumped the boy unceremoniously on his backside, "I was going to ask you if you'd like to come and meet my folks?"

The boy squinted up through the low golden bars of late sunlight, fat and heavy now as they hung through the trees. A shy smile flickered into life.

"What… You mean you want to introduce me? As a friend, I mean?"

He found himself adding the last sentence a little too quickly, and blushed as a result.

"Sure," said Evan, handing him to his feet. "Someone special. It's OK!" he added, quickly, seeing the boy's round eyes. "They're very open-minded. They just want me to be happy."

The boy grinned back at him. "Yeah," he said, that's just what my mum said this morning," and he briefly went on to tell Evan of the exchange that had taken place while he was in the toilet."

"Wow! I really am irresistible!"

"No! You're a conceited pain I the neck! I only let you hang out with me to keep you out of trouble!"

"Come on!" said Evan, grabbing his hand and taking charge. "You'll love them, honest! And they'll love you, too, cos I do…"

The boy trotted after him, his ears ringing as though someone had sounded a very loud gong next to his head. Evan had just said he *loved* him! Oh me oh my!

Evan led them away from the river, and deeper into the trees. They continued to hold hands and chatted happily as they went. Only as the sun began to turn into a low crimson ball of fire did the boy notice that Evan seemed to be becoming uneasy. He looked over his shoulder, and a frown appeared on his face.

"Are you alright?" huffed the boy, as he half-jogged to keep up: Evan had gradually increased the pace as they walked on. "I don't mind if you want to hang fire on introducing me," he added.

Evan lobbed a cheery grin at him from over his shoulder.

"Don't be soft! It'll be fine! I just want to get there before they start their dinner, that's all!"

The boy returned the smile, but wasn't entirely convinced. Something, as they say, was definitely up.

Then, as they navigated their way passed a pair of enormous beech trees, which stood like a pair of sentinels, they found themselves in a clearing and two things happened at once.

First, the boy saw something out of a storybook: a single-storey white cottage, complete with thatched roof and a garden bursting with flowers of all shapes and sizes – a rowdy riot of colour. Blue smoke curled out of the chimney and there was even an old-fashioned well in the middle of an immaculately cut lawn.

The second thing was the appearance of a figure on the far side of the clearing. Striding confidently from between the trees came a tall, slim young woman. She was very pale and her long hair was polished silver in colour, even though she couldn't have been more than twenty. It was held in place by a gleaming metallic circlet. She wore what at first he took to be motorcycling leathers, black and close-fitting, but as she approached, he could see that the material was elaborately patterned and in segments – almost like armour. And, as his eyes roamed around in astonishment, he realised that two curved handles protruded up over her shoulders, almost like wings.

Her appearance was so out of place, he stood and gawped like an idiot.

She stopped a few feet into the clearing; the dying sun caused her hair to flush and kissed the circlet on her head with fire. She was beautiful and yet terrible at the same time – and something deep within him resonated, as if with recognition. He looked, nervously at Evan, and was shocked to find his face looking white and drawn with open fear.

"Surprised to see me, Efandyr?" she called in a voice like a rising horn. "Give the boy to me. You're no warrior. Give him to me now and I may spare you."

Evan turned to look at the boy, and then the cottage, and then back to the terrifying woman. Something glinted in his left hand, and the boy saw that a silver key had magically appeared, by some elaborate sleight of hand. Evan caught his eye and smiled.

"Do you trust me?"

"Yes."

It was all that needed to be said, because it was an absolute truth.

"It's all going to be fine," he reassured, with a little wink, before suddenly yanking on his hand and shouting "run!"

The two sprinted for the cottage door: it must only have been sixty meters away, but it seemed like a mile. For once, pumped as he was with screaming adrenaline, the boy had no trouble keeping up with Evan, who surged forward like a hare.

Behind him, the boy heard a cry of rage, and a sound like metal sliding against metal.

"Fool! You have chosen death!" came the alarming cry behind them.

Everything seemed to slow down until they reached the door and Evan, in one smooth movement – no fumbling or doubt – inserted the key and turned it. As the door swung inwards, the boy glanced back over his shoulder, only to see the young woman hurtling towards him with a look of cold anger on her face. She moved like an arrow, swift and true, and was coming straight for him. In each hand, she held a long black blade, slightly curved and traced with silver runes which glowed ominously as she approached.

"Do not enter that place, boy!" she thundered – and he almost didn't, for he found himself gawking at her again in disbelief, until Evan seized him by the scruff of the neck and yanked him across the threshold. The door slammed shut, and Evan swiftly inserted the key and turned the lock. It wasn't a moment too soon, for the door handle twisted furiously and there was a muffled sound of rage, followed by a couple of impacts on the other side of the door.

The boy spun in alarm to stare at Evan, who was leaning against the wall and gasping for breath as though he was having some kind of attack. Beads of sweat stood out on his forehead; his eyes were wide and his nostrils flared. He looked really scared, which in turn scared the boy.

"By the sacred stones," he gasped, clutching at his chest, "that was close!"

"Evan?" ventured the boy in a small, querulous voice, "what's going on?"

"We have to go," said Evan, "that door won't hold her forever." And even as he spoke, the door begin to shiver slightly; as the boy watched, little traces of silver light appeared, first around its edges, and then, slowly in the natural cracks which could be found in the wood.

The boy looked wildly around. They were in what would nowadays be called a kitchen-diner. The work surface of the counter and the sink were spotlessly clean and a small wooden table and two chairs were positioned in front of a fireplace. Tied bunches of herbs and mushrooms hung from the ceiling to dry, and gave the room a pleasant, earthy smell. To the right was a simple wooden door.

"But... Is there another way out? Is that a back door?" And suddenly: "Your grandparents! Where are they?"

"They're fine," whipped out Evan, crisply, "and yes, there is another way out. Come with me."

The boy was relieved to see that Evan had recollected himself and was acting in his usual decisive manner. He found himself pulled through the second, internal door, and into a well-appointed bedroom. There was a large wooden wardrobe, some matching drawers and a double bed festooned with a fantastic patchwork quilt. A vase of roses from the garden sat on a bedside table and filled the air with a sweet perfume.

Without stopping to explain, Evan grabbed the bed and pushed. "Help me!" he commanded, so the boy did.

The bed seemed to be made of solid oak, or some such, but with both of them pushing, it scraped its way across the floor. Where it had stood, the boy found himself gazing down at what looked like a trapdoor.

"Is that a...?"

"Trapdoor! Yes. Now come on, we don't have much time."

Reaching down, Evan flipped the trapdoor open, revealing wooden slats somewhere between a ladder and some steps. As if to emphasize the need for haste, there was a loud cracking sound coming from the kitchen. A ray of silver light lasered through the wood and scorched its signature on the polished wooden floorboards.

The boy gaped. "But… How is she… What…?"

"Listen!" snapped Evan, grabbing both of his arms roughly and squeezing them. "I need you to focus. That woman… if she can, she'll kill us. I'm sorry you've got caught up in this, but that's where we are. Now, get straight down that trapdoor and I'll come behind you. If… if she gets through, I'll try to buy you some time. There's a secret passage. It leads down into a cave where Granda keeps his brewing stuff and his still. Look for a pile of old barrels. Behind them there's a small opening – it leads into another cave, and, eventually, back out." He stopped to stare into the boy's now terrified eyes. Gently, he caught his face between both hands. "Go," he whispered. "Now."

Blinking back tears, the boy struggled down into the dark interior of the trapdoor. At the bottom of the ladder, he found himself in a rock-lined tunnel which headed off in a rough approximation of a straight line. A few metres away, he made out a dim light, glowing in the darkness. With little choice, he headed towards it.

Behind him, there was a thump, which almost made him cry out, but then Evan was there, grabbing his hand and leading him on past what was revealed to be a lantern, lit and positioned in a stone recess.

"Come on! Quickly!"

The boy did as he was told, and together, they descended into the tunnel. Luckily, the floor was reasonably smooth, and lanterns were positioned every three metres or so, but even so, they were moving faster than the boy liked: what if they fell? What if they were injured?

Somewhere behind them, he felt, rather than heard, an impact.

"She's through." Evan confirmed, grimly. "The door bought us a couple of minutes. Pray to your gods that it's enough!"

On some level, the boy thought that was a strange thing to say, but now was not the time to be debating semantics. Evan was speeding up and behind them came an ululating cry of pursuit.

"Holy Mother! She's actually enjoying this!" hissed Evan. And then, they were there: the passage fell away on either side, and the boy found himself in a large stone cavern. It must have been easily twenty feet high. There were signs of human activity: some mats on the floor and an array of materials in barrels and sacks. There was also a large collection of bottles, neatly stacked into crates. Over to one side, a generator hummed contentedly to itself, and the cavern was illuminated by a pair of bright electric lights on a tall metal stand, rather like a floodlight in miniature. There was a rich, warm smell of something sweet and pungent, which immediately took the boy back to the contents of Evan's hipflask, now seemingly a distant memory. In the centre of the chamber was a large pair of brazen containers, each one probably six feet high. Evan dragged him bodily towards them.

"The stills?" he asked, as they flew past them?

Evan nodded, but the boy realised that he was none the wiser. What was a still and what was it used for? Then he realised that he was struggling to focus again...

171

They had almost reached the opposite side of the cavern when the warrior woman appeared, leaping like some sort of superhero – or indeed villain – from the passageway.

"There!" yelled Evan, and the boy saw a pile of barrels, triple stacked, so that they must have been ten feet high.

Evan pulled him around the edge and he could see a gap between the barrels and the wall. There, running like a jagged wound in the rock, was a fissure, rather less than a metre across. The boy goggled. A strange green light seemed to be emanating from the crevice, leeching out like pus from a wound. He imagined trying to fit through this unappealing opening; it made him think of his Grandmother carving shapes out of pastry with a jagged metal cutter.

"Is it safe?" he whispered.

He didn't know why, but he felt a terrible dread at the sight of this orifice; it grinned at him like a vertical maw, rocky teeth dripping with unctuous green slime. His whole being rebelled against the thought of entering it.

"What are you doing?" cried Evan, as he came up short.

"I can't go in there," explained the boy, simply, and for him, it was a simple fact. All his instincts told him to stop.

"Stop!" thundered the woman. "This time, I will bring you the justice you so deserve, little prince of lies," she cried, a look of steely determination on her face.

Evan quailed visibly as she suddenly broke into a run, his green eyes almost popping out of his head.

"Please!" he begged, almost in tears. "Follow me. It's your only chance!" He kissed him on the lips and flung himself at the opening, disappearing into the green mist instantly. The boy wrestled with his conflicting feelings. There was something wrong, here – and he was being charged by a psychopathic woman waving two swords in the air. Not quite a rock and a hard place, but not far off it. And the boy that he loved, with all of his heart, had just gone through and begged him to follow. Looking again at the woman, now barely twenty feet away, he stepped towards the fissure.

"No!" she cried. "Do not enter that place! Stay here, in my custody!"

Custody? Who the hell is this? She thinks she's a police officer now? Is she insane?

The answer was *quite possibly,* but that was of scant comfort to him.

The boy stepped away from her, standing on the brink. She stopped, very close now. Slowly she sheathed her twin swords and extended a black-gloved hand. Proud; so proud she looked – and at this distance, he saw that she really was beautiful – but in a scary, merciless way, like you might imagine a vengeful angel.

"Come," she said, her voice gentler now, but still with the ring of someone used to be being obeyed. "You must be questioned, but I do not think you will be harmed."

Slowly, he shook his head, knowing what he was going to do.

He took another step back. The sensation of the rock was chill upon his flesh.

Her eyes, which he now saw had golden irises, widened.

"What are you doing? Don't you know that place will be inimical to you? Come here boy. Don't follow him. He has practised a gross deceit upon you."

The boy licked his lips. He felt strangely calm and then he smiled, a sweet, wistful smile at her.

"But I love him. I... think. He's the only person in the world I do love."

With that, he turned and entered, catching, fleetingly, her stern expression melting into one of sadness and... pity?

He steeled himself and entered the fissure.

And then, he began to scream.

Chapter 14
Revelations

I'm not one to gloat, but it's always satisfying when one is able to accomplish one's aims in the teeth of a rival's failure.

And now at last, we shall meet in the flesh: no more mirror-gazing for me: I shall look you in the eye and you can return the compliment – if you have the courage.

Welcome to my domain, sweetling.

A pretty little fly in my web.

I shall be gentle with you.

At first.

The pain was unbelievable, like nothing he had ever experienced. It coursed through his flesh from head to toe, wracking him with exquisite, burning agony. It felt as though his flesh was trying to tear free from his bones; indeed his very bones ground and twisted within as though they were splintering apart. After a few seconds, he must have blacked out. When he came to, he was lying on a rocky platform in a small cave. Cracking his eye open, he looked to see there was no sign of the crevice through which he had entered this place. His whole body was shaking, as though recovering from a terrible trauma or shock: which, of course, it was. His clothes were damp with sweat and possibly urine, and when he tried to raise his head, he vomited a pool of honey-tinted bile on the pitted floor. It was all too much; his body couldn't take it and darkness descended again.

The second time he woke, the trembling had subsided somewhat and he felt a hand gently stroking his hair. When his sore eyes began to open, he became aware of a gentle, silvery light falling around him.

"Ssshh. It's alright. Take it easy. Don't try to sit up suddenly. You need time to adjust. Gently does it."

The boy slowly realised that his head was now resting on something. It was some sort of material; blue material. It smelt of outside and cigarettes. Then his memory began to assemble itself and he recognised it to be a denim jacket – Evan's denim jacket.

If Evan was here, then it would all be alright. An embryonic smile formed, despite the throbbing of his body and his eyes opened fully. The light surrounding him was so gentle, like moonlight, it bathed him in a cool sense of peace. It made the pain ease and engendered a feeling of tranquillity.

Then his eyes opened, and he saw its source. Evan sat next to him on the floor. He looked different: a bit older – more nineteen than fifteen – but that was a minor difference, all things considered. His skin shimmered a pale gold; his hair gleamed; each burnished curl fell perfectly, as though he had summoned a personal stylist to tend to and arrange them. His eyes, which had often seemed to glow with energy in the past now really did blaze with an inner light, like a pair of jewels with a dark centre. And slowly, he realised that the soft light emanated from him.

For a few seconds they stared at each other as Evan's hand continued to make rhythmic, soothing movements across his brow. The boy's brain struggled to function; Evan looked back at him with an almost shy smile.

"You…" the boy began, before pausing to formulate something resembling a sentence. "You're… glowing."

Evan's smile broadened a little, showing a glimpse of pearly teeth.

"Yes. This is what I really look like. In my world. In your world, I have to hide my true nature."

The boy continued to stare and came to the sudden realisation that he was no longer stunned due to the pain, which was now, unbelievably, dissipating. He realised that he had become lost at contemplating the being above him. Evan was a very good-looking lad, there was no denying it: even his mother had commented on this. But here, his beauty transcended human possibility. His appearance was so radiantly sublime, that it took the boy's breath away. He was too perfect: too divinely handsome to the point of being somehow unnatural – yes, that was it – his perfection was, on some level, disturbing. No one should look like that, without any visible flaw; his beauty was somehow chilling in its inhuman abnormality.

"You're not human, are you?"

It was an absurd question, which he knew as soon as he had uttered it.

Evan flashed a full smile at him, and it felt as though someone had grabbed his heart and given it a squeeze. God! He felt like a lice-ridden ape, newly descended from the trees in his presence. There was such a gulf between them; he should be down on his knees, like a humble supplicant...

No.

No.

The boy closed his eyes. There was something seriously weird going on here: he wasn't sure what it was, but it weakened when he couldn't see Evan's face. The feelings of awe-struck inferiority receded.

Evan laughed: a sound like the finest of silver bells caught in a gentle zephyr.

"Smart," he observed, gently caressing his eyelids. "No. I'm not. Human, that is."

"Are you..." the boy felt silly saying it, "are you an angel?"

This brought forth a full-throated burst of laughter, so infectious in its wild joy that it made the boy smile from ear to ear and open his eyes again. Evan still dazzled on every level, but he felt a little more in control now, as though he had seen through some kind of parlour trick.

"Oh no. I'm certainly not one of those. I'm afraid, my dear, that I have little by way of virtue to recommend me."

The boy steeled himself to look fully into his eyes: they shone now, a glassy green, as though back-lit. Something uneasy moved across his mind – something about those eyes... He had seen something like them before.

Frowning, he tried to sit up, and found that he was perfectly able to do so. Looking around, he found that he was in a large cavern. Clusters of crystalline stalagmites sprouted like flowers from the rocky floor. The seemed to emit a low, greenish-white light, and sang as with a low-level resonance – almost like they were humming to themselves. The walls were smeared with luminous lichen and there was a sickly sweet aroma in the air. Somewhere high above, he could hear sounds, like claws scraping against rocks.

He shivered.

"So. Where are we? You said this is your world." The boy tasted the words as he spoke them – and they were strange to him, as though someone else had taken control of his tongue. "Does that mean we're not on… Earth… anymore?"

"Pretty much," confirmed Evan, cheerfully, as though it was a simple little thing to pass from one world into another – something of little consequence, like moving from one house to another across the street.

"Right. Right… And that crazy woman with swords was…?"

Evan pulled a sour face, as of old, but it still looked good on him.

"An enemy, of course."

"Huh!" The boy slowly got to his feet, expecting to be hit by waves of pain as he did so. But no: incredibly, his body felt almost fine – as though he had just recovered from an illness and felt vaguely fragile, like frosted glass.

The boy directed one of his old, sardonic grins at the magisterial Evan. "So what happened to all your kung fu moves? Eh? How come you didn't just knock her out?"

Evan smiled and laughed. He had stood too, and now traced a finger gently down the boy's cheek.

"What a funny guy you are. Normally people are still down on their knees in awe of me at this point. You know, I admire your irreverence – and your strength of will. I think you may truly be special."

He leaned forward as he spoke, transfixing the boy with his glittering eyes. Truth be told, the boy felt rather like a popsicle being held in front of a hair-dryer, but he was determined not to show it. He could so easily have fallen to his knees in worship, but something, somewhere, warned him against such a course. Instead, he leaned into Evan's gaze, even closer, into the full-heated blast of his supernatural splendour.

"Thanks for the vote of confidence: I love being patronised by you. I take it she was too much for you to handle?"

Now this elicited a pout – a petulant one, too.

Evan sniffed.

"You know nothing after all, foolish boy! By your mundane standards, I can fight well. But that fat fool in the park? A mere punchbag – no threat at all! Aelodie Skye, however, is bred for battle. Also, she had two swords to my two fists. I wasn't going to trade blows with that one! I like my head on my neck, thank you very much…. Besides, I've always been a lover rather than a fighter. Charm opens more doors than brute force."

With that, he gave the boy a knowing look, as though there was a private joke in play. He found he didn't like that – especially not because he couldn't help feeling that he was the one being laughed at.

"Hmm. What did she want, anyway? Why was she so fired up?"

"Simple: she was trying to stop me from bringing *you* here. You had to pass through the gateway of your own free will: she was attempting to prevent this. In the event, she may even have inadvertently helped me!"

"How?" asked the boy in a now small voice. He didn't like the way this conversation was heading.

"Because she knew that my mistress wanted you: and that was enough for her to want to stop you coming here. Her aggressive mien probably provided an additional incentive to leap through the fissure, despite your instincts telling you not to. They were telling you that, weren't they?"

The boy stared hard at Evan. He was somehow different in this place – as though a mask of easy and affable charm had fallen away to reveal something coldly contemptuous and proud. What had been mellowed and in some ways endearing before glared at him now like a naked light bulb.

"Yes. They were. But I followed you anyway. Because I..."

He stopped himself there, subconsciously aware that he was exposing his unprotected core. Something was repelling him back, warning him not to abandon his defences. But it was futile after all...

"Of course you do, little sparrow," whispered Evan softly and with a wide mocking smile on his face. "That is my gift, after all."

The boy locked eyes with him then, and something fell into place like a single missing jigsaw piece. His brow creased with the effort of maintaining prolonged contact with those green, green eyes.

"Your eyes," he observed, softly – almost as if to himself… "They're tiger eyes."

He blinked then, and his own eyes became veiled by tears.

"You're a predator." He knew it to be an undeniable truth. "You're a predator and I'm your prey. Isn't that right?"

Somewhere in his mind, he heard a lilting female voice saying *"you will wish for a clean death – clean and quick…"*

Evan actually looked rather surprised by this: his eyebrows shot up, and then he laughed, lightly and cynically.

"Well," he replied, "that's all rather melodramatic if you're asking me. But I suppose you could use that analogy. Yes, I was sent to find you."

"To find me – and bring me back here."

An affable nod. "Right."

That was when the pain began in his chest and began to radiate outwards in waves, as though from an epicentre. The boy even looked down for a moment to see if there was a knife – or possibly an icicle – protruding from his heart.

"You… Do you… Do you have any… feelings for me?"

How he hated asking that question, in all its pathetic neediness.

The boy found he was breathing hard, as though struggling to catch his breath. A few coloured spots flew across the surface of his vision. He already knew what the answer was going to be, but he prayed with all his heart it wasn't so.

Evan's face softened a little. He gave a wistful smile and then shrugged helplessly.

"You were my mark. I was sent to acquire you and I used the tools that I had. It's what I was bred for. I said earlier, perhaps rather flippantly, that I'm a lover not a fighter. But that's exactly what I am. It's my gift. People can't help falling in love with me – I mean, really can't help it. I'm not just being vain."

The boy nodded, with a vacuous, goofy smile. Hadn't he seen it with his own eyes? All of those people who had been subjected to his charm for a few seconds going all googly-eyed and starstruck? And they had been mere acquaintances. Imagine if you spent hours with Evan – hours every day of the summer months. Imagine what that would do to you.

Abruptly, he gave a short, barking laugh.

"How stupid I am! You must have been having a real laugh at me, scampering around after you like some empty-headed puppy."

He grinned wildly.

Evan assumed a pensive expression.

"No. I don't take pleasure in it. It was just business – a mission that I was given to fulfil. You aren't stupid at all. In fact, you're surprisingly strong-willed. That's why I was sent in person to retrieve you. You proved to be resistant to her charms through the mirror. You were like a computer which had been cut off from the websphere; you were operating in dark mode. That's where I came in. I had to insinuate my way in, you see; to get close to you."

"Oh God, Evan!" The boy's eyes were like saucers, their pupils huge. "You didn't need a hunting knife to cut me up and cut me open, did you?"

"No. I'm rather more subtle than that, of course."

"So… why did you say all those things to me? Why did you kiss me? Why did you…" Here the boy's voice broke somewhat. "Why did you make me think you might love me?"

Evan met his imploring gaze levelly.

"I said – and did – what I needed to. I had to get you here. The emotion of love makes your kind much more pliable; once I had established such a bond with you, it was only a matter of time before you could be brought in."

Ah! But think now of the poor boy's heart: like a flower it was, a beautiful, delicate, many-petalled spring flower, caught now in a late frost which left it dying and blasted. His sweet little red heart froze inside him and shattered into jagged broken shards. His mouth tasted of the ash of despair.

He half-doubled over as though Evan had punched him in the stomach.

"I know it hurts now and I am sorry about that. It's nothing personal: I was just doing my job."

With that, he put his arms around the shaking boy can drew him into a gentle embrace; a sympathetic gesture of comfort and warmth which quite unmanned the boy and caused him to dissolve into great wracking sobs of grief; he sobbed, and coughed out tears, and mucus-laden strings of saliva. He collapsed into Evan's arms and wept with complete abandon as people do when their hearts have been cruelly broken.

To his credit, Evan held him, almost like a mother, crooning softly and gently to him as he cried for his illusory love and the terrible pain which skewered him once more – only this time its source was emotional, rather than physical; emotional - but it felt just as debilitating as when he had entered this God-forsaken place.

They remained thus, in a tragic tableau: the gentle seraph comforting the dishevelled, non-descript human. Then Evan stiffened and raised his head, frowning with concentration. Through the hissing subterranean air currents and the hypnotic humming of the crystalline stalagmites, a voice slowly took shape. Sere as old leaves, as ancient, desiccated mummies, words curled themselves around the two youths.

"Bring him. Bring the boy to me."

They caressed the air, like snake scales sliding over his face.

Under normal circumstances, their total lack of warmth, of humanity, might have set the boy's teeth on edge and triggered his flight response. But now, weak and broken as he was, he simply raised his face, smeared with dust, tears and snot, and gazed blindly into the gloom through red-raw eyes.

"Your mistress."

Statement.

"Yes."

"Well," he gave a crumpled smile to Evan, which didn't even try to reach his eyes, "this is what you came for. Mission accomplished. You'd better take me to her."

Evan 's eyes straked his face, as if searching for something.

"Be brave now, my little one," he whispered. Then he took him by the hand and slowly helped him to his feet. He put one of the boy's arms around his neck, and led him through the cavern. Strange frog-like creatures chirruped and sidled out of the way as they walked on; pairs of feral eyes gleamed out from the shadows. Nothing made a sudden move towards them, however.

On they walked, minutes fading into each other, until the boy became vaguely aware that they seemed to be heading downwards. Soon, they reached another tunnel, lit by bizarre, pulsing growths on the walls, somewhere between fungus and tumours. The tunnel gradually opened out, and they emerged into another cave, smaller than the first, but with a sweet smell of decay lingering all around. Somewhere at its heart, a sickly green light crept outwards, touching the rocks with baleful phosphorescence.

Something moved at its core.

There was something there, waiting for them.

"Aaaahhhhhh...."

Now at last, the boy's ancient mammalian instincts made themselves felt , like a prehistoric rodent gazing for the first time into the eyes of a snake. He stopped short, and the trembling took him again.

He looked at Evan, fear flashing across his face.

His beautiful companion simply squeezed his hand, and murmured, "be brave now. You must face her."

A sheer laugh echoed around them, a little too high and cracked around the edges. It was not a laugh to set one smiling in sympathy.

"Buzz, buzz, bzzzzzzz!" came a dry female voice.

Then another laugh.

"Come closer, little fly. Come enter my web…"

Chapter 15
In the Flesh

Ah! The sweet anticipation!

The moment of truth, where a long looked for rendezvous finally takes place...

Will he be all I'd hoped for?

Will he be the boy of my dreams?

Now that's a question! My dreams are as dark as the void... But still, we'll soon find out. For my bright-armoured little trickster has baited the hook and landed our prize. It seems on this occasion that brains really did outdo brawn!

I see you at last with my own eyes as you approach.

I smell your fear.

You are right to be afraid of me, for I long to get my claws into you. Call me old-fashioned, but I always like to try the goods before executing a final purchase. In this case, of course, there can be no refund for the years of effort spent on reaching this moment – only the acid burns of my extreme displeasure should you disappoint me.

The boy put one leaden foot in front of another. In the pit of his stomach he felt a kind of dread, but thanks to the numb shock of his emotional distress, it was somehow an abstract notion, cut off from the here and now.

For that small mercy, at least, perhaps he owed a debt to Evan Greenway.

They were on a trail through the crystal fields and obscene fungi; it began to curve upwards to a sort of plateau from whence emanated the nauseous green light. As they reached the final approach, the boy became aware of shadowy figures keeping pace with them, escorting them along the way. Huge, bipedal, armoured forms: eight feet tall at least, they were a weird fusion of man and beetle. Many faceted eyes glittered inhumanly at him; mandibles the size of sickles clacked and immense arms were tipped with fierce-looking claws.

The plateau itself was fringed by man-sized stalagmites, their formation so precise, they could not have naturally occurred. They were, surely, some kind of fortification – and someone had engineered them thus.

Then they were in: inside that glittering barred space. The beetle-men stopped short, cutting off the exit.

The boy blinked stupidly. A structure of sorts lay ahead of him: a kind of grotto, but made entirely from glowing crystal; in front of it lay what could only be described as a garden, but planted with row after row of fungus: brilliant-hued mushrooms to pestilent-seeming puffballs. To the right of the gardens lay the source of the light: a great whirling oval of green liquid. It showed no apparent source of support, but was suspended in mid-air in a way which must surely have distressed any physicist worth their salt. The boy stared, momentarily transfixed. The surface of this wonder had a consistency similar to mercury. It did not look as though it should exist. Periodically, little silver bursts and swirls appeared, streaking across the roiling whole as though someone had just poured a dash of cream into a particularly venomous-looking soup.

The spell was broken by the sound of rasping breath: a form stood silhouetted in the mouth of the crystal cottage and the boy suddenly felt his outer defences and layers swept away in one brief second. Never had he felt so exposed before such a pervading sense of malignity. His practised mask, developed and perfected his whole life, was torn away and tossed contemptuously aside. Then came an exhalation: like steam from some geothermic fissure, it hissed forth, conveying on a very basic level a sense of twisted delight. That was when he realised she was laughing.

"Come closer, child. Let me see you as you really are."

The boy, despite the pain of his distress, gulped and there was a pulse which ran right through his body. At that moment, he laughed: a hollow, desperate sound. *What more can she take away from me?*

Soon he would have his answer. Soon, but not quite yet.

He wiped the snot on the back of his sleeve and turned towards the shadowy figure, eliciting a gasp of delight.

"Oho! A bold one! He says little, but inside he seethes quietly. Isn't that so, sweetling?"

"You seem to have all the answers. I'm guessing you don't need mine." His voice was an empty echo, but the words were not lost on her. Slowly, she eased herself out of her glittering lair and into the light.

The boy shook – again – but the fight had gone out of him. At that moment, he wouldn't have cared if a crack in the ground had swallowed him up, never to be seen again.

The woman – if he could consider her such – moved slowly, deliberately towards him. She was a little taller than him, but also had a stoop, which probably made her seem shorter than she was. She leaned upon a crystal staff and wore long robes of grey material, overlaid with something he assumed was lace – although it could equally have been a festoon of cobwebs. Her hair was black, but with green tinges, as from algae; her skin was white as leprosy. Although she moved like an ancient, her face was smooth and unlined; thin dark lips hung around a leering mouth; her nose was proudly aquiline. Then he made eye contact. Those eyes. They were sheer black, like chips of obsidian. She had odd tattoos which receded from her brow up the line of her temple. Only, he realised, as she moved within touching distance, they weren't tattoos at all, but were more eyes, diminishing in size as they crested her forehead. All of them were focused on him. And there was not a jot of humanity or pity to be seen in any of them.

They stood, a few centimetres apart and she smiled, exposing her black-edged, pointed teeth.

"So good to have you home, little one."

Then she reached out to him. Her sinuous white fingers had three joints instead of two; they were preternaturally long, and, as she moved to caress his face, he saw that the pads were coated with long, fine, white hairs. Her touch cut through his despair; it made him nauseous, but he found he couldn't move.

"No," she whispered, as if fully aware of his thoughts, "you are caught now in my web."

The clammy, hairy fingers traced a line down his tear-stained cheek.

"Fascinating…" she continued, before pulling at his cheek like some horse-trader of old. "The blood of the Others runs strong in you, little one. You are shrouded in darkness: even I would find it difficult to sense you were you not in front of me and my full will focused upon you. Ha!"

Then one long, sharp talon sliced into his cheek, causing crimson droplets to trickle down it. She scooped some up with her ghastly finger and licked it off with a long, dark tongue. She gave a slight shudder of ecstatic excitement.

"Ah! You may well prove useful to me, for if your gifts are what I believe them to be, you will be a refined tool indeed."

She spun then, with surprising speed, to regard Evan, who was hanging back like a naughty school boy, one hand clasping the other and staring resolutely at the floor.

"You have done well, Efandyr," she crooned, "and I shall be sure to reward you."

"Serving your will is reward enough in itself," he intoned, solemnly, and the boy was simultaneously struck by his cravenness and his insincerity.

The hag must have agreed with him, for she snorted dismissively.

"Huh. You can stand down from your charm offensive for now. You are a wily vassal and useful to me. As long as this remains the case, you will be rewarded for your success."

She reached into her robes and her hand emerged with a small bag, which she threw carelessly in his direction. For all of his supine posture, Evan's hand shot out like a rattlesnake to catch it in mid-air and it vanished into his denim jacket, which was once more on his back.

With that, he inclined his head in a half-bow, turned smartly on his heels and strode off without a backward glance.

"Think no more of that one," chuckled the woman, with a strange gurgle. "He loves only himself. He is clever and beautiful, but possesses no depth of character at all. Scratch the surface and there is nothing but a desire for pleasure and self-adoration. I, on the other hand, will love you like your own mother. You may even call me Mother, if you wish, though my enemies know me as the Pale Lady."

At this, her eyes hardened all of a sudden, and her inky lips set into a severe line. She rose to her full height, no longer stooping nor with any pretence of age or infirmity. She must easily have been seven feet tall, and stared forbiddingly down at him.

"But enough of the introductions. I'm afraid I haven't time to waste on social niceties. Mr Weiss!"

Her sibilant voice cracked out suddenly, like a whip.

The boy looked around to see a shorter figure had silently appeared, hanging back at the corner of her jagged grotto. He was a little over five feet tall, and was wearing a strangely modern two-piece of a powder blue tunic and matching trousers. He also wore a white apron, which was ominously spattered with dark, reddish splashes and smears. Mr Weiss smiled, but it was all business with him. His head was a little too large for his body and his face impossibly wrinkled, like an ancient prune. The eyes, though, glinted like pieces of ice set amidst the folds of his flesh: they were sharp enough. His ears were exceedingly large, and his teeth – well, there were rather too many of them in his mouth, which was very wide, and they were crooked and of varying length.

Accompanying Mr Weiss were two even shorter, wrinklier beings than himself. They capered and leered in the sickly light.

"The pod is ready, Dread Lady," announced Mr Weiss, with a simpering expression albeit his voice was rich and deep.

"And the crystals are sufficient?"

"They are, my Lady," he replied, before sketching a bow. "Indeed, they are of considerable strength. Although they will accelerate and amplify the reaction process, there is a significant risk that the subject may not survive."

"Oh tush, my dear Mr Weiss. With this one a little more boldness is required. It is a risk I am prepared to take for the potential gain of his Gift is… considerable." This last word was hissed with serpentine glee, and the dark tongue flickered unpleasantly around her lips. "You may take him now. Monitor him closely and keep me informed of his progress. I leave him to your tender care. Please don't disappoint me."

On that note, she waved vaguely at the boy before turning and shuffling back towards her dwelling.

The sight of her back, crooked once more over her staff, seemed to act as a kind of signal to Mr Weiss, who snapped his fingers in a business-like manner. His two stunted associates scurried forward to seize the boy's arms, one apiece. For all that they were short, their grip was like iron, and they seemed to take delight in pinching and prodding him as they drew him back into the dimness of the caverns.

The boy's mouth hung open stupidly. It had all happened too fast: he had crossed into another world, had his heart broken and had been carried away by hideous creatures which clearly weren't human.

His mind rebelled.

It sought refuge somewhere else: in another time and place, down by a river, dappled in sunshine and warmed by love.

He was so lost, you see, he had nowhere else to go.

Chapter 16
Metamorphosis

To look at humans, it is easy to dismiss their worth. Small creatures in every sense of the word. True, some have touches of brilliance, but they flare like rogue matchsticks amongst the dross and then they are gone, back into the darkness, their pitifully short lives over.

I, however, pride myself on the openness of my mind to all possibilities.

Many of my kind had been using them as pawns for centuries in their petty feudal disputes: mere cannon-fodder to be moved around an ever-evolving battlefield. Then my sister and I had an idea: what if, instead of simply taking these creatures at face value and flinging them onto each other's weapons, we approached the matter rather more imaginatively?

We began to experiment.

Immediately, it was clear that we were on to something. By mixing the blood of Others with humans, we found that the results transcended the potential of both. In their dreary mundanity, humans offered a sort of inert crucible in which other more... mercurial... elements could be mixed and fused.

They were the perfect hosts.

It was all too easy, replacing individual humans here and there with... something else.

The results were exciting.

They continue to be so.

I am thrilled by the possibilities at hand.

As our experience of breeding grew, so did our understanding: a pinch of this or that; a little tweak here and there to the long chains which shape all of our natures. We learnt that different combinations yielded different results, different gifts. Some were subtle – others dazzling in their raw power.

Of course, although humans remained as blind as ever to what was going on around them, our brethren were not. Our creations may pass for human at a cursory glance, but a true

Other can always detect the preternatural fire glowing within. We cannot hide from ourselves.

Just imagine what might happen if we could.

What's that expression the humans use? A wolf in sheep's clothing.

He didn't suspect a thing until his throat was being torn out...

Now there's a thought... wouldn't you say?

They took him into a deep chamber where the hum of the crystals was enough to jar his teeth. In the low light, shadows took on ever more sinister shapes: they lowered over him, pulling him this way and that.

He didn't understand.

In his terror, he was mute; passive. A poor little doll being tugged this way and that by cruel children.

His clothes were torn from his body; he was naked; heart-touchingly vulnerable. Was there nowhere to hide anymore?

They hacked off his hair with the impersonal skill of a sheep shearer, and pinched at his flesh, before garbling to each other in a quick guttural tongue. Their wrinkly faces were all too mobile in the low light; grinning like intelligent monkeys, they went about their work. One wielded a scalpel-like knife with sudden breath-taking precision, carving elaborate scarlet swirls and symbols on his chest with the ease of a calligrapher making notes on a piece of vellum. The pain brought tears to his eyes as it struck. They held him down and pulled out one of his teeth, which they proceeded to smash into a pestle and mortar, before studying it closely, three heads nodding and bobbing like a synod of wise men deliberating some matter of intense theological interest.

There was no malice in it: it was quite impersonal: they were simply going about their business with efficient skill.

The boy wasn't sure whether that made it better or worse.

He was a piece of meat. They were skilful chefs, wielding knife and hammer to shape him into something worthy of a golden salver.

He had no voice; no recourse to complain. *This must be what it's like to be a lab rat*, he thought, somewhere in a closed corner of his mind which was still operating, albeit in emergency power mode.

Then, after he had been seasoned, sliced and marinated, he was dragged into a smaller chamber. It was lined with crystals of a pale golden hue. The light was soft; almost comforting. Why, then, did all the hairs on his arms rise up as he entered the room? It was a feeling like static electricity. Something within him gave a disturbing twist – as if in response. It wanted to get out...

In the centre of the circular space was a great, fleshy growth. It was a metre high and two long. Its sides curled up and met in an uneven line in the middle, pressed together like an enormous pair of violet lips. The thing wobbled and pulsated. It sickened him. The two flunkies held him by the arms whilst Mr Weiss stepped forward, caressing the bloated object, and smiling, crooning like an old grandmother.

As the boy watched in rapt and appalled amazement, the pustule began to undulate. Its motions made him nauseous. Even the pain of his many shallow cuts seemed to fade in the moment. Then, with a wet, tearing sound, a crack appeared: a moist, vermilion crack and the lips slowly proceeded to inch themselves apart, in a series of revolting muscular spasms.

Finally, they lay fully distended, and the boy found himself looking down into a raw-looking, fleshy capsule, two thirds full of a thick, pinkish liquid. Mr Weiss studied what lay before him, cocking a birdlike head askance for a moment, before suddenly plunging in his hands. There was a sharp twist and the thing gave an involuntary shudder. Then his hands emerged clutching an object dripping with dark pink fluids. He gave this couple of expert shakes, before producing a cloth with which he wiped it clean. It was revealed to be a clear crystal about the size of a large food tin. Smiling and humming to himself, Mr Weiss produced what looked like a cross between a hypodermic and a cut glass decanter. There was something inside its glittering chamber: something with a milky pink consistency. He looked up to see the boy staring at him, and nodded back, affably, with a little smile.

"This stuff," he said, conversationally, like a helpful doctor explaining a procedure to a prospective patient, "is... you. Or at least, a kind of essence of you."

He tapped the object casually, causing it to briefly sing, before slowly inserting it into the crystal itself. The boy goggled. He had not expected that.

"Ah!" said Mr Weiss, knowingly, as if pleased that he had noticed something. "The crystal has not fully hardened yet: it has only just been harvested and has yet to forget its organic origins. Soon, though, it will imprint with your essence and set in full. Almost as tough as a diamond, then!"

As the boy continued to stare, the strange apparatus discharged its contents into the crystal, which immediately flushed a dark, ruby red colour.

Weiss nodded, as though this was just what he had expected. He then continued to illuminate the boy's mind.

"This could be thought of as a tuning crystal. It will help to focus the energies of the crystals in this particular chamber. It will modulate them and redirect them in such a way that, hopefully, they will not turn you into porridge."

Seeing the boy's reaction to this, he emitted a loud, parrot-like squawk of laughter.

"There is never a guarantee, I'm afraid, and the risk is heightened by the Pale Lady's insistence that we expose you to the full power of the crystals in this particular hatchery. But you should take comfort in the fact that I am very experienced in my field – and that she will be angry if you die on my watch, so I will do all I can to see that you survive! Now, if you will observe, you will see that I am going to place the focusing crystal into the walls of the chamber."

With that, the ugly little fellow skipped blithely across the room, before swiping a hand over the sheer crystal wall. As the boy watched, an aperture, around twenty centimetres high and fifteen across, opened like a baleful eye. Inside it was a metallic-looking frame into which the red crystal fitted perfectly.

Immediately, there was a change to the rhythm of the crystals in the chamber. The boy felt a wild surge of joy within him, and, again, that familiar pulling in his innards as though something which had been deeply buried was now rising to the surface.

He didn't like that feeling at all.

"And now," beamed Mr Weiss, all that remains is for you to take up your position."

The boy looked around nervously. What did this mean?

The wrinkly face creased even more with a mixture of humour and exasperation.

"Well," said Weiss, "what are you waiting for? Climb into the pod, boy. In the pod."

The boy stared at Mr Weiss and then back at the pod.

Climb. In.

No!

The boy began to shake.

"Wait! What is this! You said... you said this was a hatchery. What sort of hatchery? What are you going to do?"

"Heh! You are clearly stalling for time," replied his tormentor. "But the question is reasonable, so I will answer it. The pod is to protect what you are at your core in the face of the crystals. They emit a high level of energy which will break down many of your component parts and reassemble them in a more interesting way. We are going to put you in the pod, scramble you around and then you will hatch, like a butterfly – at least in the sense of process, if not beauty."

This was clearly a very droll remark, for it elicited another squeal of mirth.

"But..." the boy's trembling had got worse. He tensed against the arms of Weiss' two assistants, but their grip was pitiless. "But I don't want to be reassembled. Please! I beg you! Don't put me in that thing. Please!"

His earlier heartbreak forgotten now, the boy began to sob and struggle.

"I want to be me! Please, please don't do this! Let me go home, let me go... I won't say anything to anyone - they wouldn't believe me if I did!"

It did him no good, however, and he was slowly, inexorably manoeuvred closer to the gyrating pod. It seemed to be expecting him, and was quivering as if with excitement. The pink ichor within churned and rippled with delight.

The boy's pleas gave way to increasingly incoherent screams now, as it became all too clear what was going to happen. He pulled and twisted with all his might, but only managed to move his captors' grip by occasional millimetres. Then, as he reached the edge of the pod, he flailed wildly with his legs, trying to kick the abomination.

"No! No! Nooo!"

Just as his shrieks reached a sort of cracked crescendo, however, he felt a sudden pain in his arm. Startled, he looked down to see that Mr Weiss had produced another hypodermic from his many pocketed off-white coat, which he had, without any warning, plunged into his upper arm. A colourless fluid drained out of the syringe and the boy felt his strength and his energy ebbing away.

"Sshh!" said Mr Weiss, with a mischievous twinkle in his eyes. "You might wake some of the other hatchlings early – and that would be a disaster…"

The boy struggled to focus on him.

"Ha ha! Lucky for you, I'm joking! All of the others, like you, are sedated before they enter the pods. Physical struggle and high levels of emotional stress are not at all conducive to a positive outcome to the process as a whole. Don't worry; you probably won't remember anything after a few more seconds until you are woken and extracted. At least, I don't think you will. Be sure to inform me if you do, as I keep meticulous logs of all my subjects and their data. Now why don't you be a good boy and count down with me from ten. Yes? Ten, nine…

Eight.

The periphery of his vision was darkening.

Seven.

Mr Weiss' face was swimming increasingly out of focus. Then it began to break up into numerous smaller versions, all of them floating around the back of his retina.

Six.

Must fight… Must try to… get…

Get? Get what?

Oh.

That.

Too late I'm afraid, for the boy was now quite unconscious and his scrawny naked form was thrown, without further ado, into the pod, which closed around him like an enormous and particularly horrid venus flytrap.

Had he still been aware, he would have seen the strange little men bustling around, tapping the crystal walls with small metallic rods, making them sing. Soon, the crystals' resonance began to increase, louder and louder it got, until it would have been unbearable for an unprotected human ear.

Mr Weiss' assistants departed, leaving the master to make a final inspection of the chamber. The crystals were starting to glow, their rays assuming an increasingly hard-edge. As they got brighter and louder, Weiss himself made a brisk withdrawal from the chamber. It wasn't quite so fast as to be undignified.

Not quite.

Back in the pod, the boy lay immersed in fluid which bubbled and seethed around him. The pod itself twisted and heaved uncomfortably in the light and the noise. At its heart, its fluids lapped at the boy, slowly stripping away small pieces of skin as he seemed to undergo a process not unlike digestion.

His only solace, as Mr Weiss had indicated, was that he was completely unaware of the whole awful process.

Wasn't he?

Chapter 17
Emergence

I do like getting presents, especially when there is an element of surprise involved. I can't help thinking that this one is something of a lucky dip. I have had him flung into the tombola and turned around and around. But what will emerge? Who can say! Will it be a prince or a pauper? And will he fit the glass slipper I have had made for him?

Ah! But you must think me flippant, and in truth, my gaiety is in part due to a certain nervousness. I have taken a gamble. All of those careful years planning... I'm afraid I am of the school of thought which declares 'nothing ventured, nothing gained.' Or at least, I think that's what it says! You humans and your colourful aphorisms!

So. I issued the orders: he will be exposed to the full power of the crystals. Mr Weiss tells me that this is risky – the boy may not survive the procedure. Or he may emerge as a twisted, unusable husk. Alternatively, he will be shaped into something marvellous – a masterwork weapon to be deployed against my foes.

Well, I have thrown the dice and now we shall see.

I hope it will be a pleasant surprise. If not, it will be back to the drawing board with this particular lineage. And Mr Weiss may well end up in one of his own pods.

Let's hope that serves to concentrate his mind.

Somewhere in a subterranean chamber, a small bell emitted sweet music.

Mr Weiss produced a silver pocket watch of exceptional craftsmanship from his pocket. He checked the time himself before snapping the case shut with a sharp click. Striding from his office, he snapped his fingers at a pair of orderlies; they had been idling away the time playing an obscure game involving the placement of ivory counters on a large grid.

Together they made their way through the coral-like tunnels of the hatcheries before arriving at their destination.

The chamber was eerily quiet. The crystals had faded into a state resembling colourless glass; their humming had ceased. In the centre of the chamber, something moved within the birthing capsule: something pressed briefly against the fleshy, taut surface and then subsided.

"The time for dreaming is over, little one. Now we must see what we have cooked up."

Mr Weiss smiled softly, a kind and hopeful expression taking shape upon his face. Then he produced a scalpel and began to cut…

They pulled him out, blinking, unaware, into the dim-lit cavern. Lean hands worked efficiently, slicing through veiny tendrils, dabbing away the thick pink fluid. Here and there, between the thicket of busy limbs could be glimpsed patches of soft white skin, new, so very new, that Mr Weiss' ministrations became positively tender.

"This is a particularly delicate stage," he informed his assistants in a low, steady voice. "There must be no bruising or tearing. The slightest damage to it now may prove irreparable. I do not need to explain what would happen to all of us if the Pale Lady's project were to be marred by carelessness on our part."

He did not. And indeed, his helpers proceeded with all due diligence, their every motion as gentle as a summer breeze – as attentive as an archaeologist cleaning dirt from an ancient artefact. And as such, gradually... something... began to emerge.

This... figure stood, half stooped, like a clockwork man in need of winding. There was no sign of physical or mental awareness. Mr Weiss stepped back to regard his handiwork.

"Has the procedure failed?" squeaked one of his interns, with a distinctly nervous edge. He was a relatively new recruit, or he would have known better.

Mr Weiss issued an irritable tsk, just for his benefit.

"The subject has just been extracted. It will take both its mind and its body time to catch up with reality. It still believes that it is in the pod, dreaming endlessly to itself."

The three of them waited patiently, hopefully for a sign. After a few minutes, there were the first signs of muscular twitches in hands and thighs and calves.

Somewhere in what had been the boy's mind, images flitted and whirled, sharp and jagged round the edges, like shards from a shattered mirror; flashes of colour and fragments of faces glittered across the blank plain of his new-formed consciousness. Soon, along with the images came broken, discordant sounds. The other senses followed on. Gradually, different pieces began to merge, to assemble, to form a whole. The boy's eyes slowly flickered open. They felt unaccountably heavy, but his vision was razor sharp: even in the low light of the birthing chamber, he was aware of the tiniest of details: a quivering pink tendril on the floor near his right foot; the precise sheen and crisp edges of the crystal around him; the small blue mole on Mr Weiss' cheek, just under his left eye.

Then he glanced downwards.

He felt strangely disconnected from reality, as though he was watching a fly-on-the wall documentary. So at first, the pale folds of his skin didn't bother him. Then, as neurons reformed their links and sentience slowly kindled, he began to appreciate his situation.

Memories. Memories of joy – and of terror. He could remember now: the warmth of the pod; its nauseating undulations. They had put him in there and left him to be... Wait! What had happened to him? What had they done?

Slowly the boy lifted his right arm. Pale, milky flesh hung in loose folds. It wobbled obscenely as he moved. Looking down at his torso and legs, the boy was reminded of a fat candle he had once seen in a church. His skin resembled layer upon layer of melted wax. He looked like a candle – a candle that had been left too close to a fire so that it had partially melted, before being moved away and setting into a new configuration.

What feelings coursed through him? Rage? Terror? Sorrow?

All of these things.

He let out a cry of grief, only to find that his voice too was muffled. Reaching up, his face resembled, to his questing fingertips, a particularly aged and sun-exposed bloodhound. His mouth seemed almost buried beneath loose folds, and great jowls wobbled at his throat.

"What have you done to me?"

His voice was unable to convey the feelings within and the words came out as strangely deadened. Struck through with revulsion and terror, the boy took a stumbling step backwards. The recent intern moved quickly to follow him, despite Mr Weiss' warning grimace.

"Do not damage it!" he hissed urgently.

But for the boy, adrenaline was already surging: the emotions which thrashed and quested for dominance within seemed, all at once, to combine into a desperate, self-pitying rage. Suddenly, it was as though time itself had slowed down. The nasty, wrinkly creature moved forward to seize his arm, but in a slow, measured way, as though he was working his way through a series of tai chi movements. Suddenly incandescent with fury, the boy swung a pale, sagging arm which landed like a club on the side of his head. The beady-eyed, sharp-toothed intern did not immediately seem to register what had happed: it was as though the signal to his brain had somehow been jammed, leading merely to an expression of vague confusion. So the boy swung again – and again – and now the creature was on his knees, a stunned look on his face and dark green liquid – blood? – leaking from his pointed nose.

Then time seemed to resume its normal course. The boy found himself breathing heavily.

"Be calm," urged Mr Weiss in a sing-song voice, paying no attention whatsoever to his fallen lackey. "You have just emerged from a birthing pod. Your current physical appearance is not necessarily permanent – merely new. Do not give into such rage. You could damage yourself profoundly."

The boy's hands were shaking now, a though he had just completed a long and arduous run. He stared again down at his warped white body; the vile, suety blanket of flesh, which hung about him like a living cloak.

"You are distressed, but all will be well," declared Weiss, in his most soothing voice. The little man stepped over his stunned colleague and offered the boy a reassuring smile, causing his eyes to sparkle and laughter lines to run wild. And, whilst the boy stared into those eyes, trying to assess Mr Weiss' words, a needle slid swiftly into his flesh.

The boy glanced down in surprise, before offering a reproachful glare as his eyes veiled and he sank to the floor.

Mr Weiss capped and stowed his hypodermic.

"Ah! But it's for the best! You might have damaged yourself in this fragile emotional state. And then where would we be?"

He went on to produce a small, leather-bound notebook from another pocket and began to make notes in tight, crabbed writing and with great urgency.

"But did you see how he moved?" he trilled, as he scribbled, possibly to his assistants – even the bruised and battered one – or perhaps just to himself. "The acceleration of physical impulses and reflexes – most advanced! And musculature seems to have been somewhat enhanced, also."

He beamed around the room. "I think," he ventured, "that the Pale Lady is going to be pleased!"

Chapter 18
Soothing the Mind

Hmmm... so it would seem that the initial indications on my latest pet are quite promising. Of course, Mr Weiss would say that, wouldn't he? And yet, I doubt he would exaggerate over-recklessly: he's too cautious for that. Just look how long he has survived being in my employ! So maybe there is something to be celebrated after all... Time will tell.

For now, the weapon is at a delicate stage: soft and malleable – and easily warped out of shape. This one must needs be treated gently. He must learn to love his new self – and to recognise his new powers. The post-hatching process will be slow and gradual – and careful. It must not be rushed: all of our hard work will be for nought if his mind is broken and he becomes too psychologically crippled to function.

Also, I must have an independent assessment of his capabilities so that I know whether Mr Weiss should be rewarded or made to suffer.

So, I must call upon another retainer of superlative skill: a master of the mind. She will see him through this dark journey. It is necessary if he is to serve me to his full effect.

I wait, meanwhile, in the shadows, observing always as I have ever done.

Do not fail me.

The sound of water tinkling down into an elaborate stone bowl, topped by a winged cherub, eased across his sense of awareness and mingled with sunshine to bathe him in warmth and contentment. The boy sighed happily, perhaps taking solace in some recent vestigial memories: recent and yet now belonging to another existence.

Stretching he yawned and sat up on the immaculate springy turf. To his right was a venerable cedar tree. A rustic swing had been suspended from a low-hanging branch and that was where she was, swinging gently, the softest of breezes stirring her honey-coloured tresses. She wore a loose-fitting white dress and delicate silver chains around her throat and right ankle. Her eyes were closed as if she was relishing the moment.

The boy stared down at his arms, with a twinge of fear, but they looked perfectly normal. In fact, they looked better than normal, as they seemed to have acquired an even, golden tan.

He looked up again and this time she was looking straight at him with eyes of cornflower blue and a smile of unaffected empathy.

"Hello," she said. "It's nice to meet you finally."

He couldn't help but look around to see if she was talking to him. None of the pretty girls at school gave him a second look and she left them in the shade.

That was when he laughed.

She smiled a bit wider, as if sharing a joke of which, in truth, she was wholly ignorant.

"What's so funny?" she enquired, in rich, throaty voice full of ready humour.

"All of this!" he exclaimed, gesturing at the beautiful gardens around them. "I'm getting used to your tactics, you see. None of this is real. You're just trying to put me at ease. Somewhere I'm still out there, mangled and deformed so I can never have a normal life again. You may well be real. In fact, I'm wondering if you have a brother. Called Evan? Because if you do I know him well and he screwed me over... so don't expect me to greet you like an old friend and open my heart a bit more for you to stomp on it."

And here his voice began to wobble as all of his recent traumas began to stir in the recess of memory. He fought to suppress them: he couldn't possibly face all of that right now; it would shatter his frail and probably illusory sense of control.

The young woman stopped swinging and looked at him earnestly.

"I am sorry," she said, and for a second he almost believed her – but he had seen too much now, and it had made him justifiably cynical. "I know you have been through a fearful ordeal."

The boy shrugged, and looked away, perhaps to hide the tears that were welling in his eyes.

"Let's get on with it," he snapped, gruffly. "Who are you and what do you want?"

If she was annoyed or offended, she didn't show it. She just smiled again, a bit more sadly, this time.

"They call me Yellow Rose," she answered, "and I have been asked to help you in your recovery. Changes such as those which you have been subjected to can take a terrible toll on the subject."

He chuckled bitterly at this.

"No, surely not! You mean been tricked into leaving your world behind so that you can be taken prisoner by some evil spider woman thing and then put inside a blender to be whizzed up so that even your own mother wouldn't recognise you? You mean some people react badly to that?"

His voice squeaked slightly and he was aware of its rapidly ascending pitch. He was also aware how petulant he sounded - a lot, in fact, like a frightened little boy trying to sound braver than he felt. His mouth snapped shut and he closed his eyes, breathing deeply.

"I know this is a dream," he whispered, his eyes still closed. "I almost don't care anymore – at least I look normal here. Just tell me what you want and then leave me alone."

There was a sigh, and then, suddenly he felt her arms wrap around him, like a mother cradling her young child.

"You poor, poor boy," she murmured, and she smelt of roses after all, close up, except for her breath which smelt like marshmallows. "You've been through so much. Too much."

Somewhere steely and cold in the boy's mind told him with certainty that this was all phoney – that actually she didn't give a damn about him. But that was just one little corner. On every other level, he was desperate – truly desperate – for some show of compassion and kindness. He drank it up like it was water in the desert. And within moments, his frayed self-control had snapped, leaving him to sob out his pain and his terror and his despair all over her pretty white dress.

If she minded, she didn't show it.

She held him close, speaking in a low, melodic voice which somehow brought him comfort.

"That's it, my love," she sang, "let out all of that pain. It's dangerous to keep it all pent up inside you. Let it out. Crying is the mind's way of venting its anguish – of drawing out the poison. You have been hurt very badly and so you have a lot of sorrow to externalise. Just let it go – and be at peace. You will feel better for it very soon."

He wasn't sure how long he wept, but eventually, he began to feel that he was all cried out. Rubbing at his puffy eyes, he sat up slowly.

She held his hands in hers and smiled. He felt suddenly loved and safe and he didn't care that it wasn't real.

"A bit better?" she asked, gently.

He nodded by way of an answer.

"You are right, of course," she continued. "This place has been manufactured for the mind – it's a kind of dream. But I don't want anything from you. Think of me as a sort of doctor. I've been asked to help you. Your mind has been wounded – your very sense of self stretched to the point of snapping. I believe that in your world, doctors sometimes place patients into a medical coma in order to create a period of time in which the body's functions slow down and they are able to administer treatment. This dream is a safe space. It's a break from the physical and psychological traumas which have recently been visited upon you. Because waking up to the new reality could just push you over the edge in terms of what your mind can cope with. You need some tender loving care and a sympathetic ear. You also need to know that, although at first glance your body seems to have been warped beyond repair, there is still hope. We believe that this is a temporary state. Think of a butterfly when it first emerges from its chrysalis: it is a drab, ugly creature, its wings stunted and shrivelled. But after time in the sun, it assumes a new and glorious shape. That could be you. It will be you. I am going to help you to face this – and to take back control of your body and your life."

It was quite a speech, and she sounded like she meant every word of it.

"So, it did all happen – they put me inside that thing and I came out looking like I'd melted?"

"Yes. That is all true. But it is the beginning of the tale, not the end. One life has been left behind but another is now beginning – one in which you will have almost unlimited potential."

"As what? An exhibit in a freak show?"

He laughed, but in truth, something in her words was kindling a sort of hope, and that was scaring him.

"Oh no, something much more wonderful than that. The Pale Lady has been watching you for years – she has great plans for you. Pointless mutilation so that you could no longer pass easily back into your human world is not part of her plan. That would be a terrible waste of time and potential."

Had she tried to cloak any of that in a genuine concern for his well-being, he would have swatted it aside with the contempt it deserved. The Pale Lady cared for nothing and no one, of that he was quite sure. But mercenary motives – a desire to make use of him somehow – that seemed entirely credible to him. What would be the point in turning him into a freak, unless it was some kind of capricious joke on the part of a being beyond his understanding?

Yellow Rose gave him a large, plain white handkerchief and he blew his nose with some enthusiasm. When he had wiped the tears and snot from his face, he sat up fully, meeting her gaze calmly and evenly.

"Alright," he said, crisply, "so where do we stand? What's next, Dr Rose?"

She smiled at him. "Now that's better! First we will go through a few basic meditative routines so that you can centre yourself and learn to control your emotions."

He grinned ruefully back at her. "I thought I'd already learnt how to do that pretty well – hide my feelings and all that. Are you telling me that actually I'm not that good?"

"Hiding," she replied, coolly, "is not the same as mastering. Emotions have their place in human interactions, but they are, essentially, a hangover from your near-animal past. With time, practise and discipline, you can evolve beyond them – like an arachnophobe who manages to allow a tarantula to crawl down their arm. Emotions, you see, are both destabilizing and irrational."

The boy looked at her, solemnly for a moment.

"Are you a Vulcan?" he enquired, gravely.

She laughed. It was a light, carefree sound.

"No. If I was, I wouldn't have a sense of humour – nor, indeed, a sense of empathy."

"But you're not human either, are you?"

The truth was, he wasn't really sure what to think on that score, but she answered him readily enough.

"Not at all. I am... something else. I am an Other."

"Another?"

"An... Other. We look remarkably similar – well, some of us more than others – but we are not human. We have staged forays into your world for centuries, but we are not of it."

He nodded, as he had suspected as much, but still felt an overwhelming lack of comprehension, like a goldfish attempting to understand algebra.

"Well, I think that's enough philosophizing for now. Let's get to work on your training."

She moved her fingers in an intricate fashion and a large, clear piece of crystal seemed to appear out of thin air, as though she was a conjurer.

"Whoa! How did you do that?" he asked, impressed despite himself.

She winked. "Easily enough. Remember that none of this is real. This is, in a practical sense, a dream – so I can create anything I wish with complete disregard for the laws of physics."

"That sounded extremely cool – and I almost understood it, too. I wish you could meet my maths teacher. I wonder what he'd make of you!"

A vision of Mr Hayes' chalky old face sprang to mind; he was blinking in astonishment as Yellow Rose sipped tea from a china cup whilst discussing theoretical physics with him. It was so incongruously strange it made him giggle like a naughty little boy half his age.

"Good," said Miss Rose, tilting her head approvingly. Laughter is good for the soul – and the mind. And now I want you to take this crystal and look into it."

She passed it over. It was around twice the size of a golf ball; it was very clear but also multi-faceted, like a large, glassy diamond. It made him think of Grandmother's cut glass decanter.

"Look into the crystal and tell me what you see."

The boy resisted the urge to snigger at this, but it made him think of some kind of Saturday night TV show. Instead, he concentrated – and almost dropped the crystal with a squawk of alarm. Various versions of his face gazed back at him from the different planes within. Some were older – some younger. In one, he looked almost like a male model: older and smoulderingly handsome, with an arrogant tilt to his mouth. In another, his features were wispy; indistinct. In the worst, his face was barely recognizable as such: it was a mass of quivering skin: pinkish wattles hung from a pasty visage. His eyes were like black pinpricks in a ball of dough. There was no nose to be seen – just a vague bump in between the eyes and the solidified rivulets of flesh which dangled from his face.

"That's what I really look like, isn't it?" he whispered, appalled at his ugliness.

"They are all versions of yourself. Some are more rooted in physicality than others. The point is, you form a concept – a sort of reality where you see yourself. Think of it as a projection. Some are idealised; some are whimsical; some are the result of subconscious fantasy – of how you would secretly like to be perceived by others. They are all valid in their own way. You must learn to look past the most simple of these – and, to some extent, all of them. There are thousands of possible variations, as you will come to realise, and all of them are ultimately fleeting and inconsequential, for they are no more real or profound than the clothes you might choose to wear from one day to the next."

"Easy for you to say, when you look like a Hollywood A-lister."

He snorted.

"This is just psycho-babble: you're trying to dress up the fact that I look like a burns victim now and I'll never have a normal life again."

"Am I?" she sang, her eyebrows leaping up her forehead and her mouth forming a round O of surprise. "Well, before you neatly categorize me and put me into a labelled box, look again. This time, look deeper."

He frowned.

"You're just trying to gloss it over. You're probably trying to help me, like a therapist or something. Is this all about my self-image? It's nice but it's not going to wash."

Her blue eyes enfolded him and they were warm and tender.

"I'm not going to ask you to trust me. You would be foolish to in this place. But try, at least. Don't give up without trying."

He met her gaze for a few seconds and then sighed, and looked back at the crystal. There they all were again – a multitude of faces, some plain, some wicked, some smiling and others twisted with rage or hate. He shivered as they all stared back at him: it reminded him of those silly ghost cartoons, where galleries of sinister portraits grimaced at passers-by and followed them with their eyes. They were all him, though. Except that they weren't. Slowly, an idea was taking shape in his mind: what Yellow Rose had said about projections – different perceptions and incarnations of his own self. He began to see past the rows of glittering, scowling, beautiful images, walking past each in turn, like a field of mirrors; suddenly he was lost inside the crystal itself, lost, and yet something drew him on. At the heart of it all, past the mute, mouthing images, something lay at the core. And as the brittle self-reflections fell away, fading like old photos left for years in the sun, he could see it: a shifting, swirling ball of energy. It was reminiscent of an image from deep space, of a roiling galaxy of shimmering stars. Silver lines twisted and intersected; glowing orbs of various colours studded the shifting ebb and flow of energies like jewels. And he knew, then, what it meant to be him – this was his very essence; it was who he was. He had never been a religious person, but it hit him with undeniable truth: this was his soul. And it was beautiful; God, it was so beautiful that he found himself lost in contemplating its transcendent splendour. He swayed like a dancer, like grass in a gentle breeze, like the water in a breaking wave. His heart beat in time with the pulsing light at the centre of it all and he bathed in the gentle light of his own vital sense of being.

Then he heard a distant, vaguely familiar voice – like a distant memory of his mother calling him for supper.

Slowly, reluctantly, he felt himself pulling back – withdrawing from the sensation of self.

When Yellow Rose's face suddenly drifted across his field of vision, he thought there was something wrong with his eyesight – until he realised that his eyes were full of tears and he wept again – albeit this time for joy.

Gently, she dabbed at his eyes with her handkerchief. Their eyes locked and an understanding passed between them.

"It was all true," he whispered in a slight, trembling voice. "They're all like painted images on playing cards compared to what lies at the heart of it all. That was my soul. It was... amazing."

She smiled at him, compassionate understanding dripping from her gaze.

"You have seen a great truth, and in doing so, have understood the greatest of illusions: that we are what we see in the mirror. It is this simple notion which has limited so many of your kind. You are so much more, my love, than the mundane, transient image which happens to be caught briefly on a piece of glass – and yet you humans allow mirrors to exert such power over you. You are ensnared by something which isn't really real – and you lose sight of the burning star at the centre of your being – the true core of what and who you are."

He reached over and took her hand, still euphoric from his brief foray, but feeling now that he had grasped a vital truth at the heart of the universe - and himself.

He felt calm; serene. Certain.

The physical was a temporary cloak – brief as the flashes of light across one's face as a train speeds through a stand of tall trees.

"It's OK," he said, "I can face it. I'm ready to wake up, now. You can bring me back."

Chapter 19
The Mentor

Would a rose by any other name smell as sweet? That is what one of your more talented versifiers asserted in a particularly sentimental play. I can't answer that question – I have other, more pressing demands on my time, you see – far too many to squander valuable moments on idle philosophical quandaries. However, where my Rose is concerned, I can attest that her sweetness and skill are second to none. I even allowed her to choose her own name – a rare boon for one of my servants – but she asked so nicely, and it seemed a trivial thing at the time. To see her weave her magic, manipulating damaged minds carefully back into place is to see an artist at work. I must say that, whilst some of my rivals like to resort – all too quickly – to brute force, I myself have always preferred subtlety to advance my cause. Finesse. That's how I like to think of my long-term strategies. Careful planning and preparation yield far more lasting gains than those won abruptly by crude martial means.

My pretty Yellow Rose shares that view, I know.

She is so lovely – and so dextrous in the application of her art – that I must watch her carefully.

Perhaps I will rename her at some point, just to remind her who's in charge. If she wasn't so astonishingly talented and valuable to me, I might take even sterner action: it's always the clever, subtle ones you have to watch, after all. I suppose you

*think me rather paranoid – not to mention a touch psychotic –
but I haven't survived this long by assuming the best about
people. Trust no one except yourself – and take particular care
with the charmingly sincere ones, for it will be one of them who
tries to quietly knife you in the back.*

*For now, though, the artist is at work, moulding and shaping my
new implement gradually into something I can use. My, but
she's clever! Perhaps it won't do too much harm to simply leave
her to it. Soon, I hope to enjoy the fruits of her labours. Let's
hope they don't prove fatal to me. My kind nature may yet
prove to be my undoing...*

Sometimes it can be nice to wake from a dream to find oneself
in the comfortable familiarity of our real lives. Granted, the boy
was beginning to feel slightly hazy as to which reality was real,
but he knew, with lead-heavy inevitability, that he would
awaken to a malformed body and a sense of grief. He had never
been especially good-looking - perhaps attractively fey from a
certain angle, to a certain type - but now he was a monster.

Slowly, his eyelids flickered open to expose his doughy white
flesh. Even they seemed to sag, and it was with an effort of will
that he widened his gaze beyond a narrow slit to feast on his
self-revulsion. Although he knew what to expect, and had
hardened himself to it, it was difficult. Even though he came
fortified with the knowledge that the physical self is transient
and not all that important after all, it was difficult to pull away
from a lifetime of fascination in how he looked – and how
others might perceive him. It was, in so many ways, a
microcosm of the human condition. As he raised his left hand to
stare at the almost web-like membrane between his fingers,

and the loose, pinkish skin on the back of his hand and wrist, he could not help but shiver in morbid fascination. Then another hand, slender and lily-white, took hold of it, and well-manicured fingers gently stroked him. He looked up quickly, to find a pair of shining blue eyes, like captured glimpses into a glorious summer sky, gazing into his with no sign at all of horror or disgust.

"I admire your self-control," he observed, wryly, "I know I must look like the elephant man. Well done for not throwing up over me!"

His voice sounded muffled again, as though he was talking through a duvet, and he knew that the folds of skin were even worse on his face. With his right hand, he reached up and took hold of an expanse of droopy skin: it was, surely, the mother of all jowls! He forced himself to stay calm, to not panic or retreat into self-pitying hysteria.

"It's just flesh," she replied, archly, "mortal flesh — one moment it's there, and then it's gone again, like dew burnt off by the rising sun."

The boy laughed outright at this, feeling his face wobble like a plate of blancmange, which was even funnier.

"Thanks," he drawled, "you really know how to pick someone up when they're down!"

"I try my best," she responded, with a smile, "though I fear that my own lack of mortality can sometimes hinder the appropriate level of empathy."

"No shit!" he snorted, with another wheezy, walrus-like splutter of laughter. "Don't beat yourself up about it. Just tell me what

I'm supposed to do now. You seemed to be saying, back in your nice garden, that there might be some hope – that there is some sort of long-term plan for me other than a starring role in a horror film."

"There is always hope," she assured him. "Come; sit up, find your feet, begin to rediscover yourself."

So he did. He sat up and looked around. He was in another subterranean chamber, but this one was lit with a soothingly gentle violet light. A small spring bubbled and gurgled nearby from a crystal-encrusted formation, and danced into a clear pool on which small white flowers seemed to float of their own accord. He was lying on a raised piece of rock which seemed to be concave in shape, and its hollow had been thickly lined with a substance somewhere between ferns and moss. It was remarkably springy and comfortable beneath him. As he looked upwards, he realised the roof above tapered to an impossibly high point, and it was from there that the light was drifting down in lazy, unhurried bars. He stared for a few moments.

"Does that go all the way up to the surface?" he mused, almost to himself.

"Yes. It was a gift, this chamber, from the Pale Lady. Few can boast of access to natural light."

He swung his legs over to the floor.

"Wow! Nothing says thank you like a cave with a view."

With that little barb launched, he tried to stand up, expecting to struggle, like an old man or an invalid. But in truth, he was fine. He actually felt remarkably chipper in a physical sense – full of energy, fizzing for release. He had to stop himself from springing around the room like a person with giant springs on his feet.

"Oh!" he exclaimed.

Yellow Rose was smiling at him with open pleasure.

"You feel good, don't you?"

"Well – yes! I guess I do! If I didn't look like someone had thrown me into a bath of acid, I might actually start doing cartwheels around your lair."

"My lair?" she cried, with a bubble of laughter, "you really don't trust me, do you? I'm not some wild beast or evil witch, you know!"

"No, of course I don't trust you! You work for that horrible old woman –why should I trust you? And as for the witch-beast thing, well, the jury's out."

"Thanks," she trilled, pleasantly, "it's good to see you're keeping an open mind about it all. Now let's see if we can't put a little of that sass and positivity to use. Please hold out your arms in front of you and do as I say."

He bobbed his head deferentially.

"My lady," he intoned, and he did as he was bid.

She reached out in turn and took both his hands in hers.

"Now," she murmured, "I am going to establish a closed link with your mind. Don't worry: you won't feel a thing. You'll just hear me talking in your head. We will be able to interface far more effectively this way, as opposed to using crude verbal communication. It will enable me to convey nuanced concepts and thoughts instantaneously into your consciousness. I will be able to show you things – and it will all be very fast indeed. I have no sinister motives. I have been asked to help you and that is my sole aim. With your permission, I will proceed."

He smiled, a little grimly. Not so long ago, the thought of someone being able to penetrate his mind, to poke around in his very consciousness – or, worse, his subconscious - would have seemed like a terrible and terrifying act of violation. Now, with the all of the events of the last few days... or weeks (objectively judging the passage of time since he and Evan had entered the portal was difficult to say the least) he found a complete lack of emotional reaction to what she proposed. Perhaps there was some slight uneasiness- but what else could she do to him now? His mind and body had been brutalised to the point of insensibility and he found that he couldn't muster much in the way of caring – not even for his own self-preservation.

So he shrugged, carelessly, and simply muttered acquiescence to her request.

"Fine: go for it."

She paused and looked at him.

"I promise I won't hurt you," she whispered, gently. "I do just want to help you."

"Are you trying to convince me or you?"

Where did that come from? Sometimes, he surprised himself. He really had become careless of his fate – reckless as to possible consequences. Here he was being provocative to the woman who would shortly be tinkering around inside him: probably not the most sensible of ideas. But then, what did sensible mean anymore?

Their eyes locked. He felt a slight dizziness, and then everything around him changed. The cave was gone. They stood on what seemed to be a gleaming white marble disc, enfolded entirely by a star studded night sky. She continued to hold his hands.

"OK, this is different," he observed, drily. "So where are we now?"

"We are still in the cave, but I have isolated your senses, to help you to focus on the here and now. Like blinkers on a horse." She had the grace to grin at this, with just a hint of mischief.

"Thanks! Will I get a lump of sugar when it's over?"

"Only if you're good."

He actually smiled at that.

"Ah... But what IS good?" he countered, a look of mock innocence on his face – or at least, that's what he hoped it looked like, on some level at least. "And why this now: couldn't you have done it all in the dream place?"

"Because this is a sharply focused, direct link between us. Dream space is more... nebulous. Think of a shower sprinkler where the water is widely distributed and falls in numerous gentle streams. That's just right for someone in need of some gentle, soothing care. What this task requires, however, is rather more... surgical."

"There you go again, making me feel great about everything. Is there actually going to be anything of me left at the end, out of interest?"

Her eyes twinkled of their own volition for a moment. He wondered how she did that.

"Oh yes," she stated, simply. "You will most definitely still be you."

He wondered why he got a slight frisson of naughtiness as she told him this, but no matter.

"Now, let us begin." Her voice changed suddenly into something clear and crisp, like a winter's morning. "I shall release your hands in a moment. The link is established: here there is no need for physical contact."

So saying, she dropped her hands to her side. He stood for a moment, his arms still outstretched, like a sleepwalker, before he did the same.

"Stretch out your fingers, and then flex them, one, two three. Now your toes. Left foot. Right foot..."

The boy simply did as he was told. He felt rather foolish on some level and it all reminded him of a film that he had half-watched at school, where some kids in black and white had had to limber up for the day before lessons commenced.

Ours is not to reason why...

The exercises were long. They were tedious. He wondered what their point was. After what seemed like hours of flexing and stretching every part of his body, he was on the verge of saying so – but something in Yellow Rose's radiant gaze stopped him from complaining.

"Good," she said, eventually. "You are becoming intimately familiar with your new body. That is essential for the next step which we must take."

He gave her what could have been an ironic look, somewhere beneath his jowls.

"It's good that you are experimenting with facial expression," she noted, like a prim school teacher. "Keep that up. Now, lift up your left hand. Stretch it our so that the skin tautens. That's right. Now, concentrate. Try to get the skin as smooth as possible."

He focused grimly and obediently on the task set and stared as the skin on his hand slowly assumed a less saggy appearance. It was still pretty droopy, though.

Suddenly he felt her inside him – actually in his head – as though there was another consciousness sharing his mind, looking out of his eyes. It was most disconcerting.

You may need a little help here, as you are unused to the procedure. So I'm going to give your nerve impulses a little... nudge. Think of it as a kind of kick start.

He really wasn't sure that he wanted anything kicking around in his mind, be he was reduced to the role of a spectator from the stands of his own id, as his functions were momentarily hijacked. Before he could formulate a response, he felt something give; something in his mind sparked and flared – a new awareness – a new... channel. It was scary and it hurt a little. He flinched, washed over by feelings of intense vertigo. He felt out of sorts in his own psyche – like a burglar caught wide-eyed in another person's house. It was an odd sensation; disorientating; it was as though someone had taken his hand, figuratively speaking, and was guiding it through a series of ritualistic motions which needed to be learnt. He watched mesmerized. And then it happened. The skin on the back of his hand began to change. Its whole texture altered, as though it had, abruptly, received alternative orders on how it should look.

The boy stared.

One hand remained wattled and waxen; the other was now lean and shapely. He stared some more and then blinked.

"There are certain things that your body manages instinctively," said Yellow Rose, patiently, "such as breathing and blinking. There are others which require conscious management, such as deciding to pick something up or to perform a back-flip. Some are easy: others require training. You will find the same with your new body. It is not a thing to be feared. It can be trained – and so can you. Soon, you will be able to do extraordinary things."

She took his still malformed hand.

"This is the easy bit. Now, you try. Picture your hand as it always was. Concentrate. Order the flesh to resolve itself according to the image in your mind. It is a straightforward command from your brain, just like any other."

The boy licked his lips, excited despite his determined cynicism. He did as she said: an image formed of his hand. His very ordinary hand: eating a sandwich; drawing a picture; beating out the time to some music. It was his hand. He let the image take shape and immersed his whole conscious being in it. Slowly, much more slowly than when Yellow Rose had helped him, he felt cogs moving around in his mind – commands and nerves were interlocking, forming new pathways.

Slowly, very slowly, as he watched, his hand began to shift, back into the familiar shape in his mind. The skin seemed to tighten, the excess folds gradually melting away, almost as if it was somehow being absorbed.

"What just happened, please?" he enquired.

"You are very special," came the reply. "You have been carefully bred to exhibit certain... abilities. The pod in the hatchery was used to trigger these abilities – to activate them from a dormant state, if you like."

He locked eyes with her again.

"What abilities are we talking about here?"

"The one we are currently exploring relates to your physical composition. Your flesh and bones are unusually elastic. The malformed state which so distressed you was simply a default. Soon, you will learn how to shape your flesh into the forms you want."

A few moments ticked by.

"I didn't get that at all," he said, having tried to process the information.

"The evidence is in front of you," she continued, gently. "Look at your hands. They have altered, have they not?"

"Well, yes."

"We start with the hands because they are easy. If you think about it, anyone can, over time, alter the shape and appearance of their body. They can become more muscular, fat, blond, brunette. There are so many possibilities. We'll continue to practise with your hands, before moving on to other more… complex tasks."

"Right."

He still felt all at sea, but an idea was beginning to germinate in his mind.

"Then we will continue. Clear your mind. Try to relax. Allow your hands to shift in between states…"

Somewhere, a little bell rang. He started to focus. He felt himself being very subtly guided, but he didn't mind this time.

Yellow Rose gave a sharp nod.

"Continue."

Chapter 20
Shifter

Free will is entirely illusory.

A bold statement, I know, but I hope it had an impact. You will note the deliberate mention of illusion: this is necessary to the successful execution of one's long-term plans. People don't like to feel pushed or forced in a certain direction, you see. They tend to push back; to rail against their oppressor. They will probably be unsuccessful, but regardless of their petty acts of rebellion, they will surely chafe at the boot on their throat – and therefore be less productive. When one's thralls are allowed to exist in a false skein of freedom, they are so much easier to manage and deploy; they fulfil their functions with greater efficacy too.

The creation of the illusion costs little in effort, but my goodness, it yields abundant rewards!

Watch now, for example, how this boy begins to adjust to the notion of his newfound abilities. A short time ago, it was all over for him – he wallowed in a slough of despair. Now, though, he is reviving. Watch, as his face takes on the new sheen of hope and excitement. He is thinking that his life might actually be worth living after all – that, just perhaps, he can enjoy his rebirth in ways that he couldn't previously imagine. He might yet be the mater of his own destiny.

Who am I to burst his bubble?

Dream on, my sweet, you will serve me all the better. Just remember that, behind your flimsy sense of self-fulfilment, you

*may follow your own road only so far, for I intend to keep you on
a long but particularly robust leash.*

They were back in the liquid light of Yellow Rose's lair, now, the
need for blinkers apparently fallen by the wayside. The boy
stood hunched in a posture of intense effort and concentration.

Hands shifted in and out of focus. After what must have been a
period of hours, he was starting to feel that he had them down
pat. He even discovered, through experimenting with different
impulses, that he could alter their tone, from pale to lightly
tanned. And then to very tanned. He looked up, delightedly, at
Yellow Rose who smiled radiantly in return, sharing his joy.

"You are proving to be an apt pupil," she remarked, "see how
quickly you're picking it up? I'd go so far as to say you're a
natural."

The boy glowed with pride at this praise, despite his practised
cynicism, so caught up was he in the moment.

The days fled by, quickly now, as he slowly expanded his
attention beyond his hands to his arms and then his legs. He felt
his way instinctively, moulding and shaping the flesh there with
increasing skill and confidence.

He looked down at his familiar skinny white legs and giggled.

"Like two pieces of string!" he declared, with mock despair to
his tutor. And then, suddenly, they assumed a golden tone and
seemed to swell slightly with additional muscle tone.

"That's better."

He winked at Yellow Rose, who raised an approving eyebrow.

"Impressive!"

For a moment, he thought that he saw a slight flicker of surprise, but if it had been so, it was gone now. It was of little consequence. The boy was enraptured; he was brimming with excitement at the possibilities which were now crowding into his head.

"What about faces?"

He turned and fired the question without warning.

"I think I get the limbs now. I assume I can do something with my face, yes?"

Yellow Rose blinked twice in quick succession.

"Oh. Well. Yes, of course. Although I had expected to wait a little longer before we ventured there. The face is by far the hardest area to master. There are so many tiny details – so many subtle signs and nuances of expression. The face is the first thing that humans look at: their brains are programmed to read faces. So, what I'm trying to say, is that they're fearfully difficult to get right."

"Even when it's my face?" he enquired, innocently.

She smiled, but again, he got the sense that she was slightly on the back-foot.

"Even then. In fact, that can make it worse, because it's the face you know best – and, deep in your psyche, it's rooted as part of your core identity – part of who you are. Sometimes, when one such as yourself, starts to experiment too quickly, they can become… disorientated. Sometimes, seeing one's own face being manipulated as though it was made of clay, can be deeply disturbing. I would caution you not to rush into things. Take your journey steadily. More haste, less speed, my pupil."

The boy reached up experimentally to touch his face. His fingers went from pale to golden as he did so. His mind felt as though fireworks were exploding across a satin sky – blazes of colour illuminated his thoughts and awareness; he felt things shifting, like gears and moving parts, but with the speed of a super-computer, as he knew, instinctively, how to sculpt his living flesh.

"It isn't a curse…" he whispered to himself, with a dawning sense of wonder. "It's a blessing… It's… incredible."

Raw self-knowledge and instinct took over once more, and before he had consciously formed the desire, or issued the mental command, he felt his face changing; the loose skin tightened abruptly, and there were little clicks from the bones in his face. He hadn't expected that, but it seemed suddenly obvious, that even his bones were no longer fixed into a single state.

He stared speculatively at his other hand, and suddenly it expanded outwards, into a large, tanned paw; bones clicked and rearranged themselves, some of them flowing now, like mercury, before reforming, as he assumed a huge, hairy hand – one that Edward Hyde would have been proud to own – and which was twice the normal size.

He gazed, spellbound, for a moment, before willing his hand back, almost instantaneously to its normal proportions.

Lost as he was in the moment, he heard a gasp of surprise and turned to find his mentor with her mouth opened into an O of surprise.

"I need a mirror, so that I can practise," he said, more as a statement than a request.

She looked at him for a moment, her mouth closing sharply and her eyes now exhibiting a mixture of shock and cool assessment, as though weighing him up. They regarded each other for a few more seconds, and then a sort of veil dropped over her eyes, hiding her thoughts and feelings. She seemed to have reached a decision.

"I feel bound to tell you," she said, in a calm, even tone, "that I have never seen anyone pick it up this quickly. I am not sure whether this is a good thing yet, but I will humour you. We will need to monitor events closely, though... Too far, too fast, and your mind could suffer permanent damage..."

He felt an absolute sense of certitude on this. There was no fear, no doubt.

"It'll be fine," he assured her. Again, it was a statement, not a question.

He watched as she approached a large crystalline outcrop, similar in shape to a fingertip, but around four feet high. The top of it had been sheared away at an angle, and was perfectly smooth, like a translucent table top. At a simple gesture from Yellow Rose, the flat, smooth surface became suddenly reflective, just like a mirror.

The boy approached. Was he nervous? Perhaps, a little, but the same kind of nerves that a loved child might have on the night before Christmas. His reflection glided into view. He wore a simple blue robe, which Yellow Rose had given to him to hide the nakedness of his newly emerged body, which he now opened. His arms and legs were pretty much as they should be. His torso quickly assumed its normal shape, even as he looked at it. His face, however, was far from normal. One side had tightened itself up, but it was taut and shiny, as though it had been burnt. It did not look like him. The other side remained swathed in pallid folds of flesh. The boy did not quail at the sight before him. He continued to stare straight at it; mental calculations whizzed through his brain and he gave a few experimental twitches, causing skin to ripple like a newly disturbed pool. Pink puckered flesh at the corner of his mouth began to curve as he suddenly began to smile. Like liquid evaporating in the sun, his skin began to move; the ripples and folds disappearing into a smooth, shining plane. That was the first step. Now the jowls had gone, but his face remained featureless, almost like a mask. Only his dark, dark eyes, staring out at him conveyed any sense of humanity. He cocked his head to one side and concentrated, hard, visualising his own face. Somewhere in the background, he was dimly aware of Yellow Rose, speaking in a low, calm voice, urging him not to rush things... He tuned her out with surprising ease. This was his body; his gift, if you like. No one else's. And he was master. It was his body – and it would respond to his commands. Of this, he was sure.

There was a sudden, jarring crunch as his cheekbones dissolved and collapsed, before reforming themselves in a familiar shape.

Click, click. His nose straightened itself and assumed its customary, slender appearance, rising up from a gentle bump in the centre of his face. The flesh around his eyes swam momentarily, before rearranging itself so that his big eyes were no longer tightly slanted, but dark orbs, gleaming now with ferocious joy.

His jaw shuddered and creaked, before moving back into its delicate, pre-transformation state.

His lips slimmed themselves down and flushed slightly pink; familiar little bumps and curves began to appear elsewhere; the skin beneath his eyes darkened slightly and the shiny, pink sheen was replaced by something softer and pale – pale as befitting someone who tended to spend his time indoors, when he wasn't being whisked away by dangerously charming acquaintances.

The boy stared at himself and found that he was smiling an almost savage smile. His own face flashed back out at him. He had done it; he wasn't sure how long he had been shaping and adjusting his tender visage, but it was now, once more, him.

He casually shrugged the robe to the floor so that he could view his entire body. He rotated, slowly, in full circles, staring and tweaking, nipping away any remaining patches of pale doughiness, and restoring his natural flesh tones.

When he was satisfied, he turned to look at Yellow Rose. She had fallen silent some time ago, but he had paid little attention: what he was doing, after all, required his absolute focus.

She was staring at him, with an expression somewhere between astonished and... fearful?

"It seems that you are something of a prodigy," she murmured. "You have done, in a few hours, what normally takes weeks of painful training and gradual progression."

He felt something flutter, very lightly, like a butterfly, across his mind and knew it was her, subtly probing and assessing him. She gave a sharp hiss of breath and was suddenly gone. He knew why, too: his mind was ablaze: he could feel the thoughts, the ideas, the countless desires, lit up now like a million brilliant stars in the firmament.

"It's too bright now," he whispered, softly.

She nodded.

He looked back into the mirror.

"I am a blank canvas. My body is a crucible. I can be whoever I want to be."

They both stared once more into the mirror, spellbound by the brief pops and crunches as he grew a few inches taller. His torso shaped itself obligingly, into a form resembling an ancient Greek statue for muscular definition. His face gained a couple of years; his cheek bones inclined slightly upwards and his lips were suddenly thicker and more sensuous. His hair gleamed black, but fell into slight waves around his face. He pouted at the aesthetic vision of glory which now looked back at him; his reflection blew him a kiss.

"Now ain't that something?" he asked, looking over his shoulder at Yellow Rose and favouring her with a lop-sided grin.

"Yes," she replied, in a faint voice. "But remember that pride comes before a fall. You are treating your very identity with a worrying degree of irreverence. You may think you can simply discard the form you grew in to over the course of your life as though it's a thing of little consequence, but you are taking a terrible risk by proceeding with such speed."

"Duly noted," he replied, but with little conviction. "I'm just making a few... adjustments, that's all."

He looked back at himself. He was almost there. After a few seconds, he knew just what to do, to finish the job, and his eyes flickered from near-black to a deep, sapphire blue. It was like the movement of a kaleidoscope window from one colour to another. It was not at all difficult.

"Perfect," he told himself, with a pleased nod.

There was a waft of fragrance as Yellow Rose moved next to him. She tentatively ran a finger down his newly toned and golden arm.

"Yes," she agreed with him, venturing a small smile, like a shy little girl.

"What do you think, then?" he asked, pirouetting and giving her a little bow.

"I think," said she, carefully, "that the Pale Lady is going to be very happy."

Chapter 21
Changeover

Oho! It never ceases to amaze and amuse me in equal measure how much store humans place in their fleshly vestments. Look at this one now: he thinks his ability to manipulate his appearance into something pleasing to a contemporary eye is a masterful gift. It is of little import. To me and mine, physical appearance is as insubstantial and transient as smoke. In what little worth can be ascribed to it, I suppose we might use it to make some sort of statement, whether on one's mood or status, in a similar manner to donning a favoured hat. It is of little consequence to me. Let others preen and obsess over such nonsense. What matters is victory, not some subjective predilection to aesthetics. I will not waste my energy on this any further.

So. Now my latest weapon is newly forged and is showing quite remarkable promise. This is pleasing, although I am not one to count my blessings: the brightest flames oft do burn out all the sooner.

His mind is full of folly and idle preoccupation; there is no discipline, no resolution. This is a mere decorative blade which will bend or break on its first use. My lovely Rose has done her part: she has saved his broken mind and restored his spirits. It is now time to pass him on to another, very different tutor: one who will add a cold edge to this gilded tool. He will quench the fires of trivial vanity and grant instead a sure and certain purpose. Which is, of course, to serve me in the furtherance of my aims, dark and dastardly as they are.

I believe you humans refer to this process as 'tough love.'

Let it begin.

It was as though the summer, rich and kind, was brought rudely to an end by the harsh spectre of winter when he came.

The boy had revelled in the joy of his new gift – and in the nurturing benevolence of his teacher, whose smiles of delight had restored him to some sort of spiritual equilibrium. Her encouragement and patience had seen him make great strides in the control and execution of 'shifting' abilities, as she referred to them. He had learnt to vary his height, his age, his ethnicity – even his gender. Now that had been a bizarre experience: one which had led him, briefly, to reconsider her constant warnings as to long-term identity issues.

But Yellow Rose's tutelage went beyond the simple development of his strange new skills: appearance was only half of the equation – the rest depending on how one acted. It was no good looking like an eighty year old and then vaulting over gates, after all. He learnt the need to embed himself within the adopted persona. It reminded him somewhat of those now far-distant school drama lessons, where he had, briefly, enjoyed pretending to be someone else – someone with another life; another set of motivating desires. No: on assuming a shape, it was vital that he act in an appropriate manner. Posture, facial expression and voice were all to be carefully considered. Voice was probably the hardest: perhaps, luckily, because he was, chronologically, an adolescent, his voice had not fully deepened into manhood: it retained an ambiguous quality which made for the use of a pleasingly indeterminate manner of speaking. Accents he was working on – and making good progress.

Somewhere in the back of his mind, he did wonder about the purpose of these exercises, and what plans he played a part in - but he tried not to allow such gloomy thoughts to intrude themselves on what had been a prolonged period of intensely exciting discovery: one might even say, enjoyment. But, of course, all good things come to an end, and so it was with the jocund delights of Miss Rose's company.

One morning – if such a term could be used in these subterranean places – he awoke from his peaceful slumbers to find Yellow Rose sitting at his side with a poignant smile on her face. He sensed immediately that this was significant.

"What is it?" he blurted, sitting up, suddenly.

"My student," she responded, in a tone which was at once proud and grave, "you have learnt all of my little tricks. From now on, they are yours and will grow in skill through your own practice. Now it is time for you to enter another phase of your training."

He felt the first delicate palpitations of fear – an anxiety giving his heart a little squeeze. He realised all at once how important this woman's kindness had been to him; she had provided him with a wellspring of comfort and stability in the wake of a physical and emotional maelstrom. The thought of having to leave… well, perhaps he had known it would have to happen sooner or later – indeed, perhaps he had thought it must end at some point – but not now, all of a sudden, out of the blue…

"But..." he stammered, afraid. "It's... it's all too quick. I... I don't feel ready. I want to stay with you."

And he clutched then, instinctively, at her hand, a little boy still in the physical guise of a Greek God.

She gave him a bright, encouraging smile, and gave his hand an answering squeeze.

"I'm afraid that events are moving quickly for both of us. I must follow my orders – as you will, too. You have learnt to have faith in yourself and to modify the mask of your flesh so that you can pass undetected almost anywhere. Now you must learn to hone your reflexes and physical reactions."

"What do you mean?" he whispered, in a small voice.

"You will learn how to avoid blows and how to wield a weapon. Your next tutor has arrived, and he will train you in the more... martial arts."

"Fighting..." he muttered, before looking her fully in the eye. "Just what have you people got planned for me?"

Yellow Rose inclined her beautiful neck, like a fabulous flower deprived of water.

"I cannot vouch for the plans of the Pale Lady: but she has invested much time and effort in you. You are a prized asset to her, and she will already have ascribed a role for you in her grand scheme."

They continued to look at each other: her bright, shining blue eyes, meeting his darker sapphires. Somewhere deep inside, he felt something germinating: a deep-seated hatred of the Pale

Lady, who sought to bind him to her will and use him in her plans. Who wrenched him now away from Yellow Rose.

"And now, my dear, we must part. I do not know if we shall ever meet again, but perhaps we will. Come, let us part as friends: life is a journey, and we must move ever onwards in its currents."

With that, she pulled him gently to his feet and gave him a tender kiss on the lips: a kiss that promised lark-song and hot azure skies. She led him across her chamber – which was now the closest thing he had to home – and there, in an opening in the rock which he had never seen before, stood a gaunt figure, as cold and drear as she was warm and joyful. His hair was silver and braided at the temples. His eyes seemed almost colourless, and his white skin was stretched tightly over his face, like parchment. His cheek bones were savage curves; his mouth an unfriendly, thin-lipped gash. He was dressed in loose-fitting black trousers and a black sleeveless jacket that exposed arms which were snowy white yet corded with muscle.

His empty eyes met the boy's and in a flat voice, he introduced himself.

"I am Octavius Gray. You will find me hard company after this lady, for I am not one for social discourse or finer feelings. I have been tasked to train you in the martial arts and this is what I shall do. If you give of your all to meet my expectations, I will treat you fairly. We will never be fiends, and I may tell you candidly that you will not like me."

The boy smiled, slightly giddily, and carefully avoided looking at Yellow Rose. He brought his heels together and nodded his head curtly. This was a new role and he would have to adapt to survive: isn't that what she had taught him?

"A pleasure to make your acquaintance, sir. Do lead on."

And with that, he left her, without a backward glance, and found himself journeying anew through the labyrinthine tunnels of the Pale Lady's domain.

Octavius Gray moved through the twists and turns swiftly and did not look back to see whether his charge was keeping up with the pace. The boy felt his muscles and reflexes straining as he ducked here to avoid a stalactite and dodged there to avoid a sudden hollow in the rocky floor into which a foot might easily slip and be twisted.

As he had noted before, his reactions and general fitness seemed somehow enhanced; at first he even relished the opportunity to stretch his muscles and to undertake such a physical challenge. It was... exhilarating. The boy grinned at the thought of it: no one would have predicted that he might develop a taste for subterranean fell-running, and yet here he was, doing just that.

Needless to say, the pleasure couldn't continue forever. After some time, the boy felt a sheen of sweat slicking his long limbs and his breath was becoming more ragged. The ghostly figure of Octavius continued to glide implacably forwards with no sign of exertion.

I think I might be built for speed rather than endurance the boy managed to observe inwardly, and with some self-deprecation, as he ran.

After the passage of a few more minutes and close to half a mile of tunnels, he actually felt his muscles starting to twitch and a stitch began to manifest unpleasantly in his abdomen. He gritted his teeth and fixed a bitter gaze on Gray's silvery head as it bobbed along in front of him – increasingly in front of him. He was determined not to show any weakness in front of this old martinet. Oh no. He was starting to understand how these beings worked: they did nothing by accident. This was a test: Mr Gray was putting him through his paces, probably so that he could enjoy the pleasure of criticizing him and shredding back his ego at the end of it all.

He wondered whether it was all part of some grand strategy: Yellow Rose was the good cop, softening him up, and now Octavius Gray was the bad cop, knocking him back on his heels.

He decided that if this was the case, Yellow Rose was oblivious to the plans; even to him, her actions had seemed completely genuine and sincere. Still, a little paranoia was probably no bad thing down here. Trust no one had to be his motto now.

He was jolted from his internal dialogue by having to pull up short to avoid hitting Octavius in the back. The old man turned to face him with exaggerated slowness; he stretched out his limbs and cracked his head from side to side, as though he had just risen from his bed after a long sleep. There was the slightest hint of perspiration, but other than that, he showed no obvious sign of fatigue. Unlike the boy, whose hair was stuck to his head with sweat and who was gasping like a fish freshly dumped on a river bank.

His instructor's strange eyes assessed him without comment, leaving the boy's imagination to fill the gap in terms of what he might be thinking. He doubted it was terribly positive.

"We have arrived," he announced, in his flat, dry voice. "You will spend some time here under my supervision. I will endeavour to inculcate you with the skills necessary for your future survival. You would do well to listen and to follow my orders to the letter. You may address me as Mr Gray or as teacher."

A pale arm gestured into a particularly large and inhospitable-looking cavern.

"Enter here. To your right you will see a patch of glowing stalagmites. Walk beyond them and you will find a chamber has been prepared for you. Water and food have been set aside for your consumption. You may have a short time to rest, meditate and prepare yourself for training. That is all."

With that, he walked off into the cavern, leaving the boy standing alone.

"Thanks for the warm welcome..." muttered the boy to himself – but somewhere deep inside, he knew it could have been much worse – and that his tribulations were just beginning...

Chapter 22
Honing the Blade

Octavius Gray exemplifies the concept of an effective tool. He is terribly proficient in the arts of personal combat; a weapon honed to perfection in the fulfilment of its purpose. He is completely lacking in subtlety and has utter contempt for social graces. I like him for that. He is... straightforward. As a weapon should be. I issue commands and he follows them. I direct him at a target and he destroys it. Sometimes it is so refreshing not having to worry about what one's minions might or might not be thinking or plotting. Warriors are so much easier to deploy and maintain. Sadly, though, most of my own schemes require rather more finesse than a blade slicing through a main artery. Most of them. I have not evolved so far that I cannot appreciate the occasional scarlet flash as an enemy dies on an edge of cold steel, as per my orders. There is something atavistically satisfying about it. Of course, seeing an enemy unravelled and ruined by a tangle of devious machinations can also be delightful. Nothing warms my heart like the depth of despair in the eyes of a foe when they realise that, for them at least, the game is over.

I am conscious, by the way, that there is an element of risk in assigning Octavius to training duties. He is a talented mentor who should instil the discipline that I require from my servants. But he can be rather... abrasive. I calculate that the risks involved in this outweigh the potential benefits. My latest recruit should now have the mental fortitude to endure his new, Spartan, regime. It will flay away childish notions and self-

absorption; it will help him to grasp that he is now a cog in a much bigger design; dwelling on personal pleasures or angst is a luxury that will no longer be available to him.

Sweat dripped from his brow, and he shook his head sharply in an effort to redirect it away from his eyes, for he needed to see the obstacles in his way.

"Faster!" barked the voice of his nemesis from somewhere behind him.

The boy pushed himself forward, leaping a spur of rock as it suddenly rose through the floor in front of him; he dodged to the left as a stalactite fell from the roof, as if perfectly timed and aimed to spear him. In the event, he was left with a slight gash on his right cheekbone.

Up ahead, a glowing blue orb marked his destination.

What would the old buzzard throw at him next?

The boy had come to expect unpleasant tactics in these relentless exercises, and hurled himself suddenly left; his hands seized upon a rocky outcrop and he flipped through the air before landing with gymnastic precision about five feet to the left of a boulder which had dropped out of nowhere. He continued to tumble in zig-zag motions for the last twelve feet, until finally the blue light enfolded him and he felt his physical aches and cuts melt magically away.

Mr Gray materialised, wraith-like, from the darkness beyond.

"Better," he remarked, rather grudgingly. "You are beginning to understand that obstacles and threats do not necessarily follow regular or predictable patterns. This may save your life at some point, if the lesson is truly embedded."

The boy slowly slicked his hair back, and cracked open one eye to look at him.

"It will be," he replied, "for I have no wish to quit this life just yet."

He knew instinctively that Gray responded best to bald statements of facts. He had no interest in expressions of emotion and contempt for puffed-up braggarts. The boy had assessed him quickly enough and had gradually fine-tuned the persona that his new tutor wanted him to have. He didn't know if the old man was conscious of his preferences, but the boy was, and he played to them. It was what his first tutor had taught him so well, and it was all part of the practice – in addition to the brutal physical regime which was now being inflicted upon him.

The current unpleasantness was designed to push his reactions and his speed. Mr Gray had designed this particular cavern himself: the very composition of its walls and floor could be shaped at will – or designed to generate random challenges. The boy was unsure whether the random fluctuations of the cavern itself – or the old man's calculated jabs – were worse. He suspected the latter.

At first, it had been a massacre. The boy had been cut to ribbons by flying shards of rock; several times he had lost consciousness in a blaze of mangled agony. The healing orbs had always repaired the damage, but the pain was very real.

And, it turned out, quite incentivising. Whilst the duck 'n' dodge exercises would not feature highly on his most pleasurable experiences list, there was no doubt that his reactions, both physical and mental, had been considerably sharpened as a result.

Mr Gray stood, still as a statue, until the blue orb finally dissipated and the boy was left healed and unscarred. Then he slowly moved forwards, in a fluid motion, like a dancer viewed at half speed.

"And now, boy, we will meditate."

He breathed deeply in and out. The boy had initially had to quell the urge to snigger at these horse-like gasps, but Mr Gray had simply reminded him that a good warrior tends to all of his weapons: and that the most important of these was the mind. So he joined in, practising the fluent sequence of movements as he had been taught and feeling all of the tension leeching out of him.

Adrenaline was a handy thing to have in a hairy situation, but the come-down left one feeling weak and shaky. This process helped to tame the more animal impulses of his part-human physiology.

After this was done, they ate a simple meal, before Mr Gray left him for half an hour with strict instructions to tend to his blades. The boy walked into his chamber and lifted up a box. It was made of beautiful wood, the grains rich and dark, but was unadorned by decoration. Very Mr Gray. Within, it was separated into two compartments: each was stuffed with a substance not unlike cotton wool. And each contained a slender knife, perfectly weighted and designed to inflict precise, surgical damage on any unlucky enough to be designated as a target.

The boy took out each knife in turn and felt them. Their weight was balanced; just as it should be. His fingers curled around the hilts, familiar now as the joystick which had served him on a games console in a past life. He practised a few ritualised movements with them, before turning to a second box. This contained a whetstone and oils and he spent the next twenty minutes carefully sharpening the blades before lovingly, sacredly, anointing them with oil. What had happened to him? A few months – or possibly years - ago, he had never so much as sliced a chicken breast in the kitchen – and here he was, cradling a pair of knives which had been designed specifically for him to use as weapons.

They were his. They had been made specifically for him by a master-craftsman. At least, that was what Mr Gray had told him. They seemed to fit his grip perfectly and they could slice through hair without even pulling at the roots. He knew: he'd tried it. His teacher had told him to name his weapons carefully, as it would help him to bond with them – and this was always a good thing for a warrior.

A warrior! Sometimes he wondered whether he had been struck with a blunt instrument and was actually lying comatose in a hospital somewhere – that all of this was simply going on in his head, as an extension of the sort of fiction he enjoyed.

But he had acceded to the request, naming his blades Pride and Fall, in part, at least, in homage to Yellow Rose, who had ever counselled against brash decision-making. Careful planning and a cool head were everything: something with which Mr Gray fully concurred, as it turned out. He had named them thus as a reminder not to get cocky: his life (apparently) depended on it!

At the appointed time, he rose from his humble pallet bed and returned to the cavern, where Mr Gray was already waiting for him and was limbering up in an ominous manner, stretching his shoulders, arms and legs. The boy knew to do likewise. They had a couple of minutes where they each prepared themselves, occasionally nodding amiably at one another like passing joggers in the park, before the sparring began.

Mr Gray was fast, despite his apparent age, and had two lethally sharp knives himself. The boy was forced to sway frantically this way and that to avoid a painful slashing: he had learnt the benefits of quick reflexes in this arena too. Of course, it helped if you could read your opponent and anticipate which way he was intending to strike – but Mr Gray was rarely so obliging as to give such helpful clues. He had been poked, sliced and bled in their numerous encounters: he was always healed, but the common thread remained that there was no teacher like pain.

The boy tried desperately to maintain a focus on the glittering blades being directed at various parts of his anatomy. Not so long ago, he would have been sliced up like so much pastrami, but since his emergence from the pod, not only had his body changed in terms of appearance, but also in its very make up. The boy had grown up with fast reflexes; he was good at catching things before they hit the floor; he could dart through a closing door or vault a fence. But now... now he was far faster than any human should be. Sometimes, when he really concentrated, it was as though Mr Gray seemed to slow down a little – just enough for him to anticipate his next move before it landed. The first time, this had happened almost by accident, leaving both himself and Mr Gray equally surprised.

"Interesting," mused his mentor, rubbing at his chin. "It seems that you are capable of a variety of battle trance. In some I have seen, this manifests as extreme strength, or preternaturally resistant skin. As per the berserkers that you may or may not have heard of. In you, however, it has produced an ability to move and operate at extreme velocity. If you can control it, you will have the chance of aiming for exceptional as opposed for good. Although," he continued, landing a swift-pointed jab to the boy's throat which had left him choking on the floor and gargling blood, "you have yet to attain the level of adequate."

The boy had not taken this personally. Mr Gray was indeed cold and unlovable, but he did not detect any malice in the man. He was like a savage predator, who struck, maimed and killed as driven by instinct or training – but he derived no pleasure from the process.

So, the latest bout continued, with each combatant swaying and moving like a ribbon of water, eyeing each other for threat and opportunity; darting at potential weak points; covering possible openings in their own defences.

They must have done this a hundred times or more and the boy, whilst conscious of his knives' names, sensed that the contests were much less one-sided now. Sometimes, it took Mr Gray more than a minute to poke a hole in his flesh. And on this occasion, more than a minute had passed, and they were still whirling around each other, probing for a weakness.

The boy cleared his mind and focused on the movement of Mr Gray's knives. They were bright sparks of deadly light in the gloom. He drew deeper on his breath, narrowly evading a slice to his face, but still not taking his eyes away from the blades.

Focus.

Focus.

For a moment, it was as though Yellow Rose was back in his head, like the first time they had experimented with his shape-shifting abilities.

Suddenly, something snapped into place. It was reminiscent of an optician sliding a different lens over one's eye whilst conducting a sight test. Everything beyond Mr Gray was filtered out into an indistinct background blur; the man himself was suddenly crystal clear, his white skin gleaming as he swung low and arced his left directly at the boy's stomach in what would have been a gutting manoeuvre. Slowly, inevitably, the blade made its inexorable journey.

Slowly!

It was as though Mr Gray was performing one of his meditative dances: his movements had been reduced in speed, possibly by half.

The boy allowed the arm to close to within a few centimetres, before he eased to one side and drove Fall straight through Mr Gray's right cheek. Milliseconds later, he felt an intense burst of pain which snuffed out his moment of triumph, as Mr Gray's right hand sliced neatly through the hamstring of his left leg.

Suddenly, the normal flow of time was restored, and both figures crashed heavily to the ground: the boy to his back and Mr Gray to his knees.

The old man's cheek was hanging open like a torn cloth; the boy could see his dull grey teeth and pink gums lying within, stained now by the blood which was dripping all over the floor from both the wound and his mouth. He gave a ghastly red smile – the first time the boy could ever remember seeing such an expression on his face. Through the bubbling blood, he chuckled.

"Never take your eye off the second blade: the first could all too easily be a feint."

Slowly he got up and a blue healing orb bloomed around them.

"Still, credit where it's due: you landed a blow on me, and there are few enough who can lay claim to that. A shame you wasted it on a superficial flesh wound rather than directing it at a mortal spot where it would have been a killing blow. That is your second lesson. Sometimes you will have only one shot: make it count or you will surely lose in a prolonged bout. You are designed for speed – for quick strikes, boy. So be quick. Aim to kill in a single blow, before your opponent has the time or will to collect themselves and muster a defence."

As the agony in his leg subsided, the boy nodded.

"Yes teacher. Next time, I'll aim for the throat."

Mr Gray gave him a look, as though trying to ascertain whether or not he was being flippant. Finally he gave a curt nod.

"Yes. Preferably in the location of a main artery. But for now, we shall have a little break from our dances. I think it high time you cut your teeth on something a little less warm and forgiving than me."

The boy raised his eyebrow at this. Of all the things he had learnt about Mr Gray, never once had he suspected that there might be a sense of humour somewhere in the man. Perhaps he should re-evaluate.

Rising smoothly to his feet, he bowed low.

"I will be guided, as ever, by what you deem best, teacher," he intoned, solemnly.

"Good. Then there is yet hope that you might survive your first week in the field."

In the field...

The boy bit his tongue. Patience is a virtue. All would be revealed to him soon enough.

Chapter 23
Dress Rehearsal

I tend to be a 'glass half empty' person: always expect the worst; it's easier to avoid disappointment that way! However, on this occasion, I am having to restrain certain feelings that can only be described as optimistic! This boy, so very uninspiring to look at, has, thus far, excelled all expectations. Of course, there is still time for him to fail and disappoint, but current indications are that he will prove to be a vassal of quite exceptional aptitude. Both of his tutors speak highly of him and vouch for his skill and ability to think on his feet. It is beginning to look as though my throw of the dice back in the hatchery, when I gambled his very life on a dramatic outcome, has come off nicely.

Sometimes, one simply has to take risks. I don't like the fact, as I have certain control issues and I dislike variables... but there you go. Not everything can be accounted and planned for. Most things, but not all. Hence my little prodigy.

Soon it will be time to put him to the test back in his own world. But first, he must survive Mr Gray's pre-release trials. Think of it as a kind of quality control.

I do hope that he succeeds. If he perishes at this stage, I shall be positively irked.

I will have to root for him from the shadows.

The boy stilled his mind and took several, controlled breaths as he awaited his next test. All that Mr Gray would tell him was that this was a 'live test.' He wasn't quite sure what he had meant by this, but he certainly had a bad feeling about it.

The cavern had morphed itself into an eerie maze of twisting passages, framed by walls varying in height from five to seven feet. The light was a mournful deep red. He moved slowly, cautiously forward, his senses straining to pick up anything that might warn him of an approach.

He didn't know who or what he was up against; he had no idea what to expect, except that he must survive. Mr Gray would give him no more information than that, saying that he would have no warnings when facing dangerous enemies in the future. He had been trained to use his body's skills to their full extent. This would be challenging, as his opponent knew this was a fight to the death too. It was as it should be.

The boy smiled grimly. Once he would have been a quivering jelly of fear by now. Back in another existence. As it was, he felt only a slow-burning hunger for life. He *would* survive all of their petty traps and games; he had gone through too much to fail now.

With infinite care, he inched himself forward to a corner before leaning out very slightly to look for any sign of movement. As he did so, he heard a faint hiss behind him. Instinctively, he somersaulted away to the left, landing on his feet and drawing his knives almost simultaneously. A figure was crouched on the top of the passage wall. It looked humanoid, but in this dim light it was hard to tell. A knife had thudded into the rock wall where a second ago he had been standing. Had he still been there, it would have taken him just below his neck. Now, it had skittered harmlessly onto the floor, having bounced ineffectually from the stone. It lay glinting ominously in the dark red light. He heard what sounded like a sharp exhalation of breath and sensed the irritation therein.

Smiling as provocatively as he could, he sketched a slight bow, whilst maintaining a visual connection, and gestured to the fallen dagger.

"Please do come and retrieve your weapon," he called, in an eminently reasonable tone of voice. "I'd hate to put you at a disadvantage."

The figure vaulted lithely down, the light glinting from a second blade.

"Talking, talking... always full of chatter and lying words," snarled a raspy feminine voice. "I do not need two knives to gut you and wear your face!"

She advanced towards him, and his heart almost faltered when she moved out into the passageway, offering him as clear a view as he was likely to get in this poor light. She was a similar height and build to him; her skin was darker, though, and bore spirals of dots around the cheekbones and the eyes. For a second he quailed inwardly, for it was the huntress from his dreams, come for him: this time when he was awake. Wasn't he? And wasn't she?

Perhaps and perhaps not.

After a brief spasm, he noted slight differences. This was not the same girl who had hunted him in his dreams – although she looked very similar. They were clearly of the same tribe... or species... or whatever these beings called themselves.

He yawned nonchalantly.

"Well if you're going to do all that, I wish you'd get on with it. I've got important business to attend to when I've finished with you, Kitty."

Straight from Yellow Rose's lessons that one: psychology is a weapon. Words can be used to charm or enrage. And anger is a dangerous thing to allow in a fight. But would it work?

Yes!

There was another hiss of rage.

"Arrogant fool! You do not realise that you are prey! But I shall teach you humility as I take the skin from your carcass!"

"Yes, yes, well don't let me keep you from your affairs. I must say, if you spend as much time as this talking to everything you hunt, I'm surprised that you catch anything at all. Unless you lull them into a stupor with the dreariness of your conversation. What do they call you? The queen of chatter? The huntress of a decent conversation?"

At the same time, he made a show of looking at his fingernails and taking his eyes off her, anticipating that this might lure her in.

It did: almost a little too well, if truth be told! She was on him in a second, a clawed hand raking at his face whilst the knife swept low to gut him. My, she was fast! Surely as fast even as the old man. It took all of his training to twist like a contortionist and avoid both blows. Her breath was hot and foetid in his face; her eyes were almost black, so big were her pupils, and her scarlet mouth was open in a savage cry of rage. He was not in a position, unfortunately, to land a mortal blow, so he had to content himself with a swift slash across her face before leaping back to face her. Crimson blood welled down her cheek, and, as he had hoped, it seemed to enrage her further.

"Sorry about that!" he sang, blithely.

"Stop… talking!"

With a shriek, she came at him again, all wild-eyed fury; he dodged this way and that, studying her moves. She seemed quite able to compensate for the absence of one of her daggers, thanks to those nasty talons, with which she repeatedly reached for him, hoping to trap or trip him, or to pull him close for a final embrace. She moved with a ferocious grace, but also relied a little too much, unless he was mistaken, on her instincts. Her attacks were feral rather than planned; she wanted to cut him up, and was trying her best to gratify this desire instantaneously – but there didn't seem to be a long-term plan.

In reality, only a few seconds had passed, but the boy felt his heart beat ominously like a drum, as he slowly entered his battle trance. Suddenly, he saw her moves as they were: savage; borne of rage and fear – and a desire to be free. A clawed hand whipped towards his chest, as if to seize his loose-fitting tunic, whilst she swung the blade wildly at his throat. Swaying slightly to his right, he dropped Pride and caught her furious hand using her own momentum to carry her forward; he felt her knife, thrown slightly off by his movement, slice up into the bottom of his jawbone. It did occur to him that her weapon might be poisoned, but he calculated that this was unlikely – both for her as a hunter and Mr Gray, who would probably insist on a level playing field. Either way, that sudden sparking of pain up his cheek from his jaw had bought him the opportunity to pull her close into an embrace of his own, whilst simultaneously sliding Fall up through her armpit, slicing through her heart and lung.

All the fight left her at once, as she sagged against him.

He felt her hot blood gushing forth, running down their bodies as they pressed together, almost like lovers. He watched as the fierce light in her eyes flickered and went out, and the life left her. It had all happened so quickly, she had barely had the time to register what had happened. He let her fall to the ground.

"It's over," he whispered, and he wasn't sure whether he was addressing this to her or himself.

He wasn't even sure whether she was real, or just another of Mr Gray's clever simulations.

A dull rumble preceded the cavern reshaping itself; the walls melted back down into the floor, making it as smooth as he had ever seen it.

He picked up his fallen knife and cleaned the other on the dead girl's tunic. If he felt anything at all, he had carefully repressed it. As he checked his weapons, a blue sphere enveloped him, and he felt the burning pain from his face disappear. The sphere had no effect on his fallen adversary, though: she remained undeniably dead.

He checked his weapons, and when he was satisfied, he sheathed them.

When he looked up, Mr Gray was standing in front of him as he had known he would be.

The old man nodded.

"Good. You were able to deploy a variety of tactics to defeat your opponent. And that was no easy matter, for she was born a killer. I did wonder if she would catch you out with her little ambush, but you were able to rise to the challenge. Well done. You have passed your final test."

"Do I get a certificate?" enquired the boy, drily.

"No!" rasped another voice behind him, dry and yet dripping with meaning. "You are granted the pleasure of entering my tender service."

He felt the hairs rise on the back of his neck.

So: it was time. The Pale Lady had come to collect.

Mr Gray had gone down on one knee, like an old knight from a storybook, so the boy turned to face her and did the same.

"It will be my honour to serve you, great lady," he intoned, and almost sounded credible.

She chortled at him.

"Heh! Do not worry about such things as courtly manners: they are one thing which I shall never expect of you. Only that your life be bound to serve the good of my realm."

And then, her long, insectile fingers were caressing his cheek, until one slid under his jaw and raised his head up from staring determinedly at the ground. He forced himself to look once more into that hideous visage.

The matted green-black hair was piled up under what looked like an elaborate bone crest, and her eyes were impossibly and unfathomably wide and black. There was not a spark of humanity to be seen; they were utterly alien. He met her gaze nonetheless, determined not to show any fear.

"I will do all that you ask of me, Lady." He could think of nothing else to say.

"Ah! The speech of a well-taught child is always pleasing to the ears. You are indeed a credit to your tutors!"

Then she leaned down a little closer, forcing even him to flinch.

"And you're quite right. You will indeed follow my orders to the letter. Now, come with me, sweetling, for there is much to discuss."

Chapter 24
Baptism

He made it, then. All of the obstacles thrown in his way and he overcame them – with a fairly significant amount of input from his tutors, and, indirectly, of course, myself. Credit where it's due, after all. Now, finally, he is ready for use. My new, shiny weapon! How I'm looking forward to trying him out!

But first, there are a few formalities that must be attended to. As Mr Gray observed, it is good practice to give one's weapons a name. In this case, as the weapon is sentient, the name is more for his benefit than mine. It will help to reinforce his new identity and function. I will also choose his name, as is the owner's privilege; it helps to make the line of command very explicit, I find.

Then there will be a couple of, shall we say, housekeeping points, before I reintroduce him back to his native plane of existence. Let's not lose sight of the fact that he will no longer be a native, though: ironic, really, isn't it? I'm afraid he is no longer human, not by any definition – although, to be fair, he never was, technically, thanks to my advanced breeding programme. One has to laugh, when one thinks about it: all of those people wandering around, completely certain that they're human when in actuality, they are a hybrid – or something else entirely. But that's another story: one that you'll become acquainted with in good time.

Well, enough talk: it's time to move things along to the final phase.

The boy stood awkwardly. He had been directed now to a crystalline chamber and was bathed in soft, damask light. It was both pleasant and strange. He looked around at the geometric patterns of the crystal: it was all perfectly regular in shape, so that he felt like he was standing inside a professionally cut gem. After a time, he decided to sit cross legged on the cold floor and meditate. It was something that Mr Gray had taught him in order to ensure a clear mind: nothing worse than internal mental clutter when you have a job to be getting on with – especially if making a mistake on that job could cost you your life.

He remained in this position for some time, before he felt a presence enter the glittering cell. He opened his eyes to find the

Pale Lady and a young girl appraising him, as one might an unusual creature in a zoo. The girl was finely featured and clearly inhuman: her hair was a lustrous vermilion colour; her eyes were entirely black and when she smiled at him, her teeth were pointed, like a cat's. She appeared to be carrying a bundle of clothes, which she now deposited on the ground at his feet.

"Leave us," rasped the Pale Lady – and she did, after shooting him another quick, curious look. A section of the crystal wall suddenly shimmered, becoming both opaque and entirely reflective – like a mirror, in fact. The girl stepped into this and instantly vanished from sight.

The boy stared for a moment, unable to hide his interest – or to repress his Grandmother's story.

He found his new mistress regarding him, impassively.

"Well?" she croaked.

"It's a portal. You can use mirrors as portals, can't you?"

She emitted a noise somewhere between a snort and a phlegmy cough. Her long, sinuous hand flicked dismissively.

"Space is easy enough to bend and shape, if you know how."

He continued to look at her, his face a shining plate of innocence and wonder.

"Stop that," she snapped. "We have things to discuss. Come closer, boy."

The boy jumped nimbly to his feet and moved closer as he was bid. A hand shot forward to seize his chin. He could feel the bristles on the end of her fingertips. He did not flinch this time, although those hands reminded him of some sort of deep-sea creature. Something nasty and white which has lived forever in darkness.

The Pale Lady seemed to have reached a decision as she looked him up and down. He still used the amended form that he had first conjured all those months ago under Yellow Rose's astonished eye. He looked like the sort of boy who gets made into a cut-out in high-street clothes shops in order to model the merchandise.

"No." she decreed. "This won't do. I need you to blend in. This form is too attractive to your kind – it will get you noticed. Do not use it when you are performing your duties for me, unless it is directly relevant to the fulfilment of an objective."

Her fingers dug into his face slightly, and he felt something pulse through him, like he was being flushed, all of a sudden, with a wave of toxins. She released him quickly, to allow him to retch, before his body convulsed into a series of painful muscular spasms. Shaking, he looked down to find that his hands looked somewhat smaller. Tentatively, he felt his face. Smooth, delicate, unremarkable features – and he knew that he had reverted back to his original human appearance.

"It's one of the things I liked about you," she went on. "The sheer mediocrity of your visage. No one is going to look at you twice: you are neither hideously malformed nor are you excessively beautiful. You will find, in your future line of work, that the ability to camouflage yourself and avoid attention is something which you will be glad of."

The boy ground his teeth and blinked a couple of tears from his eyes. The waves of pain left him feeling weak.

"You could have just asked me to change back," he hissed, clutching at his sides.

"Yes, but where's the fun in that?"

He glanced up at her, a retort forming on his lips which he immediately snuffed out. He must remember that this creature was without compassion; she was alien and utterly ruthless. He winced again as another wave of painful cramps swept through him. This was just a taste of what she could do, of that he was sure.

"My Lady," he gasped again, when his muscles had stopped rippling around inside him. He bowed and went down on one knee, the traditional posture of submission.

"Hmmm, perhaps I wasn't entirely truthful when I told you earlier that there was no need for courtly manners. The lesson is simple enough to grasp: I require your loyalty. If I find that you need to be reminded of that at any point, I shall enjoy another demonstration. You may conduct your personal life as you see fit but you will obey the chain of command, boy, is that quite clear?"

"Completely," he affirmed, in a stronger voice, now that the pain seemed to have passed.

"Good. Now don these vestments. They have been fashioned in the contemporary style of your original world. You will find that they fit you perfectly."

A little smile here, and he knew that she had planned to fling him painfully back into his old body all along. He said nothing, though, and simply put on the clothes: undergarments, a pair of jeans, a plain T-shirt and a dark jacket.

When he was finished, a mirror suddenly appeared in the wall of the chamber again. He looked almost exactly as he had on the day he met Evan Greenway, except that he was a couple of years older and his hair was a little longer, and flopped down now over his face.

"That's better," observed the Pale Lady. "Pale and uninteresting. Your own mother might well overlook you if she passed you on the street."

He said nothing. If she hoped to elicit pain by mentioning his mother, she would have to be disappointed.

The surface of the mirror suddenly swirled, and there, in front of his astonished eyes, sat his mother. She appeared to have bought a new sofa and was engaged in an animated conversation with someone whom he couldn't see. There was no sound, but the boy looked on in fascination, despite himself. The woman, his mother, got up then and approached the surface of the mirror, until her face almost filled it. She appeared to be checking her hair. In truth, she did look different from the last time he saw her. She had lost weight and looked, if anything, a bit younger and like she had started to take a pride in her appearance.

Suddenly he realised.

"She got a new mirror."

Yes. It all made sense now: she had replaced the mirror in the lounge – the one that Carl had broken all of those years ago.

His mother laughed, silently. She looked happy. Then she turned from the looking glass and ran to hug someone who had just entered the frame – probably from the kitchen.

The boy's blood ran cold. It was him. Or at least, it clearly wasn't – but it certainly looked like him.

The new him looked happy – playful, even. He was grinning and said something to his mother that caused her to double up with laughter. He had grown somewhat and broadened; his hair was now cut to a smart, mainstream style and he looked eminently likeable. There was no trace of the surly mop-headed teenager.

He didn't bother to ask who the other boy was.

"Why are you showing me this?" he asked, in a quiet, bleak voice.

"To help you understand," breathed the Pale Lady, "just how inconsequential you are in the greater scheme of things. You see how easily you were replaced. She never even knew that you were missing. Now someone else is living your life and your mother is happier than she has been for years. Having a kind and attentive son, apparently, does wonders for you."

Alright. Correction. It turned out his mother was a weak spot, after all. That would explain why he abruptly felt like a crushed tin can. It wasn't so much that he found he loved his mother after all – it was more the idea that he was so vapid – so... completely lacking in personality that his own mother hadn't noticed he had been replaced by an imposter. Or maybe she had, and she preferred the new version. Actually, that thought made it even worse.

Well done, my Lady; bravo! You know just how to snuff out the last dying spark of self-worth that might have been clinging on in the gloom of the void.

Then the mirror disappeared, and he found himself suddenly in very close proximity to her face again. An inky tongue poked out, like a blind underground creature, and probed around her cracked, dark lips before withdrawing again. Her eyes were like receding pools of utter darkness which gazed now into his very soul.

"I consider my point made. Now, on to topics which matter. This chamber is… special," she whispered, as though confiding a secret to a lover.

He shuddered.

"It is completely sealed against any attempt to scry or spy on me. No one can possibly see or hear what goes on in here. I designed it myself. It pays to be paranoid around here, because they really are all out to get me." She laughed – or at least, that's what he thought she was doing – at this little jest. At any rate, a gurgling rasp made it way out of her throat, accompanied by several strands of thick-looking saliva.

"Now, my little love…" And at this, a hand appeared again, caressing his cheek in a most alarming manner. "It is time to give you a name – and a sense of purpose."

"I… had a name…" the boy ventured, before pausing and frowning in confusion. He looked up, quickly. "Didn't I?"

When he looked into his memory for it, he was bemused to find there was nothing there: his name had simply vanished from his mind like a deleted file.

"The entity which followed my servant here through the waypoint had a name. But he no longer exists. He died back in the hatchery – you emerged from his remains, like a beautiful, deadly wasp from a broken cocoon."

Here, her fingers stroked his chin, almost fondly.

"Your name, sweetling, is Byron Black, and you will bring death and dismay to my enemies."

"Byron Black..."

He tried the name out; tasted it. It seemed, somehow, to fit. He looked up at her again, before he could stop himself, like an eager pupil with a question for teacher.

"Alright. I like it. But why Byron Black?"

She tutted, and translucent lids, like those of a reptile, lowered briefly over her eyes, before flickering up again. He braced himself for another bout of pain, but realised that the grimace she now bore was one of amusement.

"They say there's no such thing as a bad question. But that's not always true, is it? Still, in this instance, I see no harm in answering your enquiry. Your first name you bear in honour of one of your most famous poets: a man whose genius was only equalled by his volatility. I liked his style: for a human, he was really rather interesting. Not that I want you to be excessively volatile, of course. That would lead to terrible pain on your part. I'm sure I don't need to worry on that score: I have taken great care to see that your training placed a cool and thoughtful head on those slim little shoulders."

He simply nodded in acknowledgement.

"And the second name?"

"Oh really!" she cried, in a warbling voice. "Surely you can work that one out for yourself!"

He regarded her levelly.

"Death. It's the colour of death, yes?"

"Ahhh! My beautiful boy, yes, yesss!"

She leaned even closer, and for one terrifying second he thought she might actually kiss him.

"You will be the bearer of the gift of death. You will bring it to all who seek my downfall. And none but you and I will truly know of your purpose and skills. That's why I'm meeting you here. Soon, I will send you back to the world you came from. You will come to know that my kind have insinuated themselves into the very fabric of human society. But none of them will be able to blend in like you, my sweet chameleon. How will they be able to guard against a foe when they have no idea what he looks like? You don't even have the aura: it was one of the first things I noticed about you!"

"What aura?" he asked, in a faint voice.

"My kind always emit an aura - a kind of energy field. It tends to be more noticeable in relation to the power of the individual. Of course, the foolish humans are largely oblivious to it – unless they have a drop or two of Other blood in their veins. But my kind can sense it easily enough: it makes us stand out to one another as though we were haloed in unholy light. I may tell you that you are not the only one in my service who can change form, but your lack of an aura is, as far as I'm aware, unique"

As she spoke, a smile crept, slug-like, across her face, exposing green-tinged teeth.

"No. For some reason, you have no aura at all. Even I can barely sense you when you're standing next to me. That's why I decided to risk a throw of the dice – to expose you to the maximum power of the stimulus crystals in the hatchery. And I was right. The gamble paid off!"

Here, the boy, Byron, noticed that she had gripped his arm in an iron hold; lost in thought, her voice rose in triumph, screeching like a witch over her cauldron.

Her eyes rounded out like side-plates; it was most discomfiting.

"You," she growled, in a low, breathy voice, "are a stealth weapon, my love. *My* stealth weapon. They cannot sense your presence – and they won't know you're even there until the knife is at their throat. You are the piece that I have sought for many a year – the asset which could tip the scales in my favour"

Then she relaxed, releasing his bruised arm and stepping back to smile in a joyful reverie.

"You will bring death to my enemies, child, and there's nothing that they can do to prevent it."

He stood, gazing at her, his face as inscrutable as it ever was.

"Yes, my lady."

Chapter 25
Going Home

He has been forged in the fires of my ambition and quenched in cold malice. Now he is going back through the looking-glass – back to the world of the mundane humans. There I will assign him to the care of my major-domo: a man almost as tender-hearted as I am. A touch affected – even pompous, one might say – but he is scrupulously loyal to me and he gets results. Now that's the important thing!

He will need to keep a close eye on my new pet: he is precious to me and will need careful management as he acclimatises to his new role. Training aside, cold, harsh, dangerous reality is something altogether different...

What is it they say in your military speak? This is not a drill!

And so it was that Byron Black found himself standing on windswept urban street on a dour autumnal afternoon. Faint rain hissed down on him and he squinted bleakly at the house numbers in front of him.

Number 194 Berkley Road.

This was the address he had been given, shortly after leaving the tender mercies of the Pale Lady. It had been somewhere between surreal and anticlimactic in the end. Back in her spy-proof crystal chamber, a mirror had appeared. In it, though, he saw not his reflection, but a rather dingy-looking parlour, with faded floral wallpaper and a scruffy high-backed armchair in which an old woman apparently dozed in front of a television set.

"Step through, sweetling," purred the Pale Lady: so he did. He walked towards the mirror and felt a faint sensation, like static electricity and the fluttering you get in your stomach when a car drives fast down a sudden hill. Next thing he was there – in the old lady's room. And it was suddenly not just an image, but a real, living scene as his other senses kicked in: the blaring of a quiz show on the TV; the smell of lavender and, just beneath, of human sweat. He stood frozen for a moment, gawping around. After several months being held in a selection of subterranean chambers, it seemed bizarre to find himself once more in a mundane, earthly setting.

The old lady smacked her lips and then her eyes shot open. They were a bright china blue, and sat gleaming with a preternatural shrewdness in her wrinkled face.

"Ah. You must be the new boy," she stated, rather than enquired. "I've been expecting you."

She gestured towards a second armchair set parallel to hers.

"Please. Take a seat."

Her voice, like her eyes, were at odds with the impression created by the room and her own appearance: rumpled clothes with a faint air of neglect; greasy unkempt hair. The voice, though, was not at all feeble, but rich and strong, like old wine. He knew, almost instantly, that she wasn't human: she was one of them. Well, strictly speaking, he supposed that should now be one of *us*, as much as he resented it. An Other. He could sense her energy, wrapped around her in coldly shimmering ribbons.

He sat, as directed and stared blandly at her, with the suggestion of a smile on his face.

"Ooh, I can see why you've got her all excited," chuckled his hostess. "No aura at all. Just look at you, sitting there all sweet and innocent like a choirboy. No one would ever suspect that you're a trained killer, would they? Here, have a custard cream."

She waved at a small flowery plate containing biscuits.

"No thanks. The Pale Lady told me that you would instruct me how to proceed from here."

"To the point, eh? How very male you are." She grinned at him with even white teeth.

"Alright then. You're to make your way to the city centre. There, you should look for a house on Berkley Street. Number 194. Here's a street map to help you."

The boy took the proffered map without comment; his brows furrowed briefly.

"Is that where my target is?"

This produced a gale of laughter.

"Oh no, my dear, funny though it would be to tell you otherwise. That is where you'll find your Handler, Mr Golden."

"So you're not…"

"Little old me? Oh no, dear, I'm just here to greet the new arrivals and send them on their way."

He was fairly sure there was a lot more to her than that, but he simply nodded. He was already scanning the map and soon found the street in question.

"OK. Found it. Do you have anything else for me, or is that it?"

He began to rise from the chair as he spoke.

She looked at him, narrowly for a second.

"Just… watch yourself around Mr Golden. He is a man of… unusual tastes and temperament."

He returned her look sharply, trying to assess the layers of possible meaning in her words. Finally, he nodded.

"Will do, ma'am," and he allowed a smile to flicker briefly across his face, before walking briskly to the door, which led directly out onto the street.

She gazed after him for a moment or two before her lips formed a thin smile.

"Ah, the impetuosity of youth. Well, don't say I didn't warn you."

Thus it was that, in less than an hour, he found himself standing outside the property in question. Berkley Street was a genteel row of Georgian villas, built just outside the city centre itself.

194 was smartly painted and shielded from the road, he noted, by a well-trimmed hedge and closed curtains.

Someone doesn't like to be seen…

Well, that much was self-evident. It would take more than a bit of laurel and some elegant drapes to keep out the sort of prying that should most be feared, though, he observed drily. He wondered if there were any mirrors inside – and, if there were, whether they had been placed behind some miniature curtains.

Byron smiled to himself for a moment before sidling up the path and ringing the bell.

"Who is calling, please?" came a refined English accent over an intercom.

"Byron Black," he replied, without any further elaboration.

A brief pause, as if waiting for further information, and then a prim announcement.

"One moment please, my assistant will be there to greet you shortly.

The boy remained where he was and could hear bolts snicking across, followed by a well-oiled locking mechanism. The door slid smoothly open and he found himself regarding a young man, probably not a great deal older than himself. He was a little taller, but also had black hair, albeit, slicked back across his head. His features were very fine, with high, arching cheekbones and his skin was sallow and without blemish. His eyes were the colour of amber. The two exchanged measuring glances for a few moments, and Byron felt… something – some sort of internal prickling of energy of the kind he hadn't experienced for some time… some sort of connection, albeit fleeting. His opposite number blinked once, twice and he was sure that he had felt it too.

He composed himself quickly enough, however, and broke the silence.

"Hello, Mr Black. I'm Zaffre. If you'll please follow me, I'll take you to the master."

His voice was surprisingly soft, with a hint of expression he found it hard to place – resignation? Something stronger?

Zaffre gestured for him to enter a beautifully tiled hallway before closing and securing the formidable-looking door. He then gave Byron a significant look before walking down the corridor to a grand set of dark-wood stairs. He wore very expensive, shiny black shoes that made a smart noise on the tiles. He was dressed in a pristine white shirt and a close-fitting black suit. A dark blue tie completed the ensemble.

As they ascended the stairs, Byron spoke quietly to his straight back.

"So… you're Mr Golden's assistant?"

A very slight pause, followed.

"Yes. I have that privilege."

His voice was so expressionless, that Byron was sure he was hiding something. He also noted that Zaffre had no discernible aura.

Are you a mere human?

He couldn't help but wonder. He supposed the Others must have to make use of mundane humans as servants from time to time.

But that was all he had time for: they had arrived outside a polished wooden door, upon which Zaffre rapped three times.

"Enter." The voice which spoke was as rich and warm as poured syrup. Zaffre responded by opening the door and stepping smartly to one side, so that Byron could pass him. He did so without any hesitation; the assistant promptly withdrew, shutting the door almost silently behind him, and the visitor found himself in a large, well-appointed room that could quite easily have belonged to a nineteenth century gentleman. Well, apart from the troll... Or whatever it was. A hulking figure, at least seven feet tall, loomed over him. It was probably male, and had been crammed into a suit, although it sat rather less well on him than Zaffre. Its brow was corrugated and large teeth jutted up from his lower jaw. A hand the size of Byron's head descended to rest on his shoulder. It was surprisingly gentle, but the sense of threat was heavy in its restraint. The movement was accompanied by a loud electronic squealing sound, and Byron noticed that, rather incongruously, there was some sort of ultra-modern metal frame through which he had to walk – like one of those security scanners at the airport.

"If you would be so kind as to hand your weapons over to Vodrun," came the syrupy voice again. Byron took the risk of peeping around his over-sized welcoming committee to see a man of indeterminate middle-age sitting at a very large and beautiful wooden desk. His long hair was the colour of wheat and appeared to be tied at the nape of his neck by a black ribbon. He was wearing an immaculate if somewhat outmoded suit which had been cut from a very dark blue cloth. Byron noticed that the jacket had a sort of sheen to it which rather reminded him of a male peacock. He was very handsome in a classical period drama sort of way.

"I believe that you specialise in the use of knives. I take it they are concealed by some artifice or other about your person?" He flashed a gleaming smile at his visitor. "If you pass them to my security operative, then we can get down to business. Don't mind my caution: I like to take particular care when assassins come to call."

I haven't even killed anyone yet... he thought to himself. *Well, except for the girl with the pointy teeth. And she doesn't really count. Does she?*

He realised that, for the first time he had actually touched upon the moral and ethical considerations of what he had been engaged to do. Would he actually be able to go through with it? Actually killing people?

For a moment, he felt he was having an out-of-body experience, but then he was forced to focus by a cough from Vodrun the troll – or whatever he was. Well, some sort of deep, resonating vibration: it could have been a cough – or even a growl. Either way, he reached into his jacket and withdrew his knives from the hidden pockets sewn within the lining. He passed them obediently to the craggy sentinel.

"Thank you, Vodrun. Please wait outside and return the knives to Mr Black when he leaves."

The creature stepped sideways through the door and took Byron's weapons with him. The boy directed his gaze towards his host.

"You see," declared Mr Golden, in a ringing voice, pointing at the metal scanner, "although humans tend towards the uninspiring, one should always keep an open mind in terms of their technologies. Now please, do take a seat."

Byron stepped carefully up to the desk, taking in his surroundings as he did so. The room was tastefully decorated with a deep red, patterned wallpaper. Dark-wood books cases lined one wall and there was a large marble fireplace set into the wall opposite the windows: tall Georgian windows which were currently covered by heavy red drapes. A pair of cream armchairs were placed in front of the fire with an elegant round table set in between them. There was a large gilt-edged mirror hanging over the mantelpiece and somewhat to the left was a beautiful old wooden sideboard: it had some kind of lace overlay and a number of bottles and decanters, not to mention a tray of crystal glasses, were artfully arranged on it.

Byron took the proffered seat on the other side of the desk and found himself face-to-face with his new... what had they called him? Handler?

Mr Golden's eyes were blue with flecks of gold around the edges. They were gleaming with quiet amusement and his mouth was set at a very slight curve, emphasizing the expression. He extended a hand over the polished desk top.

"A pleasure to finally make your acquaintance, Mr Black. I am, of course, Henry Golden"

Byron shook it noncommittally.

"Hello, Mr Golden," he replied.

They weighed each other up for a few moments more.

Byron could not but notice the neatness of Mr Golden's desk. To the man's left sat a large, leather-bound book. To his right, an elegant fountain pen in its own holder (do people really still have those?!) a glass pot containing ink (an inkpot?) and a pad of strange looking paper which looked rather too thick and fluffy to write on – notwithstanding the fact that it already had a number of inky spots on it. On top of the pad sat a strange object rather like a library book stamper, but with a curved base rather than a flat one. Finally, just to the right of that, reposed an old-fashioned black telephone with a rotary dial. He recognised it as such as his Grandmother had only recently upgraded her own telecommunications to a push button phone.

"Ah! What a closed book we have here!" chuckled Mr Golden after a few moments. "How very silent and wan, you are, Mr Black. I find myself quite intrigued already. Come: let's sit by the fire and toast our new relationship. You must have questions that you'd like to ask?"

Here, Mr Golden rose from his chair, gesturing to the armchairs at the fireplace.

After the briefest of pauses, Byron did likewise. He was slightly surprised to find Mr Golden stepping around his desk before linking arms and guiding him across the room. It felt... uncomfortable.

"Please: sit. I'll get us a little snifter and we'll get down to business."

Byron took the seat at which he had been deposited and found himself gazing up at the mirror. He wondered who might be watching through that mirror: given its position, it was unlikely to be one of the Pale Lady's enemies. He wondered, momentarily, how that worked. Did the Others do a line in secure mirrors? The thought briefly entertained him, but the truth was, he was looking forward to leaving this place – even if it was for the purpose of bumping off some hapless foe of his wicked mistress.

Mr Golden returned a moment later, with two small crystal glasses, each containing a thick, red liquid. He could smell the alcohol rising from it.

"Chin chin!" cried Mr Golden, clinking his glass against the side of Byron's. He proceeded to take a refined sip, his head bobbing in friendly confirmation. "Do try it: it's an old and wonderful vintage!"

Byron sighed inwardly. He did not want to try it. He had no desire to be drunk under the table by Mr Golden: he did not think that would end very well. Still, this was, in effect, his new boss, and so he took a small sip himself. It didn't taste as bad as he thought it was. The liquid was thick and warm as it trickled down his throat. It left him feeling pleasantly heated within. He was sure that it must be very strong stuff! He took a second sip and was rewarded by a glorious smile from his host.

As he went to take a third sip, though, he became aware that he was struggling to lift his hand. Mr Golden moved with surprising speed to relieve him of his glass.

"Allow me!" he gushed, "we really don't want any unpleasant stains on my carpet: it was hand-made, you know!"

Byron blinked a couple of times, and tried, experimentally, to stand. He found that he could barely move his hands to the sides of the armchair, let alone push himself up.

"You are undoubtedly a clever and resourceful boy," interjected Mr Golden, "and you will work out fairly quickly that you have been drugged. There are a few ground rules that I wish to establish with you, and, because you are clever and resourceful, I have taken the precaution of immobilising you. Do not worry: the substance will wear off in an hour or so and has no long-term effect. It simply paralyses your muscular system, in effect making it impossible for you to move."

As he spoke, Mr Golden returned to his desk. He took a bunch of keys from his pocket, one of which he used to open a drawer in his desk. He removed what looked like a miniature leather briefcase, with which he walked over to the armchair.

Although his body was frozen, Byron's mind was anything but: it whizzed with frantic activity as he tried to think of a way out of this predicament. Whatever he tried simply fizzled out before it started: it was as though the signals from his brain had been cut off from the rest of his body. He tried to force himself into a more relaxed state; to remember the meditation exercises that Mr Gray had taught him. Be logical. He was – by all accounts – a prized asset to the Pale Lady. It was highly unlikely that her regional commander would seek to damage or destroy him before he could even be used. This was something else: something that he was becoming accustomed to in the higher ranks of the Others' organisation. This was some sort of proving ground – possibly a test – certainly a way of establishing absolute authority and obedience.

This was certainly a comfort in a rational sense: he doubted very much that he was going to die. However, there was a fair chance that this – whatever it was – situation would be... unpleasant. This sense of foreboding was rapidly sharpened when Mr Golden deftly relieved him of his jacket and then his shirt, leaving him exposed from the waist up, his pale skin gleaming in its vulnerability.

"You know," observed Mr Golden, as he clicked open his little briefcase, "you really are quite a pretty boy. I really do hope that I don't have to spoil that." He gave an encouraging smile, like a dentist about to conduct a scale and polish, before producing a fabric band containing a variety of slender, pointy metallic objects.

"You're probably wondering what I'm going to do to you. I can assure you that these objects are every bit as unpleasant as they look. You see, the infliction of pain is something of a hobby of mine. We all have our little peccadilloes, no? I have studied many works on the subject of torture, and I have come to realise that it is something of an art form. A true master, you see, would never truly damage the subject – at least, not physically. No. That would be the crude blunderings of some common thug. I have spent many years practising on too many subjects to count and I have reached a level of expertise which would be the envy of petty human dictators around the world. The true attainment of skill in this area lies, rather, in maximising the pain whilst minimising physical harm."

And with that, he inserted a long steel pin into the boy's ribs.

Had he been able to, Byron would have screamed: the pain was incredible.

"I'm rather proud of my narcotic formula, by the way, for whilst it paralyses the muscles, it leaves the nervous system quite intact, so that every little bit of pain can be reported back. The pin I just inserted, incidentally, has not made any contact with internal organs. It has been precisely placed so that it pierces a nerve centre. Clever, eh?"

Mr Golden looked very pleased with himself, and beamed at his prone victim.

"You'll have heard of acupuncture. I suppose you could say that this is its less benign cousin. The pins are placed precisely to cause immense pain and suffering. This will continue until they are withdrawn. See!"

And with that, he slid another long pin into the flesh at the base of Byron's neck.

Another exquisite torrent of pain swept through him. He was aware of tears forming in his eyes and then rolling down his frozen cheeks.

Mr Golden was right: the pain did not subside after the initial penetration: it was held at a constant, awful level.

A third pin, and then a fourth were added, and then his tormentor stepped back, eyeing him critically, like an artist checking the perspective on a landscape. Apparently satisfied, he returned to the side board and poured himself a large glass of red liqueur, which he sat and drank in the opposite armchair, whilst perusing a large newspaper. He gave Byron not a second glance, until somewhere a clock gave a musical chime. Then, in what could only be described as a leisurely manner, Mr Golden rose from his seat. He carefully folded the newspaper and placed it and the empty glass on the round table. Then, he strolled over and carefully removed the pins from Byron's body. The relief, as each was withdrawn, was hard to exaggerate.

"This was just a little demonstration, by the way. To show you what awaits you if I become displeased with your performance – or indeed your attitude. Shortly, you will feel the sedative wearing off. You may even harbour some resentment towards me. I urge you to quell it. If you follow orders meticulously, you will have nothing to fear. If you disappoint me, I promise you a far more rigorous procedure than this one –which, by the way, barely qualifies as a warm-up."

With that, Mr Golden placed Byron's jacket and T-shirt, both of which had been carefully folded, on his knees, before sitting down once more.

"Please speak when you can. There is no point in my beginning the briefing until you are fully functional and able to ask pertinent questions."

There was a crackle as the newspaper was taken up once more, and then Byron was left to feel his limbs gradually thawing out, with an intense feeling of pins-and-needles. He wiggled his fingers experimentally; he felt stiff, as if he had just completed a particularly punishing work-out, but his feelings were restored to him. He waited until he had complete control again before replacing his clothes. Then, having settled his breath into a steady rhythm, he spoke.

"Alright, I'm ready to hear the briefing now."

"Ah, splendid," beamed Mr Golden, looking up from his newspaper as though he had run into an old friend on the train.

"The target's name is Johan Kessel. He lives in a high-rise block in one of the more insalubrious suburbs. He runs a variety of... irritating operations from his apartment. You are to eliminate him quickly and quietly. He is of middle age and somewhat overweight, but do not be over-confident. He is probably armed and is quite happy to resort to brute violence when the occasion presents itself. How you gain access is entirely up to you. But don't mess this up, or I shall be unhappy. And we wouldn't want that, would we?"

Another bright smile followed, and Byron gave an involuntary shudder at the thought of Mr Golden feeling unhappiness towards him.

"Now, if that is all clear, we shall return to the desk."

They did so, Byron slightly shakily, although he tried his best to hide it. If Mr Golden noticed, he didn't say anything. They took their respective seats. Then, another desk drawer was unlocked and a large buff envelope was removed.

"This contains all of the details for the matter in hand. You will please sign for it in my ledger of operations. I like to run a tight ship here, you know. Some people call me old fashioned, but there's nothing quite the same as a freshly inked signature when it comes to acknowledging receipt of orders. Digital just doesn't quite do it for me. *My* records will certainly never be lost due to a systems crash!"

With another delightful smile, Mr Golden opened his large ledger at a pre-marked page. There Byron observed the date and an immaculately written summary of the mission's objectives as issued and information pack.

Mr Golden passed him the beautiful fountain pen. It felt cool and heavy, as though made from ebony.

"Please sign and date here," he ordered, indicating with his finger.

The boy did so. Mr Golden then picked up the curved library stamper and rolled it expertly over the wet signature.

"Very good," he nodded, as he retrieved his pen to counter sign and date the entry. He then picked up his telephone receiver and dialled a single digit. "Come, please."

A few seconds later, there was a muted knock at the door.

"Come in, Zaffre."

The door swung open, and the slimly elegant assistant reappeared.

"Oh, one other thing," added Mr Golden, casually. "Mr Kessel will have at least one laptop in his possession. Please bring it here, if you would, so that we can analyse its contents. There's a good chap. Now, Zaffre, please show Mr Black out. And make sure he collects his knives from Vodrun – I've a feeling he may be needing them!"

And that was it: they were dismissed with a slight inflection of his beautifully manicured fingers. Funny the sort of details you sometimes notice- or miss.

The two young men left Mr Golden's study. Byron was reunited with Pride and Fall from the formidable guard, who was stationed like a piece of grotesque sculpture out on the landing now. When they reached the bottom of the stairs, Zaffre turned and looked at him. It was a glance heavy with meaning, and possibly a touch of sympathy, but that might have been Byron projecting what he felt ought to be there.

"I'm glad to see that Mr Golden seems to approve of you," he murmured in a low voice. "I trust you will return to us safely."

Byron allowed himself a half-smile at this.

"Thanks for your concern. Your master is an... interesting character. I'll do my best to get back here with the laptop."

On an impulse, he stuck out his hand. Zaffre's lips moved almost imperceptibly, and he took it in his own long, pale hand. But instead of shaking it, he gave it a slight squeeze.

"Be careful, Mr Black. This world is full of monsters."

He nodded in acknowledgement and stepped back outside.

He had his target. Would he now graduate to be a full-blooded killer?

Who was the monster now?

Chapter 26
First Blood

One is always interested to see how one's assets perform once they are taken out of a test situation and placed in a live environment. Byron does possess manifold gifts: but will he be able to utilise them effectively when he is faced with a real life challenge? I do hope so. And I hope, too, that he avoids any embarrassing entanglements or unpleasantness that might draw unwanted attention to my operations. Well, I know that Mr Golden has employed his customary motivational strategy where that is concerned. Did you know that Mr Golden used to be one of my senior intelligence extractors? It's true! What that man can't do with a sharpened implement! I took something of a gamble with him, too, and decided to promote him to Head of Operations in Zone Three. Some disapprove of his methodology; Yellow Rose, for example, feels that his routine employment of terror may lead to future problems with agents under his command – that they might be more easily turned against me. Personally, I have always preferred terror as a means of control to love, as was recommended by the Earth philosopher Machiavelli. Everyone knows exactly where they stand, then, and indeed what the price of failure or betrayal will be. I've never been a very lovable person, I'm afraid, hence my reliance on Mr Golden's type of encouragement. He will continue to have my support – as long, of course, as he continues to get results.

Killing someone in his own world: could he do it? This wasn't some weird non-human – or at least, not at first glance. Nor was it all taking place in an alternate plane of existence, where everything was somehow more... abstract; more morally ambiguous.

Byron didn't know what Johan Kessel had done to provoke the ire of the Pale Lady – and he didn't really want to know. He found himself replaying the old adage that *ignorance is bliss.*

Well, there was no point tormenting himself with moral indecision. The fact was, if he did not complete his task, he would have the Pale Lady and Mr Golden's needles to worry about. And let's face it: if someone had to suffer, he would rather it be this Kessel guy than him. Not that he had any intention of drawing things out any longer than they needed to be.

A quick kill. A clean kill.

Who was the hunter now? And would he be just as pitiless*?*

And so he set to work. In the pack he had been given, he found a debit card, accompanied by a note which instructed him to use it as he saw fit in the execution of his mission. *Alright, then.* He booked himself into a cheap motel in the locale and bought himself a new suit. Not a really expensive one, mark you, but one of those slightly shiny ones that were worn by men lacking in either funds or taste – or both. He made himself taller than usual but slim; he added a pair of fashionable spectacles (plain glass, obviously) and gave himself a conservative haircut: short, brown; side-parting. Just so. A black leather briefcase completed the ensemble.

In the end, gaining admittance to Mr Kessel's apartment was surprisingly easy. On finding that a bookish legal clerk had come to call with news of an obscure legacy from a deceased relative, the gentleman in question ushered him in without the slightest appearance of apprehension. It helped, Byron assumed, that he looked like flimsy enough to snap in half given a strong gust of wind.

Johan Kessel, on the other hand, was not at all so winsome. He had answered the door clad in a thick red woollen dressing gown. He was several inches over six feet tall, and must have weighed twenty stone or thereabouts. He was somewhere between his late forties and early fifties, though it was hard to tell. This was not a man who looked after himself. His face was greasy and lined, with a thick growth of grizzled grey stubble. His eyes were small and mean – an effect accentuated by the fat face in which they were placed. His eyebrows were darker; his wild, unwashed hair was a mixture of grey and black. He had not looked pleased to find he had a visitor, but had relented on discovering that he had been traced as a possible beneficiary in a will. Even the thought of money was not enough to bring out a smile, though; instead he had gruffly invited Byron in and gestured towards a grimy brown sofa. He had had to make his own space, fastidiously setting aside a pizza box and a pile of newspapers. Once perched like a prim little bird on the edge of the couch, Byron peered up over his glasses to find that Johan had deposited his considerable bulk into a mismatched armchair a foot or so away.

"Well?" growled the hirsute Mr Kessel, giving a mighty snort through his nostrils. "What's all this about then? How much money we talking?"

Byron smiled brightly and placed his briefcase on the coffee table, once he had cleared a space by reorganising a number of empty mugs and beer cans. He clicked the catches open smartly and passed a couple of stapled sheets to his host.

"This is Arthur Fenwick," he intoned solemnly, as though he was a respectful funeral house director. "Mr Fenwick died some six months ago, seemingly without issue."

He had assembled these documents in the local library, as it happened, making liberal use of online images and some basic legal research. Mr Kessel gave the sheets a cursory look. He seemed caught somewhere between his evidently natural suspicion and greed. He did not seem especially bothered to peruse the history of the unfortunate Arthur Fenwick.

"So what's he left, then?"

The background sheets were tossed aside with barely a second glance – but that was fine – it was just another layer of deception to give credence to the whole charade.

"Well, Mr Kessel, it would appear that Mr Fenwick left a large house and a considerable sum in stocks and shares, not to mention a fair amount of cash. If you'll have a look at this summary sheet, I have detailed his assets and their approximate worth."

Now this one did grab his attention: he practically snatched it out of Byron's hand and began to scan it carefully, licking his flaky lips as he did so.

"Hang on, this says there's another sheet to follow," he grumbled, shooting Byron an accusing look.

"Oh, I do beg your pardon, Mr Kessel, I thought the document was printed double-sided. Here you are."

He passed him a second sheet.

"If you look towards the bottom the page, you'll see that the assets add up to a considerable sum."

The charcoal brows beetled; his fat, chapped lips pursed for a moment.

"What? Where? I can't see any total! You sure there's not another sheet missing?"

He shot Byron a disgusted glance, which communicated a profound lack of faith in his organisational capacities. How quickly one can be brought to make a judgement on another's capabilities and find them wanting.

"Ah, no!" said Byron, brightly, rising from his seat to stand in front of Mr Kessel. With his left hand he pointed towards the bottom right of the sheet. "The total is just down here, in the bottom right hand corner."

There was a grunt.

"This table here? That's the total?"

"That's right sir. That's the point which concerns you."

And with that, he leaned a little further forward and slipped his knife straight in between Johan Kessel's ribs. Once he had hit the spot, as only someone with advanced training could, without a great deal of luck, he threw his full body weight behind the blade, to ensure passage through the considerable bulk it encountered, thrusting it straight up through the big man's heart. A brief look of surprise morphed into shock, before he keeled over on the sofa. Byron checked his pulse. He was, as he should have been, quite dead. Skewering the heart remains a particularly quick and effective way of ending a life.

Speaking of which, it seemed that he was quite able to take the life of another person, after all.

He stood and mused for a moment. Did he feel bad? Was he appalled by what he had done?

No.

No guilt; no horror. Just a mission successfully completed. Nothing personal.

It almost made him think of someone else that he had once known; almost. Not quite quick enough to make it to the surface, that unhelpful thought, before it was dragged back down.

In the meantime, he had another task to complete. Byron rose from the ponderous corpse of his victim and began a methodical search of his apartment. He didn't bother with gloves, as he had found, through experimentation, that he was able to vary the whorls of his finger prints at will, just like everything else.

Sweet.

The apartment wasn't large and he soon found a laptop and a tablet. The former had a case, albeit covered in dust and some kind of unpleasant stain, under the bed. The latter he simply placed inside his briefcase. He also found a baseball bat propped near to the door. Given Mr Kessel's physical attributes, he doubted that he was a regular player. Rather, this, along with the handgun he found hidden in the sock drawer, hinted at a more violent side to Mr Kessel's otherwise sunny personality.

Once he had acquired the items requested by Mr Golden, Byron left without a backward glance. The door was fitted with a Yale lock, which snapped shut behind him on exit. He walked briskly down the stairs, bobbing his head and politely wishing any passers-by a 'good afternoon.'

An hour and twenty minutes later, he was being admitted into Mr Golden's beautiful house by his ethereal assistant.

"Welcome back, Mr Black," pronounced Zaffre, solemnly. "If that is the laptop you were asked to obtain, please leave it here on the floor. It will be examined later."

Was that the slightest hint of a smile?

"I'm glad to have survived my first posting," responded Byron, as he deposited the laptop case containing all of Kessel's equipment on the tiled floor. He flashed what he hoped was a roguish smile.

Zaffre smiled in response, but a little sadly.

"We are all glad to survive from one day to the next. Who knows what Fate has in store for us?"

Byron took a moment to look at him then. Those liquid amber eyes shone so very brightly, but there was something else in there too – something hidden. Was it pain? Suffering?

He opened his mouth as if to speak and found that his hand was half-risen, as if to offer comfort, but Zaffre turned on his heels with surprising alacrity and processed to the stairs.

"If you'll be so good as to follow me, Mr Black, your return has been eagerly anticipated by my master."

So that was that; Byron closed his mouth and followed Zaffre's slim and immaculately tailored form up the staircase. As they approached the study door, Byron felt a little fluttering of fear. He had completed his mission successfully, hadn't he? So why would Mr Golden want to make him suffer? And he knew, even as Vodrun extended a massive paw for his knives, that it wasn't a question of logic: it was something altogether more visceral. Mr Golden *enjoyed* hurting people; it gave him *pleasure.* And it created a sense of ever-present fear or doubt in those who had to work under him. Which, was, presumably, exactly what he wanted. A man who cannot be predicted, who would relish any opportunity to leave you writhing in agony... that wasn't someone you would antagonise lightly... *So, maybe*, thought, Byron, allowing himself a cheeky little grin, as he passed the door that Zaffre was now holding open for him, *maybe there is some sort of logic to it after all...*

He found the thought that actually, Mr Golden was just a regular, psychopathic sadist who had developed his own effective methods of control over the years oddly comforting.

He also made sure that there was no hint of a grin when he stepped into the study. He didn't want any more of those needles, thank you very much.

Mr Golden rose from his desk as Byron approached, wreathed in smiles. Byron noted again how good-looking he was, and, were it not for his previous encounter, he would have been put entirely at ease by his handler's manner. It was all the more chilling.

"My dear Byron!" cried Mr Golden, warmly, reaching out to give his shoulders a manly squeeze. "Am I to understand that your first mission has been successfully completed?"

"Yes, Mr Golden," he replied, forcing himself not to shy away from the physical contact. "The target is dead and I removed his laptop and a tablet from his apartment. I left them with your assistant."

A bright white smile greeted that.

"What a good boy you are!" murmured Mr Golden, gently cupping Byron's face in his hand. "This is a most promising beginning to our relationship."

A manicured thumb ran itself over Byron's bottom lip, and a dark glimmer appeared in Mr Golden's eyes. The boy maintained a steady composure, looking directly over his operator's shoulder.

Then it was all over. Mr Golden abruptly released him and returned to his desk, gesturing at Byron to sit opposite him. It was all business now. He wrote an entry in his enormous ledger, before turning it to Byron and presenting him with the antique fountain pen.

"Please sign and date this entry," he ordered, with a crisp smile.

Byron did so.

"You have made a pleasing start, Mr Black, but do not allow yourself to indulge in hubris. Pride comes before a fall! And you must be ever so careful in your role, as failure could expose our organisation to all manner of… irritations. You may have the rest of today to compose yourself. Report back here at nine o' clock tomorrow morning, and we will discuss your next mission."

Byron signed off the entry as requested, noting Mr Golden's comments about the mission parameters and their fulfilment.

When he looked up, his overseer was already leafing through some other documents. A casual flick of the wrist served as his dismissal whilst reinforcing their relative positions within the hierarchy.

Byron took his leave and then his knives, before being escorted to the door by the graceful Zaffre, who's every movement, he noticed, was fluid and controlled. It planted a seed in his mind – not much of one, but just something to wonder about...

Chapter 27
The Sword of
Judgement

I realise that I shouldn't get ahead of myself, but my mind is awash with possibilities. Who should I target next? The grotesque Mr Kessel had provided a number of services to one of my many enemies. She had been using the human internet to manipulate events in her favour. Of course, the delectable Johan was simply a small cog in a much larger enterprise, but his removal will cause some irritation and delay to the Elementals. Little acts of sabotage can be surprisingly efficacious: especially when one is able to perpetrate a large number of them.

That being said, one is only able to do all of this if one has the appropriate means. Just because someone is able to wield a blade with great skill doesn't mean they will be a superb assassin. There is all manner of careful preparation required before the killing move takes place. That scarlet crescendo is merely the tip of the iceberg. For it to happen at all requires a great deal of meticulous legwork.

I am hopeful that my sweet Byron has the wherewithal to succeed in this area. Isn't it funny? He was so lazy in his schoolboy incarnation – wouldn't do his homework or lift a finger if he didn't have to. And now look at him, swotting away, researching his victims and different potential strategies. It fair warms my old heart! Isn't that what's known as making dramatic progress? Put me in charge of your education system –

or, for that matter, Mr Golden – and you'd soon see the examination results surging upwards!

Ah! But enough of this jocularity: time flies by and I have so many people to kill. I really must get on.

The next target was a wealthy and reclusive man who lived in a grand house and had armed guards. This posed its own problems, but, through careful observation over a couple of weeks, Byron was able to formulate a strategy. It appeared that the target had few visitors, but on Monday and Thursday a distinguished looking gentleman would arrive to play chess with him between the hours of three and four in the afternoon. Byron knew this, because he followed the man home, to a less than glamorous neighbourhood and he asked him questions, posing as a plain-clothes detective investigating a case of sophisticated money-laundering. Zaffre had provided him with impressively realistic identity credentials and the rest had been quite straightforward. The chess player, he discovered, had emigrated from Belarus ten years ago, where he had been a professional player of some renown. Now, he was reduced to humouring rich men who wanted an intellectual challenge. It was an easy thing for the police detective to persuade him to stay at home on the following Monday without alerting his wealthy opponent to the fact.

Not that the guards knew any different mark you, for there, as regular as clockwork, appeared their regular visitor, dapper as ever in a dark blue suit. The only difference was that he was wearing an ivory and gold cravat instead of the usual bow tie, but they thought little of that, other than to offer a gentle joshing at the door about him making a special effort, as they frisked him down for concealed weapons.

Nor did the unfortunate target have much to say, other than to gesture, frowningly at a chess board, still in the midst of a game begun the previous Thursday.

"Come, Andrei!" he called, rather peremptorily, gesturing to a polished wooden chair before sitting down across the antique chess table. "I have been evaluating your strategy, and I think I know what you're up to! I hope to counter it today and to defeat you!"

A rich, cultured voice, used to issuing commands and, of course, to deference. This was not, it was clear, a relationship of equals.

"We shall see," said Andrei, with an indulgent smile.

Looking at the older, dynamic gentleman on the other side of the table, he thought briefly of Mr Golden, who also conducted himself like a feudal lord. How very droll that he should find himself in such a familiar situation.

Byron was pleased to see that his voice provoked no untoward reaction. That was good. He had recorded the original Andrei during the interview, and had spent a significant amount of time imitating his voice and accent.

Soon, they were in the thick of it: the chess pieces moved ponderously; one move, then a counter; another move… the man's brow crinkled with concentration.

"What are you up to? I knew I should have kept my thoughts to myself… You've changed your plan, haven't you, you rogue!"

He flashed a wolfish grin, before redirecting his attention to the board.

Of course, it was one thing preparing to play a role, but Byron's talents did not extend to playing world-class chess. Luckily, that was never part of the overall plan, of course. Quite the opposite. And so it was that he soon made his fatal move, leaving a rook dangerously exposed and the tempting opportunity of chequing his King. His opponent gawped wildly at the board for almost thirty seconds, his busy eyes scanning this way and that for a trap. There was nothing to be seen, and he swiftly moved his Queen to take advantage.

"Ha! You must be slipping old boy! Look to me like you've got your mind on something…!

And here, even as he looked up, flush in his triumph, the words froze on his lips as he felt a savage pain at his breast. His mouth opened like a fish for a moment, before he slumped forward, scattering the pieces all over the carpet.

"You were looking for danger in the wrong place," Byron gently informed him.

He wiped his specially modified cravat pin on a piece of tissue before putting it back in place.

"I believe that's cheque mate, old friend'" he chuckled, in Andrei's voice, a rather self-indulgent manifestation of gallows humour, admittedly.

He then moved his victim to sit in a nearby armchair, posed as if he was asleep. There was the faintest little spot of blood on dead man's white shirt, but it was the thinnest of blades, after all – just enough to stop a heart when correctly inserted. He didn't like to deviate from his usual weapons, but needs must…

The job done, Byron carefully picked up and rearranged the chess pieces, before sitting for some time playing solitaire on his phone. It settled his nerves, and he knew he couldn't leave early: Andrei left at four on the dot. To breach this routine would risk provoking questions. Andrei had assured him that the chess match itself was a sacred ritual which was never interrupted.

Thus, as the clock chimed four, the elegant Belarusian left the scene of the crime, and the guards simply bade him a good evening. It was a full half an hour before anyone realised that there was something wrong, and by that time, he was well away.

Or at least, Byron was. The murder trial of Andrei Voychenko made for fascinating reading in the papers over the next few weeks.

Oh well. You can't make an omelette without breaking a few eggs. *Besides*, Byron reminded himself, *better him than me.*

It seemed on this occasion that Mr Golden agreed with him.

"What a marvellous idea!" he crowed, enthusiastically. "Not only have you eliminated a significant enemy asset, but you have redirected the authorities to a completely specious target. I'm impressed, Mr Black! Come, we'll sit by the fire to toast your success, and you can talk me through it all."

It took all of Byron's willpower not to make a run for the door. They both knew that he didn't really have a choice about this. He rose grimly and moved to sit in the plush armchair next to the fire. Mr Golden gave him an innocent look as he moved to fix them both a drink. When he passed the pungent crystal glass to Byron, he made a point of resting his hand, very briefly and gently, on his upper thigh.

"Isn't this nice?" he whispered huskily into his subordinate's ear.

Byron felt like throwing the stuff into Mr Golden's face, but he maintained his iron self-control. *Never let them know what's going on in your mind,* he urged himself.

And then Mr Golden moved away, over to his chair, leaving behind a rich odour of aftershave. He gave a knowing smile before lifting his glass to his lips.

"Bottoms up, dear boy!"

Byron felt sick. It was all a big game. This man was simply playing around with him. Would he be paralysed again? Or was it all a big charade designed to keep him fearfully guessing as to what might happen next?

Well, he wouldn't give him the satisfaction of seeing his internal strife. Instead, Byron returned Mr Golden's smile with a bright, delighted grin of his own. It helped to imagine him sitting on the toilet – that's assuming that Others actually used toilets... Probably best not to get too caught up in that one.

"Thanks," said Byron, cheerily, tilting his glass in his host's direction. "Chin chin!"

They both drank swiftly and then sat looking at each other.

There was a speculative caste to Mr Golden's eyes, as if he was waiting for something.

Byron, tried to stay calm, and to keep the beating of his heart even. But it was difficult. As the seconds crawled by, he sat there, waiting for the first tell-tale signs of muscular cramps and paralysis.

The seconds turned into a minute and then two.

"Is everything alright?" enquired Mr Golden, with a concerned expression on his handsome face.

"Of course, Mr Golden. It's just that I'm not used to drinking. Please do excuse me!"

This provoked an unseemly guffaw.

"Ha! Oh my! Your face is a picture! Well, you can relax on this occasion: it's just a rather fine claret. It'll put hairs on your chest."

He winked, roguishly.

But relaxing was easier said than done, especially when Mr Golden stood again and walked over, only to drop down to a squatting position directly in front of him, with a hand on each of Byron's knees.

"But do be mindful, boy," he whispered, fixing him with a look worthy of a hungry fox staring down a chicken. "For you belong to me now, body and soul. You are mine and I will do as I please with you. Make sure that I remain happy, Mr Black, for your own sake."

He gave Byron's knees a squeeze, whilst continuing to stare coldly into his eyes. Then, after a few more seconds, he rose, and walked casually back to his desk.

"I think that'll be all for today, Mr Black. Please come and sign off for this particular assignment."

Very well. Byron knew where he stood now, and, easing himself slightly woozily out of the chair he went back to the desk, took the proffered fountain pen and signed the ledger entry with particular gusto.

"Good day, Mr Black. Please report back in two days' time for further instruction."

Then came the regal wave of dismissal.

"Certainly, sir," he affirmed, moving swiftly back to the door where he hoped Zaffre's friendly face was waiting for him.

Life must go on.

Chapter 27
The Daily Grind

Things seem, as ever, to be going to plan. I hate to be immodest, but I must admit a talent for long-term strategy. Perhaps I should take up this human game of chess? I'm sure I'd be very good at it – although it might take several years, or even decades, before I have all of the pieces just where I want them.

My latest little pet seems to be getting on nicely and seems obligingly obedient. I can't say that I completely agree with Mr Golden's methodology – some of his tastes are a little too mammalian for my liking – but as long as he gets results, I am minded to tolerate his... unusual habits.

But for now I must depart – I'm afraid I haven't time to waste on social discourse. I have a number of other irons in the fire and I am currently much engaged with a young lady who can jump between bodies: now just imagine that! Not to mention the fun I could have with her at my full disposal...

It all goes back to the human mind being incredibly resilient. Admittedly, Byron was no longer fully human. Well, not by a long chalk, in fact. But even so, things fell into a kind of routine. Funny how he had wondered whether he'd actually be able to kill someone, when it came down to it, in cold blood. It turned out he did so without compunction: to the point when, even though his job murdering people – not to put too fine a point on it - he gradually adjusted to what was demanded of him.

Always there was a mission: there was no real let-up. One after another they came. Always, he was thinking, planning, preparing. So far, through a mixture of forethought, reconnaissance and luck, he had managed to fulfil his briefs without any major upset.

But then, there was always that chance for something to go wrong – for some unexpected variable to come into play. And that, of course, would mean pain and possibly death. For him. Needless to say, although his whole life had come to revolve around death, he remained as determined as ever to avoid that particular fate himself.

And so he went on, following his orders like a good boy; tolerating – as he must – Mr Golden's unexpected mind games and increasingly unpleasant physical interactions.

The faces – the ones he killed, and the ones he wore - began to fold into one another, an endless procession of mummery and murder.

Do I even know who I am anymore?

He allowed himself to look into a mirror – something which he did very rarely these days. But hey, he supposed the worst that could have happened on that front already had... As he stood there, his face flickered, shifting from his youthful appearance to that of a middle aged black man; then an elderly white guy; finally a teenage girl.

It's a good job that I'm so grounded.

His face flashed back into sharp relief and he allowed himself a rueful grin.

Aren't I?

But there was no time to waste on this psychological self-indulgence: perhaps that was why they kept him so busy. He was expected at Berkley Road at nine so he needed to get on.

He dressed and bathed before leaving the small apartment he had called home for the last few months. Well, apartment was probably too grand a description: it was more of a bedsit, really. Something modest, in an indeterminate part of town. He didn't want anyone paying him any undue attention: and, more importantly, neither did his employers.

It was, despite Mr Golden's cultivated unpredictability, an increasingly familiar process. He had at least made some progress with the enigmatic Zaffre, who now looked somewhat pleased to see him and was in serious danger of smiling when he answered the door.

"Mr Black," he intoned, with a barely perceptible upturn in the corners of his mouth.

"Morning, Mr Zaffre," grinned Byron. "Always a pleasure. I trust you're keeping on top of... whatever you have to do when you're not answering the door to me."

There was a smile at this – but it was too quick, too shallow. Misdirection of some kind? It worried him.

The fact was, Byron had become very good at reading people: at looking out for little non-verbal clues. It was a useful skill to have when you were planning to kill someone. Ah! What would his mother say? He had finally developed an emotional awareness and he used it to facilitate assassination.

But back to the present. Normally when people smile, it's a good sign. But not with Zaffre. He was seriously self-contained. If he was smiling, there must be something wrong. Right?

"Hey... are you OK?" Byron ventured, perhaps rather haplessly. Although to be fair, what else could he have said?

Zaffre made a small noise that seemed like it might be a sort of laugh. It wasn't exactly bubbling with good humour though.

"All is well, thank you, Mr Black."

"Are you sure? I mean..." and because he didn't really know what he meant, he took Zaffre's hand in his, very gently. Quick as a flash the young man had snatched it back, as if Byron's touch was as corrosive as lime. Byron tried to hide how much this wounded him.

"I'm sorry," he said, a little stiffly. "I only wanted to..."

"Yes. Yes, I know that, Byron, but you can't, I'm afraid. Now, if you'll follow me, Mr Golden is expecting you. If we delay any further, he may become... displeased."

He turned smartly and began to walk up the stairs. Byron had little choice but to follow him. As they ascended, though, his quick eye noticed something else. A slight catch in Zaffre's left leg as he walked, as though he had injured a muscle and was trying to cover it up.

"What've you done to your leg?" he asked with exaggerated jocularity, trying to compensate for his previous awkwardness. "Is it a football injury?"

Zaffre didn't turn around or slow his pace.

"I... slipped in the kitchen."

Just the slightest of pauses, but enough to trigger another thought in Byron's mind.

"Wait." He took hold of Zaffre's jacket sleeve this time, forcing him to stop and reluctantly turn around.

"We really must get on, Mr Black."

"You didn't slip in the kitchen. Did... did he do something to you?"

Zaffre produced an exhalation that was more like an angry cough. Something rippled through his face, as though it was a mask placed over something else. His gleaming eyes shone even more than usual as he looked down at his would-be sympathiser.

"My but you're full of questions and conversation this morning, Mr Black. I appreciate your concern, but it's really nothing to do with you. Ours is merely a professional relationship, that's all."

Byron blinked, and this time he didn't quite hide his reaction to Zaffre's coldness.

Never let them know what you're thinking...

But he didn't feel like being a marble statue this time. Beneath the controlled exterior, Zaffre was a nice guy – he was sure of that. And he liked him... he was fairly sure on that score, too, though it was difficult to tell what Zaffre thought and felt.

"He did something to you, didn't he?"

Something flickered and caught light inside him.

Zaffre looked anxiously up the stairs. When he looked back at Byron, he looked as if he was about to start crying. His voice came out as a hoarse whisper, low and urgent.

"Please, please, just leave it and come upstairs to see him. We mustn't make him angry."

Byron dropped Zaffre's arm, instantly full of remorse. What was he thinking? He would get them both in trouble.

"Oh God, Zaffre, I'm so sorry. That... bastard. If there was anything I could do to help you. He shouldn't treat you like that... You're... a good guy... I..."

It was painfully lame and he knew it.

Zaffre collected himself all of a sudden. It was like a shade being replaced over a lamp.

"All well and good, Mr Black, but time is pressing."

He walked now to the top of the stairs, with Byron at his heels like a doleful hound.

They walked down the now familiar passageway where Vodrun waited at his post outside Mr Golden's door. As Byron handed over his knives, Zaffre knocked and held the door open for him to enter.

"Ah! Dear Mr Black! Always a delight to see you!" called Mr Golden, flashing a particularly winning smile at him. He seemed in a remarkably good mood. Byron tried not to think why – and was careful to repress any hint of anger or distaste.

"Good morning, Mr Golden," he replied, solemnly enough.

"Oh, but don't be in such a hurry to leave us, Zaffre," called the older man.

Zaffre paused, half way through closing the door.

"Sir?"

"Come on in, Zaffre. There's something that I would like you to be a part of today."

Without any flicker of expression, Zaffre calmly closed the door and stood respectfully in front of it, his hands linked behind his back.

"Lovely!" crooned Mr Golden, before turning back to Byron. "Now, Mr Black, before we proceed with the main order of business there is something which I feel we need to be quite clear about. And that, my dear boy, is the chain of command: and, specifically, the respect that is due to me."

Byron felt a flutter in his stomach, followed by a hint of bile at the back of his throat.

Mr Golden was deviating from the normal sequence of events. This was not good. In fact, he had learned that the happier Mr Golden looked, the more you should be worried. He was probably anticipating all of the fun he was about to have – which meant anything but for his chosen partner.

"If you would both be so good as to stand over there in front of the fire, gentlemen."

A slender hand gestured for them to move.

Mr Golden waited until they had taken their station, like a pair of raw recruits on parade for the first time. Zaffre still had his hands behind his back; Byron let his hang by his side. The commanding officer smiled encouragingly at them from his desk.

"Pretty as a picture, you two standing there!"

He let the tension build for a couple of minutes, before rising and sauntering over to them both. He appraised their appearance, still smiling, but not in a nice way. No, smiling like the cat that had got the canary, as Grandmother liked to say.

He took his time to walk around them in a slow circle, not saying a word. It was intensely uncomfortable, as he must have known. Then, as he was standing behind them, he spoke.

"It seems that we have a little dissension in the ranks. That some of the infantry are unhappy with their stations."

He let his words hang there for a few seconds, as Byron desperately weighed his odds of bluffing his way out of that one. He licked his lips, nervously. Then he felt the heat of Mr Golden's breath on the back of his neck.

"So, I'm a bastard, am I?"

The words drizzled into his right ear like honeyed poison. Mr Golden's lips were so close, they brushed against the side of his face. A hand moved across his throat and chin like a large, fleshy spider. He felt his lips being slightly squeezed, before Mr Golden inserted his index finger into the corner of his mouth. Byron's stomach lurched with mingled disgust and fear, as he felt his superior hug him close from behind, his other hand moving around to rest against his flank.

A soft laugh gently disturbed Byron's hair.

"Silly, silly boy. Do you think you can say or do anything that I don't know about? And what, I wonder, were you thinking you might do about it? Perhaps you could write a letter of complaint to the Pale Lady regarding your treatment at my hands?"

This idea seemed to particularly amuse him, and produced a bark of laughter. Then he was released, and Mr Golden sidled back over to his desk. But rather than sit down, he did what Byron had dreaded: he opened his special drawer and removed his case of metallic implements. Zaffre didn't move or make a sound, but Byron felt him tense next to him. He wished that there was something he could do, but under the potent gaze of this Other, he felt completely helpless.

"How sad I am that it has come to this, my dear boy. You know I hate to have to issue punishment."

Here he grinned at the outrageousness of the lie.

He walked back to them again, this time opening his case and placing it on the side table next to his favourite armchair.

He came to stand in front of them again, a smile flickering on his face like living flame.

"Now, Mr Black, if you would be so good as to take seat, I shall demonstrate to you the error of your ways."

He pointed at the second armchair, and Byron meekly sat himself down in it. He hated his spinelessness, but the layers of control had been laid down deeply over many months, almost without him realising it. Mr Golden had a natural talent in this respect. Now he stood surveying his recalcitrant subordinate, like a disappointed headmaster.

"You will see now just what a bastard I can be," he hissed, smiling all the more, his eyes practically gleaming with feral joy.

Then abruptly, he turned.

"Zaffre, remove your outer clothes."

Byron blinked a couple of times while his mind tried to process this unexpected twist.

Oh no. Oh shit no.

Zaffre didn't bat an eyelid. He simply shrugged himself out of his beautifully tailored suit, folding the jacket and trousers and placing them neatly over the back of Mr Golden's chair. He then removed his tie and crisp white shirt, depositing them likewise.

Byron was struck by the mechanical motion of it all, and that was when he finally began to realise: this was not an unusual event; far from it. Zaffre's movements were born of frequent practice. In a matter of moments, he had resumed his earlier pose, but now wearing just his underwear. Byron's gaze was drawn to the sight of numerous little bumps and ridges of hard skin, which dotted Zaffre's body, particularly his torso. These were made up of scar tissue, and in places, there even seemed to be a pattern, as though some kind of artwork or relief was in the back of their inflictor's mind.

These marks were not made by needles, surely?

Mr Golden stood back, admiring the visual signs of his handiwork.

"Ah," he mused, silkily, running a hand over Zaffre's tightly defined chest. "This is what we must call a labour of love!"

325

He turned then to observe Byron, who knew instinctively that he was searching for any sign of emotion. He *wanted* to see some sort of reaction – it would give him pleasure.

Byron simply returned his smile, much as it took an enormous effort of will to feign an appreciation for this torturer's efforts.

"You see, I am quite as adept with the scalpel as I am with the needles. And when you have unlimited time and opportunity, it is incumbent on one to test the boundaries of one's skill. We have spent many happy hours together, have we not, Zaffre, exploring the nature and limits of the human form."

"Yes sir," replied Zaffre calmly, as if he had been asked to furnish them with morning tea.

"You cannot understand, Mr Black, the relationship that Zaffre and I enjoy."

Here he turned to address Byron once more, whilst placing a fatherly hand on Zaffre's shoulder.

"For Zaffre is my thrall. I own him. It's as simple as that. I own him completely. Not a thing can be said to him without my knowing about it. I even feel the thrill of his pain, such is our connection. But please be at peace, Mr Black, for Zaffre has accepted his role and is content with his lot. Isn't that so?"

"Quite content, sir."

"There, now. But since you wanted to be a part of all this and you have expressed an interest in Zaffre's well-being, I feel I should at least give you the chance to see us playing together; I'm sure it will put your mind at rest and quite still any further disquiet you might have on the subject."

And with that he produced something gleaming from his nasty little case and, as Byron sat transfixed, he made a small, crimson incision near the base of Zaffre's spine.

"This is something we've been working on together of late. You observed that Zaffre has a slight limp at the moment and I'm rather afraid that this was a side-effect of our exploration. You see here, well, there is a nerve cluster which affects lower motor skills."

This was surreal. Byron felt like a first year medical student at a lecture. He looked up at Zaffre, whose face showed no reaction to the incursion of the scalpel.

Next, Mr Golden went over to his grand sideboard, from which he produced a thick linen sheet. It was difficult not to notice the bloodstains. He carefully positioned the sheet over the plush carpet.

"I chose a red carpet on purpose, you know. But still, it does no harm to be careful about these things. A good quality carpet is frightfully expensive."

A light-hearted laugh followed this observation, before he turned his baleful gaze to his assistant.

"Lie face down."

An order: an order which Zaffre obeyed without hesitation.

"Now, this particular nerve cluster has some interesting physiological effects. Observe!"

And with this, Mr Golden produced a second implement: this one looked rather like a very slender pair of elongated pliers. Without further ado, he inserted the instrument into the incision and began to manipulate it. Almost immediately Zaffre's body convulsed, his head and upper body and his feet all rising to form a U shape. Byron found the expression on his face difficult to forget. His mouth was a twisted rictus of pain and he had screwed his eyes shut.

With different movements, Mr Golden showed how he could cause Zaffre's lower body to move in numerous ways and directions.

"Isn't human anatomy a wonderful thing?"

Byron returned his smile again, albeit rather more weakly this time.

This was just the beginning.

Zaffre tried not to cry out, but after a couple of minutes, the screaming began; real, intense screams of soul-consuming agony.

Byron's hands gripped the arms of the chair so hard they went white. Still he sat there, smiling and nodding as Mr Golden continued his lecture on the human nervous system, with lots of practical demonstrations.

Oh dear God, why didn't I keep my mouth shut?

He felt tears begin to form in his eyes as Zaffre's screams turned to broken sobs. Truly, Byron was watching a master at work.

Time seemed to assume an air of suspension during the ordeal, but eventually, Mr Golden seemed to feel that he had made his point. He placed his stained surgical instruments on a silver tray and simply turned back to Zaffre.

"That will do for now. Please get dressed."

Rising shakily to his feet, Zaffre complied without comment. He did not look at Byron, not once. His body shook and twitched from residual nerve impulses. His face was wet with tears and his bottom lip was bleeding where he had bitten it.

When he was fully dressed once more, Zaffre turned back to his master, as if awaiting further instructions.

A golden smile greeted him.

"Please take the instruments down to the kitchen and sterilise them in the usual way."

"Yes sir."

And with that, he picked up the tray upon which reposed the instruments of his torture.

"Oh, and Zaffre!"

The young man paused at the door and slowly, stiffly, turned around.

"Sir?"

"All of that activity has made me quite thirsty. Please bring up a pot of Darjeeling, there's a good chap."

"Of course, sir."

With that, he was gone, a dignified, wounded phantom sliding silently out of the room.

Mr Golden stood for a moment, one hand resting on the fine marble of his fireplace. He looked like a patriarch of the past, sternly gazing upon his errant charge.

"When I took you on, Mr Black, I was very clear in setting out my expectations, was I not?"

"Yes, Mr Golden."

"It is always so very unpleasant when one is forced to discipline one's staff. I trust that there will be no repeat of your loose attitude of this morning?"

"No, Mr Golden."

"Very good. Poor Zaffre: I hope you realise the consequences of your actions. I doubt the poor boy will ever be able to look at you again without remembering what your careless words led to."

Here he smiled vaguely, as if dwelling on something that was particularly pleasing to him.

"Well, we'll say no more on the matter. If you would move back to the desk, I have a complex assignment for you."

Byron did as he was bid. Mr Golden took his customary seat across from him.

"This one could be tricky, but we think you're capable of pulling it off."

Byron looked at him expectantly.

"The target is Elys Starr. But this one is no mere human: she is an Other. Her chosen weapon is charm and she wields it most effectively against the foolish humans. I am operating under the assumption, by the way, that her paltry wiles will have no effect on you whatsoever. She is guarded and not without her own abilities when it comes to defending herself. You must be especially wary with her. Even so, she will die in just the same way as a human if you can get under her guard. Here is the file."

"Thank you, Mr Golden, I shall, of course, act on your advice."

Byron took the folder and rose from his chair.

"A wise course. And, ah, Mr Black?"

Byron turned back.

"You forgot to sign the ledger."

Mr Golden beamed at him and pressed the pen into his hand, before gesturing down to his precious leather-bound book.

"We must make sure that all of the paperwork is just so, after all!"

Chapter 28
Boss Fight

I thought it was about time to move things up a gear. I have disrupted the operations of my enemies with some success, but the removal of Elys Starr will send a very clear message, I feel. She is one of their most effective operatives, and has managed to inveigle her way into the highest level of human society.

Her death will be a sore blow to her mistress — and could, in fact, set her back by a couple of years while she tries to re-establish her lost connections and influence.

What a prize!

I do hope my little man is up to the challenge. I gather that Mr Golden has had to be very firm with him on a matter of discipline.

Well, all's well that ends well. We must have good order, mustn't we? The great problem with free will is that it's just so hard to get anything organised or achieved satisfactorily. You issue an order only to be told "No, I don't want to do that."

I'm afraid that's not how we run things in my outfit. When one issues an order, one must have every confidence that one's underlings will leap to its fulfilment. If that requires, from time to time, a little encouragement, then so be it!

Elys Starr was not a difficult woman to find, not by any measure. Given his lack of interaction with the human world at large,

Byron had never heard of her. Once he began to prowl the internet, however, he wondered how this was so.

She was rich; she was beautiful; she was rumoured to have connections with the government. She was both a socialite and an activist, and had assumed a high profile in a number of charitable and social campaigns. He found photographs of her with Government ministers and even the occasional world leader. Then there were others of her in casual clothes, holding the hands of sick, malnourished children, or, more locally, campaigning against cyber bullying in schools.

On the social side, Ms Starr was a doyenne of the tabloid press, who loved to speculate about her romantic entanglements. She had been linked to A-list actors, sports stars, politicians and even, on one occasion, a royal Prince.

The lady herself lived in an exclusive neighbourhood where, he assumed, there would be good security. Byron sat back in his chair and swivelled around a few times. *How can I get access to her?* That was the first problem to be solved. The second, which he was trying not to think too much about at this stage, was that she was an Other.

One step at a time.

The old desk-top computer hummed in tandem with Byron's mind.

Slowly, the outline of a plan began to form.

What if... what if she really is as good as she makes out?

Life had hardly inspired him to have a great deal of faith in human nature – let alone that of the Others. But he had nothing to lose by trying to push against that particular door. If she was a fake who just loved the publicity she got from her acts of selfless radiance, well, it just wouldn't work and he would have to think of a new strategy.

But what if she was the genuine article?

A kind Other: was this a contradiction in terms? His mind touched briefly on his memories of Yellow Rose. Maybe; maybe not… There was only one way to find out.

He walked to the mirror and smiled at himself. Let's see if he could remember how this went… A moment passed and he gradually grew taller, his features shifting here and there until he was once more the sapphire-eyed paragon of male beauty that he had chosen as his form back in the glory days of Yellow Rose's tutelage. He eyed himself critically. He was certainly good-looking, but Elys Starr was in her late twenties and he currently looked around nineteen. That wouldn't do at all. He made a few tweaks over the next half-hour, carefully adding a little bulk here and there and a few faint lines on his forehead and around his eyes. He was getting really quite good at this now, having studied so carefully the finer details of human faces. When he looked as though he was in his mid-twenties, he paused again and smiled in satisfaction. That would do nicely… He spent some time gazing at himself in the full-length mirror and committed every tiny detail to memory. He then practised shifting in between his usual appearance and his marvellously handsome alter-ego. Eventually he stopped and reverted to his default identity. He wasn't sure how much Mr Golden and his minions knew about his abilities; he had certainly never referred to his shape-changing in any conversation and, knowing the Pale Lady, it wouldn't surprise him if she had kept the full extent of his talents to herself. Hadn't she said as much in her crystal chamber? Byron decided not to rock any boats by appearing at Berkley Road in a wholly different guise, although he would like to see the look on Zaffre's face. Who knew what might happen if he did: perhaps it would lead to his unlooked for dismemberment by the delightful Vodrun!

With that sobering thought on his mind, he returned to Berkley Road to seek Zaffre's assistance on a couple of points. A certain nervousness tingled in his chest as the door was unlocked; what if Mr Golden was right? What if Zaffre did blame him for... for what had happened? He tried to hide his anxiety on that point: he could only wait and see. The door swung back, and Zaffre stood there, looking as chic and unflustered as ever.

"Mr Black."

Byron licked his dry lips.

"Hello, Zaffre."

They both stood there, looking at each, before Zaffre raised one ironic eyebrow.

"Would you like to come in? Or were you planning to stand on the step for a while? I can come back for you at a convenient time if you wish."

Byron actually felt himself blushing; he looked sheepishly down at his feet and then, tentatively, up at Mr Golden's assistant.

"Sorry. I... I feel a bit awkward. It's... you know..."

Zaffre gazed down his long slim nose for a moment, and then his face softened.

"You have nothing to feel awkward about, Mr Black," he answered, his voice slightly softer than usual. "Please, put yourself at ease on my part and come in."

As if to prove there were no hard feelings, he followed this up with a brief smile. Brief, but it transformed his face into some quite different, albeit fleetingly.

Byron wondered what he would look like if he was happy but swiftly pushed the thought aside. He didn't want any more trouble on that score!

He was directed to the kitchen, as he always was when it was an unscheduled visit to seek assistance in the fulfilment of a mission. Once there, Byron was offered mint tea and lemon cake, both of which he consumed absent-mindedly as he began to unfold his ideas.

"Zaffre, I'm hoping that you have some contacts that I could use."

This was his opening statement, and he knew from past experience it was entirely possible that he would have. For a solitary personal assistant who seemed incapable of a cross word, let alone violence, Zaffre had some… colourful associates.

The young man directed an inscrutable gaze at Byron.

"What sort of contacts?"

Straight to the point, then.

"A couple of hard guys who could rough someone up."

Zaffre's slim brows shot up at this.

"Oh. I see. That doesn't seem like your usual style, Mr Black. I'm not sure that Mr Golden would approve of such crude methods. Who do you have in mind as the object of this roughage?"

Byron smiled. He loved Zaffre's sardonic manner. The guy was so dry. He was frequently unsure as to how seriously he should take him when he passed comment. On this occasion, however, he knew he was going to elicit a little tremor of surprise with his answer.

"Me. That is myself. As the object of the roughing."

Zaffre paused with his teacup halfway to his mouth.

"I see."

He took a delicate sip and replaced it in the saucer.

"You are a source of constant perplexity, Mr Black."

That was about as expressive as Zaffre got.

"I take it that this has something to do with your current target?"

"Oh yes. I've no particular desire to get battered, but I have a cunning plan which I hope will make it worth the sacrifice."

"I'm not sure I dare enquire any further."

"Probably best that you don't. Suffice it to say that I am hoping for a memorable introduction to the target, after which I will use my charm and good looks to get close to her and fulfil the brief."

Zaffre's face was wonderfully still.

"Hm."

"You're not entirely convinced?"

Byron gave him an innocent look.

"Do you not think that I could be winningly attractive if I put my mind to it?"

Somewhere inside, a little part of Byron shook its metaphorical head, wondering at the changes which had taken place in him on all levels since the death of his stepfather in the dim and distant.

He peeped over his cup mischievously as he drained the last of the drink.

Zaffre gave him a cool look in return.

"I'm not sure I'm qualified to comment on that, Mr Black, but I will make some enquires to see if I can't act as an intermediary for you and the requisite... heavies."

Was that a touch of humour again? Byron gave up trying to work it out. He would wait for the contacts and put his plan into action.

It was a blustery autumnal night and Elys Starr's sleek black limousine was making its way back through the streets following a well-publicized gala dinner to raise money for a prominent international charity. It was late and the streets were almost deserted, but as she approached the end point of her journey, she was shocked to see a grim tableau of violence being played out beneath a flickering street light. There, in plain view, a young man was being savagely attacked by two unsavoury looking characters wearing crash helmets. Luckily, Ms Starr never travelled anywhere without her bodyguard, Silas; Gareth, the chauffeur, was pretty handy in a scrap too, if it came down to it.

She didn't hesitate.

"Stop the car! Silas… do something!"

Silas, who was ex-special forces and had been trained to kill people with his bare hands if need be, had learned to interpret his new commander's rather vague orders, using his considerable experience to fill in any gaps. He sprang from the car, oozing menace; at the front end, Gareth stepped out too, cracking his knuckles.

Silas smiled pleasantly as he advanced upon the thugs. In his experience, the type of men who concealed their faces and had to attack a lone victim in the dead of night would not require a great deal of threat before they took to their heels: certainly not when the numbers were even.

He was correct in his assumption. A muffled shout from inside one of the crash helmets, and they both fled into the night.

That was good enough. He had no intention of chasing them down any dark alleys, whilst leaving his employer undefended. He hoped that she wasn't going to order him to do so. By now, Ms Starr had stepped forth herself and was hurrying to the side of the victim, who was struggling to sit up. Silas noted that it was a young man. He had a split lip, a bloody nose and what would probably be a fantastic black eye the next morning.

In the light of the street lamp, Elys Starr noticed all of this too. She also noted that, beneath the blood, this young man was extremely good-looking. And… something else, which she filed to the back of her mind, for now, at least. At present, she knelt on the pavement and eyed him critically.

"How badly hurt are you? Can you walk?"

Her voice was business-like, and yet tinged with compassion.

Maybe she really is the genuine article…

Byron sat up, wincing. It was not at all difficult to put on a show of being hurt.

"I think I'm OK," he said, his voice slightly slurred and wobbly. "They only got a few punches in before you came along."

Luckily. Talk about enjoying your work…

He gave a wide grin, which he immediately regretted, given his split lip.

"My knight in… ow! Shining armour!"

Somewhere in his memory was a comparable vision of being rescued from a beating, but that had not been orchestrated by himself, and the memory was more painful than the event, so it was quickly thrust back into the murk.

He carefully stood up and she rose with him. He swayed slightly.

"Feel free to tell me to do one, but if I promise not to bleed on your upholstery, is there any chance you could give me a lift home? I only live ten minutes away."

He gave another hopeful smile at her.

"Ow!"

Her face broke into an answering smile then, full of a whimsical playfulness which seemed entirely without artifice; it was as though she exuded a natural sense of joy. And he could see then why she elicited such fascination from the media. There was a simple, carefree beauty to Elys Starr which seemed to pulse out around her. Maybe it was connected to her aura, which was very powerful, but had none of the menace that cloaked the Pale Lady or the sadistic Mr Golden. Hers was a radiant cloud of energy which made you feel glad to be alive. He liked her.

Shame I've got to kill you, really.

"Come on, my poor battered prince: climb aboard. You can have that lift, but first I'm going to take you by my place to check that you're really alright. Is that a deal, sir?"

Byron made a show of pondering her proposal and sucked air through his teeth before sketching a bow and wincing again.

"That should be fine, as long as you don't keep me too long. I have an important business meeting at three."

"Really?"

"Er... no."

Her mouth curved again into a smile.

"It's certainly good that you can maintain a sense of humour after what's just happened to you."

He shrugged helplessly.

"Can't let the bastards grind you down, can you? That's what they'd want. I'm not going to be miserable just because of them."

She gave him a shrewd look then.

"You seem to know your assailants. Well, you can tell me all about it in the car and I'll give you a shot of something hot and strong to numb the edges. I'm Elys, by the way."

She extended a hand, which he shook without hesitation.

"Will. Will Penney."

He found himself shivering as a sudden surge of energy rippled through him. It was like a kind of gentle electricity, but it took away some of the pain and left him with a strangely unlooked for sensation of hope.

He blinked a couple of times, because he hadn't expected that. Then he looked at her face and saw that her immaculate brows had furrowed slightly and her expression had darkened, as though a wisp of cloud had flitted past the sun.

The Pale Lady had been most insistent that he did not have a noticeable aura himself, but that look made him wonder.

Elys Starr looked at him again, her humour now dampened by some sense of... what? Doubt? Concern? Byron held his breath. Then she smiled.

"Come on, then: hop in!"

She gestured towards her car, whose luxurious interior called out to him to deposit his posterior upon its sumptuous leather seat. Of course, if she was anything like Mr Golden, he was probably being lulled into a false sense of security – and when they got to her place, he would be brutally tortured to extract any useful information before being killed. Ah! Such were the perils of being an assassin! Well, he would just have to hope that she hadn't somehow penetrated his disguise. Maybe she was just worried about his well-being? Or getting blood on her beautiful leather seat after all? Only time would tell.

So the street lights swung lazily by as the car made its way through the darkness. Eventually, they arrived at Ms Starr's pad: electronic gates opened to admit them and they crunched up a long gravel drive before parking outside a beautiful manor house. Byron was impressed. The sheer size of the garden, judging by the length of the drive, was more reminiscent of the country than the city.

"Wow!" uttered Byron as they all got out of the car.

He had already begun to relate his (entirely fictitious) story on the journey, but she had hushed him and told him to wait till they got back to her house. Now they were here.

"This is a serious piece of real estate."

She smiled happily.

"Yes. It's a lovely house. You can't really tell in the dark, but it has extensive grounds. That's why I bought it, to be honest. I love the feeling that I'm close to the great outdoors, even here in the heart of the city."

He returned her smile.

"Right. I think I get that. I've been stuck in some pretty grim, enclosed spaces myself."

"Yes," she said. "That would make sense."

Then she gave him that look again, like she knew there was something going on beneath his carefully cultivated cover story.

They stood for a moment and she looked up at the stars and grinned.

"Such a beautiful night! And a good one to make new friends!"

She took him by the hand and started to lead him towards the house. The chauffeur bade them good night and headed off discreetly to his own niche in the manor. The bodyguard, however, looked less enthusiastic. He frowned and followed them, before coughing significantly.

"Oh come on, Silas," she sang, merrily, "I promise I won't hurt him!"

Silas looked distinctly uncomfortable.

"It's not that, ma'am. It's just that... well, we don't know this young man, or why he was involved in the altercation we witnessed. I haven't even frisked him down. I don't think I should leave you alone until we know more about him."

Well! Some people are just born with a suspicious mind.

Truth be told, he was hoping that he didn't get frisked, as he had come armed with just one solitary knife, concealed in the lining of his coat. It would probably be missed in a cursory search, but he had a feeling that Ms Starr's protector would be rather thorough. Of course, he had a cover story at the ready, but it would make things a bit awkward. All he could do was stand with a look of surprised alarm on his face.

"Oh! Of course... I am so sorry – it never occurred to me..."

He stepped forward obligingly to be examined, lifting his arms from his sides.

But then she intervened, as he hoped that she would.

"Oh for goodness' sake, Silas! The poor man has just been viciously attacked. I'm just going to make him a coffee, have a chat and then I'll call him a taxi. It'll be fine." Here she smiled sweetly and put her hand on Silas' arm. He looked for all the world like an overprotective father, and lots of gloomy, doubtful emotions rippled out across his face.

"If you say so, ma'am." And he directed a look at Byron, which pretty much said *you mess with her, and you really will get battered.*

"I do. You're a good man and very diligent in the execution of your duties. But I'll be fine. Will's a nice guy – no threat at all. I have a real feel for people. You wouldn't hurt me, would you, Will?"

She turned to him, all guileless smiles and big eyes.

Shit.

Either she was too trusting to be true – or she was playing a very clever game and was sending him a not-so subtle message.

He smiled back at her and raised one hand.

"Scout's honour. I'm a complete non-violent pacifist."

"There you go. Now just clear off to bed, Silas. It's really late and you must be shattered. Go on: that's an order."

He did so, but reluctantly. Byron knew he would have to play this one very carefully. For now, though, his target was blithely inviting him into her own house for a coffee. It would be rude not to accept – not to mention a terrible waste of opportunity.

They went through to the kitchen, which was surprisingly shiny and modern for such an old building. She made a pot of coffee, and they began to talk about what had happened and why. The coffee made, and smelling rather inviting, it had to be said, she led him through to a small reception room. It was tastefully decorated and had a wide, glowing coal fire at its heart.

"This room is my little snug," she confided to him, gesturing for them both to sit on a remarkably comfortable sofa, whilst she passed him a drink.

"I like to come here in autumn and winter and curl up in front of the fire with a good book and a hot chocolate."

He sank back into the rich upholstery.

"It's lovely," he answered, smiling contentedly. And for once he meant what he was saying.

She sat right next to him.

"So, Will, why don't you tell me what tonight was all about. My instincts are that you've got quite a tale to tell."

He laughed aloud at this.

"You probably wouldn't believe the half of it!"

"Try me."

So he did. As they sipped their coffee and the fire crackled merrily in front of them, he reeled out his whole story for her. He was a human rights activist, working for a well-known charity. He had been acting on a tip-off from someone who flatly refused to go to the police. He was trying to get evidence that he could present to the authorities to push them into action. He had received a threatening phone call two days ago, urging him to back off, but he refused to do so! (He hoped that he told that bit with the requisite indignant passion…) Tonight, he had been taking photos of a large, run-down building being used as a holding facility by people traffickers. Unfortunately, he had been spotted and pursued through the back streets. One of the men had taken his camera and legged it, leaving the two they saw on the kerb side giving him a good kicking.

That pretty much brought it to a close.

She listened patiently, only occasionally asking questions.

Patience was a quality he admired; it was why he was now reeling off this cock-and-bull account of derring-do, rather than just trying to knife her on the sofa the moment she sat down. He liked to listen to his instincts too; they were telling him that this one needed to be reeled in very gently. Besides, there was always the danger that the hired help might be lurking around for a while, ready to intervene with a chair leg should he make an untoward move on his lovely employer.

She was lovely, by the way. She possessed physical beauty, as per the photos in the gossipy tabloids. But she was even more beautiful in the flesh, for she had a living spirit which animated her features and made one feel at ease, just by being in the same room. Being close to her made his soul stir, like a desiccated seed in the desert.

One hour turned to two, with just the pair of them chatting like old friends.

So far, things had gone pretty much as well as could be hoped. He knew that the critical moment was fast approaching. It was just as he was beginning to reposition himself on the sofa when she paused, and stared thoughtfully into the fading coals in the fire.

"It's a good story," she said, turning back and smiling brightly. "And recounted with such plausible spirit."

He froze.

"Thanks. I think…"

He maintained his easy grin, which was quite a feat given the sudden lurch in his stomach.

"But there's a lot more to you than that, isn't there, Will? Assuming that's your real name."

They both sat and looked at each other for a moment. Then she stood up and poured out two glasses of something which smelt richly alcoholic before returning to the couch. She passed one to him.

"Are you sure there's nothing else that you'd like to tell me, Will?"

Her eyes were a dark violet colour and were focused on him intently – though without any obvious anger.

He looked down at the glass she gave him, and hesitated in spite of himself. What would happen if he drank this? Would she reach under the sofa and produce a meat cleaver to slice him up while he lay there helpless? Was it deadly poison?

She suddenly laughed: a sound like a fast-flowing brook. Her eyes twinkled and she smiled.

"It's alright. I'm not planning anything untoward. Don't feel you have to drink that if you don't want to."

He looked up quickly and gave her a weak smile. The truth was, he was thinking of Mr Golden, all smiles and bonhomie, just as he was about to carve someone up.

"No... I, er... It's just that..."

Stammering fool! He cursed his suddenly jangling nerves.

Gently, she took the glass out of his hand and placed it on the table. Then she reached back and took his hand in hers.

"I'm not going to hurt you. In fact, I want to help you."

This conversation was hurtling out of control like a runaway train.

"Right," he ventured.

"There is an emptiness at your core. Something might have been there once, but no longer. You are tinged with darkness, Will. I don't mean that you're evil, because I don't think that you are. But you have suffered greatly. I sense that you only manage to stumble from day to day by numbing your emotions to the point where you can't really feel anything at all.

"What do you mean?"

His voice squeaked like a boy on the cusp of manhood – which maybe wasn't too far from the truth.

She maintained eye contact, searching for something in his own gaze.

"You know what I am, don't you?"

It was posed as a gentle question, but they both knew the answer.

He knew he should deny it, that he should launch into some bluster, but he felt suddenly tired, like he couldn't carry on with the endless lies and deception any more. He swallowed.

"Yes. You're an Other."

She laughed.

"Is that what you call us? How funny! But I can smell the foetid odour of the depths on you. If they wanted to recruit a human as a spy, they should have taken more care not to taint him with their malign essence. Who is it that you work for?"

He was hardly going to tell her that, now, was he?

"Henry Golden sent me."

Oh.

Perhaps now he was beginning to understand why killing Others was a lot harder than it looked.

She nodded thoughtfully and then returned her attention to him.

"Yes. That makes sense. The Pale Lady's chief agent in this part of the world. I have been engaged in numerous skirmishes with him over the years. He is a thoroughly unpleasant man, is he not?"

Byron found himself nodding in agreement and again felt uncomfortably like he used to do as a gauche schoolboy.

She lifted her hand suddenly and stroked his cheek. Whereas Mr Golden's touch made his flesh crawl, this was unaccountably gentle. He closed his eyes and leaned into her touch. She gasped then, as he began to relax; to drop the many layers that he had constructed to protect himself, to hide away the raw, scarlet wound at the centre of his being.

"You poor, poor child," she whispered, pulling him into a gentle embrace. "You have suffered so very much. I had no idea. They have done awful things to you, haven't they?"

Whatever she was doing to him was beginning to dissolve his self-control. He could barely hold his current form. Her aura pulsed around him, like a shining, golden cloud of love.

She rested his head on her shoulder.

"Listen. You don't have to be afraid any more. I know what they will have threatened you with, but I can protect you from their vengeance. They can't hurt you here. I want to help you. Let me and together we'll end your misery and heal the damage that has been inflicted on you. You can help me to combat Mr Golden and his vile schemes instead. Doesn't that sound more appealing? To have me as your guide?"

Oh but it did, and he nodded, dumbly. Just the thought of Mr Golden's face on hearing the news of his defection brought a smile unbidden to his face. But then he thought of Zaffre and his smile faltered. It wouldn't go so easily for him.

He couldn't just abandon him to his fate.

"There's another boy. Mr Golden's holding him at his house. Do you think you could help him, too?"

She studied his earnest expression.

"I can't make any promises. If we could somehow get him out of the house, then maybe... I take it he is subject to Mr Golden's tender mercies too?

Byron nodded.

"Look, there's always hope. If we work together then we can defeat him and his foul mistress."

Her eyes shone and he believed her. Or at least her sincerity.

Her smile blossomed like a brilliant white flower in the night. It made him feel like any goal could be achieved if he strove for it.

"That's the spirit," she whispered, softly, before adding, "and what is your name, by the way? I take it that it's not Will?"

"No."

He looked back up at her.

"I had a name, once. I had a name and another life, but they took them away from me. I can't even remember what I was called back then. Or how long ago that was."

"Oh. But that's... so *sad*!"

Her voice was resonant with feeling and he realised that she was right: it was really, truly, terribly sad. His whole life had gone, and what was he now? Just a highly trained serf – little better than one of those slave gladiators that Roman lords used to keep. His life... His name... They were scarce remembered whispers of something that no longer existed. That boy was dead and all that was left was an empty husk that served without question, advancing the cause of the Pale Lady and leaving nothing but death and despair in his wake.

Was that what he had come to?

He was a shade, after all; his soul had withered away and he had no one; nothing; a life with no meaning except to kill the next target... and the next. If he was to die this night, no one would weep for him.

In the face of her luminous compassion, he began to laugh, even as he felt tears running hot down his face.

Oh God! He was crying!

Never let them know what's in your mind...

But he couldn't help it. He was suddenly consumed by the meaningless tragedy of his own existence and he couldn't stop himself from releasing at least some of the pain and fear that he had buried so deep, so toxically deep, over the intervening months or years. He didn't even know how old he was, for God's sake!

"Poor child."

He found himself enveloped again in her fragrant warmth. He knew that she was the genuine article. She would help him. She would protect him. She would weep for him.

They swayed together for a while, the sobbing young man cradled by the beautiful older woman with the shining eyes.

"It's alright," she whispered, taking him back to his first meeting with Yellow Rose. "I've got you now. You're safe here. Let the

351

pain flow out: it'll poison you if you keep it locked inside you. Sshhh. Don't worry. You're free from them now."

The fire crackled and hissed, its dying embers beginning to darken, and there was the faintest chill creeping in at the edges of the room. The two were locked together in a warm embrace until finally Elys Starr gave a sigh and her hands slipped away from him as though he was covered suddenly in oil.

Byron caught her as she fell back, and lay her gently on the sofa. The hilt of his knife protruded incongruously from her ribs, where a dark stain was spreading out across the midnight blue fabric she had worn that evening.

"I'm sorry," he coughed, with tears and snot dripping from his face. And he was, too. His shoulders shuddered anew as he gazed down on her face, caught somewhere between puzzlement and affection. "I'm... so... sorry," he uttered in a broken voice, and he reached down with a shaking hand to stroke her dark brown hair.

As he spoke, he felt his form slipping away, the handsome young man about town melting away into a distressed teenager, slender, bruised and battered and torn apart by the realisation that his life had become an exercise in meaningless futility.

Elys Starr's eyes widened very slightly at the transformation; she was unable to speak.

"They've got their hooks in me too deep, you see," he continued, trying desperately to restrain his sobbing so that he didn't wake the whole house. "I've got to finish the job... I just have to... I know you would've helped me... Please... please forgive me..."

His voice fell to a shattered whisper; tears fell on her upturned face like rain drops.

She formed the ghost of a smile and one of her hands moved very slightly as if to comfort him; then the light went out in her eyes.

As the weeping boy watched, a soft, golden radiance seemed to leech out of her, bathing them for a few seconds in a gentle light.

She was gone.

Elys Starr was dead.

He had completed his contract.

He sat a few minutes more. With her death, the emotional wave which had blasted him out of all composure began to recede. His customary controls began to kick in. He took some deep breaths.

This won't do at all. Pull yourself together.

Mr Gray's face sprang unbidden to his mind. He regulated his breathing and felt for his centre, seeking for calm.

After some minutes, he had restored his equilibrium and proceeded to wipe his nose attentively on a tissue. Once he had regained his customary cold control, he shifted back into the Will Penney persona, just in case he was seen leaving. There would probably be cameras outside and he would have to match the description given by the bodyguard.

He steeled himself to look down on her once more; just a corpse after all. Tears were past all use. He reached decisively down and withdrew his knife with a swift pull, causing her to jerk slightly at the roughness of the action. He cleaned it off on the fabric of the sofa. Then he looked down at her for the last time.

"Sorry about that. But better you than me."

Chapter 29
Clocking In

Oho! What a triumph! What a coup! I must admit, I did wonder if he'd rise to this particular challenge – and yet again, my wonderful Byron has shown his calibre.

The communications networks are ablaze with the news that Elys Starr has been killed. I gather that most of the factions are pointing the finger in my direction. Good. It will give them pause for thought. Now that they have seen this little demonstration of my power, then they might think twice before antagonising me. Perhaps, in the longer term, some of them might even think about a reunification under my inspired leadership.

Great events often follow key moments in history.

But I mustn't get too carried away. Pardon my megalomaniac fantasies. I freely admit to craving universal domination. Perhaps – one day?

For now, I shall revel in the joy of this moment, secure in the knowledge that my representatives in the human world have struck a terrible blow against the organisation of one of my most effective enemies.

I shall be sure to pass on my appreciation to Mr Golden for his expert management of the situation – and of course to the boy, who is serving me so very well, just as I had hoped.

I knew he wouldn't let me down!

It was so late it was early when Byron finally got back to his apartment. He felt tired to the core: not just physically tired, but tired of the life which clung to him now like a heavy, suffocating, cloak.

He shook it off. He wasn't one, these days, to indulge in morbid introspection. There was no point: he couldn't change anything anyway, so it was just an exercise in reviewing how shit it all was.

He crashed out for an unknown period of time and certainly didn't dream about Elys Starr or her offer of a sweeter life. That really would be self-destructive. It wasn't for him. He had done too many bad things, now; he was in too deep. He couldn't even begin to imagine turning on the Pale Lady or Mr Golden.

Best to make as good a job out of it as he was able.

Wasn't it?

He tossed and turned, restless in his bed, before being dragged back into the land of the living by the sound of his phone ringing.

He fished around for it on the bedside table before grunting incoherently into it.

Zaffre's voice was cool as spring water.

"And good morning to you, Mr Black. I take it that you had a late night, and as such I am loth to tear you from your well-earned rest. However, Mr Golden is in a state of some excitement, and has requested your presence at the earliest convenience."

Byron rubbed at his face and yawned colossally.

"Right," he croaked, "so as soon as possible, then. OK Zaffre, I'll be there in half an hour."

"Your esprit de corps is, as ever, much appreciated, Mr Black. I'll be sure to have a strong coffee ready for your arrival."

"No!"

It came out a little too quickly and evaporated the last vestiges of sleep.

"I beg your pardon?"

"Ah, not coffee, please."

Not lovely, rich-smelling coffee and kindness; please, not that.

"Of course. I'll make it tea, then. We'll see you shortly, Mr Black."

The phone went dead and Byron got up. Splashing his face with water, he stared into the mirror.

Are you watching me, you old hag?

His slightly elfin face looked tired and worn – older than it should be. His black hair had resolved itself into a spectacularly dramatic bedhead. He decided that Mr Golden could wait a few minutes more and forced himself through the shower, which brought about at least some partial revivication.

Finally, he threw on some clean clothes and made his way to Berkley Road. Back to his master. He gave a long-suffering sigh.

He'd had his chance for a new life and had turned it down just about as equivocally as was possible. Who's to say she was the real deal anyway? She probably just wanted to use him like all the others. The other Others, that was.

Bleak as it was, he clung to that thought for comfort as he knocked on the door.

Zaffre answered it and actually greeted him with a smile. Or at least, his sculpted lips curved in a generally upward direction.

"Hi Zaffre. Sorry I'm a bit late. I couldn't function without a shower."

"Not to worry, Mr Black. I'll have your tea on standby; for now, it might be politic to go straight up, as Mr Golden is extremely keen to see you."

And Mr Golden always gets what he wants.

"Roger that."

They made their time-honoured pilgrimage up the grand stairs. Byron surrendered his knives and he was ushered in by Zaffre.

He found Mr Golden to be almost frenetic with excitement. He leapt up from his desk, a wild grin on his face.

"Ah! My boy! My little miracle worker!"

He strode forward and actually embraced Byron with some enthusiasm. If the boy felt at all uncomfortable, even when Mr Golden's hand slid some way past his lower back, then he didn't show it. Not even when his master's hot breath roiled at his ear, murmuring what a good boy he was and how very pleased he was with his performance. He just stood there, smiling blandly, with his arms half raised, as if unsure where he was meant to put them.

Finally, he was released from Mr Golden's tactile appreciation. The man himself took a step back and smiled indulgently down at his underling.

"You see, Mr Black, that although I am a harsh task-master, I can be *very* appreciative of those who serve me well."

Here he made a point of running his thumb gently across Byron's chin.

"*Very* appreciative," he repeated, in a slightly husky voice, which made Byron far more nervous than when he was in the bad books.

Mr Golden then joined his hands behind his back and strode over to the fireplace, rather like the lord of the manor. He turned back to face Byron.

"I had a very positive feeling about you when you first arrived and my best hopes have so far been indulged. That is no mean feat, Mr Black. You have risen to every challenge we have set for you thus far. Well done. Clearly, you are able to adapt and learn, becoming ever more proficient with every kill that you make."

"Thank you, sir."

Byron allowed a faint smile to touch his lips as if in modest appreciation of the compliment.

I am a killer, after all.

But he didn't really like to think of that. He killed because he had to. Unlike Mr Golden, he took no pleasure in acts of violence. He preferred to get the job done quickly and clinically instead. He dreaded that one day he might actually enjoy his work.

Mr Golden was nodding, with a smug expression of extreme satisfaction on his face.

"The mighty Elys Starr, fallen at last," he mused. "How I have dreamt of this day! That woman has been a thorn in my flesh for years, seeking to frustrate my plans, constantly blunting my efforts with her meddlesome do-goodery!"

His eyes flicked greedily back to Byron and he licked his lips.

"How did she die? Did you make her suffer? Was there much pain?"

Byron coolly returned his gaze and produced an answering smile, right on cue.

"There was a certain amount of pain as I sliced through her ribs, but she started to cry out and so I was forced to finish her quickly. There was security in the house, you see, sir."

He tried not to think of that beautiful face looking up at him with such gentle hope, even as the light bled out from her.

Mr Golden rubbed his hands and nodded knowledgeably.

"Of course, of course. It has to be business before pleasure. I quite understand. I am glad that she had a taste of pain before she perished, though, for all of the nuisance that she has caused me in our tiresome conflict."

There was something of a pause, then, as Mr Golden's mind seemed preoccupied by something else.

"Well, as I say, Mr Black, you have performed well. You may have tomorrow as a day of self-indulgence. And tonight, to show my appreciation, you will dine here with me at Berkley Road. Zaffre is a marvellous cook and I, of course, can be very good company. Shall we say eight o' clock?"

Byron gave a great big smile.

"That's really very kind of you, Mr Golden. I shall look forward to it very much."

"Of course you will," replied the Other, silkily. "A good time shall be had by all." This was followed by a glance which made Byron think of a dog eyeing a large piece of steak.

"Ah! But we must put our social pleasures aside for a while. There are still matters of business to attend to."

He gestured to the desk, where the both sat down.

A pristine manilla folder was waiting there.

"Now for your next target. After Miss Starr, you should find this rather easy to accomplish, although the target is a mid-ranking Government minister, so the job is not without its difficulties. There will be security to be bypassed. Also, the Pale Lady is keen that you cast suspicion for the murder on the minister's wife – although she was rather vague on how that might be achieved."

Byron allowed himself a knowing smile at this, warmed by the knowledge that she had kept his illustrious mentor in the dark as to the finer points of his ability after all. The subliminal message was not lost on Mr Golden, whose lips pursed in an expression of mild irritation.

"I'll start to prepare tomorrow, Mr Golden," Byron assured him, with an open look of innocent enthusiasm.

The pout slowly faded away.

"Ah! Volunteering to work even though I kindly gave you the day off. Now that's the sort of attitude that will get you far in our organisation."

"Yes, sir."

Mr Golden reached across the desk to give his hand a squeeze. It was just a little too hard to be comfortable.

"Who knows to what dizzying heights you will have climbed after a few more years under my... guiding hand."

Mr Golden winked at this. Byron blushed quite fetchingly.

"Now: where were we? Ah yes, we must sign the job off. Mr Black: if you would be so kind?"

Byron was presented with the ledger. He reached expectantly for the fountain pen, but was surprised to see Mr Golden walking around the desk to pass it over to him. As he did so, the older man surprised Byron even more by kneeling down at his feet.

"Please sign the ledger," he ordered loudly, placing the pen into Byron's startled hand. Then, leaning forward, he placed one hand on Byron's thigh and whispered, "I wonder, my dear boy, if you could indulge my... curiosity?"

Byron looked down at the manicured fingers as they crept slowly higher, like shiny pink caterpillars.

"Of course, Mr Golden. Anything you like."

He gave Mr Golden a soft, knowing smile.

The older man leaned in even closer.

"I knew you were a good boy," he murmured. "And I do so hate secrets. If I don't know your full capabilities, then I may not make the best use of you as an asset. The Pale Lady can be quite... careful with information sometimes. I respect her judgement, of course, but in this matter, I would be most obliged if you could fill in any... blanks. She has intimated that you have certain... unusual abilities."

"You could certainly say that," said Byron, with a bold grin.

Mr Golden must have liked it, for he gave his upper thigh a quick, encouraging pinch. He could hardly keep the hunger from his face.

"So: you'll tell me what it is that you can do?"

"You are my master. I can have no secrets from you. I want you to trust me completely, sir."

"What a wonderful boy you are!" Mr Golden exclaimed, moving imperceptibly forwards. "I grow more and more delighted with you..."

Byron continued to smile, happily.

"Thank you, sir. I hope that we will have many happy years working together."

"Yes, yes. I hope so too. But now, please tell me: what's your naughty secret? Are you able to blend in with your surroundings like a chameleon? That's my current working theory."

"Ha! In a manner of speaking, I suppose that's true!"

"In a manner of speaking?"

"Yes," said Byron, and he suddenly shifted, his entire appearance melting and reforming like wax, so that Mr Golden felt for a moment that he was looking into a mirror. It was all quite easy. Byron had practised taking on Mr Golden's form on numerous occasions: at first as an act of defiance and later because he had a feeling that it might come in useful one of these days.

Mr Golden's face drooped in astonishment.

"Oh!"

This was all he could manage, as he stared, mesmerised at the vision before him. It would appear that, even for an Other, seeing a literal double was something of an indelible experience.

"But... that's..."

He began to raise his gaze up to Byron's, but got no further as his doppelganger thrust the fountain pen, with all his strength, through Mr Golden's left eye.

It was a high quality piece of workmanship; the steel nib came to an almost precise point, which was more than a match for the jelly of Mr Golden's astonished gaze. The pen travelled smoothly on. Byron gave it an additional sharp whack to lodge it fully in his superior's brain.

As he had hoped, although Mr Golden's mouth flared open and shut, like a fish, he made no sound. It appeared that the nerve centres in the brain had a particularly potent effect upon the subject. His upper body went into spasms and blood and ichor ran like extraordinary tears down his cheek.

The second Mr Golden leaned forward.

"How about you sign that off, you bastard?"

There was a strange gurgling noise and then Mr Golden keeled over onto his plush red carpet. He twitched a few times, and lay still. A greenish-black liquid began to flow out of his mouth and ears, pooling in his pale blond hair.

Something left the room: a kind of oppressive weight, and Byron knew that Mr Golden was no more. He went to work quickly, undressing the corpse carefully to minimise contact between the cloth and the blood. This job accomplished, he removed his own clothes and swapped them for those of his erstwhile employer.

He had no idea if this was going to work, or indeed if he would still be alive in an hour's time. He hadn't even known that he was going to bump off his boss, truth be told, but it had felt like the right thing to do at the time. Now, to escape from the very heart of the Pale Lady's organisation. He carefully buttoned Mr Golden's jacket. It was going to be high-risk, but it had to be worth a shot, didn't it? It wasn't like he had a great deal to live for under the current arrangements anyway.

Sometimes, you just have to gamble everything on a throw of the dice.

Byron looked himself up and down in his new attire. The suit was beautifully cut, but so heavily impregnated with Mr Golden's scent and essence that it made him feel slightly sick.

Stay focused. Pull yourself together.

Byron dragged the body to the corner of the room, where he draped it, fittingly, with the sheeting used by Mr Golden when he had tortured Zaffre. It was hardly a fool proof hiding place, but it only had to buy him a few minutes' grace to get out. He was hoping the rest would be achieved through some particularly bold acting.

Here goes nothing.

Byron closed his eyes, visualising his loathsome master. He held his head high and strode to the door. Just beyond, the troll stood sentinel like a block of granite.

Byron shot him a contemptuous glance.

"Vodrun: I need to speak to Zaffre about a... personal issue. Please see that Mr Black does not leave the study before my return."

It was bloody good, he had to admit. The crisp voice; the slight sneer; the overweening arrogance. It was almost faultless. He even considered asking for his knives, but decided that was too much of a risk. He would have to sacrifice those beautiful weapons of Mr Gray's. His only objective now was to go downstairs and get out of the building. So much quicker and easier than trying to fight his way out or clambering out of a window.

Vodrun rumbled something unintelligible in reply and he began to walk coolly past.

Then there was trouble...

"You! Wait there!"

The troll suddenly surged to his feet, surprisingly fast for something so seemingly ponderous.

Byron feigned outrage.

"How dare you!" he spat.

Vodrun loomed closer and emitted a bizarre noise, rather like a drain emptying. The gleaming gimlet eyes, nestled beneath craggy brows, swivelled around, before locking on to him and turning to an alarming shade of red.

"You smell wrong!" accused the behemothic warden. "You not him!"

He loomed over him, distended nostrils flaring, before opening his maw to emit a deafening, spittle-flecked roar.

Battling Vodrun, with or without a fountain pen (without, actually, as he had left it embedded in its owner) was not what Byron had had in mind, but it seemed that he had little choice in the matter. A huge fist swept towards him, and it took all of his honed reflexes to dart out of the way.

"You come here!" roared the troll, smashing an antique wooden table as if it was made of papier-mâché.

"You'll forgive me if I decline!" he squawked, ducking another fist which punched a foot-wide hole in the wall behind him.

His concrete-skinned assailant issued another bellow of rage, before lowering his head and charging.

"Shit!"

Byron ran frantically down the passageway leading to the stairs. He was fast and preternaturally agile, but there was no room for manoeuvre here. Vodrun smashed straight through the ornate wooden bannister, landing like a bulldozer on the stairs in front of him, cutting off his escape. The whole house shook. Each breath a growl, the monstrous bodyguard advanced up the stairs, which groaned and creaked in protest of his weight.

"My, but they certainly built things to last in those days!" trilled Byron, hoping to distract his approaching nemesis.

Vodrun casually swiped away a few stair rails in a gesture of seething aggression.

"Well, perhaps not bannisters," added Byron, squeakily.

"You talk too much! Vodrun will smash your head and feast on your flesh!"

"Well, at least we both know where we stand," began the assassin, but he was cut off by the troll suddenly generating another burst of intense speed, this time charging up the stairs.

"You... are... certainly light on... your feet!"

Byron found that he needed every ounce of concentration as he ducked this way and that, dodging blows just one of which would have splattered him over the wall.

"For a... big... fell-ahhh!"

Too late Byron realised that he had underestimated both Vodrun's speed and grasp of tactics. The creature was anticipating his movements, and as the boy dodged neatly to one side to avoid one blow, he suddenly understood that this had been a feint: the second fist was hurtling towards his face like a pile-driver. It was too huge and the space was too confined to entirely avoid it.

Desperately, he flung himself backwards. He had exceptional reflexes, which meant that he managed to evade the full impact – but the massive mitt still caught him a glancing blow that sent him sprawling down the hall. Byron struggled to sit up. His face hurt like hell, and he suspected that his cheek bone had been fractured. It felt as though a bell-ringing convention was being held in his head and there were spots before his eyes.

"Stupid human. You not mess with Vodrun!"

Enormous knobbly hands reached down and lifted him up from the floor like a stray sock. Byron found himself staring into blood-red eyes entirely devoid of pit; only blood-lust dwelt therein. Vodrun dangled him one-handed by the scruff of his neck, a sodden kitten about to be put out of its misery. He raised his other huge paw, placing his thumb and finger on either side of Byron's temples.

""Now we will end this. Vodrun will squash your head."

"Well at least it'll be quick," mumbled Byron, now suspecting that his jaw might also be fractured. "I don't suppose there's anything I can do to change your mind?"

"No."

He felt the roughness of Vodrun's fat digits against the side of his head and then the first feeling of intense pressure.

He let out a loud scream and the troll seemed to smile.

"Maybe not so quick?"

Great. Even the bloody troll was a sadist in this place.

The pressure eased slightly and then started again with a vengeance. He could feel the bones in his skull straining not to fold in on themselves.

"You got nothing funny to say now, little man?"

The troll released the pressure again and gave a sort of hideous grimace.

"You have no more words for Vodrun?"

There was a grating sound which may or may not have been laughter.

Then it stopped abruptly.

This is it, then...

But Vodrun's gnarled features had taken on a different expression – almost one of confusion. He gazed down, his red eyes blinking stupidly.

This time, Byron heard the impact: a nasty thud, and he felt the troll sway like a great tree beneath an axe blade.

His vision was distinctly blurry, but he thought he could see two pinpricks of bright light on the front of Vodrun's suit jacket.

The was another grating sound. The beast seemed to be struggling to move now. Byron was dropped like an afterthought as the troll slowly rotated to look back down the stairs.

"What you..."

Sadly, Byron was not to discover the full nature of this partially formed question, as at that precise moment, the back of Vodrun's head exploded. Something hit the wall behind him. Hard. There was a sound akin to an ice shelf splitting away from a glacier – a great creaking, groaning, gust of despair.

"Shit!"

Byron just had enough presence of mind to scoot backwards, to avoid being crushed beneath the troll's colossal body.

Behind this, came the sound of footsteps, slow and measured, ascending the stairs. They clacked on the wood. Byron pulled himself up onto his elbows, to see a pristine form come into view behind the latest corpse. Zaffre pointed a silver and ebony crossbow down at Vodrun's head and loosed a glittering bolt at close range. Other than the sound of the contact, and the tremor which shook the fallen troll, there was no other reaction.

"Better safe than sorry where trolls are concerned. Diamond-tipped bolts are required to penetrate their hides. Mr Golden had me keep a few downstairs, just in case Vodrun ever went rogue. And for the record, they have an exceptional sense of smell."

"Err… thanks?"

Byron tried to grin and yelped as his face hurt so much.

Zaffre raised the crossbow to point at him.

"Now, why don't you change out of that particular form. It holds very few pleasant associations for me. If you'd be so kind."

Byron ogled the crossbow nervously. If a diamond-tipped bolt could pierce a troll, it would have no problem with his peach-like skin. Luckily, this time, the weapon seemed to be unloaded.

Zaffre seemed to know what he was thinking.

"Hurry up, or I might change my mind."

Almost instantaneously, Byron snapped back into his usual form.

Zaffre lowered the crossbow and failed to hide his wonder.

"Now that is really something to behold," he whispered, before approaching Byron, who had struggled back up to his feet. Gently, he lifted his free hand to trace a finger down Byron's uninjured cheek.

"Is this what you really look like?"

"I think so," replied Byron, shakily. "I can't remember very much from... before. I might have made a few changes without realising. I... try not to stand out, so it's best to have a plain, boring face..."

Zaffre's expression of wonder softened and suddenly he smiled: a real, bright smile that came from the heart. His amber eyes glowed with humour.

"Shut up you idiot!"

Byron gaped in surprise.

"You're not plain; you're beautiful. Don't you know?"

And with that, he leaned suddenly forward and hugged him close, taking care to be gentle with his battered face. The crossbow dropped heavily to the floor and Byron closed his eyes as he revelled the unlooked-for physical contact. Somewhere inside, what was left of his fragmented, freeze-dried heart, gave a little a little tremor, like a faded memory of what it had once been.

It was difficult to say who was the most shocked: the young man who had just witnessed a shape-changer or his former colleague, now enfolded in his arms.

Eventually, Zaffre broke off and stepped back.

"I've been waiting a long time to do that, Mr Black."

"Then... you really don't hate me? I... I wasn't sure whether you were just trying to cover it all up back in the kitchen. I..."

Zaffre shook his head.

"There was only one person to blame for that and it wasn't you. He wanted you to feel guilty – and maybe for me to blame you. But I always knew, you were just looking out for me. It just made me... like you even more."

"Oh."

Byron closed his mouth.

"Right. Glad that's all cleared up then."

He felt a dangerously large and painful smile forming on his own face.

They grinned at each other for a while.

"How did you kill him?" Zaffre suddenly enquired. "I knew he was dead straight away. I couldn't feel him in my head any more, crawling around like a maggot, feeding on my thoughts and feelings. We were... linked, you see. The last thing I got from him, in an unguarded moment, was an image of himself but in your clothes."

Byron was slightly startled by the directness of the question.

"Oh. I, er, shoved his pen through his eye."

"You mean the one he keeps on his desk for that bloody ledger?"

"Yeah."

Zaffre gave a chortle at this.

"How very poetic! Truly, mightier than the sword."

"Sorry?"

"It doesn't matter. Listen, we need to go – to get out of here. The Pale Lady will probably know that Golden is dead, just like I did. She'll be sending... agents to investigate what happened. And then you and I are going to be number one on her hit list."

Byron nodded.

"I wasn't planning on hanging around to waltz with a troll. Don't worry, I've got an escape plan all worked out."

He paused then and looked shyly at Zaffre.

"Do you want to... I mean, you could come..."

Zaffre placed a finger on his lips. He looked suddenly sad, and shook his head.

"In many ways I would love to come with you. Maybe one day we'll see each other again. But we have to go our separate ways, I think. We'll need to be really careful for a long time. And I can't change like you. If we stay together, it'll make it easier for the Pale Lady to find us both."

He knew he was right; Zaffre's logic was impeccable. He kind of thought the same thing. But... it still made him feel sad.

"I get so lonely."

This escaped his lips unbidden, just like the tears which suddenly slid from his eyes.

"You're the only person I know, now – the only friend I've got in this world. That's all."

Zaffre's face softened and he embraced him again, before speaking gently into his ear.

"That was then. You're free now. You can go anywhere – be anyone. There's nothing to stop you making friends and a life for yourself, Byron." He stepped back. "Look: the cage door is open. Get out, while you can. Don't let them keep you a prisoner in a cell without bars."

Byron laughed through his blubbing.

"Hey! You're really savvy for a butler, Zaffre."

Zaffre smiled.

"And you're very sweet, for an assassin."

He held out a long, pale brown hand.

"Goodbye, Mr Black. And good luck. Who knows: maybe we'll meet again in some distant, far-flung location yet to be discovered. Thanks. You set me free. Now you need to do the same for yourself."

They shook hands, and, without another word, Zaffre walked smartly back down the stairs and straight out of the front door.

Byron gaped after him, admiringly, for a moment.

You've been here for too long.

The voice came unbidden to his mind, and he knew it was true. Returning to the study, he recovered his knives, before taking care of a couple of other items in the room itself. He used the crossbow to shatter Mr Golden's enormous gilt-edged mirror and fed the ledger to his fire. This done, he slipped down the stairs in Zaffre's wake.

Around thirty minutes later, a young shop assistant in a high street clothes store dwelt briefly on something that had struck her as odd. She could have sworn that the only person she had seen going into the changing room just after she returned from her break was a skinny-looking white guy in a funny suit. He looked like one of those really pretty emo kids, but his suit was too big for him. Strangely, the only person she had seen coming out again was an athletic looking mixed race lad of about nineteen or twenty wearing jeans and a dark jacket. He had given her a friendly smile as he walked past. And the funny thing was, she couldn't remember the second guy going in, any more than she could remember the first one coming out.

As it happened, it was a busy day on the high street, and she didn't have time to ponder the puzzle for too long. There were so many people coming in and out that she'd obviously missed a couple, that's all. She hoped that neither gentleman had been filching the merchandise!

It was, perhaps, just as well that it was one of her colleagues who found a suit – not one of theirs, either – folded neatly and abandoned under a changing room seat. It looked a bit old-fashioned, to tell the truth, and smelt strongly of cologne. After consulting with the manager, she dropped it at a charity shop on her way home.

Time, ceaseless time, flowed on like an unstoppable river.

Somewhere in a run-down tower block, in an insalubrious part of town, an old man struggled and wheezed up the stairs. He had accepted the arm of a kind lady, but once he got inside the door, he moved with surprising alacrity. Putting a pizza in the oven, he casually vaulted over the back of a worn out sofa, where he ensconced himself happily in front of a high-end games console. Putting on his headphones, he began to exchange banter with some unknown online buddy or other, in an incongruously youthful voice, before demonstrating his superb reflexes by sniping someone who had happened to peep around the edge of a window for a split second. He laughed raucously at his accomplishment, even as he was subjected to an earful of abuse.

He seemed to be having the time of his life.

Epilogue

Words cannot express my ire at the extent of this betrayal. To have one of my own turn on me in such a fashion... The sheer ingratitude after all the resources I expended to make him what he is today: so much better than human. Did I not bless him with powers that his kind can only dream of? I made him a king amongst men.

Alas, it seems that once again my trusting nature has brought about a bitter disappointment.

Mr Golden must take a measure of the blame, too. It seems that he mismanaged the boy to the point where he actually turned on his own handler. I can still hardly believe it! Perhaps I should have heeded Yellow Rose's warning and monitored events more closely myself.

Now Mr Golden is dead and I am left to pick up the pieces. Just at the moment of my triumph, when I sought to press home my advantage with the elimination of Elys Starr, my own director of operations is likewise terminated. Now I too face the annoyance of having to rebuild my organisation and to draw together an extensive list of complex contacts and organisations. A difficult job made all the more fraught by his insistence on using that wretched journal, the remains of which were found in the fireplace of his study. There's no point in keeping detailed records if they can be burnt to a crisp by some opportunistic saboteur!

No doubt my rivals will be toasting my misfortune and smiling to themselves... Bah!

Well, there is a lesson here for me. Perhaps I have grown too lax or complacent of late. I will proceed with greater caution than ever. As for the organisation, what are a few more years to me?

I am not some short lived homo sapien. If it takes a decade to rebuild, then so be it.

And as for my wicked assassin and his little assistant, justice will be served. I will devote all available resources into tracking them down and then... well, let's just say that Mr Golden was an enthusiastic amateur in the stimulation of pain compared to my countless years of expertise. Oh yes, punishment must be seen to be administered, lest some begin to think that I am losing my grip.

I will find you, boy, and when I do, I'll strip you away, layer by layer. I will have my vengeance – and you, sweetling, will wish that you had died when you had the chance.

26607664R00220

Printed in Great Britain
by Amazon